OZ

⋅⋅—⋅⋅⋅◀ The ▶⋅⋅⋅—⋅⋅

Complete
COLLECTION

⋅⋅ ——— ⋅⋅⋅ ——— ⋅⋅

VOLUME
4

*Follow the yellow brick road to your nearest bookstore
and discover the magic of a land called*

OZ

OZ, the COMPLETE COLLECTION, VOLUME 1
The WONDERFUL WIZARD of OZ
The MARVELOUS LAND of OZ
OZMA of OZ

OZ, the COMPLETE COLLECTION, VOLUME 2
DOROTHY and the WIZARD in OZ
The ROAD to OZ
The EMERALD CITY of OZ

OZ, the COMPLETE COLLECTION, VOLUME 3
The PATCHWORK GIRL of OZ
TIK-TOK of OZ
The SCARECROW of OZ

OZ, the COMPLETE COLLECTION, VOLUME 4
RINKITINK in OZ
The LOST PRINCESS of OZ
The TIN WOODMAN of OZ

OZ, the COMPLETE COLLECTION, VOLUME 5
The MAGIC of OZ
GLINDA of OZ
The ROYAL BOOK of OZ

Read them all!

Oz

····◄ The ►····

Complete
COLLECTION
VOLUME
4

·•·———··———·•·

L. Frank Baum

Includes:

RINKITINK in OZ

The LOST PRINCESS of OZ

The TIN WOODMAN of OZ

Aladdin

NEW YORK LONDON TORONTO SYDNEY NEW DELHI

🏮ALADDIN
An imprint of Simon & Schuster Children's Publishing Division
1230 Avenue of the Americas, New York, NY 10020
This Aladdin edition March 2013
Rinkitink in Oz originally published in 1916
The Lost Princess of Oz originally published in 1917
The Tin Woodman of Oz originally published in 1918
All rights reserved, including the right of reproduction in whole or in part in any form.
ALADDIN is a trademark of Simon & Schuster, Inc., and related logo is a registered trademark of Simon & Schuster, Inc.
For information about special discounts for bulk purchases, please contact Simon & Schuster Special Sales at 1-866-506-1949 or business@simonandschuster.com.
The Simon & Schuster Speakers Bureau can bring authors to your live event. For more information or to book an event contact the Simon & Schuster Speakers Bureau at 1-866-248-3049 or visit our website at www.simonspeakers.com.
Designed by Jane Archer (www.psbella.com)
The text of this book was set in Baskerville.
Manufactured in the United States of America 0518 MTN
10 9 8 7 6
Library of Congress Control Number 2012950402
ISBN 978-1-4424-8893-9 (hc)
ISBN 978-1-4424-8550-1 (pbk)
ISBN 978-1-4424-8555-6 (eBook)
These books were originally published individually.

Contents

Rinkitink

in

To my new grandson
Robert Alison Baum

Introducing this Story

Here is a story with a boy hero, and a boy of whom you have never before heard. There are girls in the story, too, including our old friend Dorothy, and some of the characters wander a good way from the Land of Oz before they all assemble in the Emerald City to take part in Ozma's banquet. Indeed, I think you will find this story quite different from the other histories of Oz, but I hope you will not like it the less on that account.

If I am permitted to write another Oz book it will tell of some thrilling adventures encountered by Dorothy, Betsy Bobbin, Trot and the Patchwork Girl right in the Land of Oz, and how they discovered some amazing creatures that never could have existed outside a fairyland. I have an idea that about the time you are reading this story of Rinkitink I shall be writing that story of Adventures in Oz.

Don't fail to write me often and give me your advice and suggestions, which I always appreciate. I get a good many letters from my readers, but every one is a joy to me and I answer them as soon as I can find time to do so.

L. Frank Baum, Royal Historian of Oz

"Ozcot" at Hollywood in California, 1916

Chapter 1

The PRINCE of PINGAREE

If you have a map of the Land of Oz handy, you will find that the great Nonestic Ocean washes the shores of the Kingdom of Rinkitink, between which and the Land of Oz lies a strip of the country of the Nome King and a Sandy Desert. The Kingdom of Rinkitink isn't very big and lies close to the ocean, all the houses and the King's palace being built near the shore. The people live much upon the water, boating and fishing, and the wealth of Rinkitink is gained from trading along the coast and with the islands nearest it.

Four days' journey by boat to the north of Rinkitink is the Island of Pingaree, and as our story begins here I must tell you something about this island. At the north end of Pingaree, where it is widest, the land is a mile from shore to shore, but at the south end it is scarcely half a mile broad; thus, although Pingaree is four miles long, from north to south, it cannot be called a very big island. It is exceedingly pretty, however, and to the gulls who approach it from the sea it must resemble a huge green wedge lying upon the waters, for its grass and trees give it the color of an emerald.

The grass came to the edge of the sloping shores; the beautiful trees occupied all the central portion of Pingaree, forming a continuous grove where the branches met high overhead and there was just space beneath them for the cosy houses of the inhabitants. These houses were scattered everywhere throughout the island, so that there was no town or city, unless the whole island might be called a city. The canopy of leaves, high overhead, formed a shelter from sun and rain, and the dwellers in the grove could all look past the straight tree-trunks and across the grassy slopes to the purple waters of the Nonestic Ocean.

At the big end of the island, at the north, stood the royal palace of King Kitticut, the lord and Ruler of Pingaree. It was a beautiful palace, built entirely of snow-white marble and capped by domes of burnished gold, for the King was exceedingly wealthy. All along the coast of Pingaree were found the largest and finest pearls in the whole world.

These pearls grew within the shells of big oysters, and

the people raked the oysters from their watery beds, sought out the milky pearls and carried them dutifully to their King. Therefore, once every year his Majesty was able to send six of his boats, with sixty rowers and many sacks of the valuable pearls, to the Kingdom of Rinkitink, where there was a city called Gilgad, in which King Rinkitink's palace stood on a rocky headland and served, with its high towers, as a lighthouse to guide sailors to the harbor. In Gilgad the pearls from Pingaree were purchased by the King's treasurer, and the boats went back to the island laden with stores of rich merchandise and such supplies of food as the people and the royal family of Pingaree needed.

The Pingaree people never visited any other land but that of Rinkitink, and so there were few other lands that knew there was such an island. To the southwest was an island called the Isle of Phreex, where the inhabitants had no use for pearls. And far north of Pingaree—six days' journey by boat, it was said—were twin islands named Regos and Coregos, inhabited by a fierce and warlike people.

Many years before this story really begins, ten big boatloads of those fierce warriors of Regos and Coregos visited Pingaree, landing suddenly upon the north end of the island. There they began to plunder and conquer, as was their custom, but the people of Pingaree, although neither so big nor so strong as their foes, were able to defeat them and drive them all back to the sea, where a great storm overtook the raiders from Regos and Coregos and destroyed them and their boats, not a single warrior returning to his own country.

This defeat of the enemy seemed the more wonderful because the pearl fishers of Pingaree were mild and peaceful in disposition and seldom quarreled even among themselves. Their only weapons were their oyster rakes; yet the fact remains that they drove their fierce enemies from Regos and Coregos from their shores.

King Kitticut was only a boy when this remarkable battle was fought, and now his hair was grey; but he remembered the day well and, during the years that followed, his one constant fear was of another invasion of his enemies. He feared they might send a more numerous army to his island, both for conquest and revenge, in which case there could be little hope of successfully opposing them.

This anxiety on the part of King Kitticut led him to keep a sharp lookout for strange boats, one of his men patrolling the beach constantly, but he was too wise to allow any fear to make him or his subjects unhappy. He was a good King and lived very contentedly in his fine palace, with his fair Queen Garee and their one child, Prince Inga.

The wealth of Pingaree increased year by year; and the happiness of the people increased, too. Perhaps there was no place, outside the Land of Oz, where contentment and peace were more manifest than on this pretty island, hidden in the bosom of the Nonestic Ocean. Had these conditions remained undisturbed, there would have been no need to speak of Pingaree in this story.

Prince Inga, the heir to all the riches and the kingship of Pingaree, grew up surrounded by every luxury; but he was a manly little fellow, although somewhat too grave and thoughtful, and he could never bear to be idle a single minute. He knew where the finest oysters lay hidden along the coast and was as successful in finding pearls as any of the men of the island, although he was so slight and small. He had a little boat of his own and a rake for dragging up the oysters and he was very proud indeed when he could carry a big white pearl to his father.

There was no school upon the island, as the people of Pingaree were far removed from the state of civilization that gives our modern children such advantages as schools and learned professors, but the King owned several manuscript books, the pages being made of sheepskin. Being a man of intelligence, he was able to teach his son something of reading, writing and arithmetic.

When studying his lessons Prince Inga used to go into the grove near his father's palace and climb into the branches of a tall tree, where he had built a platform with a comfortable seat to rest upon, all hidden by the canopy of leaves. There, with no one to disturb him, he would pore over the sheepskin on which were written the queer characters of the Pingaresc language.

King Kitticut was very proud of his little son, as well he might be, and he soon felt a high respect for Inga's judgment and thought that he was worthy to be taken into the confidence of his father in many matters of state. He taught the boy the needs of the people and how to rule them justly, for some day he knew that Inga would be King in his place. One day he called his son to his side and said to him:

"Our island now seems peaceful enough, Inga, and we are happy and prosperous, but I cannot forget those terrible people of Regos and Coregos. My constant fear is that they will send a fleet of boats to search for those of their race whom we defeated many years ago, and whom the sea afterwards destroyed. If the warriors come in great numbers we may be unable to oppose them, for my people are little trained to fighting at best; they surely would cause us much injury and suffering."

"Are we, then, less powerful than in my grandfather's day?" asked Prince Inga.

The King shook his head thoughtfully.

"It is not that," said he. "That you may fully understand that marvelous battle, I must confide to you a great secret. I have in my possession three Magic Talismans, which I have ever guarded with utmost care, keeping the knowledge of their existence from anyone else. But, lest I should die, and the secret be lost, I have decided to tell you what these talismans are and where they are hidden. Come with me, my son."

He led the way through the rooms of the palace until they came to the great banquet hall. There, stopping in the center of the room, he stooped down and touched a hidden spring in the tiled floor. At once one of the tiles sank downward and the King reached within the cavity and drew out a silken bag.

This bag he proceeded to open, showing Inga that it contained three great pearls, each one as big around as a marble. One had a blue tint and one was of a delicate rose color, but the third was pure white.

"These three pearls," said the King, speaking in a solemn, impressive voice, "are the most wonderful the world has ever known. They were gifts to one of my ancestors from the Mermaid Queen, a powerful fairy whom he once had the good fortune to rescue from her enemies. In gratitude for this favor she presented him with these pearls. Each of the three possesses an astonishing power, and whoever is their owner may count himself a fortunate man. This one having the blue tint will give to the person who carries it a strength so great that no power can resist him. The one with the pink glow will protect its owner from all dangers that may threaten him, no matter from what source they may come. The third pearl—this one of pure white—can speak, and its words are always wise and helpful."

"What is this, my father!" exclaimed the Prince, amazed; "do you tell me that a pearl can speak? It sounds impossible."

"Your doubt is due to your ignorance of fairy powers,"

returned the King, gravely. "Listen, my son, and you will know that I speak the truth."

He held the white pearl to Inga's ear and the Prince heard a small voice say distinctly: "Your father is right. Never question the truth of what you fail to understand, for the world is filled with wonders."

"I crave your pardon, dear father," said the Prince, "for clearly I heard the pearl speak, and its words were full of wisdom."

"The powers of the other pearls are even greater," resumed the King. "Were I poor in all else, these gems would make me richer than any other monarch the world holds."

"I believe that," replied Inga, looking at the beautiful pearls with much awe. "But tell me, my father, why do you fear the warriors of Regos and Coregos when these marvelous powers are yours?"

"The powers are mine only while I have the pearls upon my person," answered King Kitticut, "and I dare not carry them constantly for fear they might be lost. Therefore, I keep them safely hidden in this recess. My only danger lies in the chance that my watchmen might fail to discover the approach of our enemies and allow the warrior invaders to seize me before I could secure the pearls. I should, in that case, be quite powerless to resist. My father owned the magic pearls at the time of the Great Fight, of which you have so often heard, and the pink pearl protected him from harm, while the blue pearl enabled him and his people to drive away the enemy. Often have I suspected that the destroying storm was caused by the fairy mermaids, but that is a matter of which I have no proof."

"I have often wondered how we managed to win that battle," remarked Inga thoughtfully. "But the pearls will assist us in case the warriors come again, will they not?"

"They are as powerful as ever," declared the King. "Really, my son, I have little to fear from any foe. But lest I die and the secret be lost to the next King, I have now given it into your keeping. Remember that these pearls are the rightful heritage of all Kings of Pingaree. If at any time I should be taken from you, Inga, guard this treasure well and do not forget where it is hidden."

"I shall not forget," said Inga.

Then the King returned the pearls to their hiding place and the boy went to his own room to ponder upon the wonderful secret his father had that day confided to his care.

Chapter 2

The COMING of KING RINKITINK

A few days after this, on a bright and sunny morning when the breeze blew soft and sweet from the ocean and the trees waved their leaf-laden branches, the Royal Watchman, whose duty it was to patrol the shore, came running to the King with news that a strange boat was approaching the island.

At first the King was sore afraid and made a step toward the hidden pearls, but the next moment he reflected that one boat, even if filled with enemies, would be powerless to injure him, so he curbed his fear and went down to the beach to discover who the strangers might be. Many of the men of

Pingaree assembled there also, and Prince Inga followed his father. Arriving at the water's edge, they all stood gazing eagerly at the oncoming boat.

It was quite a big boat, they observed, and covered with a canopy of purple silk, embroidered with gold. It was rowed by twenty men, ten on each side. As it came nearer, Inga could see that in the stern, seated upon a high, cushioned chair of state, was a little man who was so very fat that he was nearly as broad as he was high. This man was dressed in a loose silken robe of purple that fell in folds to his feet, while upon his head was a cap of white velvet curiously worked with golden threads and having a circle of diamonds sewn around the band. At the opposite end of the boat stood an oddly shaped cage, and several large boxes of sandalwood were piled near the center of the craft.

As the boat approached the shore the fat little man got upon his feet and bowed several times in the direction of those who had assembled to greet him, and as he bowed he flourished his white cap in an energetic manner. His face was round as an apple and nearly as rosy. When he stopped bowing he smiled in such a sweet and happy way that Inga thought he must be a very jolly fellow.

The prow of the boat grounded on the beach, stopping its speed so suddenly that the little man was caught unawares and nearly toppled headlong into the sea. But he managed to catch hold of the chair with one hand and the hair of one of his rowers with the other, and so steadied himself. Then, again waving his jeweled cap around his head, he cried in a merry voice:

"Well, here I am at last!"

"So I perceive," responded King Kitticut, bowing with much dignity.

The fat man glanced at all the sober faces before him and burst into a rollicking laugh. Perhaps I should say it was half laughter and half a chuckle of merriment, for the sounds he emitted were quaint and droll and tempted every hearer to laugh with him.

"Heh, heh—ho, ho, ho!" he roared. "Didn't expect me, I see. Keek-eek-eek-eek! This is funny—it's really funny. Didn't know I was coming, did you? Hoo, hoo, hoo, hoo! This is certainly amusing. But I'm here, just the same."

"Hush up!" said a deep, growling voice. "You're making yourself ridiculous."

Everyone looked to see where this voice came from; but none could guess who had uttered the words of rebuke. The rowers of the boat were all solemn and silent and certainly no one on the shore had spoken. But the little man did not seem astonished in the least, or even annoyed.

King Kitticut now addressed the stranger, saying courteously:

"You are welcome to the Kingdom of Pingaree. Perhaps you will deign to come ashore and at your convenience inform us whom we have the honor of receiving as a guest."

"Thanks; I will," returned the little fat man, waddling from his place in the boat and stepping, with some difficulty, upon the sandy beach. "I am King Rinkitink, of the City of Gilgad in the Kingdom of Rinkitink, and I have come to Pingaree to see for myself the monarch who sends to my city so many beautiful pearls. I have long wished to visit this island; and so, as I said before, here I am!"

"I am pleased to welcome you," said King Kitticut. "But why has your Majesty so few attendants? Is it not dangerous for the King of a great country to make distant journeys in one frail boat, and with but twenty men?"

"Oh, I suppose so," answered King Rinkitink, with a laugh. "But what else could I do? My subjects would not allow me to go anywhere at all, if they knew it. So I just ran away."

"Ran away!" exclaimed King Kitticut in surprise.

"Funny, isn't it? Heh, heh, heh—woo, hoo!" laughed Rinkitink, and this is as near as I can spell with letters the jolly sounds of his laughter. "Fancy a King running away from his own people—hoo, hoo—keek, eek, eek, eek! But I had to, don't you see!"

"Why?" asked the other King.

"They're afraid I'll get into mischief. They don't trust me. Keek-eek-eek—Oh, dear me! Don't trust their own King. Funny, isn't it?"

"No harm can come to you on this island," said Kitticut,

pretending not to notice the odd ways of his guest. "And, whenever it pleases you to return to your own country, I will send with you a fitting escort of my own people. In the meantime, pray accompany me to my palace, where everything shall be done to make you comfortable and happy."

"Much obliged," answered Rinkitink, tipping his white cap over his left ear and heartily shaking the hand of his brother monarch. "I'm sure you can make me comfortable if you've plenty to eat. And as for being happy—ha, ha, ha, ha!—why, that's my trouble. I'm *too* happy. But stop! I've brought you some presents in those boxes. Please order your men to carry them up to the palace."

"Certainly," answered King Kitticut, well pleased, and at once he gave his men the proper orders.

"And, by the way," continued the fat little King, "let them also take my goat from his cage."

"A goat!" exclaimed the King of Pingaree.

"Exactly; my goat Bilbil. I always ride him wherever I go, for I'm not at all fond of walking, being a trifle stout—eh, Kitticut?—a trifle stout! Hoo, hoo, hoo—keek, eek!"

The Pingaree people started to lift the big cage out of the boat, but just then a gruff voice cried: "Be careful, you villains!" and as the words seemed to come from the goat's mouth the men were so astonished that they dropped the cage upon the sand with a sudden jar.

"There! I told you so!" cried the voice angrily. "You've

rubbed the skin off my left knee. Why on earth didn't you handle me gently?"

"There, there, Bilbil," said King Rinkitink soothingly; "don't scold, my boy. Remember that these are strangers, and we their guests." Then he turned to Kitticut and remarked: "You have no talking goats on your island, I suppose."

"We have no goats at all," replied the King; "nor have we any animals, of any sort, who are able to talk."

"I wish my animal couldn't talk, either," said Rinkitink, winking comically at Inga and then looking toward the cage. "He is very cross at times, and indulges in language that is not respectful. I thought, at first, it would be fine to have a talking goat, with whom I could converse as I rode about my city on his back; but—keek-eek-eek-eek!—the rascal treats me as if I were a chimney sweep instead of a King. Heh, heh, heh, keek, eek! A chimney sweep—hoo, hoo, hoo!—and me a King! Funny, isn't it?" This last was addressed to Prince Inga, whom he chucked familiarly under the chin, to the boy's great embarrassment.

"Why do you not ride a horse?" asked King Kitticut.

"I can't climb upon his back, being rather stout; that's why. Kee, kee, keek, eek!—rather stout—hoo, hoo, hoo!" He paused to wipe the tears of merriment from his eyes and then added: "But I can get on and off Bilbil's back with ease."

He now opened the cage and the goat deliberately walked out and looked about him in a sulky manner. One of the rowers brought from the boat a saddle made of red velvet and beautifully embroidered with silver thistles, which he fastened upon the goat's back. The fat King put his leg over the saddle and seated himself comfortably, saying:

"Lead on, my noble host, and we will follow."

"What! Up that steep hill?" cried the goat. "Get off my back at once, Rinkitink, or I won't budge a step.

"But—consider, Bilbil," remonstrated the King. "How am I to get up that hill unless I ride?"

"Walk!" growled Bilbil.

"But I'm too fat. Really, Bilbil, I'm surprised at you. Haven't I brought you all this distance so you may see something of the world and enjoy life? And now you are so ungrateful as to refuse to carry me! Turn about is fair play, my boy. The boat carried you to this shore, because you can't swim, and now you must carry me up the hill, because I can't climb. Eh, Bilbil, isn't that reasonable?"

"Well, well, well," said the goat, surlily, "keep quiet and I'll carry you. But you make me very tired, Rinkitink, with your ceaseless chatter."

After making this protest Bilbil began walking up the hill, carrying the fat King upon his back with no difficulty whatever.

Prince Inga and his father and all the men of Pingaree were much astonished to overhear this dispute between King Rinkitink and his goat; but they were too polite to make critical remarks in the presence of their guests. King Kitticut walked beside the goat and the Prince followed after, the men coming last with the boxes of sandalwood.

When they neared the palace, the Queen and her maidens came out to meet them and the royal guest was escorted in state to the splendid Throne Room of the palace. Here the boxes were opened and King Rinkitink displayed all the beautiful silks and laces and jewelry with which they were filled. Every one of the courtiers and ladies received a handsome present, and the King and Queen had many rich gifts and Inga not a few. Thus the time passed pleasantly until the Chamberlain announced that dinner was served.

Bilbil the goat declared that he preferred eating of the sweet, rich grass that grew abundantly in the palace grounds, and Rinkitink said that the beast could never bear being shut up in a stable; so they removed the saddle from his back and allowed him to wander wherever he pleased.

During the dinner Inga divided his attention between admiring the pretty gifts he had received and listening to the jolly sayings of the fat King, who laughed when he was not eating and ate when he was not laughing and seemed to enjoy himself immensely.

"For four days I have lived in that narrow boat," said he, "with no other amusement than to watch the rowers and quarrel with Bilbil; so I am very glad to be on land again with such friendly and agreeable people."

"You do us great honor," said King Kitticut, with a polite bow.

"Not at all—not at all, my brother. This Pingaree must be a wonderful island, for its pearls are the admiration of all the world; nor will I deny the fact that my kingdom would be a poor one without the riches and glory it derives from the trade in your pearls. So I have wished for many years to come here to see you, but my people said: 'No! Stay at home and behave yourself, or we'll know the reason why.'"

"Will they not miss your Majesty from your palace at Gilgad?" inquired Kitticut.

"I think not," answered Rinkitink. "You see, one of my clever subjects has written a parchment entitled 'How to be Good,' and I believed it would benefit me to study it, as I consider the accomplishment of being good one of the fine arts. I had just scolded severely my Lord High Chancellor for coming to breakfast without combing his eyebrows, and was so sad and regretful at having hurt the poor man's feelings that I decided to shut myself up in my own room and study the scroll until I knew how to be good—hee, heek, keek, eek, eek!— to be good! Clever idea, that, wasn't it? Mighty clever! And I issued a decree that no one should enter my room, under pain of my royal displeasure, until I was ready to come out. They're awfully afraid of my royal displeasure, although not a bit afraid of me. Then I put the parchment in my pocket and escaped through the back door to my boat—and here I am. Oo, hoo-hoo, keek-eek! Imagine the fuss there would be in Gilgad if my subjects knew where I am this very minute!"

"I would like to see that parchment," said the solemn-eyed Prince Inga, "for if it indeed teaches one to be good it must be worth its weight in pearls."

"Oh, it's a fine essay," said Rinkitink, "and beautifully written with a goosequill. Listen to this: You'll enjoy it—tee, hee, hee!—enjoy it."

He took from his pocket a scroll of parchment tied with a black ribbon, and having carefully unrolled it, he proceeded to read as follows:

"'A Good Man is One who is Never Bad.' How's that, eh? Fine thought, what? 'Therefore, in order to be Good, you must avoid those Things which are Evil.' Oh, hoo-hoo-hoo!—how clever! When I get back I shall make the man who wrote that a royal hippolorum, for, beyond question, he is the wisest man in my kingdom—as he has often told me himself." With this, Rinkitink lay back in his chair and chuckled his queer chuckle until he coughed, and coughed until he choked and choked until he sneezed. And he wrinkled his face in such a jolly, droll way that few could keep from laughing with him, and even the good Queen was forced to titter behind her fan.

When Rinkitink had recovered from his fit of laughter and had wiped his eyes upon a fine lace handkerchief, Prince Inga said to him:

"The parchment speaks truly."

"Yes, it is true beyond doubt," answered Rinkitink, "and if I could persuade Bilbil to read it he would be a much better goat than he is now. Here is another selection: 'To avoid saying Unpleasant Things, always Speak Agreeably.' That would hit Bilbil, to a dot. And here is one that applies to you, my Prince: 'Good Children are seldom punished, for the reason that they deserve no punishment.' Now, I think that is neatly put, and shows the author to be a deep thinker. But the advice that has impressed me the most is in the following paragraph: 'You may not find it as Pleasant to be Good as it is to be Bad, but Other People will find it more Pleasant.' Haw-hoo-ho! keek-eek! 'Other people will find it more pleasant!'—hee, hee, heek, keek!— 'more pleasant.' Dear me—dear me! Therein lies a noble incentive to be good, and whenever I get time I'm surely going to try it."

Then he wiped his eyes again with the lace handkerchief and, suddenly remembering his dinner, seized his knife and fork and began eating.

Chapter 3

The WARRIORS from the NORTH

K ing Rinkitink was so much pleased
with the Island of Pingaree that he
continued his stay day after day and
week after week, eating good dinners,
talking with King Kitticut and sleeping. Once in a while he
would read from his scroll. "For," said he, "whenever I return
home, my subjects will be anxious to know if I have learned
'How to be Good,' and I must not disappoint them."

The twenty rowers lived on the small end of the island,
with the pearl fishers, and seemed not to care whether they
ever returned to the Kingdom of Rinkitink or not. Bilbil the
goat wandered over the grassy slopes, or among the trees,

and passed his days exactly as he pleased. His master seldom cared to ride him. Bilbil was a rare curiosity to the islanders, but since there was little pleasure in talking with the goat they kept away from him. This pleased the creature, who seemed well satisfied to be left to his own devices.

Once Prince Inga, wishing to be courteous, walked up to the goat and said: "Good morning, Bilbil."

"It isn't a good morning," answered Bilbil grumpily. "It is cloudy and damp, and looks like rain."

"I hope you are contented in our kingdom," continued the boy, politely ignoring the other's harsh words.

"I'm not," said Bilbil. "I'm never contented; so it doesn't matter to me whether I'm in your kingdom or in some other kingdom. Go away—will you?"

"Certainly," answered the Prince, and after this rebuff he did not again try to make friends with Bilbil.

Now that the King, his father, was so much occupied with his royal guest, Inga was often left to amuse himself, for a boy could not be allowed to take part in the conversation of two great monarchs. He devoted himself to his studies, therefore, and day after day he climbed into the branches of his favorite tree and sat for hours in his "tree-top rest," reading his father's precious manuscripts and thinking upon what he read.

You must not think that Inga was a mollycoddle or a prig, because he was so solemn and studious. Being a King's son and heir to a throne, he could not play with the other boys of Pingaree, and he lived so much in the society of the King and Queen, and was so surrounded by the pomp and dignity of a court, that he missed all the jolly times that boys usually have. I have no doubt that had he been able to live as other boys do, he would have been much like other boys; as it was, he was subdued by his surroundings, and more grave and thoughtful than one of his years should be.

Inga was in his tree one morning when, without warning, a great fog enveloped the Island of Pingaree. The boy could scarcely see the tree next to that in which he sat, but the leaves above him prevented the dampness from wetting him, so he curled himself up in his seat and fell fast asleep.

All that forenoon the fog continued. King Kitticut, who sat in his palace talking with his merry visitor, ordered the candles lighted, that they might be able to see one another. The good Queen, Inga's mother, found it was too dark to work at her embroidery, so she called her maidens together and told them wonderful stories of bygone days, in order to pass away the dreary hours.

But soon after noon the weather changed. The dense fog rolled away like a heavy cloud and suddenly the sun shot his bright rays over the island.

"Very good!" exclaimed King Kitticut. "We shall have a pleasant afternoon, I am sure," and he blew out the candles.

Then he stood a moment motionless, as if turned to stone,

for a terrible cry from without the palace reached his ears—a cry so full of fear and horror that the King's heart almost stopped beating. Immediately there was a scurrying of feet as everyone in the palace, filled with dismay, rushed outside to see what had happened. Even fat little Rinkitink sprang from his chair and followed his host and the others through the arched vestibule.

After many years the worst fears of King Kitticut were realized.

Landing upon the beach, which was but a few steps from the palace itself, were hundreds of boats, every one filled with a throng of fierce warriors. They sprang upon the land with wild shouts of defiance and rushed to the King's palace, waving aloft their swords and spears and battle-axes.

King Kitticut, so completely surprised that he was bewildered, gazed at the approaching host with terror and grief.

"They are the men of Regos and Coregos!" he groaned. "We are, indeed, lost!"

Then he bethought himself, for the first time, of his wonderful pearls. Turning quickly, he ran back into the palace and hastened to the hall where the treasures were hidden. But the leader of the warriors had seen the King enter the palace and bounded after him, thinking he meant to escape. Just as the King had stooped to press the secret spring in the tiles, the warrior seized him from the rear and threw him backward upon the floor, at the same time shouting to his men to fetch ropes and bind the prisoner. This they did very quickly and King Kitticut soon found himself helplessly bound and in the power of his enemies. In this sad condition he was lifted by the warriors and carried outside, when the good King looked upon a sorry sight.

The Queen and her maidens, the officers and servants of the royal household and all who had inhabited this end of the Island of Pingaree had been seized by the invaders and bound with ropes. At once they began carrying their victims to the boats, tossing them in as unceremoniously as if they had been bales of merchandise.

The King looked around for his son Inga, but failed to find the boy among the prisoners. Nor was the fat King, Rinkitink, to be seen anywhere about.

The warriors were swarming over the palace like bees in a hive, seeking anyone who might be in hiding, and after the search had been prolonged for some time the leader asked impatiently: "Do you find anyone else?"

"No," his men told him. "We have captured them all."

"Then," commanded the leader, "remove everything of value from the palace and tear down its walls and towers, so that not one stone remains upon another!"

While the warriors were busy with this task we will return to the boy Prince, who, when the fog lifted and the sun came out, wakened from his sleep and began to climb down from his perch in the tree. But the terrifying cries of the people, mingled with the shouts of the rude warriors, caused him to pause and listen eagerly.

Then he climbed rapidly up the tree, far above his platform, to the topmost swaying branches. This tree, which Inga called his own, was somewhat taller than the other trees that surrounded it, and when he had reached the top he pressed aside the leaves and saw a great fleet of boats upon the shore—strange boats, with banners that he had never seen before. Turning to look upon his father's palace, he found it surrounded by a horde of enemies. Then Inga knew the truth: that the island had been invaded by the barbaric warriors from the north. He grew so faint from the terror of it all that he might have fallen had he not wound his arms around a limb and clung fast until the dizzy feeling passed away. Then with his sash he bound himself to the limb and again ventured to look out through the leaves.

The warriors were now engaged in carrying King Kitticut and Queen Garee and all their other captives down to the boats, where they were thrown in and chained one to another. It was a dreadful sight for the Prince to witness, but he sat very still, concealed from the sight of anyone below by the bower of leafy branches around him. Inga knew very well that he could do nothing to help his beloved parents, and that if he came down he would only be forced to share their cruel fate.

Now a procession of the Northmen passed between the boats and the palace, bearing the rich furniture, splendid draperies and rare ornaments of which the royal palace had been robbed, together with such food and other plunder as they could lay their hands upon. After this, the men of Regos and Coregos threw ropes around the marble domes and towers and hundreds of warriors tugged at these ropes until the domes and towers toppled and fell in ruins upon the ground. Then the walls themselves were torn down, till little remained of the beautiful palace but a vast heap of white marble blocks tumbled and scattered upon the ground.

Prince Inga wept bitter tears of grief as he watched the ruin of his home; yet he was powerless to avert the destruction. When the palace had been demolished, some of the warriors entered their boats and rowed along the coast of the island, while the others marched in a great body down the length of the island itself. They were so numerous that they formed a line stretching from shore to shore and they destroyed every house they came to and took every inhabitant prisoner.

The pearl fishers who lived at the lower end of the island tried to escape in their boats, but they were soon overtaken and made prisoners, like the others. Nor was there any attempt to resist the foe, for the sharp spears and pikes and swords of the invaders terrified the hearts of the defenseless people of Pingaree, whose sole weapons were their oyster rakes.

When night fell the whole of the Island of Pingaree had been conquered by the men of the North, and all its people were slaves of the conquerors. Next morning the men of Regos and Coregos, being capable of no further mischief, departed from the scene of their triumph, carrying their prisoners with them and taking also every boat to be found upon the island. Many of the boats they had filled with rich plunder, with pearls and silks and velvets, with silver and gold ornaments and all the treasure that had made Pingaree famed as one of the richest kingdoms in the world. And the hundreds of slaves they had captured would be set to work in the mines of Regos and the grain fields of Coregos.

So complete was the victory of the Northmen that it is no wonder the warriors sang songs of triumph as they hastened back to their homes. Great rewards were awaiting them when they showed the haughty King of Regos and the terrible Queen of Coregos the results of their ocean raid and conquest.

Chapter 4

The DESERTED ISLAND

All through that terrible night Prince Inga remained hidden in his tree. In the morning he watched the great fleet of boats depart for their own country, carrying his parents and his countrymen with them, as well as everything of value the Island of Pingaree had contained.

Sad, indeed, were the boy's thoughts when the last of the boats had become a mere speck in the distance, but Inga did not dare leave his perch of safety until all of the craft of the invaders had disappeared beyond the horizon. Then he came down, very slowly and carefully, for he was weak from hunger and the long and weary watch, as he had been in the tree for twenty-four hours without food.

The sun shone upon the beautiful green isle as brilliantly as if no ruthless invader had passed and laid it in ruins. The birds still chirped among the trees and the butterflies darted from flower to flower as happily as when the land was filled with a prosperous and contented people.

Inga feared that only he was left of all his nation. Perhaps he might be obliged to pass his life there alone. He would not starve, for the sea would give him oysters and fish, and the trees fruit; yet the life that confronted him was far from enticing.

The boy's first act was to walk over to where the palace had stood and search the ruins until he found some scraps of food that had been overlooked by the enemy. He sat upon a block of marble and ate of this, and tears filled his eyes as he gazed upon the desolation around him. But Inga tried to bear up bravely, and having satisfied his hunger he walked over to the well, intending to draw a bucket of drinking water.

Fortunately, this well had been overlooked by the invaders and the bucket was still fastened to the chain that wound around a stout wooden windlass. Inga took hold of the crank and began letting the bucket down into the well, when suddenly he was startled by a muffled voice crying out:

"Be careful, up there!"

The sound and the words seemed to indicate that the voice came from the bottom of the well, so Inga looked down. Nothing could be seen, on account of the darkness.

"Who are you?" he shouted.

"It's I—Rinkitink," came the answer, and the depths of the well echoed: "Tink-i-tink-i-tink!" in a ghostly manner.

"Are you in the well?" asked the boy, greatly surprised.

"Yes, and nearly drowned. I fell in while running from those terrible warriors, and I've been standing in this damp hole ever since, with my head just above the water. It's lucky the well was no deeper, for had my head been under water, instead of above it—hoo, hoo, hoo, keek, eek!—under instead of over, you know—why, then I wouldn't be talking to you now! Ha, hoo, hee!" And the well dismally echoed: "Ha, hoo, hee!" which you must imagine was a laugh half merry and half sad.

"I'm awfully sorry," cried the boy, in answer. "I wonder you have the heart to laugh at all. But how am I to get you out?"

"I've been considering that all night," said Rinkitink, "and I believe the best plan will be for you to let down the bucket to me, and I'll hold fast to it while you wind up the chain and so draw me to the top."

"I will try to do that," replied Inga, and he let the bucket down very carefully until he heard the King call out:

"I've got it! Now pull me up—slowly, my boy, slowly—so I won't rub against the rough sides."

Inga began winding up the chain, but King Rinkitink was so fat that he was very heavy and by the time the boy had managed to pull him halfway up the well his strength was gone. He clung to the crank as long as possible, but suddenly it slipped from his grasp and the next minute he heard Rinkitink fall "plump!" into the water again.

"That's too bad!" called Inga, in real distress; "but you were so heavy I couldn't help it."

"Dear me!" gasped the King, from the darkness below, as he spluttered and coughed to get the water out of his mouth. "Why didn't you tell me you were going to let go?"

"I hadn't time," said Inga, sorrowfully.

"Well, I'm not suffering from thirst," declared the King, "for there's enough water inside me to float all the boats of Regos and Coregos—or at least it feels that way. But never mind! So long as I'm not actually drowned, what does it matter?"

"What shall we do next?" asked the boy anxiously.

"Call someone to help you," was the reply.

"There is no one on the island but myself," said the boy; "—excepting you," he added, as an afterthought.

"I'm not on it—more's the pity!—but *in* it," responded Rinkitink. "Are the warriors all gone?"

"Yes," said Inga, "and they have taken my father and mother, and all our people, to be their slaves," he added, trying in vain to repress a sob.

"So—so!" said Rinkitink softly; and then he paused a moment, as if in thought. Finally he said: "There are worse things than slavery, but I never imagined a well could be one of them. Tell me, Inga, could you let down some food to me? I'm nearly starved, and if you could manage to send me down some food I'd be *well* fed—hoo, hoo, heek, keek, eek!—well fed. Do you see the joke, Inga?"

"Do not ask me to enjoy a joke just now, your Majesty," begged Inga in a sad voice; "but if you will be patient I will try to find something for you to eat."

He ran back to the ruins of the palace and began searching for bits of food with which to satisfy the hunger of the King, when to his surprise he observed the goat, Bilbil, wandering among the marble blocks.

"What!" cried Inga. "Didn't the warriors get you, either?"

"If they had," calmly replied Bilbil, "I shouldn't be here."

"But how did you escape?" asked the boy.

"Easily enough. I kept my mouth shut and stayed away from the rascals," said the goat. "I knew that the soldiers would not care for a skinny old beast like me, for to the eye of a stranger I seem good for nothing. Had they known I could talk, and that my head contained more wisdom than a hundred of their own noddles, I might not have escaped so easily."

"Perhaps you are right," said the boy.

"I suppose they got the old man?" carelessly remarked Bilbil.

"What old man?"

"Rinkitink."

"Oh, no! His Majesty is at the bottom of the well," said Inga, "and I don't know how to get him out again."

"Then let him stay there," suggested the goat.

"That would be cruel. I am sure, Bilbil, that you are fond of the good King, your master, and do not mean what you say. Together, let us find some way to save poor King Rinkitink. He is a very jolly companion, and has a heart exceedingly kind and gentle."

"Oh, well; the old boy isn't so bad, taken altogether," admitted Bilbil, speaking in a more friendly tone. "But his bad jokes and fat laughter tire me dreadfully, at times."

Prince Inga now ran back to the well, the goat following more leisurely.

"Here's Bilbil!" shouted the boy to the King. "The enemy didn't get him, it seems."

"That's lucky for the enemy," said Rinkitink. "But it's lucky for me, too, for perhaps the beast can assist me out of this hole. If you can let a rope down the well, I am sure that you and Bilbil, pulling together, will be able to drag me to the earth's surface."

"Be patient and we will make the attempt," replied Inga encouragingly, and he ran to search the ruins for a rope. Presently he found one that had been used by the warriors in toppling over the towers, which in their haste they had neglected to remove, and with some difficulty he untied the knots and carried the rope to the mouth of the well.

Bilbil had lain down to sleep and the refrain of a merry song came in muffled tones from the well, proving that Rinkitink was making a patient endeavor to amuse himself.

"I've found a rope!" Inga called down to him; and then the boy proceeded to make a loop in one end of the rope, for the King to put his arms through, and the other end he placed over the drum of the windlass. He now aroused Bilbil and fastened the rope firmly around the goat's shoulders.

"Are you ready?" asked the boy, leaning over the well.

"I am," replied the King.

"And I am not," growled the goat, "for I have not yet had my nap out. Old Rinki will be safe enough in the well until I've slept an hour or two longer."

"But it is damp in the well," protested the boy, "and King Rinkitink may catch the rheumatism, so that he will have to ride upon your back wherever he goes."

Hearing this, Bilbil jumped up at once.

"Let's get him out," he said earnestly.

"Hold fast!" shouted Inga to the King. Then he seized the rope and helped Bilbil to pull. They soon found the task more difficult than they had supposed. Once or twice the King's weight threatened to drag both the boy and the goat into the well, to keep Rinkitink company. But they pulled sturdily, being aware of this danger, and at last the King popped out of the hole and fell sprawling full length upon the ground.

For a time he lay panting and breathing hard to get his breath back, while Inga and Bilbil were likewise worn out from their long strain at the rope; so the three rested quietly upon the grass and looked at one another in silence.

Finally Bilbil said to the King:

"I'm surprised at you. Why were you so foolish as to fall down that well? Don't you know it's a dangerous thing to do? You might have broken your neck in the fall, or been drowned in the water."

"Bilbil," replied the King solemnly, "you're a goat. Do you imagine I fell down the well on purpose?"

"I imagine nothing," retorted Bilbil. "I only know you were there."

"There? Heh-heh-heek-keek-eek! To be sure I was there," laughed Rinkitink. "There in a dark hole, where there was no light; there in a watery well, where the wetness soaked me through and through—keek-eek-eek-eek!—through and through!"

"How did it happen?" inquired Inga.

"I was running away from the enemy," explained the King, "and I was carelessly looking over my shoulder at the same time, to see if they were chasing me. So I did not see the well, but stepped into it and found myself tumbling down to the bottom. I struck the water very neatly and began struggling to keep myself from drowning, but presently I found that when I stood upon my feet on the bottom of the well, that my chin was just above the water. So I stood still and yelled for help; but no one heard me."

"If the warriors had heard you," said Bilbil, "they would have pulled you out and carried you away to be a slave. Then you would have been obliged to work for a living, and that would be a new experience."

"Work!" exclaimed Rinkitink. "Me work? Hoo, hoo, heek-keek-eek! How absurd! I'm so stout—not to say chubby—not to say fat—that I can hardly walk, and I couldn't earn my salt at hard work. So I'm glad the enemy did not find me, Bilbil. How many others escaped?"

"That I do not know," replied the boy, "for I have not yet had time to visit the other parts of the island. When you have rested and satisfied your royal hunger, it might be well for us to look around and see what the thieving warriors of Regos and Coregos have left us."

"An excellent idea," declared Rinkitink. "I am somewhat feeble from my long confinement in the well, but I can ride upon Bilbil's back and we may as well start at once."

Hearing this, Bilbil cast a surly glance at his master but said nothing, since it was really the goat's business to carry King Rinkitink wherever he desired to go.

They first searched the ruins of the palace, and where the kitchen had once been they found a small quantity of food that had been half hidden by a block of marble. This they carefully placed in a sack to preserve it for future use, the little fat King having first eaten as much as he cared for. This consumed some time, for Rinkitink had been exceedingly hungry and liked to eat in a leisurely manner. When he had finished the meal he straddled Bilbil's back and set out to explore the island, Prince Inga walking by his side.

They found on every hand ruin and desolation. The houses of the people had been pilfered of all valuables and then torn down or burned. Not a boat had been left upon the shore, nor was there a single person, man or woman or child, remaining upon the island, save themselves. The only inhabitants of Pingaree now consisted of a fat little King, a boy and a goat.

Even Rinkitink, merry hearted as he was, found it hard to laugh in the face of this mighty disaster. Even the goat, contrary to its usual habit, refrained from saying anything disagreeable. As for the poor boy whose home was now a wilderness, the tears came often to his eyes as he marked the ruin of his dearly loved island.

When, at nightfall, they reached the lower end of Pingaree and found it swept as bare as the rest, Inga's grief was almost more than he could bear. Everything had been swept from him— parents, home and country—in so brief a time that his bewilderment was equal to his sorrow.

Since no house remained standing, in which they might sleep, the three wanderers crept beneath the overhanging branches of a cassa tree and curled themselves up as comfortably as possible. So tired and exhausted were they by the day's anxieties and griefs that their troubles soon faded into the mists of dreamland. Beast and King and boy slumbered peacefully together until wakened by the singing of the birds which greeted the dawn of a new day.

Chapter 5

The THREE PEARLS

When King Rinkitink and Prince Inga had bathed themselves in the sea and eaten a simple breakfast, they began wondering what they could do to improve their condition. "The poor people of Gilgad," said Rinkitink cheerfully, "are little likely ever again to behold their King in the flesh, for my boat and my rowers are gone with everything else. Let us face the fact that we are imprisoned for life upon this island, and that our lives will be short unless we can secure more to eat than is in this small sack."

"I'll not starve, for I can eat grass," remarked the goat in a pleasant tone—or a tone as pleasant as Bilbil could assume.

"True, quite true," said the King. Then he seemed thoughtful for a moment and turning to Inga he asked: "Do you think, Prince, that if the worst comes, we could eat Bilbil?"

The goat gave a groan and cast a reproachful look at his master as he said:

"Monster! Would you, indeed, eat your old friend and servant?"

"Not if I can help it, Bilbil," answered the King pleasantly. "You would make a remarkably tough morsel, and my teeth are not as good as they once were."

While this talk was in progress Inga suddenly remembered the three pearls which his father had hidden under the tiled floor of the banquet hall. Without doubt King Kitticut had been so suddenly surprised by the invaders that he had found no opportunity to get the pearls, for otherwise the fierce warriors would have been defeated and driven out of Pingaree. So they must still be in their hiding place, and Inga believed they would prove of great assistance to him and his comrades in this hour of need. But the palace was a mass of ruins; perhaps he would be unable now to find the place where the pearls were hidden.

He said nothing of this to Rinkitink, remembering that his father had charged him to preserve the secret of the pearls and of their magic powers. Nevertheless, the thought of securing the wonderful treasures of his ancestors gave the boy new hope.

He stood up and said to the King:

"Let us return to the other end of Pingaree. It is more pleasant than here in spite of the desolation of my father's palace. And there, if anywhere, we shall discover a way out of our difficulties."

This suggestion met with Rinkitink's approval and the little party at once started upon the return journey. As there was no occasion to delay upon the way, they reached the big end of the island about the middle of the day and at once began searching the ruins of the palace.

They found, to their satisfaction, that one room at the bottom of a tower was still habitable, although the roof was broken in and the place was somewhat littered with stones. The King was, as he said, too fat to do any hard work, so he sat down on a block of marble and watched Inga clear the room of its rubbish. This done, the boy hunted through the ruins until he discovered a stool and an armchair that had not been broken beyond use. Some bedding and a mattress were also found, so that by nightfall the little room had been made quite comfortable.

The following morning, while Rinkitink was still sound asleep and Bilbil was busily cropping the dewy grass that edged the shore, Prince Inga began to search the tumbled heaps of marble for the place where the royal banquet hall had been. After climbing over the ruins for a time he reached a flat place which he recognized, by means of the tiled flooring and the broken furniture scattered about, to be the great hall he was seeking. But in the center of the floor, directly over the spot where the pearls were hidden, lay several large and heavy blocks of marble, which had been torn from the dismantled walls.

This unfortunate discovery for a time discouraged the boy, who realized how helpless he was to remove such vast obstacles; but it was so important to secure the pearls that he dared not give way to despair until every human effort had been made, so he sat him down to think over the matter with great care.

Meantime Rinkitink had risen from his bed and walked out upon the lawn, where he found Bilbil reclining at ease upon the greensward.

"Where is Inga?" asked Rinkitink, rubbing his eyes with his knuckles because their vision was blurred with too much sleep.

"Don't ask me," said the goat, chewing with much satisfaction a cud of sweet grasses.

"Bilbil," said the King, squatting down beside the goat and resting his fat chin upon his hands and his elbows on his knees, "allow me to confide to you the fact that I am bored, and need amusement. My good friend Kitticut has been kidnapped by the barbarians and taken from me, so there is no one to converse with me intelligently. I am the King and you are the goat. Suppose you tell me a story."

"Suppose I don't," said Bilbil, with a scowl, for a goat's face is very expressive.

"If you refuse, I shall be more unhappy than ever, and I know your disposition is too sweet to permit that. Tell me a story, Bilbil."

The goat looked at him with an expression of scorn. Said he:

"One would think you are but four years old, Rinkitink! But there—I will do as you command. Listen carefully, and the story may do you some good—although I doubt if you understand the moral."

"I am sure the story will do me good," declared the King, whose eyes were twinkling.

"Once on a time," began the goat.

"When was that, Bilbil?" asked the King gently.

"Don't interrupt; it is impolite. Once on a time there was a King with a hollow inside his head, where most people have their brains, and—"

"Is this a true story, Bilbil?"

"And the King with a hollow head could chatter words, which had no sense, and laugh in a brainless manner at senseless things. That part of the story is true enough, Rinkitink."

"Then proceed with the tale, sweet Bilbil. Yet it is hard to believe that any King could be brainless—unless, indeed, he proved it by owning a talking goat."

Bilbil glared at him a full minute in silence. Then he resumed his story:

"This empty-headed man was a King by accident, having

been born to that high station. Also the King was empty-headed by the same chance, being born without brains."

"Poor fellow!" quoth the King. "Did he own a talking goat?"

"He did," answered Bilbil.

"Then he was wrong to have been born at all. Cheek-eek-eek-eek, oo, hoo!" chuckled Rinkitink, his fat body shaking with merriment. "But it's hard to prevent oneself from being born; there's no chance for protest, eh, Bilbil?"

"Who is telling this story, I'd like to know," demanded the goat, with anger.

"Ask someone with brains, my boy; I'm sure I can't tell," replied the King, bursting into one of his merry fits of laughter.

Bilbil rose to his hoofs and walked away in a dignified manner, leaving Rinkitink chuckling anew at the sour expression of the animal's face.

"Oh, Bilbil, you'll be the death of me, some day—I'm sure you will!" gasped the King, taking out his lace handkerchief to wipe his eyes; for, as he often did, he had laughed till the tears came.

Bilbil was deeply vexed and would not even turn his head to look at his master. To escape from Rinkitink he wandered among the ruins of the palace, where he came upon Prince Inga.

"Good morning, Bilbil," said the boy. "I was just going to find you, that I might consult you upon an important matter. If you will kindly turn back with me I am sure your good judgment will be of great assistance."

The angry goat was quite mollified by the respectful tone in which he was addressed, but he immediately asked:

"Are you also going to consult that empty-headed King over yonder?"

"I am sorry to hear you speak of your kind master in such a way," said the boy gravely. "All men are deserving of respect, being the highest of living creatures, and Kings deserve respect more than others, for they are set to rule over many people."

"Nevertheless," said Bilbil with conviction, "Rinkitink's head is certainly empty of brains."

"That I am unwilling to believe," insisted Inga. "But anyway his heart is kind and gentle and that is better than being wise. He is merry in spite of misfortunes that would cause others to weep and he never speaks harsh words that wound the feelings of his friends."

"Still," growled Bilbil, "he is—"

"Let us forget everything but his good nature, which puts new heart into us when we are sad," advised the boy.

"But he is—"

"Come with me, please," interrupted Inga, "for the matter of which I wish to speak is very important."

Bilbil followed him, although the boy still heard the goat muttering that the King had no brains. Rinkitink, seeing them turn into the ruins, also followed, and upon joining them asked for his breakfast.

Inga opened the sack of food and while he and the King ate of it the boy said:

"If I could find a way to remove some of the blocks of marble which have fallen in the banquet hall, I think I could find means for us to escape from this barren island."

"Then," mumbled Rinkitink, with his mouth full, "let us move the blocks of marble."

"But how?" inquired Prince Inga. "They are very heavy."

"Ah, how, indeed?" returned the King, smacking his lips contentedly. "That is a serious question. But—I have it! Let us see what my famous parchment says about it." He wiped his fingers upon a napkin and then, taking the scroll from a pocket inside his embroidered blouse, he unrolled it and read the following words: "Never step on another man's toes."

The goat gave a snort of contempt; Inga was silent; the King looked from one to the other inquiringly.

"That's the idea, exactly!" declared Rinkitink.

"To be sure," said Bilbil scornfully, "it tells us exactly how to move the blocks of marble."

"Oh, does it?" responded the King, and then for a moment he rubbed the top of his bald head in a perplexed manner. The next moment he burst into a peal of joyous laughter. The goat looked at Inga and sighed.

"What did I tell you?" asked the creature. "Was I right, or was I wrong?"

"This scroll," said Rinkitink, "is indeed a masterpiece. Its advice is of tremendous value. 'Never step on another man's toes.' Let us think this over. The inference is that we should step upon our own toes, which were given us for that purpose. Therefore, if I stepped upon another man's toes, I would be the other man. Hoo, hoo, hoo!—the other man—hee, hee, heek-keek-eek! Funny, isn't it?"

"Didn't I say—" began Bilbil.

"No matter what you said, my boy," roared the King. "No fool could have figured that out as nicely as I did."

"We have still to decide how to remove the blocks of marble," suggested Inga anxiously.

"Fasten a rope to them, and pull," said Bilbil. "Don't pay any more attention to Rinkitink, for he is no wiser than the man who wrote that brainless scroll. Just get the rope, and we'll fasten Rinkitink to one end of it for a weight and I'll help you pull."

"Thank you, Bilbil," replied the boy. "I'll get the rope at once."

Bilbil found it difficult to climb over the ruins to the floor of the banquet hall, but there are few places a goat cannot get to when it makes the attempt, so Bilbil succeeded at last, and even fat little Rinkitink finally joined them, though much out of breath.

Inga fastened one end of the rope around a block of marble and then made a loop at the other end to go over Bilbil's head.

When all was ready the boy seized the rope and helped the goat to pull; yet, strain as they might, the huge block would not stir from its place. Seeing this, King Rinkitink came forward and lent his assistance, the weight of his body forcing the heavy marble to slide several feet from where it had lain.

But it was hard work and all were obliged to take a long rest before undertaking the removal of the next block.

"Admit, Bilbil," said the King, "that I am of some use in the world."

"Your weight was of considerable help," acknowledged the goat, "but if your head were as well filled as your stomach the task would be still easier."

When Inga went to fasten the rope a second time he was rejoiced to discover that by moving one more block of marble he could uncover the tile with the secret spring. So the three pulled with renewed energy and to their joy the block moved and rolled upon its side, leaving Inga free to remove the treasure when he pleased.

But the boy had no intention of allowing Bilbil and the King to share the secret of the royal treasures of Pingaree; so, although both the goat and its master demanded to know why the marble blocks had been moved, and how it would benefit them, Inga begged them to wait until the next morning, when he hoped to be able to satisfy them that their hard work had not been in vain.

Having little confidence in this promise of a mere boy, the goat grumbled and the King laughed; but Inga paid no heed to their ridicule and set himself to work rigging up a fishing rod, with line and hook. During the afternoon he waded out to some rocks near the shore and fished patiently until he had captured enough yellow perch for their supper and breakfast.

"Ah," said Rinkitink, looking at the fine catch when Inga returned to the shore; "these will taste delicious when they are cooked; but do you know how to cook them?"

"No," was the reply. "I have often caught fish, but never cooked them. Perhaps your Majesty understands cooking."

"Cooking and majesty are two different things," laughed the little King. "I could not cook a fish to save me from starvation."

"For my part," said Bilbil, "I never eat fish, but I can tell you how to cook them, for I have often watched the palace cooks at their work." And so, with the goat's assistance, the boy and the King managed to prepare the fish and cook them, after which they were eaten with good appetite.

That night, after Rinkitink and Bilbil were both fast asleep, Inga stole quietly through the moonlight to the desolate banquet hall. There, kneeling down, he touched the secret spring as his father had instructed him to do and to his joy the tile sank downward and disclosed the opening. You may imagine how the boy's heart throbbed with excitement as he slowly thrust his hand into the cavity and felt around to see if the precious pearls were still there. In a moment his fingers touched the silken bag and, without pausing to close the recess, he pressed the treasure against his breast and ran out into the moonlight to examine it. When he reached a bright place he started to open the bag, but he observed Bilbil lying asleep upon the grass nearby. So, trembling with the fear of discovery, he ran to another place, and when he paused he heard Rinkitink snoring lustily. Again he fled and made his way to the seashore, where he squatted under a bank and began to untie the cords that fastened the mouth of the bag. But now another fear assailed him.

"If the pearls should slip from my hand," he thought, "and roll into the water, they might be lost to me forever. I must find some safer place."

Here and there he wandered, still clasping the silken bag in both hands, and finally he went to the grove and climbed into the tall tree where he had made his platform and seat. But here it was pitch dark, so he found he must wait patiently until morning before he dared touch the pearls. During those hours of waiting he had time for reflection and reproached himself for being so frightened by the possession of his father's treasures.

"These pearls have belonged to our family for generations," he mused, "yet no one has ever lost them. If I use ordinary care I am sure I need have no fears for their safety."

When the dawn came and he could see plainly, Inga opened the bag and took out the Blue Pearl. There was no possibility of his being observed by others, so he took time to examine it wonderingly, saying to himself: "This will give me strength."

Taking off his right shoe he placed the Blue Pearl within it, far up in the pointed toe. Then he tore a piece from his handkerchief and stuffed it into the shoe to hold the pearl in place. Inga's shoes were long and pointed, as were all the shoes worn in Pingaree, and the points curled upward, so that there was quite a vacant space beyond the place where the boy's toes reached when the shoe was upon his foot.

After he had put on the shoe and laced it up he opened the bag and took out the Pink Pearl. "This will protect me from danger," said Inga, and removing the shoe from his left foot he carefully placed the pearl in the hollow toe. This, also, he secured in place by means of a strip torn from his hand-kerchief.

Having put on the second shoe and laced it up, the boy drew from the silken bag the third pearl—that which was pure white—and holding it to his ear he asked, "Will you advise me what to do, in this my hour of misfortune?"

Clearly the small Voice of the Pearl made answer:

"I advise you to go to the Islands of Regos and Coregos, where you may liberate your parents from slavery."

"How could I do that?" exclaimed Prince Inga, amazed at receiving such advice.

"Tonight," spoke the Voice of the Pearl, "there will be a storm, and in the morning a boat will strand upon the shore.

Take this boat and row to Regos and Coregos."

"How can I, a weak boy, pull the boat so far?" he inquired, doubting the possibility.

"The Blue Pearl will give you strength," was the reply.

"But I may be shipwrecked and drowned, before ever I reach Regos and Coregos," protested the boy.

"The Pink Pearl will protect you from harm," murmured the voice, soft and low but very distinct.

"Then I shall act as you advise me," declared Inga, speaking firmly because this promise gave him courage, and as he removed the pearl from his ear it whispered:

"The wise and fearless are sure to win success."

Restoring the White Pearl to the depths of the silken bag, Inga fastened it securely around his neck and buttoned his waist above it to hide the treasure from all prying eyes. Then he slowly climbed down from the tree and returned to the room where King Rinkitink still slept.

The goat was browsing upon the grass but looked cross and surly. When the boy said good morning as he passed, Bilbil made no response whatever. As Inga entered the room the King awoke and asked:

"What is that mysterious secret of yours? I've been dreaming about it, and I haven't got my breath yet from tugging at those heavy blocks. Tell me the secret."

"A secret told is no longer a secret," replied Inga, with a laugh. "Besides, this is a family secret, which it is proper I should keep to myself. But I may tell you one thing, at least: We are going to leave this island tomorrow morning."

The King seemed puzzled by this statement.

"I'm not much of a swimmer," said he, "and, though I'm fat enough to float upon the surface of the water, I'd only bob around and get nowhere at all."

"We shall not swim, but ride comfortably in a boat," promised Inga.

"There isn't a boat on this island!" declared Rinkitink, looking upon the boy with wonder.

"True," said Inga. "But one will come to us in the morning." He spoke positively, for he had perfect faith in the promise of the White Pearl; but Rinkitink, knowing nothing of the three marvelous jewels, began to fear that the little Prince had lost his mind through grief and misfortune.

For this reason the King did not question the boy further but tried to cheer him by telling him witty stories. He laughed at all the stories himself, in his merry, rollicking way, and Inga joined freely in the laughter because his heart had been lightened by the prospect of rescuing his dear parents. Not since the fierce warriors had descended upon Pingaree had the boy been so hopeful and happy.

With Rinkitink riding upon Bilbil's back, the three made a tour of the island and found in the central part some bushes and trees bearing ripe fruit. They gathered this freely, for— aside from the fish which Inga caught—it was the only food they now had, and the less they had, the bigger Rinkitink's appetite seemed to grow.

"I am never more happy," said he with a sigh, "than when I am eating."

Toward evening the sky became overcast and soon a great storm began to rage. Prince Inga and King Rinkitink took refuge within the shelter of the room they had fitted up and there Bilbil joined them. The goat and the King were somewhat disturbed by the violence of the storm, but Inga did not mind it, being pleased at this evidence that the White Pearl might be relied upon.

All night the wind shrieked around the island; thunder rolled, lightning flashed and rain came down in torrents. But with morning the storm abated and when the sun arose no sign of the tempest remained save a few fallen trees.

Chapter 6

The MAGIC BOAT

Prince Inga was up with the sun and, accompanied by Bilbil, began walking along the shore in search of the boat which the White Pearl had promised him. Never for an instant did he doubt that he would find it and before he had walked any great distance a dark object at the water's edge caught his eye.

"It is the boat, Bilbil!" he cried joyfully, and running down to it he found it was, indeed, a large and roomy boat. Although stranded upon the beach, it was in perfect order and had suffered in no way from the storm.

Inga stood for some moments gazing upon the handsome craft and wondering where it could have come from. Certainly it was unlike any boat he had ever seen. On the outside it was painted a lustrous black, without any other color to relieve it; but all the inside of the boat was lined with pure silver, polished so highly that the surface resembled a mirror and glinted brilliantly in the rays of the sun. The seats had white velvet cushions upon them and the cushions were splendidly embroidered with threads of gold. At one end, beneath the broad seat, was a small barrel with silver hoops, which the boy found was filled with fresh, sweet water. A great chest of sandalwood, bound and ornamented with silver, stood in the other end of the boat. Inga raised the lid and discovered the chest filled with sea-biscuits, cakes, tinned meats and ripe, juicy melons; enough good and wholesome food to last the party a long time.

Lying upon the bottom of the boat were two shining oars, and overhead, but rolled back now, was a canopy of silver cloth to ward off the heat of the sun.

It is no wonder the boy was delighted with the appearance of this beautiful boat; but on reflection he feared it was too large for him to row any great distance. Unless, indeed, the Blue Pearl gave him unusual strength.

While he was considering this matter, King Rinkitink came waddling up to him and said:

"Well, well, well, my Prince, your words have come true! Here is the boat, for a certainty, yet how it came here—and how you knew it would come to us—are puzzles that mystify me. I do not question our good fortune, however, and my heart is bubbling with joy, for in this boat I will return at once to my City of Gilgad, from which I have remained absent altogether too long a time."

"I do not wish to go to Gilgad," said Inga.

"That is too bad, my friend, for you would be very welcome. But you may remain upon this island, if you wish," continued Rinkitink, "and when I get home I will send some of my people to rescue you."

"It is my boat, your Majesty," said Inga quietly.

"May be, may be," was the careless answer, "but I am King of a great country, while you are a boy Prince without any kingdom to speak of. Therefore, being of greater importance than you, it is just and right that I take your boat and return to my own country in it."

"I am sorry to differ from your Majesty's views," said Inga, "but instead of going to Gilgad I consider it of greater importance that we go to the islands of Regos and Coregos."

"Hey? What!" cried the astounded King. "To Regos and Coregos! To become slaves of the barbarians, like the King, your father? No, no, my boy! Your Uncle Rinki may have an empty noddle, as Bilbil claims, but he is far too wise to put his head in the lion's mouth. It's no fun to be a slave."

"The people of Regos and Coregos will not enslave us," declared Inga. "On the contrary, it is my intention to set free my dear parents, as well as all my people, and to bring them back again to Pingaree."

"Cheek-eek-eek-eek-eek! How funny!" chuckled Rinki-tink, winking at the goat, which scowled in return. "Your audacity takes my breath away, Inga, but the adventure has its charm, I must confess. Were I not so fat, I'd agree to your plan at once, and could probably conquer that horde of fierce warriors without any assistance at all—any at all—eh, Bilbil? But I grieve to say that I am fat, and not in good fighting trim. As for your determination to do what I admit I can't do, Inga, I fear you forget that you are only a boy, and rather small at that."

"No, I do not forget that," was Inga's reply.

"Then please consider that you and I and Bilbil are not strong enough, as an army, to conquer a powerful nation of skilled warriors. We could attempt it, of course, but you are too young to die, while I am too old. Come with me to my City of Gilgad, where you will be greatly honored. I'll have my professors teach you how to be good. Eh? What do you say?"

Inga was a little embarrassed how to reply to these arguments, which he knew King Rinkitink considered were wise; so, after a period of thought, he said:

"I will make a bargain with your Majesty, for I do not wish to fail in respect to so worthy a man and so great a King as yourself. This boat is mine, as I have said, and in my father's absence you have become my guest; therefore I claim that I am entitled to some consideration, as well as you."

"No doubt of it," agreed Rinkitink. "What is the bargain you propose, Inga?"

"Let us both get into the boat, and you shall first try to row us to Gilgad. If you succeed, I will accompany you right willingly; but should you fail, I will then row the boat to Regos, and you must come with me without further protest."

"A fair and just bargain!" cried the King, highly pleased. "Yet, although I am a man of mighty deeds, I do not relish the prospect of rowing so big a boat all the way to Gilgad. But I will do my best and abide by the result."

The matter being thus peaceably settled, they prepared to embark. A further supply of fruits was placed in the boat and Inga also raked up a quantity of the delicious oysters that abounded on the coast of Pingaree but which he had before been unable to reach for lack of a boat. This was done at the suggestion of the ever-hungry Rinkitink, and when the oysters had been stowed in their shells behind the water barrel and a plentiful supply of grass brought aboard for Bilbil, they decided they were ready to start on their voyage.

It proved no easy task to get Bilbil into the boat, for he was a remarkably clumsy goat and once, when Rinkitink gave him a push, he tumbled into the water and nearly drowned before they could get him out again. But there was no thought of leaving the quaint animal behind. His power of speech made him seem almost human in the eyes of the boy, and the fat King was so accustomed to his surly companion that nothing could have induced him to part with him. Finally Bilbil fell sprawling into the bottom of the boat, and Inga helped him to get to the front end, where there was enough space for him to lie down.

Rinkitink now took his seat in the silver-lined craft and the boy came last, pushing off the boat as he sprang aboard, so that it floated freely upon the water.

"Well, here we go for Gilgad!" exclaimed the King, picking up the oars and placing them in the row-locks. Then he began to row as hard as he could, singing at the same time an odd sort of a song that ran like this:

> *"The way to Gilgad isn't bad*
> *For a stout old King and a brave young lad,*
> *For a cross old goat with a dripping coat,*
> *And a silver boat in which to float.*
> *So our hearts are merry, light and glad*
> *As we speed away to fair Gilgad!"*

"Don't, Rinkitink; please don't! It makes me seasick," growled Bilbil.

Rinkitink stopped rowing, for by this time he was all out of breath and his round face was covered with big drops of perspiration. And when he looked over his shoulder he found to his dismay that the boat had scarcely moved a foot from its former position.

Inga said nothing and appeared not to notice the King's failure. So now Rinkitink, with a serious look on his fat, red face, took off his purple robe and rolled up the sleeves of his tunic and tried again.

However, he succeeded no better than before and when he heard Bilbil give a gruff laugh and saw a smile upon the boy Prince's face, Rinkitink suddenly dropped the oars and began shouting with laughter at his own defeat. As he wiped his brow with a yellow silk handkerchief he sang in a merry voice:

> *"A sailor bold am I, I hold,*
> *But boldness will not row a boat.*
> *So I confess I'm in distress*
> *And just as useless as the goat."*

"Please leave me out of your verses," said Bilbil with a snort of anger.

"When I make a fool of myself, Bilbil, I'm a goat," replied Rinkitink.

"Not so," insisted Bilbil. "Nothing could make you a member of my superior race."

"Superior? Why, Bilbil, a goat is but a beast, while I am a King!"

"I claim that superiority lies in intelligence," said the goat.

Rinkitink paid no attention to this remark, but turning to Inga he said:

"We may as well get back to the shore, for the boat is too heavy to row to Gilgad or anywhere else. Indeed, it will be hard for us to reach land again."

"Let me take the oars," suggested Inga. "You must not forget our bargain."

"No, indeed," answered Rinkitink. "If you can row us to Regos, or to any other place, I will go with you without protest."

So the King took Inga's place at the stern of the boat and the boy grasped the oars and commenced to row. And now, to the great wonder of Rinkitink—and even to Inga's surprise—the oars became light as feathers as soon as the Prince took hold of them. In an instant the boat began to glide rapidly through the water and, seeing this, the boy turned its prow toward the north. He did not know exactly where Regos and Coregos were located, but he did know that the islands lay to the north of Pingaree, so he decided to trust to luck and the guidance of the pearls to carry him to them.

Gradually the Island of Pingaree became smaller to their view as the boat sped onward, until at the end of an hour they had lost sight of it altogether and were wholly surrounded by the purple waters of the Nonestic Ocean.

Prince Inga did not tire from the labor of rowing; indeed, it seemed to him no labor at all. Once he stopped long enough to place the poles of the canopy in the holes that had been made for them, in the edges of the boat, and to spread the canopy of silver over the poles, for Rinkitink had complained of the sun's heat. But the canopy shut out the hot rays and rendered the interior of the boat cool and pleasant.

"This is a glorious ride!" cried Rinkitink, as he lay back in the shade. "I find it a decided relief to be away from that dismal island of Pingaree.

"It may be a relief for a short time," said Bilbil, "but you are going to the land of your enemies, who will probably stick your fat body full of spears and arrows."

"Oh, I hope not!" exclaimed Inga, distressed at the thought.

"Never mind," said the King calmly, "a man can die but once, you know, and when the enemy kills me I shall beg him to kill Bilbil, also, that we may remain together in death as in life."

"They may be cannibals, in which case they will roast and eat us," suggested Bilbil, who wished to terrify his master.

"Who knows?" answered Rinkitink, with a shudder. "But cheer up, Bilbil; they may not kill us after all, or even capture us; so let us not borrow trouble. Do not look so cross, my sprightly quadruped, and I will sing to amuse you."

"Your song would make me more cross than ever," grumbled the goat.

"Quite impossible, dear Bilbil. You couldn't be more surly if you tried. So here is a famous song for you."

While the boy rowed steadily on and the boat rushed fast over the water, the jolly King, who never could be sad or serious for many minutes at a time, lay back on his embroidered cushions and sang as follows:

"A merry maiden went to sea—
Sing too-ral-oo-ral-i-do!
She sat upon the Captain's knee
And looked around the sea to see
What she could see, but she couldn't see me—
Sing too-ral-oo-ral-i-do!

"How do you like that, Bilbil?"

"I don't like it," complained the goat. "It reminds me of the alligator that tried to whistle."

"Did he succeed, Bilbil?" asked the King.

"He whistled as well as you sing."

"Ha, ha, ha, ha, heek, keek, eek!" chuckled the King. "He must have whistled most exquisitely, eh, my friend?"

"I am not your friend," returned the goat, wagging his ears in a surly manner.

"I am yours, however," was the King's cheery reply; "and to prove it I'll sing you another verse."

"Don't, I beg of you!"

But the King sang as follows:

"The wind blew off the maiden's shoe—
Sing too-ral-oo-ral-i-do!
And the shoe flew high to the sky so blue
And the maiden knew 'twas a new shoe, too;
But she couldn't pursue the shoe, 'tis true—
Sing too-ral-oo-ral-i-do!

"Isn't that sweet, my pretty goat?"

"Sweet, do you ask?" retorted Bilbil. "I consider it as sweet as candy made from mustard and vinegar."

"But not as sweet as your disposition, I admit. Ah, Bilbil, your temper would put honey itself to shame."

"Do not quarrel, I beg of you," pleaded Inga. "Are we not sad enough already?"

"But this is a jolly quarrel," said the King, "and it is the way Bilbil and I often amuse ourselves. Listen, now, to the last verse of all:

"The maid who shied her shoe now cried—
Sing too-ral-oo-ral-i-do!
Her tears were fried for the Captain's bride
Who ate with pride her sobs, beside,
And gently sighed 'I'm satisfied'—
Sing to-ral-oo-ral-i-do!"

"Worse and worse!" grumbled Bilbil, with much scorn. "I

am glad that is the last verse, for another of the same kind might cause me to faint."

"I fear you have no ear for music," said the King.

"I have heard no music, as yet," declared the goat. "You must have a strong imagination, King Rinkitink, if you consider your songs music. Do you remember the story of the bear that hired out for a nursemaid?"

"I do not recall it just now," said Rinkitink, with a wink at Inga.

"Well, the bear tried to sing a lullaby to put the baby to sleep."

"And then?" said the King.

"The bear was highly pleased with its own voice, but the baby was nearly frightened to death."

"Heh, heh, heh, heh, whoo, hoo, hoo! You are a merry rogue, Bilbil," laughed the King; "a merry rogue in spite of your gloomy features. However, if I have not amused you, I have at least pleased myself, for I am exceedingly fond of a good song. So let us say no more about it."

All this time the boy Prince was rowing the boat. He was not in the least tired, for the oars he held seemed to move of their own accord. He paid little heed to the conversation of Rinkitink and the goat, but busied his thoughts with plans of what he should do when he reached the islands of Regos and Coregos and confronted his enemies. When the others finally became silent, Inga inquired.

"Can you fight, King Rinkitink?"

"I have never tried," was the answer. "In time of danger I have found it much easier to run away than to face the foe."

"But *could* you fight?" asked the boy.

"I might try, if there was no chance to escape by running. Have you a proper weapon for me to fight with?"

"I have no weapon at all," confessed Inga.

"Then let us use argument and persuasion instead of fighting. For instance, if we could persuade the warriors of Regos to lie down, and let me step on them, they would be crushed with ease."

Prince Inga had expected little support from the King, so he was not discouraged by this answer. After all, he reflected, a conquest by battle would be out of the question, yet the White Pearl would not have advised him to go to Regos and Coregos had the mission been a hopeless one. It seemed to him, on further reflection, that he must rely upon circumstances to determine his actions when he reached the islands of the barbarians.

By this time Inga felt perfect confidence in the Magic Pearls. It was the White Pearl that had given him the boat, and the Blue Pearl that had given him strength to row it. He believed that the Pink Pearl would protect him from any danger that might arise; so his anxiety was not for himself, but for his companions. King Rinkitink and the goat had no magic to protect them, so Inga resolved to do all in his power to keep them from harm.

For three days and three nights the boat with the silver lining sped swiftly over the ocean. On the morning of the fourth day, so quickly had they traveled, Inga saw before him the shores of the two great islands of Regos and Coregos.

"The pearls have guided me aright!" he whispered to himself. "Now, if I am wise, and cautious, and brave, I believe I shall be able to rescue my father and mother and my people."

···—···◄ Chapter 7 ►···—···

The TWIN ISLANDS

The Island of Regos was ten miles wide and forty miles long and it was ruled by a big and powerful King named Gos. Near to the shores were green and fertile fields, but farther back from the sea were rugged hills and mountains, so rocky that nothing would grow there. But in these mountains were mines of gold and silver, which the slaves of the King were forced to work, being confined in dark underground passages for that purpose. In the course of time huge caverns had been hollowed out by the slaves, in which they lived and slept, never seeing the light of day. Cruel overseers with whips stood over these poor people, who had been captured in many countries by the raiding parties of King Gos, and the overseers were quite willing to lash the slaves with their whips if they faltered a moment in their work.

Between the green shores and the mountains were for-ests of thick, tangled trees, between which narrow paths had been cut to lead up to the caves of the mines. It was on the level green meadows, not far from the ocean, that the great City of Regos had been built, wherein was located the pal-ace of the King. This city was inhabited by thousands of the fierce warriors of Gos, who frequently took to their boats and spread over the sea to the neighboring islands to conquer and pillage, as they had done at Pingaree. When they were not absent on one of these expeditions, the City of Regos swarmed with them and so became a dangerous place for any peaceful person to live in, for the warriors were as lawless as their King.

The Island of Coregos lay close beside the Island of Regos; so close, indeed, that one might have thrown a stone from one shore to another. But Coregos was only half the size of Regos and instead of being mountainous it was a rich and pleasant country, covered with fields of grain. The fields of Coregos furnished food for the warriors and citizens of both countries, while the mines of Regos made them all rich.

Coregos was ruled by Queen Cor, who was wedded to King Gos; but so stern and cruel was the nature of this Queen that the people could not decide which of their sovereigns they dreaded most.

Queen Cor lived in her own City of Coregos, which lay on that side of her island facing Regos, and her slaves, who were mostly women, were made to plow the land and to plant and harvest the grain.

From Regos to Coregos stretched a bridge of boats, set close together, with planks laid across their edges for people to walk upon. In this way it was easy to pass from one island to the other and in times of danger the bridge could be quickly removed.

The native inhabitants of Regos and Coregos consisted of the warriors, who did nothing but fight and ravage, and the trembling servants who waited on them. King Gos and Queen Cor were at war with all the rest of the world. Other islanders hated and feared them, for their slaves were badly treated and absolutely no mercy was shown to the weak or ill.

When the boats that had gone to Pingaree returned loaded with rich plunder and a host of captives, there was much rejoicing in Regos and Coregos and the King and Queen gave a fine feast to the warriors who had accomplished so great a conquest. This feast was set for the warriors in the grounds of King Gos's palace, while with them in the great Throne Room all the captains and leaders of the fighting men were assembled with King Gos and Queen Cor, who had come from her island to attend the ceremony. Then all the goods that had been stolen from the King of Pingaree were divided according to rank, the King and Queen taking half, the captains a quarter, and the rest being divided amongst the warriors.

The day following the feast King Gos sent King Kitticut and all the men of Pingaree to work in his mines under the mountains, having first chained them together so they could not escape. The gentle Queen of Pingaree and all her women, together with the captured children, were given to Queen Cor, who set them to work in her grain fields.

Then the Rulers and warriors of these dreadful islands thought they had done forever with Pingaree. Despoiled of all its wealth, its houses torn down, its boats captured and all its people enslaved, what likelihood was there that they might ever again hear of the desolated island? So the people of Regos and Coregos were surprised and puzzled when one morning they observed approaching their shores from the direction of the south a black boat containing a boy, a fat man and a goat. The warriors asked one another who these could be, and where they had come from? No one ever came to those islands of their own accord, that was certain.

Prince Inga guided his boat to the south end of the Island of Regos, which was the landing place nearest to the city, and when the warriors saw this action they went down to the shore to meet him, being led by a big captain named Buzzub.

"Those people surely mean us no good," said Rinkitink uneasily to the boy. "Without doubt they intend to capture us and make us their slaves."

"Do not fear, sir," answered Inga, in a calm voice. "Stay

quietly in the boat with Bilbil until I have spoken with these men."

He stopped the boat a dozen feet from the shore, and standing up in his place made a grave bow to the multitude confronting him. Said the big Captain Buzzub in a gruff voice:

"Well, little one, who may you be? And how dare you come, uninvited and all alone, to the Island of Regos?"

"I am Inga, Prince of Pingaree," returned the boy, "and I have come here to free my parents and my people, whom you have wrongfully enslaved."

When they heard this bold speech a mighty laugh arose from the band of warriors, and when it had subsided the captain said:

"You love to jest, my baby Prince, and the joke is fairly good. But why did you willingly thrust your head into the lion's mouth? When you were free, why did you not stay free? We did not know we had left a single person in Pingaree! But since you managed to escape us then, it is really kind of you to come here of your own free will, to be our slave. Who is the funny fat person with you?"

"It is his Majesty, King Rinkitink, of the great City of Gilgad. He has accompanied me to see that you render full restitution for all you have stolen from Pingaree."

"Better yet!" laughed Buzzub. "He will make a fine slave for Queen Cor, who loves to tickle fat men, and see them jump."

King Rinkitink was filled with horror when he heard this, but the Prince answered as boldly as before, saying:

"We are not to be frightened by bluster, believe me; nor are we so weak as you imagine. We have magic powers so great and terrible that no host of warriors can possibly withstand us, and therefore I call upon you to surrender your city and your island to us, before we crush you with our mighty powers."

The boy spoke very gravely and earnestly, but his words only aroused another shout of laughter. So while the men of Regos were laughing Inga drove the boat well up onto the sandy beach and leaped out. He also helped Rinkitink out, and when the goat had unaided sprung to the sands, the King got upon Bilbil's back, trembling a little internally, but striving to look as brave as possible.

There was a bunch of coarse hair between the goat's ears, and this Inga clutched firmly in his left hand. The boy knew the Pink Pearl would protect not only himself, but all whom he touched, from any harm, and as Rinkitink was astride the goat and Inga had his hand upon the animal, the three could not be injured by anything the warriors could do. But Captain Buzzub did not know this, and the little group of three seemed so weak and ridiculous that he believed their capture would be easy. So he turned to his men and with a wave of his hand said:

"Seize the intruders!"

Instantly two or three of the warriors stepped forward to obey, but to their amazement they could not reach any of the three; their hands were arrested as if by an invisible wall of iron. Without paying any attention to these attempts at capture, Inga advanced slowly and the goat kept pace with him. And when Rinkitink saw that he was safe from harm he gave one of his big, merry laughs, and it startled the warriors and made them nervous. Captain Buzzub's eyes grew big with surprise as the three steadily advanced and forced his men backward; nor was he free from terror himself at the magic that protected these strange visitors. As for the warriors, they presently became terror-stricken and fled in a panic up the slope toward the city, and Buzzub was obliged to chase after them and shout threats of punishment before he could halt them and form them into a line of battle.

All the men of Regos bore spears and bows-and-arrows, and some of the officers had swords and battle-axes; so Buzzub ordered them to stand their ground and shoot and slay the strangers as they approached. This they tried to do. Inga being in advance, the warriors sent a flight of sharp arrows straight at the boy's breast, while others cast their long spears at him.

It seemed to Rinkitink that the little Prince must surely perish as he stood facing this hail of murderous missiles; but the power of the Pink Pearl did not desert him, and when the arrows and spears had reached to within an inch of his body they bounded back again and fell harmlessly at his feet. Nor were Rinkitink or Bilbil injured in the least, although they stood close beside Inga.

Buzzub stood for a moment looking upon the boy in silent wonder. Then, recovering himself, he shouted in a loud voice:

"Once again! All together, my men. No one shall ever defy our might and live!"

Again a flight of arrows and spears sped toward the three, and since many more of the warriors of Regos had by this time joined their fellows, the air was for a moment darkened by the deadly shafts. But again all fell harmless before the power of the Pink Pearl, and Bilbil, who had been growing very angry at the attempts to injure him and his party, suddenly made a bolt forward, casting off Inga's hold, and butted into the line of warriors, who were standing amazed at their failure to conquer.

Taken by surprise at the goat's attack, a dozen big warriors tumbled in a heap, yelling with fear, and their comrades, not knowing what had happened but imagining that their foes were attacking them, turned about and ran to the city as hard as they could go. Bilbil, still angry, had just time to catch the big captain as he turned to follow his men, and Buzzub first sprawled headlong upon the ground, then rolled over two or three times, and finally jumped up and ran yelling after his defeated warriors. This butting on the part of the goat was very hard upon King Rinkitink, who nearly fell off Bilbil's back at the shock of encounter; but the little fat King wound his arms around the goat's neck and shut his eyes and clung on with all his might. It was not until he heard Inga say triumphantly, "We have won the fight without striking a blow!" that

Rinkitink dared open his eyes again. Then he saw the warriors rushing into the City of Regos and barring the heavy gates, and he was very much relieved at the sight.

"Without striking a blow!" said Bilbil indignantly. "That is not quite true, Prince Inga. You did not fight, I admit, but I struck a couple of times to good purpose, and I claim to have conquered the cowardly warriors unaided."

"You and I together, Bilbil," said Rinkitink mildly. "But the next time you make a charge, please warn me in time, so that I may dismount and give you all the credit for the attack."

There being no one now to oppose their advance, the three walked to the gates of the city, which had been closed against them. The gates were of iron and heavily barred, and upon the top of the high walls of the city a host of the warriors now appeared armed with arrows and spears and other weapons. For Buzzub had gone straight to the palace of King Gos and reported his defeat, relating the powerful magic of the boy, the fat King and the goat, and had asked what to do next.

The big captain still trembled with fear, but King Gos did not believe in magic, and called Buzzub a coward and a weakling. At once the King took command of his men personally, and he ordered the walls manned with warriors and instructed them to shoot to kill if any of the three strangers approached the gates.

Of course, neither Rinkitink nor Bilbil knew how they had been protected from harm and so at first they were inclined to resent the boy's command that the three must always keep together and touch one another at all times. But when Inga explained that his magic would not otherwise save them from injury, they agreed to obey, for they had now seen enough to convince them that the Prince was really protected by some invisible power.

As they came before the gates another shower of arrows and spears descended upon them, and as before not a single missile touched their bodies. King Gos, who was upon the wall, was greatly amazed and somewhat worried, but he depended upon the strength of his gates and commanded his men to continue shooting until all their weapons were gone.

Inga let them shoot as much as they wished, while he stood before the great gates and examined them carefully.

"Perhaps Bilbil can batter down the gates, suggested Rinkitink.

"No," replied the goat; "my head is hard, but not harder than iron."

"Then," returned the King, "let us stay outside; especially as we can't get in."

But Inga was not at all sure they could not get in. The gates opened inward, and three heavy bars were held in place by means of stout staples riveted to the sheets of steel. The boy had been told that the power of the Blue Pearl would enable him to accomplish any feat of strength, and he believed that this was true.

The warriors, under the direction of King Gos, continued to hurl arrows and darts and spears and axes and huge stones upon the invaders, all without avail. The ground below was thickly covered with weapons, yet not one of the three before the gates had been injured in the slightest manner. When everything had been cast that was available and not a single weapon of any sort remained at hand, the amazed warriors saw the boy put his shoulder against the gates and burst asunder the huge staples that held the bars in place. A thousand of their men could not have accomplished this feat, yet the small, slight boy did it with seeming ease. The gates burst open, and Inga advanced into the city street and called upon King Gos to surrender.

But Gos was now as badly frightened as were his warriors. He and his men were accustomed to war and pillage and they had carried terror into many countries, but here was a small boy, a fat man and a goat who could not be injured by all his skill in warfare, his numerous army and thousands of death-dealing weapons. Moreover, they not only defied King Gos's entire army but they had broken in the huge gates of the city—as easily as if they had been made of paper—and such an exhibition of enormous strength made the wicked King fear for his life. Like all bullies and marauders, Gos was a coward at heart, and now a panic seized him and he turned and fled before the calm advance of Prince Inga of Pingaree. The warriors were like their master, and having thrown all their

weapons over the wall and being helpless to oppose the strangers, they all swarmed after Gos, who abandoned his city and
crossed the bridge of boats to the Island of Coregos. There
was a desperate struggle among these cowardly warriors to
get over the bridge, and many were pushed into the water
and obliged to swim; but finally every fighting man of Regos
had gained the shore of Coregos and then they tore away the
bridge of boats and drew them up on their own side, hoping
the stretch of open water would prevent the magic invaders
from following them.

The humble citizens and serving people of Regos, who had
been terrified and abused by the rough warriors all their lives,
were not only greatly astonished by this sudden conquest of
their masters but greatly delighted. As the King and his army
fled to Coregos, the people embraced one another and danced
for very joy, and then they turned to see what the conquerors
of Regos were like.

Chapter 8

RINKITINK MAKES a GREAT MISTAKE

The fat King rode his goat through the streets of the conquered city and the boy Prince walked proudly beside him, while all the people bent their heads humbly to their new masters, whom they were prepared to serve in the same manner they had King Gos.

Not a warrior remained in all Regos to oppose the triumphant three; the bridge of boats had been destroyed; Inga and his companions were free from danger—for a time, at least.

The jolly little King appreciated this fact and rejoiced that he had escaped all injury during the battle. How it had all happened he could not tell, nor even guess, but he was content in being safe and free to take possession of the enemy's city. So, as they passed through the lines of respectful civilians on their way to the palace, the King tipped his crown back on his bald head and folded his arms and sang in his best voice the following lines:

> *"Oh, here comes the army of King Rinkitink!*
> *It isn't a big one, perhaps you may think,*
> *But it scattered the warriors quicker than wink—*
> *Rink-i-tink, tink-i-tink, tink!*
>
> *Our Bilbil's a hero and so is his King;*
> *Our foemen have vanished like birds on the wing;*
> *I guess that as fighters we're quite the real thing—*
> *Rink-i-tink, tink-i-tink, tink!"*

"Why don't you give a little credit to Inga?" inquired the goat. "If I remember aright, he did a little of the conquering himself."

"So he did," responded the King, "and that's the reason I'm sounding our own praise, Bilbil. Those who do the least, often shout the loudest and so get the most glory. Inga did so much that there is danger of his becoming more important than we are, and so we'd best say nothing about him."

When they reached the palace, which was an immense

building, furnished throughout in regal splendor, Inga took formal possession and ordered the majordomo to show them the finest rooms the building contained. There were many pleasant apartments, but Rinkitink proposed to Inga that they share one of the largest bedrooms together.

"For," said he, "we are not sure that old Gos will not return and try to recapture his city, and you must remember that I have no magic to protect me. In any danger, were I alone, I might be easily killed or captured, while if you are by my side you can save me from injury."

The boy realized the wisdom of this plan, and selected a fine big bedroom on the second floor of the palace, in which he ordered two golden beds placed and prepared for King Rinkitink and himself. Bilbil was given a suite of rooms on the other side of the palace, where servants brought the goat fresh-cut grass to eat and made him a soft bed to lie upon.

That evening the boy Prince and the fat King dined in great state in the lofty-domed dining hall of the palace, where forty servants waited upon them. The royal chef, anxious to win the favor of the conquerors of Regos, prepared his finest and most savory dishes for them, which Rinkitink ate with much appetite and found so delicious that he ordered the royal chef brought into the banquet hall and presented him with a gilt button which the King cut from his own jacket.

"You are welcome to it," said he to the chef, "because I have eaten so much that I cannot use that lower button at all."

Rinkitink was mightily pleased to live in a comfortable palace again and to dine at a well spread table. His joy grew every moment, so that he came in time to be as merry and cheery as before Pingaree was despoiled. And, although he had been much frightened during Inga's defiance of the army of King Gos, he now began to turn the matter into a joke.

"Why, my boy," said he, "you whipped the big black-bearded King exactly as if he were a schoolboy, even though you used no warlike weapon at all upon him. He was cowed through fear of your magic, and that reminds me to demand from you an explanation. How did you do it, Inga? And where did the wonderful magic come from?"

Perhaps it would have been wise for the Prince to have explained about the magic pearls, but at that moment he was not inclined to do so. Instead, he replied:

"Be patient, your Majesty. The secret is not my own, so please do not ask me to divulge it. Is it not enough, for the present, that the magic saved you from death today?"

"Do not think me ungrateful," answered the King earnestly. "A million spears fell on me from the wall, and several stones as big as mountains, yet none of them hurt me!"

"The stones were not as big as mountains, sire," said the Prince with a smile. "They were, indeed, no larger than your head."

"Are you sure about that?" asked Rinkitink.

"Quite sure, your Majesty."

"How deceptive those things are!" sighed the King. "This argument reminds me of the story of Tom Tick, which my father used to tell."

"I have never heard that story," Inga answered.

"Well, as he told it, it ran like this:

"When Tom walked out, the sky to spy,
A naughty gnat flew in his eye;
But Tom knew not it was a gnat—
He thought, at first, it was a cat.

"And then, it felt so very big,
He thought it surely was a pig
Till, standing still to hear it grunt,
He cried: 'Why, it's an elephunt*!'*

"But—when the gnat flew out again
And Tom was free from all his pain,
He said: 'There flew into my eye
A leetle, teenty-tiny fly.'"

"Indeed," said Inga, laughing, "the gnat was much like your stones that seemed as big as mountains."

After their dinner they inspected the palace, which was filled with valuable goods stolen by King Gos from many nations. But the day's events had tired them and they retired early to their big sleeping apartment.

"In the morning," said the boy to Rinkitink, as he was undressing for bed, "I shall begin the search for my father and mother and the people of Pingaree. And, when they are found and rescued, we will all go home again, and be as happy as we were before."

They carefully bolted the door of their room, that no one might enter, and then got into their beds, where Rinkitink fell asleep in an instant. The boy lay awake for a while thinking over the day's adventures, but presently he fell sound asleep also, and so weary was he that nothing disturbed his slumber until he awakened next morning with a ray of sunshine in his eyes, which had crept into the room through the open window by King Rinkitink's bed.

Resolving to begin the search for his parents without any unnecessary delay, Inga at once got out of bed and began to dress himself, while Rinkitink, in the other bed, was still sleeping peacefully. But when the boy had put on both his stockings and began looking for his shoes, he could find but one of them. The left shoe, that containing the Pink Pearl, was missing.

Filled with anxiety at this discovery, Inga searched through the entire room, looking underneath the beds and divans and chairs and behind the draperies and in the corners and every other possible place a shoe might be. He tried the door, and found it still bolted; so, with growing uneasiness, the boy was forced to admit that the precious shoe was not in the room.

With a throbbing heart he aroused his companion.

"King Rinkitink," said he, "do you know what has become of my left shoe?"

"Your shoe!" exclaimed the King, giving a wide yawn and rubbing his eyes to get the sleep out of them. "Have you lost a shoe?"

"Yes," said Inga. "I have searched everywhere in the room, and cannot find it."

"But why bother me about such a small thing?" inquired Rinkitink. "A shoe is only a shoe, and you can easily get another one. But, stay! Perhaps it was your shoe which I threw at the cat last night."

"The cat!" cried Inga. "What do you mean?"

"Why, in the night," explained Rinkitink, sitting up and beginning to dress himself, "I was wakened by the mewing of a cat that sat upon a wall of the palace, just outside my window. As the noise disturbed me, I reached out in the dark and caught up something and threw it at the cat, to frighten the creature away. I did not know what it was that I threw, and I was too sleepy to care; but probably it was your shoe, since it is now missing."

"Then," said the boy, in a despairing tone of voice, "your carelessness has ruined me, as well as yourself, King Rinkitink, for in that shoe was concealed the magic power which protected us from danger."

The King's face became very serious when he heard this and he uttered a low whistle of surprise and regret.

"Why on earth did you not warn me of this?" he demanded. "And why did you keep such a precious power in an old shoe? And why didn't you put the shoe under a pillow? You were very wrong, my lad, in not confiding to me, your faithful friend, the secret, for in that case the shoe would not now be lost."

To all this Inga had no answer. He sat on the side of his bed, with hanging head, utterly disconsolate, and seeing this, Rinkitink had pity for his sorrow.

"Come!" cried the King; "let us go out at once and look for the shoe which I threw at the cat. It must even now be lying in the yard of the palace."

This suggestion roused the boy to action. He at once threw open the door and in his stocking feet rushed down the staircase, closely followed by Rinkitink. But although they looked on both sides of the palace wall and in every possible crack and corner where a shoe might lodge, they failed to find it.

After a half hour's careful search the boy said sorrowfully:

"Someone must have passed by, as we slept, and taken the precious shoe, not knowing its value. To us, King Rinkitink, this will be a dreadful misfortune, for we are surrounded by dangers from which we have now no protection. Luckily I have the other shoe left, within which is the magic power that gives me strength; so all is not lost."

Then he told Rinkitink, in a few words, the secret of the wonderful pearls, and how he had recovered them from the ruins and hidden them in his shoes, and how they had enabled him to drive King Gos and his men from Regos and to capture the city. The King was much astonished, and when the story was concluded he said to Inga:

"What did you do with the other shoe?"

"Why, I left it in our bedroom," replied the boy.

"Then I advise you to get it at once," continued Rinkitink, "for we can ill afford to lose the second shoe, as well as the one I threw at the cat."

"You are right!" cried Inga, and they hastened back to their bedchamber.

On entering the room they found an old woman sweeping and raising a great deal of dust.

"Where is my shoe?" asked the Prince, anxiously.

The old woman stopped sweeping and looked at him in a stupid way, for she was not very intelligent.

"Do you mean the one odd shoe that was lying on the floor when I came in?" she finally asked.

"Yes—yes!" answered the boy. "Where is it? Tell me where it is!"

"Why, I threw it on the dust-heap, outside the back gate," said she, "for, it being but a single shoe, with no mate, it can be of no use to anyone."

"Show us the way to the dust-heap—at once!" commanded

the boy, sternly, for he was greatly frightened by this new misfortune which threatened him.

The old woman hobbled away and they followed her, constantly urging her to hasten; but when they reached the dust-heap no shoe was to be seen.

"This is terrible!" wailed the young Prince, ready to weep at his loss. "We are now absolutely ruined, and at the mercy of our enemies. Nor shall I be able to liberate my dear father and mother."

"Well," replied Rinkitink, leaning against an old barrel and looking quite solemn, "the thing is certainly unlucky, any way we look at it. I suppose someone has passed along here and, seeing the shoe upon the dust-heap, has carried it away. But no one could know the magic power the shoe contains and so will not use it against us. I believe, Inga, we must now depend upon our wits to get us out of the scrape we are in."

With saddened hearts they returned to the palace, and entering a small room where no one could observe them or overhear them, the boy took the White Pearl from its silken bag and held it to his ear, asking:

"What shall I do now?"

"Tell no one of your loss," answered the Voice of the Pearl. "If your enemies do not know that you are powerless, they will fear you as much as ever. Keep your secret, be patient, and fear not!"

Inga heeded this advice and also warned Rinkitink to say nothing to anyone of the loss of the shoes and the powers they contained. He sent for the shoemaker of King Gos, who soon brought him a new pair of red leather shoes that fitted him quite well. When these had been put upon his feet, the Prince, accompanied by the King, started to walk through the city.

Wherever they went the people bowed low to the conqueror, although a few, remembering Inga's terrible strength, ran away in fear and trembling. They had been used to severe masters and did not yet know how they would be treated by King Gos's successor. There being no occasion for the boy to exercise the powers he had displayed the previous day, his present helplessness was not suspected by any of the citizens of Regos, who still considered him a wonderful magician.

Inga did not dare to fight his way to the mines, at present, nor could he try to conquer the Island of Coregos, where his mother was enslaved; so he set about the regulation of the City of Regos, and having established himself with great state in the royal palace he began to govern the people by kindness, having consideration for the most humble.

The King of Regos and his followers sent spies across to the island they had abandoned in their flight, and these spies returned with the news that the terrible boy conqueror was still occupying the city. Therefore none of them ventured to go back to Regos but continued to live upon the neighboring island of Coregos, where they passed the days in fear and trembling and sought to plot and plan ways how they might overcome the Prince of Pingaree and the fat King of Gilgad.

·····—··◄ Chapter 9 ►··—·····

A PRESENT for ZELLA

Now it so happened that on the morning of that same day when the Prince of Pingaree suffered the loss of his priceless shoes, there chanced to pass along the road that wound beside the royal palace a poor charcoal-burner named Nikobob, who was about to return to his home in the forest.

Nikobob carried an axe and a bundle of torches over his shoulder and he walked with his eyes to the ground, being deep in thought as to the strange manner in which the powerful King Gos and his city had been conquered by a boy Prince who had come from Pingaree.

Suddenly the charcoal-burner espied a shoe lying upon the

ground, just beyond the high wall of the palace and directly in his path. He picked it up and, seeing it was a pretty shoe, although much too small for his own foot, he put it in his pocket.

Soon after, on turning a corner of the wall, Nikobob came to a dust-heap where, lying amidst a mass of rubbish, was another shoe—the mate to the one he had before found. This also he placed in his pocket, saying to himself:

"I have now a fine pair of shoes for my daughter Zella, who will be much pleased to find I have brought her a present from the city."

And while the charcoal-burner turned into the forest and trudged along the path toward his home, Inga and Rinkitink were still searching for the missing shoes. Of course, they could not know that Nikobob had found them, nor did the honest man think he had taken anything more than a pair of cast-off shoes which nobody wanted.

Nikobob had several miles to travel through the forest before he could reach the little log cabin where his wife, as well as his little daughter Zella, awaited his return, but he was used to long walks and tramped along the path whistling cheerfully to beguile the time.

Few people, as I said before, ever passed through the dark and tangled forests of Regos, except to go to the mines in the mountain beyond, for many dangerous creatures lurked in the wild jungles, and King Gos never knew, when he sent a messenger to the mines, whether he would reach there safely or not.

The charcoal-burner, however, knew the wild forest well, and especially this part of it lying between the city and his home. It was the favorite haunt of the ferocious beast Choggenmugger, dreaded by every dweller in the Island of Regos. Choggenmugger was so old that everyone thought it must have been there since the world was made, and each year of its life the huge scales that covered its body grew thicker and harder and its jaws grew wider and its teeth grew sharper and its appetite grew more keen than ever.

In former ages there had been many dragons in Regos, but Choggenmugger was so fond of dragons that he had eaten all of them long ago. There had also been great serpents and crocodiles in the forest marshes, but all had gone to feed the hunger of Choggenmugger. The people of Regos knew well there was no use opposing the Great Beast, so when one unfortunately met with it he gave himself up for lost.

All this Nikobob knew well, but fortune had always favored him in his journeys through the forest, and although he had at times met many savage beasts and fought them with his sharp axe, he had never to this day encountered the terrible Choggenmugger. Indeed, he was not thinking of the Great Beast at all as he walked along, but suddenly he heard a crashing of broken trees and felt a trembling of the earth and saw the immense jaws of Choggenmugger opening before him.

Then Nikobob gave himself up for lost and his heart almost ceased to beat.

He believed there was no way of escape. No one ever dared oppose Choggenmugger. But Nikobob hated to die without showing the monster, in some way, that he was eaten only under protest. So he raised his axe and brought it down upon the red, protruding tongue of the monster—and cut it clean off!

For a moment the charcoal-burner scarcely believed what his eyes saw, for he knew nothing of the pearls he carried in his pocket or the magic power they lent his arm. His success, however, encouraged him to strike again, and this time the huge scaly jaw of Choggenmugger was severed in twain and the beast howled in terrified rage.

Nikobob took off his coat, to give himself more freedom of action, and then he earnestly renewed the attack. But now the axe seemed blunted by the hard scales and made no impression upon them whatever. The creature advanced with glaring, wicked eyes, and Nikobob seized his coat under his arm and turned to flee.

That was foolish, for Choggenmugger could run like the wind. In a moment it overtook the charcoal-burner and snapped its four rows of sharp teeth together. But they did not touch Nikobob, because he still held the coat in his grasp, close to his body, and in the coat pocket were Inga's shoes, and in the points of the shoes were the magic pearls. Finding himself uninjured, Nikobob put on his coat, again seized his axe, and in a short time had chopped Choggenmugger into many small pieces—a task that proved not only easy but very agreeable.

"I must be the strongest man in all the world!" thought the charcoal-burner, as he proudly resumed his way, "for Choggen-mugger has been the terror of Regos since the world began, and I alone have been able to destroy the beast. Yet it is singular that never before did I discover how powerful a man I am."

He met no further adventure and at midday reached a little clearing in the forest where stood his humble cabin.

"Great news! I have great news for you," he shouted, as his wife and little daughter came to greet him. "King Gos has been conquered by a boy Prince from the far island of Pingaree, and I have this day—unaided—destroyed Choggenmugger by the might of my strong arm."

This was, indeed, great news. They brought Nikobob into the house and set him in an easy chair and made him tell everything he knew about the Prince of Pingaree and the fat King of Gilgad, as well as the details of his wonderful fight with mighty Choggenmugger.

"And now, my daughter," said the charcoal-burner, when all his news had been related for at least the third time, "here is a pretty present I have brought you from the city."

With this he drew the shoes from the pocket of his coat and handed them to Zella, who gave him a dozen kisses in payment and was much pleased with her gift. The little girl had never worn shoes before, for her parents were too poor to buy her such luxuries, so now the possession of these, which were not much worn, filled the child's heart with joy. She admired the red leather and the graceful curl of the pointed toes. When she tried them on her feet, they fitted as well as if made for her.

All the afternoon, as she helped her mother with the housework, Zella thought of her pretty shoes. They seemed more important to her than the coming to Regos of the conquering Prince of Pingaree, or even the death of Choggenmugger.

When Zella and her mother were not working in the cabin, cooking or sewing, they often searched the neighboring forest for honey which the wild bees cleverly hid in hollow trees. The day after Nikobob's return, as they were starting out after honey, Zella decided to put on her new shoes, as they would keep the twigs that covered the ground from hurting her feet. She was used to the twigs, of course, but what is the use of having nice, comfortable shoes, if you do not wear them?

So she danced along, very happily, followed by her mother, and presently they came to a tree in which was a deep hollow. Zella thrust her hand and arm into the space and found that the tree was full of honey, so she began to dig it out with a wooden paddle. Her mother, who held the pail, suddenly cried in warning:

"Look out, Zella; the bees are coming!" and then the good woman ran fast toward the house to escape.

Zella, however, had no more than time to turn her head when a thick swarm of bees surrounded her, angry because they had caught her stealing their honey and intent on stinging the girl as a punishment. She knew her danger and expected to be badly injured by the multitude of stinging bees, but to her surprise the little creatures were unable to fly close enough to her to stick their dart-like stingers into her flesh. They swarmed about her in a dark cloud, and their angry buzzing was terrible to hear, yet the little girl remained unharmed.

When she realized this, Zella was no longer afraid but continued to ladle out the honey until she had secured all that was in the tree. Then she returned to the cabin, where her mother was weeping and bemoaning the fate of her darling child, and the good woman was greatly astonished to find Zella had escaped injury.

Again they went to the woods to search for honey, and although the mother always ran away whenever the bees came near them, Zella paid no attention to the creatures but kept at her work, so that before supper time came the pails were again filled to overflowing with delicious honey.

"With such good fortune as we have had this day," said her mother, "we shall soon gather enough honey for you to carry to Queen Cor." For it seems the wicked Queen was very fond of honey and it had been Zella's custom to go, once every year, to the City of Coregos, to carry the Queen a supply of sweet honey for her table. Usually she had but one pail.

"But now," said Zella, "I shall be able to carry two pailsful to the Queen, who will, I am sure, give me a good price for it."

"True," answered her mother, "and, as the boy Prince may take it into his head to conquer Coregos, as well as Regos, I think it best for you to start on your journey to Queen Cor tomorrow morning. Do you not agree with me, Nikobob?" she added, turning to her husband, the charcoal-burner, who was eating his supper.

"I agree with you," he replied. "If Zella must go to the City of Coregos, she may as well start tomorrow morning."

·—··◄ ᴄhapter 10 ►··—··

The CUNNING of QUEEN COR

You may be sure the Queen of Coregos was not well pleased to have King Gos and all his warriors living in her city after they had fled from their own. They were savage natured and quarrelsome men at all times, and their tempers had not improved since their conquest by the Prince of Pingaree. Moreover, they were eating up Queen Cor's provisions and crowding the houses of her own people, who grumbled and complained until their Queen was heartily tired.

"Shame on you!" she said to her husband, King Gos, "to be driven out of your city by a boy, a roly-poly King and a billy goat! Why do you not go back and fight them?"

"No human can fight against the powers of magic," returned the King in a surly voice. "That boy is either a fairy or under the protection of fairies. We escaped with our lives only because we were quick to run away; but, should we return to Regos, the same terrible power that burst open the city gates would crush us all to atoms."

"Bah! you are a coward," cried the Queen, tauntingly.

"I am not a coward," said the big King. "I have killed in battle scores of my enemies; by the might of my sword and my good right arm I have conquered many nations; all my life people have feared me. But no one would dare face the tremendous power of the Prince of Pingaree, boy though he is. It would not be courage, it would be folly, to attempt it."

"Then meet his power with cunning," suggested the Queen. "Take my advice, and steal over to Regos at night, when it is dark, and capture or destroy the boy while he sleeps."

"No weapon can touch his body," was the answer. "He bears a charmed life and cannot be injured."

"Does the fat King possess magic powers, or the goat?" inquired Cor.

"I think not," said Gos. "We could not injure them, indeed, any more than we could the boy, but they did not seem to have any unusual strength, although the goat's head is harder than a battering-ram."

"Well," mused the Queen, "there is surely some way to conquer that slight boy. If you are afraid to undertake the job,

I shall go myself. By some stratagem I shall manage to make him my prisoner. He will not dare to defy a Queen, and no magic can stand against a woman's cunning."

"Go ahead, if you like," replied the King, with an evil grin, "and if you are hung up by the thumbs or cast into a dungeon, it will serve you right for thinking you can succeed where a skilled warrior dares not make the attempt."

"I'm not afraid," answered the Queen. "It is only soldiers and bullies who are cowards."

In spite of this assertion, Queen Cor was not so brave as she was cunning. For several days she thought over this plan and that, and tried to decide which was most likely to succeed. She had never seen the boy Prince but had heard so many tales of him from the defeated warriors, and especially from Captain Buzzub, that she had learned to respect his power.

Spurred on by the knowledge that she would never get rid of her unwelcome guests until Prince Inga was overcome and Regos regained for King Gos, the Queen of Coregos finally decided to trust to luck and her native wit to defeat a simple-minded boy, however powerful he might be. Inga could not suspect what she was going to do, because she did not know herself. She intended to act boldly and trust to chance to win.

It is evident that had the cunning Queen known that Inga had lost all his magic, she would not have devoted so much time to the simple matter of capturing him, but like all others she was impressed by the marvelous exhibition of power he had shown in capturing Regos, and had no reason to believe the boy was less powerful now.

One morning Queen Cor boldly entered a boat, and, taking four men with her as an escort and bodyguard, was rowed across the narrow channel to Regos. Prince Inga was sitting in the palace playing checkers with King Rinkitink when a servant came to him, saying that Queen Cor had arrived and desired an audience with him.

With many misgivings lest the wicked Queen discover that he had now lost his magic powers, the boy ordered her to be admitted, and she soon entered the room and bowed low before him, in mock respect.

Cor was a big woman, almost as tall as King Gos. She had flashing black eyes and the dark complexion you see on gypsies. Her temper, when irritated, was something dreadful, and her face wore an evil expression which she tried to cover by smiling sweetly—often when she meant the most mischief.

"I have come," said she in a low voice, "to render homage to the noble Prince of Pingaree. I am told that your Highness is the strongest person in the world, and invincible in battle, and therefore I wish you to become my friend, rather than my enemy."

Now Inga did not know how to reply to this speech. He disliked the appearance of the woman and was afraid of her and he was unused to deception and did not know how to mask his real feelings. So he took time to think over his answer, which he finally made in these words:

"I have no quarrel with your Majesty, and my only reason for coming here is to liberate my father and mother, and my people, whom you and your husband have made your slaves, and to recover the goods King Gos has plundered from the Island of Pingaree. This I hope soon to accomplish, and if you really wish to be my friend, you can assist me greatly."

While he was speaking Queen Cor had been studying the boy's face stealthily, from the corners of her eyes, and she said to herself: "He is so small and innocent that I believe I can capture him alone, and with ease. He does not seem very terrible and I suspect that King Gos and his warriors were frightened at nothing." Then, aloud, she said to Inga:

"I wish to invite you, mighty Prince, and your friend, the great King of Gilgad, to visit my poor palace at Coregos, where all my people shall do you honor. Will you come?"

"At present," replied Inga, uneasily, "I must refuse your kind invitation."

"There will be feasting, and dancing girls, and games and fireworks," said the Queen, speaking as if eager to entice him and at each word coming a step nearer to where he stood.

"I could not enjoy them while my poor parents are slaves," said the boy, sadly.

"Are you sure of that?" asked Queen Cor, and by that time she was close beside Inga. Suddenly she leaned forward and threw both of her long arms around Inga's body, holding him in a grasp that was like a vise.

Now Rinkitink sprang forward to rescue his friend, but Cor kicked out viciously with her foot and struck the King squarely on his stomach—a very tender place to be kicked, especially if one is fat. Then, still hugging Inga tightly, the Queen called aloud:

"I've got him! Bring in the ropes."

Instantly the four men she had brought with her sprang into the room and bound the boy hand and foot. Next they seized Rinkitink, who was still rubbing his stomach, and bound him likewise.

With a laugh of wicked triumph, Queen Cor now led her captives down to the boat and returned with them to Coregos.

Great was the astonishment of King Gos and his warriors when they saw that the mighty Prince of Pingaree, who had put them all to flight, had been captured by a woman. Cowards as they were, they now crowded around the boy and jeered at him, and some of them would have struck him had not the Queen cried out:

"Hands off! He is my prisoner, remember—not yours."

"Well, Cor, what are you going to do with him?" inquired King Gos.

"I shall make him my slave, that he may amuse my idle hours. For he is a pretty boy, and gentle, although he did frighten all of you big warriors so terribly."

The King scowled at this speech, not liking to be ridiculed, but he said nothing more. He and his men returned that same day to Regos, after restoring the bridge of boats. And they held a wild carnival of rejoicing, both in the King's palace and in the city, although the poor people of Regos who were not warriors were all sorry that the kind young Prince had been captured by his enemies and could rule them no longer.

When her unwelcome guests had all gone back to Regos and the Queen was alone in her palace, she ordered Inga and Rinkitink brought before her and their bonds removed. They came sadly enough, knowing they were in serious straits and at the mercy of a cruel mistress. Inga had taken counsel of the White Pearl, which had advised him to bear up bravely under his misfortune, promising a change for the better very soon. With this promise to comfort him, Inga faced the Queen with a dignified bearing that indicated both pride and courage.

"Well, youngster," said she, in a cheerful tone because she was pleased with her success, "you played a clever trick on my poor husband and frightened him badly, but for that prank I am inclined to forgive you. Hereafter I intend you to be my page, which means that you must fetch and carry for me at my will. And let me advise you to obey my every whim without question or delay, for when I am angry I become ugly, and when I am ugly someone is sure to feel the lash. Do you understand me?"

Inga bowed, but made no answer. Then she turned to Rinkitink and said:

"As for you, I cannot decide how to make you useful to

me, as you are altogether too fat and awkward to work in the fields. It may be, however, that I can use you as a pincushion."

"What!" cried Rinkitink in horror, "would you stick pins into the King of Gilgad?"

"Why not?" returned Queen Cor. "You are as fat as a pincushion, as you must yourself admit, and whenever I needed a pin I could call you to me." Then she laughed at his frightened look and asked: "By the way, are you ticklish?"

This was the question Rinkitink had been dreading. He gave a moan of despair and shook his head.

"I should love to tickle the bottom of your feet with a feather," continued the cruel woman. "Please take off your shoes."

"Oh, your Majesty!" pleaded poor Rinkitink, "I beg you to allow me to amuse you in some other way. I can dance, or I can sing you a song."

"Well," she answered, shaking with laughter, "you may sing a song—if it be a merry one. But you do not seem in a merry mood."

"I *feel* merry—indeed, your Majesty, I do!" protested Rinkitink, anxious to escape the tickling. But even as he professed to "feel merry" his round, red face wore an expression of horror and anxiety that was really comical.

"Sing, then!" commanded Queen Cor, who was greatly amused.

Rinkitink gave a sigh of relief and after clearing his throat

and trying to repress his sobs he began to sing this song—
gently, at first, but finally roaring it out at the top of his voice:

> *"Oh!*
> *There was a Baby Tiger lived in a men-ag-er-ie—*
> *Fizzy-fezzy-fuzzy—they wouldn't set him free;*
> *And ev'rybody thought that he was gentle as could be—*
> *Fizzy-fezzy-fuzzy—Ba-by Ti-ger!*

> *"Oh!*
> *They patted him upon his head and shook him by the paw—*
> *Fizzy-fezzy-fuzzy—he had a bone to gnaw;*
> *But soon he grew the biggest Tiger that you ever saw—*
> *Fizzy-fezzy-fuzzy—what a Ti-ger!*

> *"Oh!*
> *One day they came to pet the brute and he began to fight—*
> *Fizzy-fezzy-fuzzy-how he did scratch and bite!*
> *He broke the cage and in a rage he darted out of sight—*
> *Fizzy-fezzy-fuzzy was a Ti-ger!"*

"And is there a moral to the song?" asked Queen Cor,
when King Rinkitink had finished his song with great spirit.

"If there is," replied Rinkitink, "it is a warning not to fool
with tigers."

The little Prince could not help smiling at this shrewd

answer, but Queen Cor frowned and gave the King a sharp look.

"Oh," said she; "I think I know the difference between a tiger and a lapdog. But I'll bear the warning in mind, just the same."

For, after all her success in capturing them, she was a little afraid of these people who had once displayed such extraordinary powers.

Chapter 11

ZELLA GOES to COREGOS

The forest in which Nikobob lived with his wife and daughter stood between the mountains and the City of Regos, and a well-beaten path wound among the trees, leading from the city to the mines. This path was used by the King's messengers, and captured prisoners were also sent by this way from Regos to work in the underground caverns.

Nikobob had built his cabin more than a mile away from this path, that he might not be molested by the wild and lawless soldiers of King Gos, but the family of the charcoal-burner was surrounded by many creatures scarcely less dangerous to encounter, and often in the night they could hear savage animals growling and prowling about the cabin. Because Nikobob minded his own business and never hunted the wild creatures to injure them, the beasts had come to regard him as one of the natural dwellers in the forest and did not molest him or his family. Still Zella and her mother seldom wandered far from home, except on such errands as carrying honey to Coregos, and at these times Nikobob cautioned them to be very careful.

So when Zella set out on her journey to Queen Cor, with the two pails of honey in her hands, she was undertaking a dangerous adventure and there was no certainty that she would return safely to her loving parents. But they were poor, and Queen Cor's money, which they expected to receive for the honey, would enable them to purchase many things that were needed; so it was deemed best that Zella should go. She was a brave little girl and poor people are often obliged to take chances that rich ones are spared.

A passing woodchopper had brought news to Nikobob's cabin that Queen Cor had made a prisoner of the conquering Prince of Pingaree and that Gos and his warriors were again back in their city of Regos; but these struggles and conquests were matters which, however interesting, did not concern the poor charcoal-burner or his family. They were more anxious over the report that the warriors had become more reckless than ever before, and delighted in annoying all the common people; so Zella was told to keep away from the beaten path as much as possible, that she might not encounter any of the King's soldiers.

"When it is necessary to choose between the warriors and the wild beasts," said Nikobob, "the beasts will be found the more merciful."

The little girl had put on her best attire for the journey and her mother threw a blue silk shawl over her head and shoulders. Upon her feet were the pretty red shoes her father had brought her from Regos. Thus prepared, she kissed her parents good-bye and started out with a light heart, carrying the pails of honey in either hand.

It was necessary for Zella to cross the path that led from the mines to the city, but once on the other side she was not likely to meet with anyone, for she had resolved to cut through the forest and so reach the bridge of boats without entering the City of Regos, where she might be interrupted. For an hour or two she found the walking easy enough, but then the forest, which in this part was unknown to her, became badly tangled. The trees were thicker and creeping vines intertwined between them. She had to turn this way and that to get through at all, and finally she came to a place where a network of vines and branches effectually barred her farther progress.

Zella was dismayed, at first, when she encountered this obstacle, but setting down her pails she made an endeavor to push the branches aside. At her touch they parted as if by magic, breaking asunder like dried twigs, and she found she could pass freely. At another place a great log had fallen across her way, but the little girl lifted it easily and cast it aside, although six ordinary men could scarcely have moved it.

The child was somewhat worried at this evidence of a strength she had heretofore been ignorant that she possessed. In order to satisfy herself that it was no delusion, she tested her new-found power in many ways, finding that nothing was too big nor too heavy for her to lift. And, naturally enough, the girl gained courage from these experiments and became confident that she could protect herself in any emergency. When, presently, a wild boar ran toward her, grunting horribly and threatening her with its great tusks, she did not climb a tree to escape, as she had always done before on meeting such creatures, but stood still and faced the boar. When it had come quite close and Zella saw that it could not injure her—a fact that astonished both the beast and the girl—she suddenly reached down and seizing it by one ear threw the great beast far off amongst the trees, where it fell headlong to the earth, grunting louder than ever with surprise and fear.

The girl laughed merrily at this incident and, picking up her pails, resumed her journey through the forest. It is not recorded whether the wild boar told his adventure to the other beasts or they had happened to witness his defeat, but certain it is that Zella was not again molested. A brown bear watched her pass without making any movement in her direction and a great puma—a beast much dreaded by all men—crept out of her path as she approached, and disappeared among the trees.

Thus everything favored the girl's journey and she made

such good speed that by noon she emerged from the forest's edge and found she was quite near to the bridge of boats that led to Coregos. This she crossed safely and without meeting any of the rude warriors she so greatly feared, and five minutes later the daughter of the charcoal-burner was seeking admittance at the back door of Queen Cor's palace.

The EXCITEMENT of
BILBIL the GOAT

Our story must now return to one of our characters whom we have been forced to neglect. The temper of Bilbil the goat was not sweet under any circumstances, and whenever he had a grievance he was inclined to be quite grumpy. So, when his master settled down in the palace of King Gos for a quiet life with the boy Prince, and passed his time in playing checkers and eating and otherwise enjoying himself, he had no use whatever for Bilbil, and shut the goat in an upstairs room to prevent his wandering through the city and quarreling with the citizens. But this Bilbil did not like at all. He became very cross and disagreeable at being left alone and he did not speak nicely to the servants who came to bring him food; therefore those people decided not to wait upon him any more, resenting his conversation and not liking to be scolded by a lean, scraggly goat, even though it belonged to a conqueror. The servants kept away from the room and Bilbil grew more hungry and more angry every hour. He tried to eat the rugs and ornaments, but found them not at all nourishing. There was no grass to be had unless he escaped from the palace.

When Queen Cor came to capture Inga and Rinkitink, both the prisoners were so filled with despair at their own misfortune that they gave no thought whatever to the goat, who was left in his room. Nor did Bilbil know anything of the changed fortunes of his comrades until he heard shouts and boisterous laughter in the courtyard below. Looking out of a window, with the intention of rebuking those who dared thus to disturb him, Bilbil saw the courtyard quite filled with warriors and knew from this that the palace had in some way again fallen into the hands of the enemy.

Now, although Bilbil was often exceedingly disagreeable to King Rinkitink, as well as to the Prince, and sometimes used harsh words in addressing them, he was intelligent enough to know them to be his friends, and to know that King Gos and his people were his foes. In sudden anger, provoked by the sight of the warriors and the knowledge that he was in the power of the dangerous men of Regos, Bilbil butted his head

against the door of his room and burst it open. Then he ran
to the head of the staircase and saw King Gos coming up the
stairs followed by a long line of his chief captains and warriors.

The goat lowered his head, trembling with rage and
excitement, and just as the King reached the top stair the animal dashed forward and butted his Majesty so fiercely that the
big and powerful King, who did not expect an attack, doubled
up and tumbled backward. His great weight knocked over the
man just behind him and he in turn struck the next warrior
and upset him, so that in an instant the whole line of Bilbil's
foes was tumbling heels over head to the bottom of the stairs,
where they piled up in a heap, struggling and shouting and
in the mix-up hitting one another with their fists, until every
man of them was bruised and sore.

Finally King Gos scrambled out of the heap and rushed up
the stairs again, very angry indeed. Bilbil was ready for him
and a second time butted the King down the stairs; but now
the goat also lost his balance and followed the King, landing
full upon the confused heap of soldiers. Then he kicked out so
viciously with his heels that he soon freed himself and dashed
out of the doorway of the palace.

"Stop him!" cried King Gos, running after.

But the goat was now so wild and excited that it was not
safe for anyone to stand in his way. None of the men were
armed and when one or two tried to head off the goat, Bilbil
sent them sprawling upon the ground. Most of the warriors,

however, were wise enough not to attempt to interfere with his flight.

Coursing down the street, Bilbil found himself approaching the bridge of boats and without pausing to think where it might lead him he crossed over and proceeded on his way. A few moments later a great stone building blocked his path. It was the palace of Queen Cor, and seeing the gates of the courtyard standing wide open, Bilbil rushed through them without slackening his speed.

Chapter 13

ZELLA SAVES the PRINCE

The wicked Queen of Coregos was in a very bad humor this morning, for one of her slave drivers had come from the fields to say that a number of slaves had rebelled and would not work.

"Bring them here to me!" she cried savagely. "A good whipping may make them change their minds."

So the slave driver went to fetch the rebellious ones and Queen Cor sat down to eat her breakfast, an ugly look on her face.

Prince Inga had been ordered to stand behind his new mistress with a big fan of peacock's feathers, but he was so unused to such service that he awkwardly brushed her ear with the fan.

At once she flew into a terrible rage and slapped the Prince twice with her hand—blows that tingled, too, for her hand was big and hard and she was not inclined to be gentle. Inga took the blows without shrinking or uttering a cry, although they stung his pride far more than his body. But King Rinkitink, who was acting as the Queen's butler and had just brought in her coffee, was so startled at seeing the young Prince punished that he tipped over the urn and the hot coffee streamed across the lap of the Queen's best morning gown.

Cor sprang from her seat with a scream of anger and poor Rinkitink would doubtless have been given a terrible beating had not the slave driver returned at this moment and attracted the woman's attention. The overseer had brought with him all of the women slaves from Pingaree, who had been loaded down with chains and were so weak and ill they could scarcely walk, much less work in the fields.

Prince Inga's eyes were dimmed with sorrowful tears when he discovered how his poor people had been abused, but his own plight was so helpless that he was unable to aid them. Fortunately the boy's mother, Queen Garee, was not among these slaves, for Queen Cor had placed her in the royal dairy to make butter.

"Why do you refuse to work?" demanded Cor in a harsh voice, as the slaves from Pingaree stood before her, trembling and with downcast eyes.

"Because we lack strength to perform the tasks your

overseers demand," answered one of the women.

"Then you shall be whipped until your strength returns!" exclaimed the Queen, and turning to Inga, she commanded: "Get me the whip with the seven lashes."

As the boy left the room, wondering how he might manage to save the unhappy women from their undeserved punishment, he met a girl entering by the back way, who asked:

"Can you tell me where to find her Majesty, Queen Cor?"

"She is in the chamber with the red dome, where green dragons are painted upon the walls," replied Inga; "but she is in an angry and ungracious mood today. Why do you wish to see her?"

"I have honey to sell," answered the girl, who was Zella, just come from the forest. "The Queen is very fond of my honey."

"You may go to her, if you so desire," said the boy, "but take care not to anger the cruel Queen, or she may do you a mischief."

"Why should she harm me, who brings her the honey she so dearly loves?" inquired the child innocently. "But I thank you for your warning; and I will try not to anger the Queen."

As Zella started to go, Inga's eyes suddenly fell upon her shoes and instantly he recognized them as his own. For only in Pingaree were shoes shaped in this manner: high at the heel and pointed at the toes.

"Stop!" he cried in an excited voice, and the girl obeyed,

wonderingly. "Tell me," he continued, more gently, "where did you get those shoes?"

"My father brought them to me from Regos," she answered.

"From Regos!"

"Yes. Are they not pretty?" asked Zella, looking down at her feet to admire them. "One of them my father found by the palace wall, and the other on an ash-heap. So he brought them to me and they fit me perfectly."

By this time Inga was trembling with eager joy, which of course the girl could not understand.

"What is your name, little maid?" he asked.

"I am called Zella, and my father is Nikobob, the charcoal-burner."

"Zella is a pretty name. I am Inga, Prince of Pingaree," said he, "and the shoes you are now wearing, Zella, belong to me. They were not cast away, as your father supposed, but were lost. Will you let me have them again?"

Zella's eyes filled with tears.

"Must I give up my pretty shoes, then?" she asked. "They are the only ones I have ever owned."

Inga was sorry for the poor child, but he knew how important it was that he regain possession of the Magic Pearls. So he said, pleadingly:

"Please let me have them, Zella. See! I will exchange for them the shoes I now have on, which are newer and prettier than the others."

The girl hesitated. She wanted to please the boy Prince, yet she hated to exchange the shoes which her father had brought her as a present.

"If you will give me the shoes," continued the boy, anxiously, "I will promise to make you and your father and mother rich and prosperous. Indeed, I will promise to grant any favors you may ask of me," and he sat down upon the floor and drew off the shoes he was wearing and held them toward the girl.

"I'll see if they will fit me," said Zella, taking off her left shoe—the one that contained the Pink Pearl—and beginning to put on one of Inga's.

Just then Queen Cor, angry at being made to wait for her whip with the seven lashes, rushed into the room to find Inga. Seeing the boy sitting upon the floor beside Zella, the woman sprang toward him to beat him with her clenched fists; but Inga had now slipped on the shoe and the Queen's blows could not reach his body.

Then Cor espied the whip lying beside Inga and snatching it up she tried to lash him with it—all to no avail.

While Zella sat horrified by this scene, the Prince, who realized he had no time to waste, reached out and pulled the right shoe from the girl's foot, quickly placing it upon his own. Then he stood up and, facing the furious but astonished Queen, said to her in a quiet voice:

"Madam, please give me that whip."

"I won't!" answered Cor. "I'm going to lash those Pingaree women with it."

The boy seized hold of the whip and with irresistible strength drew it from the Queen's hand. But she drew from her bosom a sharp dagger and with the swiftness of lightning aimed a blow at Inga's heart. He merely stood still and smiled, for the blade rebounded and fell clattering to the floor.

Then, at last, Queen Cor understood the magic power that had terrified her husband but which she had ridiculed in her ignorance, not believing in it. She did not know that Inga's power had been lost, and found again, but she realized the boy was no common foe and that unless she could still manage to outwit him her reign in the Island of Coregos was ended. To gain time, she went back to the red-domed chamber and seated herself in her throne, before which were grouped the weeping slaves from Pingaree.

Inga had taken Zella's hand and assisted her to put on the shoes he had given her in exchange for his own. She found them quite comfortable and did not know she had lost anything by the transfer.

"Come with me," then said the boy Prince, and led her into the presence of Queen Cor, who was giving Rinkitink a scolding. To the overseer Inga said.

"Give me the keys which unlock these chains, that I may set these poor women at liberty."

"Don't you do it!" screamed Queen Cor.

"If you interfere, madam," said the boy, "I will put you into a dungeon."

By this Rinkitink knew that Inga had recovered his Magic Pearls and the little fat King was so overjoyed that he danced and capered all around the room. But the Queen was alarmed at the threat and the slave driver, fearing the conqueror of Regos, tremblingly gave up the keys.

Inga quickly removed all the shackles from the women of his country and comforted them, telling them they should work no more but would soon be restored to their homes in Pingaree. Then he commanded the slave driver to go and get all the children who had been made slaves, and to bring them to their mothers. The man obeyed and left at once to perform his errand, while Queen Cor, growing more and more uneasy, suddenly sprang from her throne and before Inga could stop her had rushed through the room and out into the courtyard of the palace, meaning to make her escape. Rinkitink followed her, running as fast as he could go.

It was at this moment that Bilbil, in his mad dash from Regos, turned in at the gates of the courtyard, and as he was coming one way and Queen Cor was going the other they bumped into each other with great force. The woman sailed through the air, over Bilbil's head, and landed on the ground outside the gates, where her crown rolled into a ditch and she picked herself up, half dazed, and continued her flight.

Bilbil was also somewhat dazed by the unexpected encounter, but he continued his rush rather blindly and so struck poor Rinkitink, who was chasing after Queen Cor. They rolled over one another a few times and then Rinkitink sat up and Bilbil sat up and they looked at each other in amazement.

"Bilbil," said the King, "I'm astonished at you!"

"Your Majesty," said Bilbil, "I expected kinder treatment at your hands."

"You interrupted me," said Rinkitink.

"There was plenty of room without your taking my path," declared the goat.

And then Inga came running out and said. "Where is the Queen?"

"Gone," replied Rinkitink, "but she cannot go far, as this is an island. However, I have found Bilbil, and our party is again reunited. You have recovered your magic powers, and again we are masters of the situation. So let us be thankful."

Saying this, the good little King got upon his feet and limped back into the Throne Room to help comfort the women.

Presently the children of Pingaree, who had been gathered together by the overseer, were brought in and restored to their mothers, and there was great rejoicing among them, you may be sure.

"But where is Queen Garee, my dear mother?" questioned Inga; but the women did not know and it was some time before the overseer remembered that one of the slaves from Pingaree had been placed in the royal dairy. Perhaps this was the woman the boy was seeking.

Inga at once commanded him to lead the way to the butter-house, but when they arrived there Queen Garee was nowhere in the place, although the boy found a silk scarf which he recognized as one that his mother used to wear. Then they began a search throughout the island of Coregos, but could not find Inga's mother anywhere.

When they returned to the palace of Queen Cor, Rinkitink discovered that the bridge of boats had again been removed, separating them from Regos, and from this they suspected that Queen Cor had fled to her husband's island and had taken Queen Garee with her. Inga was much perplexed what to do and returned with his friends to the palace to talk the matter over.

Zella was now crying because she had not sold her honey and was unable to return to her parents on the island of Regos, but the boy Prince comforted her and promised she should be protected until she could be restored to her home. Rinkitink found Queen Cor's purse, which she had had no time to take with her, and gave Zella several gold pieces for the honey. Then Inga ordered the palace servants to prepare a feast for all the women and children of Pingaree and to prepare for them beds in the great palace, which was large enough to accommodate them all.

Then the boy and the goat and Rinkitink and Zella went into a private room to consider what should be done next.

Chapter 14

The ESCAPE

Our fault," said Rinkitink, "is that we conquer only one of these twin islands at a time. When we conquered Regos, our foes all came to Coregos, and now that we have conquered Coregos, the Queen has fled to Regos. And each time they removed the bridge of boats, so that we could not follow them."

"What has become of our own boat, in which we came from Pingaree?" asked Bilbil.

"We left it on the shore of Regos," replied the Prince, "but I wonder if we could not get it again."

"Why don't you ask the White Pearl?" suggested Rinkitink.

"That is a good idea," returned the boy, and at once he drew the White Pearl from its silken bag and held it to his ear. Then he asked: "How may I regain our boat?"

The Voice of the Pearl replied: "Go to the south end of the Island of Coregos, and clap your hands three times and the boat will come to you."

"Very good!" cried Inga, and then he turned to his companions and said: "We shall be able to get our boat whenever we please; but what then shall we do?"

"Take me home in it!" pleaded Zella.

"Come with me to my City of Gilgad," said the King, "where you will be very welcome to remain forever."

"No," answered Inga, "I must rescue my father and mother, as well as my people. Already I have the women and children of Pingaree, but the men are with my father in the mines of Regos, and my dear mother has been taken away by Queen Cor. Not until all are rescued will I consent to leave these islands."

"Quite right!" exclaimed Bilbil.

"On second thought," said Rinkitink, "I agree with you. If you are careful to sleep in your shoes, and never take them off again, I believe you will be able to perform the task you have undertaken."

They counseled together for a long time as to their mode of action and it was finally considered best to make the attempt to liberate King Kitticut first of all, and with him the men from Pingaree. This would give them an army to assist them and afterward they could march to Regos and compel Queen Cor to give up the Queen of Pingaree. Zella told them that they could go in their boat along the shore of Regos to a point opposite the mines, thus avoiding any conflict with the warriors of King Gos.

This being considered the best course to pursue, they resolved to start on the following morning, as night was even now approaching. The servants being all busy in caring for the women and children, Zella undertook to get a dinner for Inga and Rinkitink and herself and soon prepared a fine meal in the palace kitchen, for she was a good little cook and had often helped her mother. The dinner was served in a small room overlooking the gardens and Rinkitink thought the best part of it was the sweet honey, which he spread upon the biscuits that Zella had made. As for Bilbil, he wandered through the palace grounds and found some grass that made him a good dinner.

During the evening Inga talked with the women and cheered them, promising soon to reunite them with their husbands who were working in the mines and to send them back to their own island of Pingaree.

Next morning the boy rose bright and early and found that Zella had already prepared a nice breakfast. And after the meal they went to the most southern point of the island, which was not very far away, Rinkitink riding upon Bilbil's back and Inga and Zella following behind them, hand in hand.

When they reached the water's edge the boy advanced and clapped his hands together three times, as the White Pearl had told him to do. And in a few moments they saw in the distance the black boat with the silver lining, coming swiftly toward them from the sea. Presently it grounded on the beach and they all got into it.

Zella was delighted with the boat, which was the most beautiful she had ever seen, and the marvel of its coming to them through the water without anyone to row it made her a little afraid of the fairy craft. But Inga picked up the oars and began to row and at once the boat shot swiftly in the direction of Regos. They rounded the point of that island where the city was built and noticed that the shore was lined with warriors who had discovered their boat but seemed undecided whether to pursue it or not. This was probably because they had received no commands what to do, or perhaps they had learned to fear the magic powers of these adventurers from Pingaree and were unwilling to attack them unless their King ordered them to.

The coast on the western side of the Island of Regos was very uneven and Zella, who knew fairly well the location of the mines from the inland forest path, was puzzled to decide which mountain they now viewed from the sea was the one where the entrance to the underground caverns was located. First she thought it was this peak, and then she guessed it was that; so considerable time was lost through her uncertainty.

They finally decided to land and explore the country, to

see where they were, so Inga ran the boat into a little rocky cove where they all disembarked. For an hour they searched for the path without finding any trace of it and now Zella believed they had gone too far to the north and must return to another mountain that was nearer to the city.

Once again they entered the boat and followed the winding coast south until they thought they had reached the right place. By this time, however, it was growing dark, for the entire day had been spent in the search for the entrance to the mines, and Zella warned them that it would be safer to spend the night in the boat than on the land, where wild beasts were sure to disturb them. None of them realized at this time how fatal this day of search had been to their plans and perhaps if Inga had realized what was going on he would have landed and fought all the wild beasts in the forest rather than quietly remain in the boat until morning.

However, knowing nothing of the cunning plans of Queen Cor and King Gos, they anchored their boat in a little bay and cheerfully ate their dinner, finding plenty of food and drink in the boat's lockers. In the evening the stars came out in the sky and tipped the waves around their boat with silver. All around them was delightfully still save for the occasional snarl of a beast on the neighboring shore.

They talked together quietly of their adventures and their future plans and Zella told them her simple history and how hard her poor father was obliged to work, burning charcoal to sell for enough money to support his wife and child. Nikobob might be the humblest man in all Regos, but Zella declared he was a good man, and honest, and it was not his fault that his country was ruled by so wicked a King.

Then Rinkitink, to amuse them, offered to sing a song, and although Bilbil protested in his gruff way, claiming that his master's voice was cracked and disagreeable, the little King was encouraged by the others to sing his song, which he did.

"A red-headed man named Ned was dead;
Sing fiddle-cum-faddle-cum-fi-do!
In battle he had lost his head;
Sing fiddle-cum-faddle-cum-fi-do!
'Alas, poor Ned,' to him I said,
'How did you lose your head so red?'
Sing fiddle-cum-faddle-cum-fi-do!

"Said Ned: 'I for my country bled,'
Sing fiddle-cum-faddle-cum-fi-do!
'Instead of dying safe in bed;'
Sing fiddle-cum-faddle-cum-fi-do!
'If I had only fled, instead,
I then had been a head ahead.'
Sing fiddle-cum-faddle-cum-fi-do!

"I said to Ned—"

"Do stop, your Majesty!" pleaded Bilbil. "You're making my head ache."

"But the song isn't finished," replied Rinkitink, "and as for your head aching, think of poor Ned, who hadn't any head at all!"

"I can think of nothing but your dismal singing," retorted Bilbil. "Why didn't you choose a cheerful subject, instead of telling how a man who was dead lost his red head? Really, Rinkitink, I'm surprised at you."

"I know a splendid song about a live man," said the King.

"Then don't sing it," begged Bilbil.

Zella was both astonished and grieved by the disrespectful words of the goat, for she had quite enjoyed Rinkitink's singing and had been taught a proper respect for Kings and those high in authority. But as it was now getting late they decided to go to sleep, that they might rise early the following morning, so they all reclined upon the bottom of the big boat and covered themselves with blankets which they found stored underneath the seats for just such occasions. They were not long in falling asleep and did not waken until daybreak.

After a hurried breakfast, for Inga was eager to liberate his father, the boy rowed the boat ashore and they all landed and began searching for the path. Zella found it within the next half hour and declared they must be very close to the entrance to the mines; so they followed the path toward the north, Inga going first, and then Zella following him, while Rinkitink brought up the rear riding upon Bilbil's back.

Before long they saw a great wall of rock towering before them, in which was a low arched entrance, and on either side of this entrance stood a guard, armed with a sword and a spear. The guards of the mines were not so fierce as the warriors of King Gos, their duty being to make the slaves work at their tasks and guard them from escaping; but they were as cruel as their cruel master wished them to be, and as cowardly as they were cruel.

Inga walked up to the two men at the entrance and said:

"Does this opening lead to the mines of King Gos?"

"It does," replied one of the guards, "but no one is allowed to pass out who once goes in."

"Nevertheless," said the boy, "we intend to go in and we shall come out whenever it pleases us to do so. I am the Prince of Pingaree, and I have come to liberate my people, whom King Gos has enslaved."

Now when the two guards heard this speech they looked at one another and laughed, and one of them said: "The King was right, for he said the boy was likely to come here and that he would try to set his people free. Also the King commanded that we must keep the little Prince in the mines, and set him to work, together with his companions."

"Then let us obey the King," replied the other man.

Inga was surprised at hearing this, and asked:

"When did King Gos give you this order?"

"His Majesty was here in person last night," replied the man, "and went away again but an hour ago. He suspected you were coming here and told us to capture you if we could."

This report made the boy very anxious, not for himself but for his father, for he feared the King was up to some mischief. So he hastened to enter the mines and the guards did nothing to oppose him or his companions, their orders being to allow him to go in but not to come out.

The little group of adventurers passed through a long rocky corridor and reached a low, wide cavern where they found a dozen guards and a hundred slaves, the latter being hard at work with picks and shovels digging for gold, while the guards stood over them with long whips.

Inga found many of the men from Pingaree among these slaves, but King Kitticut was not in this cavern; so they passed through it and entered another corridor that led to a second cavern. Here also hundreds of men were working, but the boy did not find his father amongst them, and so went on to a third cavern.

The corridors all slanted downward, so that the farther they went the lower into the earth they descended, and now they found the air hot and close and difficult to breathe. Flaming torches were stuck into the walls to give light to the workers, and these added to the oppressive heat.

The third and lowest cavern was the last in the mines, and here were many scores of slaves and many guards to keep them at work. So far, none of the guards had paid any attention to Inga's party, but allowed them to proceed as they would, and while the slaves cast curious glances at the boy and girl and man and goat, they dared say nothing. But now the boy walked up to some of the men of Pingaree and asked news of his father, telling them not to fear the guards as he would protect them from the whips.

Then he learned that King Kitticut had indeed been working in this very cavern until the evening before, when King Gos had come and taken him away—still loaded with chains.

"Seems to me," said King Rinkitink, when he heard this report, "that Gos has carried your father away to Regos, to prevent us from rescuing him. He may hide poor Kitticut in a dungeon, where we cannot find him."

"Perhaps you are right," answered the boy, "but I am determined to find him, wherever he may be."

Inga spoke firmly and with courage, but he was greatly disappointed to find that King Gos had been before him at the mines and had taken his father away. However, he tried not to feel disheartened, believing he would succeed in the end, in spite of all opposition. Turning to the guards, he said:

"Remove the chains from these slaves and set them free."

The guards laughed at this order, and one of them brought forward a handful of chains, saying: "His Majesty has commanded us to make you, also, a slave, for you are never to leave these caverns again."

Then he attempted to place the chains on Inga, but the

boy indignantly seized them and broke them apart as easily as if they had been cotton cords. When a dozen or more of the guards made a dash to capture him, the Prince swung the end of the chain like a whip and drove them into a corner, where they cowered and begged for mercy.

Stories of the marvelous strength of the boy Prince had already spread to the mines of Regos, and although King Gos had told them that Inga had been deprived of all his magic power, the guards now saw this was not true, so they deemed it wise not to attempt to oppose him.

The chains of the slaves had all been riveted fast to their ankles and wrists, but Inga broke the bonds of steel with his hands and set the poor men free—not only those from Pingaree but all who had been captured in the many wars and raids of King Gos. They were very grateful, as you may suppose, and agreed to support Prince Inga in whatever action he commanded.

He led them to the middle cavern, where all the guards and overseers fled in terror at his approach, and soon he had broken apart the chains of the slaves who had been working in that part of the mines. Then they approached the first cavern and liberated all there.

The slaves had been treated so cruelly by the servants of King Gos that they were eager to pursue and slay them, in revenge; but Inga held them back and formed them into companies, each company having its own leader. Then he called the leaders together and instructed them to march in good order along the path to the City of Regos, where he would meet them and tell them what to do next.

They readily agreed to obey him, and, arming themselves with iron bars and pick-axes which they brought from the mines, the slaves began their march to the city.

Zella at first wished to be left behind, that she might make her way to her home, but neither Rinkitink nor Inga thought it was safe for her to wander alone through the forest, so they induced her to return with them to the city.

The boy beached his boat this time at the same place as when he first landed at Regos, and while many of the warriors stood on the shore and before the walls of the city, not one of them attempted to interfere with the boy in any way. Indeed, they seemed uneasy and anxious, and when Inga met Captain Buzzub the boy asked if anything had happened in his absence.

"A great deal has happened," replied Buzzub. "Our King and Queen have run away and left us, and we don't know what to do."

"Run away!" exclaimed Inga. "Where did they go to?"

"Who knows?" said the man, shaking his head despondently. "They departed together a few hours ago, in a boat with forty rowers, and they took with them the King and Queen of Pingaree!"

····—·< ☉hapter 15 ··—····

The FLIGHT of the RULERS

Now it seems that when Queen Cor fled from her island to Regos, she had wit enough, although greatly frightened, to make a stop at the royal dairy, which was near to the bridge, and to drag poor Queen Garee from the butter-house and across to Regos with her. The warriors of King Gos had never before seen the terrible Queen Cor frightened, and therefore when she came running across the bridge of boats, dragging the Queen of Pingaree after her by one arm, the woman's great fright had the effect of terrifying the waiting warriors.

"Quick!" cried Cor. "Destroy the bridge, or we are lost."

While the men were tearing away the bridge of boats the Queen ran up to the palace of Gos, where she met her husband.

"That boy is a wizard!" she gasped. "There is no standing against him."

"Oh, have you discovered his magic at last?" replied Gos, laughing in her face. "Who, now, is the coward?"

"Don't laugh!" cried Queen Cor. "It is no laughing matter. Both our islands are as good as conquered, this very minute. What shall we do, Gos?"

"Come in," he said, growing serious, "and let us talk it over."

So they went into a room of the palace and talked long and earnestly.

"The boy intends to liberate his father and mother, and all the people of Pingaree, and to take them back to their island," said Cor. "He may also destroy our palaces and make us his slaves. I can see but one way, Gos, to prevent him from doing all this, and whatever else he pleases to do."

"What way is that?" asked King Gos.

"We must take the boy's parents away from here as quickly as possible. I have with me the Queen of Pingaree, and you can run up to the mines and get the King. Then we will carry them away in a boat and hide them where the boy cannot find them, with all his magic. We will use the King and Queen of Pingaree as hostages, and send word to the boy wizard that if he does not go away from our islands and allow us to rule them undisturbed, in our own way, we will put his father and mother to death. Also we will say that as long as we are let alone his parents will be safe, although still safely hidden. I believe, Gos, that in this way we can compel Prince Inga to obey us, for he seems very fond of his parents."

"It isn't a bad idea," said Gos, reflectively; "but where can we hide the King and Queen, so that the boy cannot find them?"

"In the country of the Nome King, on the mainland away at the south," she replied. "The nomes are our friends, and they possess magic powers that will enable them to protect the prisoners from discovery. If we can manage to get the King and Queen of Pingaree to the Nome Kingdom before the boy knows what we are doing, I am sure our plot will succeed."

Gos gave the plan considerable thought in the next five minutes, and the more he thought about it the more clever and reasonable it seemed. So he agreed to do as Queen Cor suggested and at once hurried away to the mines, where he arrived before Prince Inga did. The next morning he carried King Kitticut back to Regos.

While Gos was gone, Queen Cor busied herself in preparing a large and swift boat for the journey. She placed in it several bags of gold and jewels with which to bribe the nomes, and selected forty of the strongest oarsmen in Regos to row the boat. The instant King Gos returned with his royal prisoner all was ready for departure. They quickly entered the boat with their two important captives and without a word of explanation to any of their people they commanded the oarsmen to start, and were soon out of sight upon the broad expanse of the Nonestic Ocean.

Inga arrived at the city some hours later and was much distressed when he learned that his father and mother had been spirited away from the islands.

"I shall follow them, of course," said the boy to Rinkitink, "and if I cannot overtake them on the ocean I will search the world over until I find them. But before I leave here I must arrange to send our people back to Pingaree."

Chapter 16

NIKOBOB REFUSES a CROWN

Almost the first persons that Zella saw when she landed from the silver-lined boat at Regos were her father and mother. Nikobob and his wife had been greatly worried when their little daughter failed to return from Coregos, so they had set out to discover what had become of her. When they reached the City of Regos, that very morning, they were astonished to hear news of all the strange events that had taken place; still, they found comfort when told that Zella had been seen in the boat of Prince Inga, which had gone to the north. Then, while they wondered what this could mean, the silver-lined boat appeared again, with their daughter in it, and they ran down to the shore to give her a welcome and many joyful kisses.

Inga invited the good people to the palace of King Gos, where he conferred with them, as well as with Rinkitink and Bilbil.

"Now that the King and Queen of Regos and Coregos have run away," he said, "there is no one to rule these islands. So it is my duty to appoint a new Ruler, and as Nikobob, Zella's father, is an honest and worthy man, I shall make him the King of the Twin Islands."

"Me?" cried Nikobob, astounded by this speech. "I beg your Highness, on my bended knees, not to do so cruel a thing as to make me King!"

"Why not?" inquired Rinkitink. "I'm a King, and I know how it feels. I assure you, good Nikobob, that I quite enjoy my high rank, although a jeweled crown is rather heavy to wear in hot weather."

"With you, noble sir, it is different," said Nikobob, "for you are far from your kingdom and its trials and worries and may do as you please. But to remain in Regos, as King over these fierce and unruly warriors, would be to live in constant anxiety and peril, and the chances are that they would murder me within a month. As I have done no harm to anyone and have tried to be a good and upright man, I do not think that I should be condemned to such a dreadful fate."

"Very well," replied Inga, "we will say no more about your

being King. I merely wanted to make you rich and prosperous, as I had promised Zella."

"Please forget that promise," pleaded the charcoal-burner, earnestly; "I have been safe from molestation for many years, because I was poor and possessed nothing that anyone else could envy. But if you make me rich and prosperous I shall at once become the prey of thieves and marauders and probably will lose my life in the attempt to protect my fortune."

Inga looked at the man in surprise.

"What, then, can I do to please you?" he inquired.

"Nothing more than to allow me to go home to my poor cabin," said Nikobob.

"Perhaps," remarked King Rinkitink, "the charcoal-burner has more wisdom concealed in that hard head of his than we gave him credit for. But let us use that wisdom, for the present, to counsel us what to do in this emergency."

"What you call my wisdom," said Nikobob, "is merely common sense. I have noticed that some men become rich, and are scorned by some and robbed by others. Other men become famous, and are mocked at and derided by their fellows. But the poor and humble man who lives unnoticed and unknown escapes all these troubles and is the only one who can appreciate the joy of living."

"If I had a hand, instead of a cloven hoof, I'd like to shake hands with you, Nikobob," said Bilbil the goat. "But the poor man must not have a cruel master, or he is undone."

During the council they found, indeed, that the advice of the charcoal-burner was both shrewd and sensible, and they profited much by his words.

Inga gave Captain Buzzub the command of the warriors and made him promise to keep his men quiet and orderly—if he could. Then the boy allowed all of King Gos's former slaves, except those who came from Pingaree, to choose what boats they required and to stock them with provisions and row away to their own countries. When these had departed, with grateful thanks and many blessings showered upon the boy Prince who had set them free, Inga made preparations to send his own people home, where they were told to rebuild their houses and then erect a new royal palace. They were then to await patiently the coming of King Kitticut or Prince Inga.

"My greatest worry," said the boy to his friends, "is to know whom to appoint to take charge of this work of restoring Pingaree to its former condition. My men are all pearl fishers, and although willing and honest, have no talent for directing others how to work."

While the preparations for departure were being made, Nikobob offered to direct the men of Pingaree, and did so in a very capable manner. As the island had been despoiled of all its valuable furniture and draperies and rich cloths and paintings and statuary and the like, as well as gold and silver and ornaments, Inga thought it no more than just that they be replaced by the spoilers. So he directed his people to search through the storehouses of King Gos and to regain all their goods and chattels that could be found. Also he instructed them to take as much else as they required to make their new homes comfortable, so that many boats were loaded full of goods that would enable the people to restore Pingaree to its former state of comfort.

For his father's new palace the boy plundered the palaces of both Queen Cor and King Gos, sending enough wares away with his people to make King Kitticut's new residence as handsomely fitted and furnished as had been the one which the ruthless invaders from Regos had destroyed.

It was a great fleet of boats that set out one bright, sunny morning on the voyage to Pingaree, carrying all the men, women and children and all the goods for refitting their homes. As he saw the fleet depart, Prince Inga felt that he had already successfully accomplished a part of his mission, but he vowed he would never return to Pingaree in person until he could take his father and mother there with him; unless, indeed, King Gos wickedly destroyed his beloved parents, in which case Inga would become the King of Pingaree and it would be his duty to go to his people and rule over them.

It was while the last of the boats were preparing to sail for Pingaree that Nikobob, who had been of great service in getting them ready, came to Inga in a thoughtful mood and said:

"Your Highness, my wife and my daughter Zella have been urging me to leave Regos and settle down in your island, in a new home. From what your people have told me, Pingaree is a better place to live than Regos, and there are no cruel warriors or savage beasts there to keep one in constant fear for the safety of those he loves. Therefore, I have come to ask to go with my family in one of the boats."

Inga was much pleased with this proposal and not only granted Nikobob permission to go to Pingaree to live, but instructed him to take with him sufficient goods to furnish his new home in a comfortable manner. In addition to this, he appointed Nikobob general manager of the buildings and of the pearl fisheries, until his father or he himself arrived, and the people approved this order because they liked Nikobob and knew him to be just and honest.

As soon as the last boat of the great flotilla had disappeared from the view of those left at Regos, Inga and Rinkitink prepared to leave the island themselves. The boy was anxious to overtake the boat of King Gos, if possible, and Rinkitink had no desire to remain in Regos.

Buzzub and the warriors stood silently on the shore and watched the black boat with its silver lining depart, and I am sure they were as glad to be rid of their unwelcome visitors as Inga and Rinkitink and Bilbil were to leave.

The boy asked the White Pearl what direction the boat of King Gos had taken and then he followed after it, rowing hard and steadily for eight days without becoming at all weary. But, although the black boat moved very swiftly, it failed to overtake the barge which was rowed by Queen Cor's forty picked oarsmen.

·—··◄ Chapter 17 ►··—··

The NOME KING

The Kingdom of the Nomes does not border on the Nonestic Ocean, from which it is separated by the Kingdom of Rinkitink and the Country of the Wheelers, which is a part of the Land of Ev. Rinkitink's country is separated from the country of the Nomes by a row of high and steep mountains, from which it extends to the sea. The Country of the Wheelers is a sandy waste that is open on one side to the Nonestic Ocean and on the other side has no barrier to separate it from the Nome Country, therefore it was on the coast of the Wheelers that King Gos landed—in a spot quite deserted by any of the curious inhabitants of that country.

The Nome Country is very large in extent, and is only separated from the Land of Oz, on its eastern borders, by a Deadly Desert that cannot be crossed by mortals, unless they are aided by the fairies or by magic.

The nomes are a numerous and mischievous people, living in underground caverns of wide extent, connected one with another by arches and passages. The word "nome" means "one who knows," and these people are so called because they know where all the gold and silver and precious stones are hidden in the earth—a knowledge that no other living creatures share with them. The nomes are busy people, constantly digging up gold in one place and taking it to another place, where they secretly bury it, and perhaps this is the reason they alone know where to find it. The nomes were ruled, at the time of which I write, by a King named Kaliko.

King Gos had expected to be pursued by Inga in his magic boat, so he made all the haste possible, urging his forty rowers to their best efforts night and day. To his joy he was not overtaken but landed on the sandy beach of the Wheelers on the morning of the eighth day.

The forty rowers were left with the boat, while Queen Cor and King Gos, with their royal prisoners, who were still chained, began the journey to the Nome King.

It was not long before they passed the sands and reached the rocky country belonging to the nomes, but they were still a long way from the entrance to the underground caverns in which lived the Nome King. There was a dim path, winding between stones and boulders, over which the walking was quite difficult, especially as the path led up hills that were small mountains, and then down steep and abrupt slopes where any misstep might mean a broken leg. Therefore it was the second day of their journey before they climbed halfway up a rugged mountain and found themselves at the entrance of the Nome King's caverns.

On their arrival, the entrance seemed free and unguarded, but Gos and Cor had been there before, and they were too wise to attempt to enter without announcing themselves, for the passage to the caves was full of traps and pitfalls. So King Gos stood still and shouted, and in an instant they were surrounded by a group of crooked nomes, who seemed to have sprung from the ground.

One of these had very long ears and was called The Long-Eared Hearer. He said: "I heard you coming early this morning."

Another had eyes that looked in different directions at the same time and were curiously bright and penetrating. He could look over a hill or around a corner and was called The Lookout. Said he: "I saw you coming yesterday."

"Then," said King Gos, "perhaps King Kaliko is expecting us."

"It is true," replied another nome, who wore a gold collar around his neck and carried a bunch of golden keys. "The mighty Nome King expects you, and bids you follow me to his presence."

With this he led the way into the caverns and Gos and Cor followed, dragging their weary prisoners with them, for poor King Kitticut and his gentle Queen had been obliged to carry, all through the tedious journey, the bags of gold and jewels which were to bribe the Nome King to accept them as slaves.

Through several long passages the guide led them and at last they entered a small cavern which was beautifully decorated and set with rare jewels that flashed from every part of the wall, floor and ceiling. This was a waiting-room for visitors, and there their guide left them while he went to inform King Kaliko of their arrival.

Before long they were ushered into a great domed chamber, cut from the solid rock and so magnificent that all of them—the King and Queen of Pingaree and the King and Queen of Regos and Coregos—drew long breaths of astonishment and opened their eyes as wide as they could.

In an ivory throne sat a little round man who had a pointed beard and hair that rose to a tall curl on top of his head. He was dressed in silken robes, richly embroidered, which had large buttons of cut rubies. On his head was a diamond crown and in his hand he held a golden sceptre with a big jeweled ball at one end of it. This was Kaliko, the King and Ruler of all the nomes. He nodded pleasantly enough to his visitors and said in a cheery voice:

"Well, your Majesties, what can I do for you?"

"It is my desire," answered King Gos, respectfully, "to place in your care two prisoners, whom you now see before you. They must be carefully guarded, to prevent them from escaping, for they have the cunning of foxes and are not to be trusted. In return for the favor I am asking you to grant, I have brought your Majesty valuable presents of gold and precious gems."

He then commanded Kitticut and Garee to lay before the Nome King the bags of gold and jewels, and they obeyed, being helpless.

"Very good," said King Kaliko, nodding approval, for like all the nomes he loved treasures of gold and jewels. "But who are the prisoners you have brought here, and why do you place them in my charge instead of guarding them yourself? They seem gentle enough, I'm sure."

"The prisoners," returned King Gos, "are the King and Queen of Pingaree, a small island north of here. They are very evil people and came to our islands of Regos and Coregos to conquer them and slay our poor people. Also they intended to plunder us of all our riches, but by good fortune we were able to defeat and capture them. However, they have a son who is a terrible wizard and who by magic art is trying to find this awful King and Queen of Pingaree, and to set them free, that they may continue their wicked deeds. Therefore, as we have no magic to defend ourselves with, we have brought the prisoners to you for safe keeping."

"Your Majesty," spoke up King Kitticut, addressing the Nome King with great indignation, "do not believe this tale, I implore you. It is all a lie!"

"I know it," said Kaliko. "I consider it a clever lie, though, because it is woven without a thread of truth. However, that is none of my business. The fact remains that my good friend King Gos wishes to put you in my underground caverns, so that you will be unable to escape. And why should I not please him in this little matter? Gos is a mighty King and a great warrior, while your island of Pingaree is desolated and your people scattered. In my heart, King Kitticut, I sympathize with you, but as a matter of business policy we powerful Kings must stand together and trample the weaker ones under our feet."

King Kitticut was surprised to find the King of the nomes so candid and so well informed, and he tried to argue that he and his gentle wife did not deserve their cruel fate and that it would be wiser for Kaliko to side with them than with the evil King of Regos. But Kaliko only shook his head and smiled, saying:

"The fact that you are a prisoner, my poor Kitticut, is evidence that you are weaker than King Gos, and I prefer to deal with the strong. By the way," he added, turning to the King of Regos, "have these prisoners any connection with the Land of Oz?"

"Why do you ask?" said Gos.

"Because I dare not offend the Oz people," was the reply. "I am very powerful, as you know, but Ozma of Oz is far more powerful than I; therefore, if this King and Queen of Pingaree happened to be under Ozma's protection, I would have nothing to do with them."

"I assure your Majesty that the prisoners have nothing to do with the Oz people," Gos hastened to say. And Kitticut, being questioned, admitted that this was true.

"But how about that wizard you mentioned?" asked the Nome King.

"Oh, he is merely a boy; but he is very ferocious and obstinate and he is assisted by a little fat sorcerer called Rinkitink and a talking goat."

"Oho! A talking goat, do you say? That certainly sounds like magic; and it also sounds like the Land of Oz, where all the animals talk," said Kaliko, with a doubtful expression.

But King Gos assured him the talking goat had never been to Oz.

"As for Rinkitink, whom you call a sorcerer," continued the Nome King, "he is a neighbor of mine, you must know, but as we are cut off from each other by high mountains beneath which a powerful river runs, I have never yet met King Rinkitink. But I have heard of him, and from all reports he is a jolly rogue, and perfectly harmless. However, in spite of your false statements and misrepresentations, I will earn the treasure you have brought me, by keeping your prisoners safe in my caverns."

"Make them work," advised Queen Cor. "They are rather delicate, and to make them work will make them suffer delightfully."

"I'll do as I please about that," said the Nome King sternly. "Be content that I agree to keep them safe."

The bargain being thus made and concluded, Kaliko first examined the gold and jewels and then sent it away to his royal storehouse, which was well filled with like treasure. Next the captives were sent away in charge of the nome with the golden collar and keys, whose name was Klik, and he escorted them to a small cavern and gave them a good supper.

"I shall lock your door," said Klik, "so there is no need of your wearing those heavy chains any longer." He therefore removed the chains and left King Kitticut and his Queen alone. This was the first time since the Northmen had carried them away from Pingaree that the good King and Queen had been alone together and free of all bonds, and as they embraced lovingly and mingled their tears over their sad fate they were also grateful that they had passed from the control of the heartless King Gos into the more considerate care of King Kaliko. They were still captives but they believed they would be happier in the underground caverns of the nomes than in Regos and Coregos.

Meantime, in the King's royal cavern a great feast had

been spread. King Gos and Queen Cor, having triumphed in their plot, were so well pleased that they held high revelry with the jolly Nome King until a late hour that night. And the next morning, having cautioned Kaliko not to release the prisoners under any consideration without their orders, the King and Queen of Regos and Coregos left the caverns of the nomes to return to the shore of the ocean where they had left their boat.

Chapter 18

INGA PARTS with His PINK PEARL

The White Pearl guided Inga truly in his pursuit of the boat of King Gos, but the boy had been so delayed in sending his people home to Pingaree that it was a full day after Gos and Cor landed on the shore of the Wheeler Country that Inga's boat arrived at the same place.

There he found the forty rowers guarding the barge of Queen Cor, and although they would not or could not tell the boy where the King and Queen had taken his father and mother, the White Pearl advised him to follow the path to the country and the caverns of the nomes.

Rinkitink didn't like to undertake the rocky and mountainous journey, even with Bilbil to carry him, but he would not desert Inga, even though his own kingdom lay just beyond a range of mountains which could be seen towering southwest of them. So the King bravely mounted the goat, who always grumbled but always obeyed his master, and the three set off at once for the caverns of the nomes.

They traveled just as slowly as Queen Cor and King Gos had done, so when they were about halfway they discovered the King and Queen coming back to their boat. The fact that Gos and Cor were now alone proved that they had left Inga's father and mother behind them; so, at the suggestion of Rinkitink, the three hid behind a high rock until the King of Regos and the Queen of Coregos, who had not observed them, had passed them by. Then they continued their journey, glad that they had not again been forced to fight or quarrel with their wicked enemies.

"We might have asked them, however, what they had done with your poor parents," said Rinkitink.

"Never mind," answered Inga. "I am sure the White Pearl will guide us aright."

For a time they proceeded in silence and then Rinkitink began to chuckle with laughter in the pleasant way he was wont to do before his misfortunes came upon him.

"What amuses your Majesty?" inquired the boy.

"The thought of how surprised my dear subjects would be

if they realized how near to them I am, and yet how far away. I have always wanted to visit the Nome Country, which is full of mystery and magic and all sorts of adventures, but my devoted subjects forbade me to think of such a thing, fearing I would get hurt or enchanted."

"Are you afraid, now that you are here?" asked Inga.

"A little, but not much, for they say the new Nome King is not as wicked as the old King used to be. Still, we are undertaking a dangerous journey and I think you ought to protect me by lending me one of your pearls."

Inga thought this over and it seemed a reasonable request.

"Which pearl would you like to have?" asked the boy.

"Well, let us see," returned Rinkitink; "you may need strength to liberate your captive parents, so you must keep the Blue Pearl. And you will need the advice of the White Pearl, so you had best keep that also. But in case we should be separated I would have nothing to protect me from harm, so you ought to lend me the Pink Pearl."

"Very well," agreed Inga, and sitting down upon a rock he removed his right shoe and after withdrawing the cloth from the pointed toe took out the Pink Pearl—the one which protected from any harm the person who carried it.

"Where can you put it, to keep it safely?" he asked.

"In my vest pocket," replied the King. "The pocket has a flap to it and I can pin it down in such a way that the pearl cannot get out and become lost. As for robbery, no one with evil intent can touch my person while I have the pearl."

So Inga gave Rinkitink the Pink Pearl and the little King placed it in the pocket of his red-and-green brocaded velvet vest, pinning the flap of the pocket down tightly.

They now resumed their journey and finally reached the entrance to the Nome King's caverns. Placing the White Pearl to his ear, Inga asked: "What shall I do now?" and the Voice of the Pearl replied: "Clap your hands together four times and call aloud the word 'Klik.' Then allow yourselves to be conducted to the Nome King, who is now holding your father and mother captive."

Inga followed these instructions and when Klik appeared in answer to his summons the boy requested an audience of the Nome King. So Klik led them into the presence of King Kaliko, who was suffering from a severe headache, due to his revelry the night before, and therefore was unusually cross and grumpy.

"I know what you've come for," said he, before Inga could speak. "You want to get the captives from Regos away from me; but you can't do it, so you'd best go away again."

"The captives are my father and mother, and I intend to liberate them," said the boy firmly.

The King stared hard at Inga, wondering at his audacity. Then he turned to look at King Rinkitink and said:

"I suppose you are the King of Gilgad, which is in the Kingdom of Rinkitink."

"You've guessed it the first time," replied Rinkitink.

"How round and fat you are!" exclaimed Kaliko.

"I was just thinking how fat and round *you* are," said Rinkitink. "Really, King Kaliko, we ought to be friends, we're so much alike in everything but disposition and intelligence."

Then he began to chuckle, while Kaliko stared hard at him, not knowing whether to accept his speech as a compliment or not. And now the nome's eyes wandered to Bilbil, and he asked:

"Is that your talking goat?"

Bilbil met the Nome King's glowering look with a gaze equally surly and defiant, while Rinkitink answered: "It is, your Majesty."

"Can he really talk?" asked Kaliko, curiously.

"He can. But the best thing he does is to scold. Talk to his Majesty, Bilbil."

But Bilbil remained silent and would not speak.

"Do you always ride upon his back?" continued Kaliko, questioning Rinkitink.

"Yes," was the answer, "because it is difficult for a fat man to walk far, as perhaps you know from experience.

"That is true," said Kaliko. "Get off the goat's back and let me ride him a while, to see how I like it. Perhaps I'll take him away from you, to ride through my caverns."

Rinkitink chuckled softly as he heard this, but at once got off Bilbil's back and let Kaliko get on. The Nome King was a little awkward, but when he was firmly astride the saddle he called in a loud voice: "Giddap!"

When Bilbil paid no attention to the command and refused to stir, Kaliko kicked his heels viciously against the goat's body, and then Bilbil made a sudden start. He ran swiftly across the great cavern, until he had almost reached the opposite wall, when he stopped so abruptly that King Kaliko sailed over his head and bumped against the jeweled wall. He bumped so hard that the points of his crown were all mashed out of shape and his head was driven far into the diamond-studded band of the crown, so that it covered one eye and a part of his nose. Perhaps this saved Kaliko's head from being cracked against the rock wall, but it was hard on the crown.

Bilbil was highly pleased at the success of his feat and Rinkitink laughed merrily at the Nome King's comical appearance; but Kaliko was muttering and growling as he picked himself up and struggled to pull the battered crown from his head, and it was evident that he was not in the least amused. Indeed, Inga could see that the King was very angry, and the boy knew that the incident was likely to turn Kaliko against the entire party.

The Nome King sent Klik for another crown and ordered his workmen to repair the one that was damaged. While he waited for the new crown he sat regarding his visitors with a scowling face, and this made Inga more uneasy than ever. Finally, when the new crown was placed upon his head, King Kaliko said: "Follow me, strangers!" and led the way to a small door at one end of the cavern.

Inga and Rinkitink followed him through the doorway and found themselves standing on a balcony that overlooked an enormous domed cave—so extensive that it seemed miles to the other side of it. All around this circular cave, which was brilliantly lighted from an unknown source, were arches connected with other caverns.

Kaliko took a gold whistle from his pocket and blew a shrill note that echoed through every part of the cave. Instantly nomes began to pour in through the side arches in great numbers, until the immense space was packed with them as far as the eye could reach. All were armed with glittering weapons of polished silver and gold, and Inga was amazed that any King could command so great an army.

They began marching and countermarching in very orderly array until another blast of the gold whistle sent them scurrying away as quickly as they had appeared. And as soon as the great cave was again empty Kaliko returned with his visitors to his own royal chamber, where he once more seated himself upon his ivory throne.

"I have shown you," said he to Inga, "a part of my body-guard. The royal armies, of which this is only a part, are as numerous as the sands of the ocean, and live in many thousands of my underground caverns. You have come here thinking to force me to give up the captives of King Gos and Queen

Cor, and I wanted to convince you that my power is too mighty for anyone to oppose. I am told that you are a wizard, and depend upon magic to aid you; but you must know that the nomes are not mortals, and understand magic pretty well themselves, so if we are obliged to fight magic with magic the chances are that we are a hundred times more powerful than you can be. Think this over carefully, my boy, and try to realize that you are in my power. I do not believe you can force me to liberate King Kitticut and Queen Garee, and I know that you cannot coax me to do so, for I have given my promise to King Gos. Therefore, as I do not wish to hurt you, I ask you to go away peaceably and let me alone."

"Forgive me if I do not agree with you, King Kaliko," answered the boy. "However difficult and dangerous my task may be, I cannot leave your dominions until every effort to release my parents has failed and left me completely discouraged."

"Very well," said the King, evidently displeased. "I have warned you, and now if evil overtakes you it is your own fault. I've a headache today, so I cannot entertain you properly, according to your rank; but Klik will attend you to my guest chambers and tomorrow I will talk with you again."

This seemed a fair and courteous way to treat one's declared enemies, so they politely expressed the wish that Kaliko's headache would be better, and followed their guide, Klik, down a well-lighted passage and through several archways until they finally reached three nicely furnished bed-chambers which were cut from solid grey rock and well lighted and aired by some mysterious method known to the nomes.

The first of these rooms was given King Rinkitink, the second was Inga's and the third was assigned to Bilbil the goat. There was a swinging rock door between the third and second rooms and another between the second and first, which also had a door that opened upon the passage. Rinkitink's room was the largest, so it was here that an excellent dinner was spread by some of the nome servants, who, in spite of their crooked shapes, proved to be well trained and competent.

"You are not prisoners, you know," said Klik; "neither are you welcome guests, having declared your purpose to oppose our mighty King and all his hosts. But we bear you no ill will, and you are to be well fed and cared for as long as you remain in our caverns. Eat hearty, sleep tight, and pleasant dreams to you."

Saying this, he left them alone and at once Rinkitink and Inga began to counsel together as to the best means to liberate King Kitticut and Queen Garee. The White Pearl's advice was rather unsatisfactory to the boy, just now, for all that the Voice said in answer to his questions was: "Be patient, brave and determined."

Rinkitink suggested that they try to discover in what part of the series of underground caverns Inga's parents had been confined, as that knowledge was necessary before they could take any action; so together they started out, leaving Bilbil asleep in his room, and made their way unopposed through many corridors and caverns.

In some places were great furnaces, where gold dust was being melted into bricks. In other rooms workmen were fashioning the gold into various articles and ornaments. In one cavern immense wheels revolved which polished precious gems, and they found many caverns used as storerooms, where treasure of every sort was piled high. Also they came to the barracks of the army and the great kitchens.

There were nomes everywhere—countless thousands of them—but none paid the slightest heed to the visitors from the earth's surface. Yet, although Inga and Rinkitink walked until they were weary, they were unable to locate the place where the boy's father and mother had been confined, and when they tried to return to their own rooms they found that they had hopelessly lost themselves amid the labyrinth of passages. However, Klik presently came to them, laughing at their discomfiture, and led them back to their bedchambers.

Before they went to sleep they carefully barred the door from Rinkitink's room to the corridor, but the doors that connected the three rooms one with another were left wide open.

In the night Inga was awakened by a soft grating sound that filled him with anxiety because he could not account for it. It was dark in his room, the light having disappeared as soon as he got into bed, but he managed to feel his way to the door that led to Rinkitink's room and found it tightly closed and immovable. Then he made his way to the opposite door, leading to Bilbil's room, to discover that also had been closed and fastened.

The boy had a curious sensation that all of his room—the walls, floor and ceiling—was slowly whirling as if on a pivot, and it was such an uncomfortable feeling that he got into bed again, not knowing what else to do. And as the grating noise had ceased and the room now seemed stationary, he soon fell asleep again.

When the boy wakened, after many hours, he found the room again light. So he dressed himself and discovered that a small table, containing a breakfast that was smoking hot, had suddenly appeared in the center of his room. He tried the two doors, but finding that he could not open them he ate some breakfast, thoughtfully wondering who had locked him in and why he had been made a prisoner. Then he again went to the door which he thought led to Rinkitink's chamber and to his surprise the latch lifted easily and the door swung open.

Before him was a rude corridor hewn in the rock and dimly lighted. It did not look inviting, so Inga closed the door, puzzled to know what had become of Rinkitink's room and the King, and went to the opposite door. Opening this, he found a solid wall of rock confronting him, which effectually prevented his escape in that direction.

The boy now realized that King Kaliko had tricked him,

and while professing to receive him as a guest had plotted to separate him from his comrades. One way had been left, however, by which he might escape and he decided to see where it led to.

So, going to the first door, he opened it and ventured slowly into the dimly lighted corridor. When he had advanced a few steps he heard the door of his room slam shut behind him. He ran back at once, but the door of rock fitted so closely into the wall that he found it impossible to open it again. That did not matter so much, however, for the room was a prison and the only way of escape seemed ahead of him.

Along the corridor he crept until, turning a corner, he found himself in a large domed cavern that was empty and deserted. Here also was a dim light that permitted him to see another corridor at the opposite side; so he crossed the rocky floor of the cavern and entered a second corridor. This one twisted and turned in every direction but was not very long, so soon the boy reached a second cavern, not so large as the first. This he found vacant also, but it had another corridor leading out of it, so Inga entered that. It was straight and short and beyond was a third cavern, which differed little from the others except that it had a strong iron grating at one side of it.

All three of these caverns had been roughly hewn from the rock and it seemed they had never been put to use, as had all the other caverns of the nomes he had visited. Standing in the third cavern, Inga saw what he thought was still another corridor at its farther side, so he walked toward it. This opening was dark, and that fact, and the solemn silence all around him, made him hesitate for a while to enter it. Upon reflection, however, he realized that unless he explored the place to the very end he could not hope to escape from it, so he boldly entered the dark corridor and felt his way cautiously as he moved forward.

Scarcely had he taken two paces when a crash resounded back of him and a heavy sheet of steel closed the opening into the cavern from which he had just come. He paused a moment, but it still seemed best to proceed, and as Inga advanced in the dark, holding his hands outstretched before him to feel his way, handcuffs fell upon his wrists and locked themselves with a sharp click, and an instant later he found he was chained to a stout iron post set firmly in the rock floor.

The chains were long enough to permit him to move a yard or so in any direction and by feeling the walls he found he was in a small circular room that had no outlet except the passage by which he had entered, and that was now closed by the door of steel. This was the end of the series of caverns and corridors.

It was now that the horror of his situation occurred to the boy with full force. But he resolved not to submit to his fate without a struggle, and realizing that he possessed the Blue Pearl, which gave him marvelous strength, he quickly broke the chains and set himself free of the handcuffs. Next he twisted the steel door from its hinges, and creeping along the short passage, found himself in the third cave.

But now the dim light, which had before guided him, had vanished; yet on peering into the gloom of the cave he saw what appeared to be two round disks of flame, which cast a subdued glow over the floor and walls. By this dull glow he made out the form of an enormous man, seated in the center of the cave, and he saw that the iron grating had been removed, permitting the man to enter.

The giant was unclothed and its limbs were thickly covered with coarse red hair. The round disks of flame were its two eyes and when it opened its mouth to yawn Inga saw that its jaws were wide enough to crush a dozen men between the great rows of teeth.

Presently the giant looked up and perceived the boy crouching at the other side of the cavern, so he called out in a hoarse, rude voice:

"Come hither, my pretty one. We will wrestle together, you and I, and if you succeed in throwing me I will let you pass through my cave."

The boy made no reply to the challenge. He realized he was in dire peril and regretted that he had lent the Pink Pearl to King Rinkitink. But it was now too late for vain regrets, although he feared that even his great strength would avail him little against this hairy monster. For his arms were not long enough to span a fourth of the giant's huge body, while the monster's powerful limbs would be likely to crush out Inga's life before he could gain the mastery.

Therefore the Prince resolved to employ other means to combat this foe, who had doubtless been placed there to bar his return. Retreating through the passage he reached the room where he had been chained and wrenched the iron post from its socket. It was a foot thick and four feet long, and being of solid iron was so heavy that three ordinary men would have found it hard to lift.

Returning to the cavern, the boy swung the great bar above his head and dashed it with mighty force full at the giant. The end of the bar struck the monster upon its forehead, and with a single groan it fell full length upon the floor and lay still.

When the giant fell, the glow from its eyes faded away, and all was dark. Cautiously, for Inga was not sure the giant was dead, the boy felt his way toward the opening that led to the middle cavern. The entrance was narrow and the darkness was intense, but, feeling braver now, the boy stepped boldly forward. Instantly the floor began to sink beneath him and in great alarm he turned and made a leap that enabled him to grasp the rocky sides of the wall and regain a footing in the passage through which he had just come.

Scarcely had he obtained this place of refuge when a mighty crash resounded throughout the cavern and the sound of a rushing torrent came from far below. Inga felt in his pocket and found several matches, one of which he lighted and held before him. While it flickered he saw that the entire floor of the cavern had fallen away, and knew that had he not instantly regained his footing in the passage he would have plunged into the abyss that lay beneath him.

By the light of another match he saw the opening at the other side of the cave and the thought came to him that possibly he might leap across the gulf. Of course, this could never be accomplished without the marvelous strength lent him by the Blue Pearl, but Inga had the feeling that one powerful spring might carry him over the chasm into safety. He could not stay where he was, that was certain, so he resolved to make the attempt.

He took a long run through the first cave and the short corridor; then, exerting all his strength, he launched himself over the black gulf of the second cave. Swiftly he flew and, although his heart stood still with fear, only a few seconds elapsed before his feet touched the ledge of the opposite passageway and he knew he had safely accomplished the wonderful feat.

Only pausing to draw one long breath of relief, Inga quickly traversed the crooked corridor that led to the last cavern of the three. But when he came in sight of it he paused abruptly, his eyes nearly blinded by a glare of strong light which burst upon them. Covering his face with his hands, Inga retreated behind a projecting corner of rock and by gradually getting his eyes used to the light he was finally able to gaze without blinking upon the strange glare that had so quickly changed the condition of the cavern. When he had passed through this vault it had been entirely empty. Now the flat floor of rock was covered everywhere with a bed of glowing coals, which shot up little tongues of red and white flames. Indeed, the entire cave was one monster furnace and the heat that came from it was fearful.

Inga's heart sank within him as he realized the terrible obstacle placed by the cunning Nome King between him and the safety of the other caverns. There was no turning back, for it would be impossible for him again to leap over the gulf of the second cave, the corridor at this side being so crooked that he could get no run before he jumped. Neither could he leap over the glowing coals of the cavern that faced him, for it was much larger than the middle cavern. In this dilemma he feared his great strength would avail him nothing and he bitterly reproached himself for parting with the Pink Pearl, which would have preserved him from injury.

However, it was not in the nature of Prince Inga to despair for long, his past adventures having taught him confidence and courage, sharpened his wits and given him the genius of invention. He sat down and thought earnestly on the means of escape from his danger and at last a clever idea came to his mind. This is the way to get ideas: never to let adverse circumstances discourage you, but to believe there is a way out of every difficulty, which may be found by earnest thought.

There were many points and projections of rock in the walls of the crooked corridor in which Inga stood and some of these rocks had become cracked and loosened, although still clinging to their places. The boy picked out one large piece, and, exerting all his strength, tore it away from the wall. He then carried it to the cavern and tossed it upon the burning coals, about ten feet away from the end of the passage. Then he returned for another fragment of rock, and wrenching it free from its place, he threw it ten feet beyond the first one, toward the opposite side of the cave. The boy continued this work until he had made a series of stepping-stones reaching straight across the cavern to the dark passageway beyond, which he hoped would lead him back to safety if not to liberty.

When his work had been completed, Inga did not long hesitate to take advantage of his stepping-stones, for he knew his best chance of escape lay in his crossing the bed of coals before the rocks became so heated that they would burn his feet. So he leaped to the first rock and from there began jumping from one to the other in quick succession. A withering wave of heat at once enveloped him, and for a time he feared he would suffocate before he could cross the cavern; but he held his breath, to keep the hot air from his lungs, and maintained his leaps with desperate resolve.

Then, before he realized it, his feet were pressing the cooler rocks of the passage beyond and he rolled helpless upon the floor, gasping for breath. His skin was so red that it resembled the shell of a boiled lobster, but his swift motion had prevented his being burned, and his shoes had thick soles, which saved his feet.

After resting a few minutes, the boy felt strong enough to go on. He went to the end of the passage and found that the rock door by which he had left his room was still closed, so he returned to about the middle of the corridor and was thinking what he should do next, when suddenly the solid rock before him began to move and an opening appeared through which shone a brilliant light. Shielding his eyes, which were somewhat dazzled, Inga sprang through the opening and found himself in one of the Nome King's inhabited caverns, where before him stood King Kaliko, with a broad grin upon his features, and Klik, the King's chamberlain, who looked surprised, and King Rinkitink seated astride Bilbil the goat, both of whom seemed pleased that Inga had rejoined them.

Chapter 19

RINKITINK CHUCKLES

We will now relate what happened to Rinkitink and Bilbil that morning, while Inga was undergoing his trying experience in escaping the fearful dangers of the three caverns.

The King of Gilgad wakened to find the door of Inga's room fast shut and locked, but he had no trouble in opening his own door into the corridor, for it seems that the boy's room, which was the middle one, whirled around on a pivot, while the adjoining rooms occupied by Bilbil and Rinkitink remained stationary. The little King also found a breakfast magically served in his room, and while he was eating it, Klik came to him and stated that his Majesty, King Kaliko, desired his presence in the royal cavern.

So Rinkitink, having first made sure that the Pink Pearl was still in his vest pocket, willingly followed Klik, who ran on some distance ahead. But no sooner had Rinkitink set foot in the passage than a great rock, weighing at least a ton, became dislodged and dropped from the roof directly over his head. Of course, it could not harm him, protected as he was by the Pink Pearl, and it bounded aside and crashed upon the floor, where it was shattered by its own weight.

"How careless!" exclaimed the little King, and waddled after Klik, who seemed amazed at his escape.

Presently another rock above Rinkitink plunged downward, and then another, but none touched his body. Klik seemed much perplexed at these continued escapes and certainly Kaliko was surprised when Rinkitink, safe and sound, entered the royal cavern.

"Good morning," said the King of Gilgad. "Your rocks are getting loose, Kaliko, and you'd better have them glued in place before they hurt someone." Then he began to chuckle: "Hoo, hoo, hoo-hee, hee-heek, keek, eek!" and Kaliko sat and frowned because he realized that the little fat King was poking fun at him.

"I asked your Majesty to come here," said the Nome King, "to show you a curious skein of golden thread which my workmen have made. If it pleases you, I will make you a present of it."

With this he held out a small skein of glittering gold twine, which was really pretty and curious. Rinkitink took it in his hand and at once the golden thread began to unwind— so swiftly that the eye could not follow its motion. And, as it unwound, it coiled itself around Rinkitink's body, at the same time weaving itself into a net, until it had enveloped the little King from head to foot and placed him in a prison of gold.

"Aha!" cried Kaliko; "*this* magic worked all right, it seems."

"Oh, did it?" replied Rinkitink, and stepping forward he walked right through the golden net, which fell to the floor in a tangled mass.

Kaliko rubbed his chin thoughtfully and stared hard at Rinkitink.

"I understand a good bit of magic," said he, "but your Majesty has a sort of magic that greatly puzzles me, because it is unlike anything of the sort that I ever met with before."

"Now, see here, Kaliko," said Rinkitink; "if you are trying to harm me or my companions, give it up, for you will never succeed. We're harm-proof, so to speak, and you are merely wasting your time trying to injure us.

"You may be right, and I hope I am not so impolite as to argue with a guest," returned the Nome King. "But you will pardon me if I am not yet satisfied that you are stronger than my famous magic. However, I beg you to believe that I bear you no ill will, King Rinkitink; but it is my duty to destroy you, if possible, because you and that insignificant boy Prince have openly threatened to take away my captives and have positively refused to go back to the earth's surface and let me alone. I'm very tender-hearted, as a matter of fact, and I like you immensely, and would enjoy having you as a friend, but—" Here he pressed a button on the arm of his throne chair and the section of the floor where Rinkitink stood suddenly opened and disclosed a black pit beneath, which was a part of the terrible Bottomless Gulf.

But Rinkitink did not fall into the pit; his body remained suspended in the air until he put out his foot and stepped to the solid floor, when the opening suddenly closed again.

"I appreciate your Majesty's friendship," remarked Rinkitink, as calmly as if nothing had happened, "but I am getting tired with standing. Will you kindly send for my goat, Bilbil, that I may sit upon his back to rest?"

"Indeed I will!" promised Kaliko. "I have not yet completed my test of your magic, and as I owe that goat a slight grudge for bumping my head and smashing my second-best crown, I will be glad to discover if the beast can also escape my delightful little sorceries."

So Klik was sent to fetch Bilbil and presently returned with the goat, which was very cross this morning because it had not slept well in the underground caverns.

Rinkitink lost no time in getting upon the red velvet saddle which the goat constantly wore, for he feared the Nome King would try to destroy Bilbil and knew that as long as his body touched that of the goat the Pink Pearl would protect them both; whereas, if Bilbil stood alone, there was no magic to save him.

Bilbil glared wickedly at King Kaliko, who moved uneasily in his ivory throne. Then the Nome King whispered a moment in the ear of Klik, who nodded and left the room.

"Please make yourselves at home here for a few minutes, while I attend to an errand," said the Nome King, getting up from the throne. "I shall return pretty soon, when I hope to find you pieceful—ha, ha, ha!—that's a joke you can't appreciate now but will later. Be pieceful—that's the idea. Ho, ho, ho! How funny." Then he waddled from the cavern, closing the door behind him.

"Well, why didn't you laugh when Kaliko laughed?" demanded the goat, when they were left alone in the cavern.

"Because he means mischief of some sort," replied Rinkitink, "and we'll laugh after the danger is over, Bilbil. There's an old adage that says: 'He laughs best who laughs last,' and the only way to laugh last is to give the other fellow a chance. Where did that knife come from, I wonder."

For a long, sharp knife suddenly appeared in the air near them, twisting and turning from side to side and darting here and there in a dangerous manner, without any support whatever. Then another knife became visible—and another and another—until all the space in the royal cavern seemed filled with them. Their sharp points and edges darted toward

Rinkitink and Bilbil perpetually and nothing could have saved them from being cut to pieces except the protecting power of the Pink Pearl. As it was, not a knife touched them and even Bilbil gave a gruff laugh at the failure of Kaliko's clever magic.

The goat wandered here and there in the cavern, carrying Rinkitink upon his back, and neither of them paid the slightest heed to the knives, although the glitter of the hundreds of polished blades was rather trying to their eyes. Perhaps for ten minutes the knives darted about them in bewildering fury; then they disappeared as suddenly as they had appeared.

Kaliko cautiously stuck his head through the doorway and found the goat chewing the embroidery of his royal cloak, which he had left lying over the throne, while Rinkitink was reading his manuscript on "How to be Good" and chuckling over its advice. The Nome King seemed greatly disappointed as he came in and resumed his seat on the throne. Said Rinkitink with a chuckle:

"We've really had a peaceful time, Kaliko, although not the pieceful time you expected. Forgive me if I indulge in a laugh—hoo, hoo, hoo-hee, heek-keek-eek! And now, tell me; aren't you getting tired of trying to injure us?"

"Eh-heh," said the Nome King. "I see now that your magic can protect you from all my arts. But is the boy Inga as well protected as your Majesty and the goat?"

"Why do you ask?" inquired Rinkitink, uneasy at the question because he remembered he had not seen the little Prince of Pingaree that morning.

"Because," said Kaliko, "the boy has been undergoing trials far greater and more dangerous than any you have encountered, and it has been hundreds of years since anyone has been able to escape alive from the perils of my Three Trick Caverns."

King Rinkitink was much alarmed at hearing this, for although he knew that Inga possessed the Blue Pearl, that would only give to him marvelous strength, and perhaps strength alone would not enable him to escape from danger. But he would not let Kaliko see the fear he felt for Inga's safety, so he said in a careless way:

"You're a mighty poor magician, Kaliko, and I'll give you my crown if Inga hasn't escaped any danger you have threatened him with."

"Your whole crown is not worth one of the valuable diamonds in my crown," answered the Nome King, "but I'll take it. Let us go at once, therefore, and see what has become of the boy Prince, for if he is not destroyed by this time I will admit he cannot be injured by any of the magic arts which I have at my command."

He left the room, accompanied by Klik, who had now rejoined his master, and by Rinkitink riding upon Bilbil. After traversing several of the huge caverns they entered one that was somewhat more bright and cheerful than the others, where the Nome King paused before a wall of rock. Then Klik pressed a secret spring and a section of the wall opened and disclosed the corridor where Prince Inga stood facing them.

"Tarts and tadpoles!" cried Kaliko in surprise. "The boy is still alive!"

·····◄ Chapter 20 ►·····

DOROTHY to the RESCUE

O ne day when Princess Dorothy of Oz was visiting Glinda the Good, who is Ozma's Royal Sorceress, she was looking through Glinda's Great Book of Records—wherein is inscribed all important events that happen in every part of the world— when she came upon the record of the destruction of Pingaree, the capture of King Kitticut and Queen Garee and all their people, and the curious escape of Inga, the boy Prince, and of King Rinkitink and the talking goat. Turning over some of the following pages, Dorothy read how Inga had found the Magic Pearls and was rowing the silver-lined boat to Regos to try to rescue his parents.

The little girl was much interested to know how well Inga succeeded, but she returned to the palace of Ozma at the Emerald City of Oz the next day and other events made her forget the boy Prince of Pingaree for a time. However, she was one day idly looking at Ozma's Magic Picture, which shows any scene you may wish to see, when the girl thought of Inga and commanded the Magic Picture to show what the boy was doing at that moment.

It was the time when Inga and Rinkitink had followed the King of Regos and Queen of Coregos to the Nome King's country and she saw them hiding behind the rock as Cor and Gos passed them by after having placed the King and Queen of Pingaree in the keeping of the Nome King. From that time Dorothy followed, by means of the Magic Picture, the adventures of Inga and his friend in the Nome King's caverns, and the danger and helplessness of the poor boy aroused the little girl's pity and indignation.

So she went to Ozma and told the lovely girl Ruler of Oz all about Inga and Rinkitink.

"I think Kaliko is treating them dreadfully mean," declared Dorothy, "and I wish you'd let me go to the Nome Country and help them out of their troubles."

"Go, my dear, if you wish to," replied Ozma, "but I think it would be best for you to take the Wizard with you."

"Oh, I'm not afraid of the nomes," said Dorothy, "but I'll be glad to take the Wizard, for company. And may we use your Magic Carpet, Ozma?"

"Of course. Put the Magic Carpet in the Red Wagon and have the Sawhorse take you and the Wizard to the edge of the desert. While you are gone, Dorothy, I'll watch you in the Magic Picture, and if any danger threatens you I'll see you are not harmed."

Dorothy thanked the Ruler of Oz and kissed her good-bye, for she was determined to start at once. She found the Wizard of Oz, who was planting shoetrees in the garden, and when she told him Inga's story he willingly agreed to accompany the little girl to the Nome King's caverns. They had both been there before and had conquered the nomes with ease, so they were not at all afraid.

The Wizard, who was a cheery little man with a bald head and a winning smile, harnessed the Wooden Sawhorse to the Red Wagon and loaded on Ozma's Magic Carpet. Then he and Dorothy climbed to the seat and the Sawhorse started off and carried them swiftly through the beautiful Land of Oz to the edge of the Deadly Desert that separated their fairyland from the Nome Country.

Even Dorothy and the clever Wizard would not have dared to cross this desert without the aid of the Magic Carpet, for it would have quickly destroyed them; but when the roll of carpet had been placed upon the edge of the sands, leaving just enough lying flat for them to stand upon, the carpet straightway began to unroll before them and as they walked on it continued to unroll, until they had safely passed over the stretch of Deadly Desert and were on the border of the Nome King's dominions.

This journey had been accomplished in a few minutes, although such a distance would have required several days' travel had they not been walking on the Magic Carpet. On arriving they at once walked toward the entrance to the caverns of the nomes.

The Wizard carried a little black bag containing his tools of wizardry, while Dorothy carried over her arm a covered basket in which she had placed a dozen eggs, with which to conquer the nomes if she had any trouble with them.

Eggs may seem to you to be a queer weapon with which to fight, but the little girl well knew their value. The nomes are immortal; that is, they do not perish, as mortals do, *unless they happen to come in contact with an egg*. If an egg touches them—either the outer shell or the inside of the egg—the nomes lose their charm of perpetual life and thereafter are liable to die through accident or old age, just as all humans are.

For this reason the sight of an egg fills a nome with terror and he will do anything to prevent an egg from touching him, even for an instant. So, when Dorothy took her basket of eggs with her, she knew that she was more powerfully armed than if she had a regiment of soldiers at her back.

Chapter 21

The WIZARD FINDS an ENCHANTMENT

After Kaliko had failed in his attempts to destroy his guests, as has been related, the Nome King did nothing more to injure them but treated them in a friendly manner. He refused, however, to permit Inga to see or to speak with his father and mother, or even to know in what part of the underground caverns they were confined.

"You are able to protect your lives and persons, I freely admit," said Kaliko; "but I firmly believe you have no power, either of magic or otherwise, to take from me the captives I have agreed to keep for King Gos."

Inga would not agree to this. He determined not to leave the caverns until he had liberated his father and mother, although he did not then know how that could be accomplished. As for Rinkitink, the jolly King was well fed and had a good bed to sleep upon, so he was not worrying about anything and seemed in no hurry to go away.

Kaliko and Rinkitink were engaged in pitching a game with solid gold quoits, on the floor of the royal chamber, and Inga and Bilbil were watching them, when Klik came running in, his hair standing on end with excitement, and cried out that the Wizard of Oz and Dorothy were approaching.

Kaliko turned pale on hearing this unwelcome news and, abandoning his game, went to sit in his ivory throne and try to think what had brought these fearful visitors to his domain.

"Who is Dorothy?" asked Inga.

"She is a little girl who once lived in Kansas," replied Klik, with a shudder, "but she now lives in Ozma's palace at the Emerald City and is a Princess of Oz—which means that she is a terrible foe to deal with."

"Doesn't she like the nomes?" inquired the boy.

"It isn't that," said King Kaliko, with a groan, "but she insists on the nomes being goody-goody, which is contrary to their natures. Dorothy gets angry if I do the least thing that is wicked, and tries to make me stop it, and that naturally makes me downhearted. I can't imagine why she has come here just now, for I've been behaving very well lately. As for that Wizard of Oz, he's chock-full of magic that I can't overcome, for he learned it from Glinda, who is the most powerful sorceress in the world. Woe is me! Why didn't Dorothy and the Wizard stay in Oz, where they belong?"

Inga and Rinkitink listened to this with much joy, for at once the idea came to them both to plead with Dorothy to help them. Even Bilbil pricked up his ears when he heard the Wizard of Oz mentioned, and the goat seemed much less surly, and more thoughtful than usual.

A few minutes later a nome came to say that Dorothy and the Wizard had arrived and demanded admittance, so Klik was sent to usher them into the royal presence of the Nome King.

As soon as she came in the little girl ran up to the boy Prince and seized both his hands.

"Oh, Inga!" she exclaimed, "I'm so glad to find you alive and well."

Inga was astonished at so warm a greeting. Making a low bow he said:

"I don't think we have met before, Princess."

"No, indeed," replied Dorothy, "but I know all about you and I've come to help you and King Rinkitink out of your troubles." Then she turned to the Nome King and continued: "You ought to be ashamed of yourself, King Kaliko, to treat an honest Prince and an honest King so badly."

"I haven't done anything to them," whined Kaliko, trembling as her eyes flashed upon him.

"No; but you tried to, an' that's just as bad, if not worse," said Dorothy, who was very indignant. "And now I want you to send for the King and Queen of Pingaree and have them brought here *immejitly!*"

"I won't," said Kaliko.

"Yes, you will!" cried Dorothy, stamping her foot at him. "I won't have those poor people made unhappy any longer, or separated from their little boy. Why, it's *dreadful*, Kaliko, an' I'm su'prised at you. You must be more wicked than I thought you were."

"I can't do it, Dorothy," said the Nome King, almost weeping with despair. "I promised King Gos I'd keep them captives. You wouldn't ask me to break my promise, would you?"

"King Gos was a robber and an outlaw," she said, "and p'r'aps you don't know that a storm at sea wrecked his boat, while he was going back to Regos, and that he and Queen Cor were both drowned."

"Dear me!" exclaimed Kaliko. "Is that so?"

"I saw it in Glinda's Record Book," said Dorothy. "So now you trot out the King and Queen of Pingaree as quick as you can."

"No," persisted the contrary Nome King, shaking his head. "I won't do it. Ask me anything else and I'll try to please you, but I can't allow these friendly enemies to triumph over me.

"In that case," said Dorothy, beginning to remove the cover from her basket, "I'll show you some eggs."

"Eggs!" screamed the Nome King in horror. "Have you eggs in that basket?"

"A dozen of 'em," replied Dorothy.

"Then keep them there—I beg—I implore you!—and I'll do anything you say," pleaded Kaliko, his teeth chattering so that he could hardly speak.

"Send for the King and Queen of Pingaree," said Dorothy.

"Go, Klik," commanded the Nome King, and Klik ran away in great haste, for he was almost as much frightened as his master.

It was an affecting scene when the unfortunate King and Queen of Pingaree entered the chamber and with sobs and tears of joy embraced their brave and adventurous son. All the others stood silent until greetings and kisses had been exchanged and Inga had told his parents in a few words of his vain struggles to rescue them and how Princess Dorothy had finally come to his assistance.

Then King Kitticut shook the hands of his friend King Rinkitink and thanked him for so loyally supporting his son Inga, and Queen Garee kissed little Dorothy's forehead and blessed her for restoring her husband and herself to freedom.

The Wizard had been standing near Bilbil the goat and now he was surprised to hear the animal say:

"Joyful reunion, isn't it? But it makes me tired to see grown people cry like children."

"Oho!" exclaimed the Wizard. "How does it happen, Mr.

Goat, that you, who have never been to the Land of Oz, are able to talk?"

"That's my business," returned Bilbil in a surly tone.

The Wizard stooped down and gazed fixedly into the animal's eyes. Then he said, with a pitying sigh: "I see; you are under an enchantment. Indeed, I believe you to be Prince Bobo of Boboland."

Bilbil made no reply but dropped his head as if ashamed.

"This is a great discovery," said the Wizard, addressing Dorothy and the others of the party. "A good many years ago a cruel magician transformed the gallant Prince of Boboland into a talking goat, and this goat, being ashamed of his condition, ran away and was never after seen in Boboland, which is a country far to the south of here but bordering on the Deadly Desert, opposite the Land of Oz. I heard of this story long ago and know that a diligent search has been made for the enchanted Prince, without result. But I am well assured that, in the animal you call Bilbil, I have discovered the unhappy Prince of Boboland."

"Dear me, Bilbil," said Rinkitink, "why have you never told me this?"

"What would be the use?" asked Bilbil in a low voice and still refusing to look up.

"The use?" repeated Rinkitink, puzzled.

"Yes, that's the trouble," said the Wizard. "It is one of the most powerful enchantments ever accomplished, and the magician is now dead and the secret of the anti-charm lost. Even I, with all my skill, cannot restore Prince Bobo to his proper form. But I think Glinda might be able to do so and if you will all return with Dorothy and me to the Land of Oz, where Ozma will make you welcome, I will ask Glinda to try to break this enchantment."

This was willingly agreed to, for they all welcomed the chance to visit the famous Land of Oz. So they bade good-bye to King Kaliko, whom Dorothy warned not to be wicked any more if he could help it, and the entire party returned over the Magic Carpet to the Land of Oz. They filled the Red Wagon, which was still waiting for them, pretty full; but the Sawhorse didn't mind that and with wonderful speed carried them safely to the Emerald City.

·——·•◁ Chapter 22 ▷•·——·

OZMA'S BANQUET

Ozma had seen in her Magic Picture the liberation of Inga's parents and the departure of the entire party for the Emerald City, so with her usual hospitality she ordered a splendid banquet prepared and invited all her quaint friends who were then in the Emerald City to be present that evening to meet the strangers who were to become her guests.

Glinda, also, in her wonderful Record Book had learned of the events that had taken place in the caverns of the Nome King and she became especially interested in the enchantment of the Prince of Boboland. So she hastily prepared several of her most powerful charms and then summoned her flock of sixteen white storks, which swiftly bore her to Ozma's palace. She arrived there before the Red Wagon did and was warmly greeted by the girl Ruler.

Realizing that the costume of Queen Garee of Pingaree must have become sadly worn and frayed, owing to her hardships and adventures, Ozma ordered a royal outfit prepared for the good Queen and had it laid in her chamber ready for her to put on as soon as she arrived, so she would not be shamed at the banquet. New costumes were also provided for King Kitticut and King Rinkitink and Prince Inga, all cut and made and embellished in the elaborate and becoming style then prevalent in the Land of Oz, and as soon as the party arrived at the palace Ozma's guests were escorted by her servants to their rooms, that they might bathe and dress themselves.

Glinda the Sorceress and the Wizard of Oz took charge of Bilbil the goat and went to a private room where they were not likely to be interrupted. Glinda first questioned Bilbil long and earnestly about the manner of his enchantment and the ceremony that had been used by the magician who enchanted him. At first Bilbil protested that he did not want to be restored to his natural shape, saying that he had been forever disgraced in the eyes of his people and of the entire world by being obliged to exist as a scrawny, scraggly goat. But Glinda pointed out that any person who incurred the enmity of a wicked magician was liable to suffer a similar fate, and assured him that his misfortune would make him better beloved by his subjects when he returned to them freed from his dire enchantment.

Bilbil was finally convinced of the truth of this assertion and agreed to submit to the experiments of Glinda and the Wizard, who knew they had a hard task before them and were not at all sure they could succeed. We know that Glinda is the most complete mistress of magic who has ever existed, and she was wise enough to guess that the clever but evil magician who had enchanted Prince Bobo had used a spell that would puzzle any ordinary wizard or sorcerer to break; therefore she had given the matter much shrewd thought and hoped she had conceived a plan that would succeed. But because she was not positive of success she would have no one present at the incantation except her assistant, the Wizard of Oz.

First she transformed Bilbil the goat into a lamb, and this was done quite easily. Next she transformed the lamb into an ostrich, giving it two legs and feet instead of four. Then she tried to transform the ostrich into the original Prince Bobo, but this incantation was an utter failure. Glinda was not discouraged, however, but by a powerful spell transformed the ostrich into a Tottenhot. Then the Tottenhot was transformed into a mifket, which was a great step in advance and, finally, Glinda transformed the mifket into a handsome young man, tall and shapely, who fell on his knees before the great Sorceress and gratefully kissed her hand, admitting that he had now recovered his proper shape and was indeed Prince Bobo of Boboland.

This process of magic, successful though it was in the end, had required so much time that the banquet was now awaiting their presence. Bobo was already dressed in princely raiment and although he seemed very much humbled by his recent lowly condition, they finally persuaded him to join the festivities.

When Rinkitink saw that his goat had now become a Prince, he did not know whether to be sorry or glad, for he felt that he would miss the companionship of the quarrelsome animal he had so long been accustomed to ride upon, while at the same time he rejoiced that poor Bilbil had come to his own again.

Prince Bobo humbly begged Rinkitink's forgiveness for having been so disagreeable to him, at times, saying that the nature of a goat had influenced him and the surly disposition he had shown was a part of his enchantment. But the jolly King assured the Prince that he had really enjoyed Bilbil's grumpy speeches and forgave him readily. Indeed, they all discovered the young Prince Bobo to be an exceedingly courteous and pleasant person, although he was somewhat reserved and dignified.

Ah, but it was a great feast that Ozma served in her gorgeous banquet hall that night and everyone was as happy as could be. The Shaggy Man was there, and so was Jack Pumpkinhead and the Tin Woodman and Cap'n Bill. Beside Princess

Dorothy sat Tiny Trot and Betsy Bobbin, and the three little girls were almost as sweet to look upon as was Ozma, who sat at the head of her table and outshone all her guests in loveliness.

King Rinkitink was delighted with the quaint people of Oz and laughed and joked with the tin man and the pumpkin-headed man and found Cap'n Bill a very agreeable companion. But what amused the jolly King most were the animal guests, which Ozma always invited to her banquets and seated at a table by themselves, where they talked and chatted together as people do but were served the sort of food their natures required. The Hungry Tiger and Cowardly Lion and the Glass Cat were much admired by Rinkitink, but when he met a mule named Hank, which Betsy Bobbin had brought to Oz, the King found the creature so comical that he laughed and chuckled until his friends thought he would choke. Then while the banquet was still in progress, Rinkitink composed and sang a song to the mule and they all joined in the chorus, which was something like this:

> *"It's very queer how big an ear*
> *Is worn by Mr. Donkey;*
> *And yet I fear he could not hear*
> *If it were on a monkey.*
> *'Tis thick and strong and broad and long*
> *And also very hairy;*

It's quite becoming to our Hank
But might disgrace a fairy!"

This song was received with so much enthusiasm that
Rinkitink was prevailed upon to sing another. They gave him
a little time to compose the rhyme, which he declared would
be better if he could devote a month or two to its composition,
but the sentiment he expressed was so admirable that no one
criticized the song or the manner in which the jolly little King
sang it.

Dorothy wrote down the words on a piece of paper, and
here they are:

"We're merry comrades all, tonight,
Because we've won a gallant fight
And conquered all our foes.
We're not afraid of anything,
So let us gayly laugh and sing
Until we seek repose.

"We've all our grateful hearts can wish;
King Gos has gone to feed the fish,
Queen Cor has gone, as well;
King Kitticut has found his own,
Prince Bobo soon will have a throne
Relieved of magic spell.

"So let's forget the horrid strife
That fell upon our peaceful life
And caused distress and pain;
For very soon across the sea
We'll all be sailing merrily
To Pingaree again."

·—·< Chapter 23 >·—·

The PEARL KINGDOM

It was unfortunate that the famous Scarecrow—the most popular person in all Oz, next to Ozma—was absent at the time of the banquet, for he happened just then to be making one of his trips through the country; but the Scarecrow had a chance later to meet Rinkitink and Inga and the King and Queen of Pingaree and Prince Bobo, for the party remained several weeks at the Emerald City, where they were royally entertained, and where both the gentle Queen Garee and the noble King Kitticut recovered much of their good spirits and composure and tried to forget their dreadful experiences.

At last, however, the King and Queen desired to return

to their own Pingaree, as they longed to be with their people again and see how well they had rebuilt their homes. Inga also was anxious to return, although he had been very happy in Oz, and King Rinkitink, who was happy anywhere except at Gilgad, decided to go with his former friends to Pingaree. As for Prince Bobo, he had become so greatly attached to King Rinkitink that he was loth to leave him.

On a certain day they all bade good-bye to Ozma and Dorothy and Glinda and the Wizard and all their good friends in Oz, and were driven in the Red Wagon to the edge of the Deadly Desert, which they crossed safely on the Magic Carpet. They then made their way across the Nome Kingdom and the Wheeler Country, where no one molested them, to the shores of the Nonestic Ocean. There they found the boat with the silver lining still lying undisturbed on the beach.

There were no important adventures during the trip and on their arrival at the pearl kingdom they were amazed at the beautiful appearance of the island they had left in ruins. All the houses of the people had been rebuilt and were prettier than before, with green lawns before them and flower gardens in the back yards. The marble towers of King Kitticut's new palace were very striking and impressive, while the palace itself proved far more magnificent than it had been before the warriors from Regos destroyed it.

Nikobob had been very active and skillful in directing all this work, and he had also built a pretty cottage for himself, not far from the King's palace, and there Inga found Zella, who was living very happy and contented in her new home. Not only had Nikobob accomplished all this in a comparatively brief space of time, but he had started the pearl fisheries again and when King Kitticut returned to Pingaree he found a quantity of fine pearls already in the royal treasury.

So pleased was Kitticut with the good judgment, industry and honesty of the former charcoal-burner of Regos, that he made Nikobob his Lord High Chamberlain and put him in charge of the pearl fisheries and all the business matters of the island kingdom.

They all settled down very comfortably in the new palace and the Queen gathered her maids about her once more and set them to work embroidering new draperies for the royal throne. Inga placed the three Magic Pearls in their silken bag and again deposited them in the secret cavity under the tiled flooring of the banquet hall, where they could be quickly secured if danger ever threatened the now prosperous island.

King Rinkitink occupied a royal guest chamber built especially for his use and seemed in no hurry to leave his friends in Pingaree. The fat little King had to walk wherever he went and so missed Bilbil more and more; but he seldom walked far and he was so fond of Prince Bobo that he never regretted Bilbil's disenchantment.

Indeed, the jolly monarch was welcome to remain forever in Pingaree, if he wished to, for his merry disposition set smiles on the faces of all his friends and made everyone near him as jolly as he was himself. When King Kitticut was not too busy with affairs of state he loved to join his guest and listen to his brother monarch's songs and stories. For he found Rinkitink to be, with all his careless disposition, a shrewd philosopher, and in talking over their adventures one day the King of Gilgad said:

"The beauty of life is its sudden changes. No one knows what is going to happen next, and so we are constantly being surprised and entertained. The many ups and downs should not discourage us, for if we are down, we know that a change is coming and we will go up again; while those who are up are almost certain to go down. My grandfather had a song which well expresses this and if you will listen I will sing it."

"Of course I will listen to your song," returned Kitticut, "for it would be impolite not to."

So Rinkitink sang his grandfather's song:

"A mighty King once ruled the land—
But now he's baking pies.
A pauper, on the other hand,
Is ruling, strong and wise.

"A tiger once in jungles raged—
But now he's in a zoo;
A lion, captive-born and caged,
Now roams the forest through.

"A man once slapped a poor boy's pate
And made him weep and wail.
The boy became a magistrate
And put the man in jail.

"A sunny day succeeds the night;
It's summer—then it snows!
Right oft goes wrong and wrong comes right,
As ev'ry wise man knows."

Chapter 24

The CAPTIVE KING

One morning, just as the royal party was finishing breakfast, a servant came running to say that a great fleet of boats was approaching the island from the south. King Kitticut sprang up at once, in great alarm, for he had much cause to fear strange boats. The others quickly followed him to the shore to see what invasion might be coming upon them.

Inga was there with the first, and Nikobob and Zella soon joined the watchers. And presently, while all were gazing eagerly at the approaching fleet, King Rinkitink suddenly cried out:

"Get your pearls, Prince Inga—get them quick!"

"Are these our enemies, then?" asked the boy, looking with surprise upon the fat little King, who had begun to tremble violently.

"They are my people of Gilgad!" answered Rinkitink, wiping a tear from his eye. "I recognize my royal standards flying from the boats. So, please, dear Inga, get out your pearls to protect me!"

"What can you fear at the hands of your own subjects?" asked Kitticut, astonished.

But before his frightened guest could answer the question Prince Bobo, who was standing beside his friend, gave an amused laugh and said:

"You are caught at last, dear Rinkitink. Your people will take you home again and oblige you to reign as King."

Rinkitink groaned aloud and clasped his hands together with a gesture of despair, an attitude so comical that the others could scarcely forbear laughing.

But now the boats were landing upon the beach. They were fifty in number, beautifully decorated and upholstered and rowed by men clad in the gay uniforms of the King of Gilgad. One splendid boat had a throne of gold in the center, over which was draped the King's royal robe of purple velvet, embroidered with gold buttercups.

Rinkitink shuddered when he saw this throne; but now a tall man, handsomely dressed, approached and knelt upon the grass before his King, while all the other occupants of the boats shouted joyfully and waved their plumed hats in the air.

"Thanks to our good fortune," said the man who kneeled, "we have found your Majesty at last!"

"Pinkerbloo," answered Rinkitink sternly, "I must have you hanged, for thus finding me against my will."

"You think so now, your Majesty, but you will never do it," returned Pinkerbloo, rising and kissing the King's hand.

"Why won't I?" asked Rinkitink.

"Because you are much too tender-hearted, your Majesty."

"It may be—it may be," agreed Rinkitink, sadly. "It is one of my greatest failings. But what chance brought you here, my Lord Pinkerbloo?"

"We have searched for you everywhere, sire, and all the people of Gilgad have been in despair since you so mysteriously disappeared. We could not appoint a new King, because we did not know but that you still lived; so we set out to find you, dead or alive. After visiting many islands of the Nonestic Ocean we at last thought of Pingaree, from where come the precious pearls; and now our faithful quest has been rewarded."

"And what now?" asked Rinkitink.

"Now, your Majesty, you must come home with us, like a good and dutiful King, and rule over your people," declared the man in a firm voice.

"I will not."

"But you must—begging your Majesty's pardon for the contradiction."

"Kitticut," cried poor Rinkitink, "you must save me from being captured by these, my subjects. What! Must I return to Gilgad and be forced to reign in splendid state when I much prefer to eat and sleep and sing in my own quiet way? They will make me sit in a throne three hours a day and listen to dry and tedious affairs of state; and I must stand up for hours at the court receptions, till I get corns on my heels; and forever must I listen to tiresome speeches and endless petitions and complaints!"

"But someone must do this, your Majesty," said Pinkerbloo respectfully, "and since you were born to be our King you cannot escape your duty."

"'Tis a horrid fate!" moaned Rinkitink. "I would die willingly, rather than be a King—if it did not hurt so terribly to die."

"You will find it much more comfortable to reign than to die, although I fully appreciate your Majesty's difficult position and am truly sorry for you," said Pinkerbloo.

King Kitticut had listened to this conversation thoughtfully, so now he said to his friend:

"The man is right, dear Rinkitink. It is your duty to reign, since fate has made you a King, and I see no honorable escape for you. I shall grieve to lose your companionship, but I feel the separation cannot be avoided."

Rinkitink sighed.

"Then," said he, turning to Lord Pinkerbloo, "in three

days I will depart with you for Gilgad; but during those three days I propose to feast and make merry with my good friend King Kitticut."

Then all the people of Gilgad shouted with delight and eagerly scrambled ashore to take their part in the festival.

Those three days were long remembered in Pingaree, for never—before nor since—has such feasting and jollity been known upon that island. Rinkitink made the most of his time and everyone laughed and sang with him by day and by night.

Then, at last, the hour of parting arrived and the King of Gilgad and Ruler of the Dominion of Rinkitink was escorted by a grand procession to his boat and seated upon his golden throne. The rowers of the fifty boats paused, with their glittering oars pointed into the air like gigantic uplifted sabres, while the people of Pingaree—men, women and children—stood upon the shore shouting a royal farewell to the jolly King.

Then came a sudden hush, while Rinkitink stood up and, with a bow to those assembled to witness his departure, sang the following song, which he had just composed for the occasion.

"Farewell, dear Isle of Pingaree—
The fairest land in all the sea!
No living mortals, kings or churls,
Would scorn to wear thy precious pearls.

"King Kitticut, 'tis with regret
I'm forced to say farewell; and yet
Abroad no longer can I roam
When fifty boats would drag me home.

"Good-bye, my Prince of Pingaree;
A noble King some time you'll be
And long and wisely may you reign
And never face a foe again!"

They cheered him from the shore; they cheered him from the boats; and then all the oars of the fifty boats swept downward with a single motion and dipped their blades into the purple-hued waters of the Nonestic Ocean.

As the boats shot swiftly over the ripples of the sea Rinkitink turned to Prince Bobo, who had decided not to desert his former master and his present friend, and asked anxiously:

"How did you like that song, Bilbil—I mean Bobo? Is it a masterpiece, do you think?"

And Bobo replied with a smile:

"Like all your songs, dear Rinkitink, the sentiment far excels the poetry."

The
Lost
Princess
of
OZ

To My Readers

Some of my youthful readers are developing wonderful imaginations. This pleases me. Imagination has brought mankind through the Dark Ages to its present state of civilization. Imagination led Columbus to discover America. Imagination led Franklin to discover electricity. Imagination has given us the steam engine, the telephone, the talking-machine and the automobile, for these things had to be dreamed of before they became realities. So I believe that dreams—day dreams, you know, with your eyes wide open and your brain-machinery whizzing—are likely to lead to the betterment of the world. The imaginative child will become the imaginative man or woman most apt to create, to invent, and therefore to foster civilization. A prominent educator tells me that fairy tales arc of untold value in developing imagination in the young. I believe it.

Among the letters I receive from children are many containing suggestions of "what to write about in the next Oz Book." Some of the ideas advanced are mighty interesting, while others are too extravagant to be seriously considered— even in a fairy tale. Yet I like them all, and I must admit that the main idea in "The Lost Princess of Oz" was suggested to me by a sweet little girl of eleven who called to see me and to talk about the Land of Oz. Said she: "I s'pose if Ozma ever got lost, or stolen, ev'rybody in Oz would be dreadful sorry."

That was all, but quite enough foundation to build this present story on. If you happen to like the story, give credit to my little friend's clever hint.

L. Frank Baum, Royal Historian of Oz

"Ozcot" at Hollywood in California, 1917

— ◄ Chapter 1 ►— ◄

A Terrible Loss

There could be no doubt of the fact: Princess Ozma, the lovely girl Ruler of the Fairyland of Oz, was lost. She had completely disappeared. Not one of her subjects—not even her closest friends—knew what had become of her.

It was Dorothy who first discovered it. Dorothy was a little Kansas girl who had come to the Land of Oz to live and had been given a delightful suite of rooms in Ozma's royal palace, just because Ozma loved Dorothy and wanted her to live as near her as possible so the two girls might be much together.

Dorothy was not the only girl from the outside world who had been welcomed to Oz and lived in the royal palace. There was another named Betsy Bobbin, whose adventures had led her to seek refuge with Ozma, and still another named Trot, who had been invited, together with her faithful companion Cap'n Bill, to make her home in this wonderful fairyland. The three girls all had rooms in the palace and were great chums; but Dorothy was the dearest friend of their gracious Ruler and only she at any hour dared to seek Ozma in her royal apartments. For Dorothy had lived in Oz much longer than the other girls and had been made a Princess of the realm.

Betsy was a year older than Dorothy and Trot was a year younger, yet the three were near enough of an age to become great playmates and to have nice times together. It was while the three were talking together one morning in Dorothy's room that Betsy proposed they make a journey into the Munchkin Country, which was one of the four great countries of the Land of Oz ruled by Ozma. "I've never been there yet," said Betsy Bobbin, "but the Scarecrow once told me it is the prettiest country in all Oz."

"I'd like to go, too," added Trot.

"All right," said Dorothy, "I'll go and ask Ozma. Perhaps she will let us take the Sawhorse and the Red Wagon, which would be much nicer for us than having to walk all the way. This Land of Oz is a pretty big place, when you get to all the edges of it."

So she jumped up and went along the halls of the splendid palace until she came to the royal suite, which filled all the front of the second floor. In a little waiting room sat Ozma's maid, Jellia Jamb, who was busily sewing. "Is Ozma up yet?" inquired Dorothy.

"I don't know, my dear," replied Jellia. "I haven't heard a word from her this morning. She hasn't even called for her bath or her breakfast, and it is far past her usual time for them."

"That's strange!" exclaimed the little girl.

"Yes," agreed the maid; "but of course no harm could have happened to her. No one can die or be killed in the Land of Oz and Ozma is herself a powerful fairy, and she has no enemies, so far as we know. Therefore I am not at all worried about her, though I must admit her silence is unusual."

"Perhaps," said Dorothy thoughtfully, "she has overslept. Or she may be reading or working out some new sort of magic to do good to her people."

"Any of these things may be true," replied Jellia Jamb, "so I haven't dared disturb our royal mistress. You, however, are a privileged character, Princess, and I am sure that Ozma wouldn't mind at all if you went in to see her."

"Of course not," said Dorothy, and opening the door of the outer chamber, she went in. All was still here. She walked into another room, which was Ozma's boudoir, and then, pushing back a heavy drapery richly broidered with threads of pure gold, the girl entered the sleeping-room of the fairy Ruler of Oz. The bed of ivory and gold was vacant; the room was vacant; not a trace of Ozma was to be found.

Very much surprised, yet still with no fear that anything had happened to her friend, Dorothy returned through the boudoir to the other rooms of the suite. She went into the music room, the library, the laboratory, the bath, the wardrobe, and even into the great Throne Room, which adjoined the royal suite, but in none of these places could she find Ozma.

So she returned to the anteroom where she had left the maid, Jellia Jamb, and said:

"She isn't in her rooms now, so she must have gone out."

"I don't understand how she could do that without my see-ing her," replied Jellia, "unless she made herself invisible."

"She isn't there, anyhow," declared Dorothy.

"Then let us go find her," suggested the maid, who appeared to be a little uneasy. So they went into the corridors, and there Dorothy almost stumbled over a queer girl who was dancing lightly along the passage.

"Stop a minute, Scraps!" she called, "Have you seen Ozma this morning?"

"Not I!" replied the queer girl, dancing nearer. "I lost both my eyes in a tussle with the Woozy, last night, for the creature scraped 'em both off my face with his square paws. So I put the eyes in my pocket and this morning Button-Bright led me to Aunt Em, who sewed 'em on again. So I've seen nothing at all today, except during the last five minutes. So of course I haven't seen Ozma."

"Very well, Scraps," said Dorothy, looking curiously at the eyes, which were merely two round, black buttons sewed upon the girl's face.

There were other things about Scraps that would have seemed curious to one seeing her for the first time. She was commonly called "The Patchwork Girl," because her body and limbs were made from a gay-colored patchwork quilt which had been cut into shape and stuffed with cotton. Her head was a round ball stuffed in the same manner and fastened to her shoulders. For hair she had a mass of brown yarn, and to make a nose for her a part of the cloth had been pulled out into the shape of a knob and tied with a string to hold it in place. Her mouth had been carefully made by cutting a slit in the proper place and lining it with red silk, adding two rows of pearls for teeth and a bit of red flannel for a tongue.

In spite of this queer make-up, the Patchwork Girl was magically alive and had proved herself not the least jolly and agreeable of the many quaint characters who inhabit the astonishing Fairyland of Oz. Indeed, Scraps was a general favorite, although she was rather flighty and erratic and did and said many things that surprised her friends. She was seldom still, but loved to dance, to turn handsprings and somersaults, to climb trees and to indulge in many other active sports.

"I'm going to search for Ozma," remarked Dorothy, "for she isn't in her rooms and I want to ask her a question."

"I'll go with you," said Scraps, "for my eyes are brighter than yours, and they can see farther."

"I'm not sure of that," returned Dorothy. "But come along, if you like."

Together they searched all through the great palace and even to the farthest limits of the palace grounds, which were quite extensive, but nowhere could they find a trace of Ozma. When Dorothy returned to where Betsy and Trot awaited her, the little girl's face was rather solemn and troubled, for never before had Ozma gone away without telling her friends where she was going, or without an escort that befitted her royal state.

She was gone, however, and none had seen her go. Dorothy had met and questioned the Scarecrow, Tik-Tok, the Shaggy Man, Button-Bright, Cap'n Bill, and even the wise and powerful Wizard of Oz, but not one of them had seen Ozma since she parted with her friends the evening before and had gone to her own rooms.

"She didn't say anything las' night about going anywhere," observed little Trot.

"No, and that's the strange part of it," replied Dorothy. "Usually Ozma lets us know of everything she does."

"Why not look in the Magic Picture?" suggested Betsy Bobbin. "That will tell us where she is, in just one second."

"Of course!" cried Dorothy. "Why didn't I think of that before?" And at once the three girls hurried away to Ozma's boudoir, where the Magic Picture always hung. This wonderful Magic Picture was one of the royal Ozma's greatest treasures. There was a large gold frame in the center of which was a bluish-grey canvas on which various scenes constantly appeared and disappeared. If one who stood before it wished to see what any person—anywhere in the world—was doing, it was only necessary to make the wish and the scene in the Magic Picture would shift to the scene where that person was and show exactly what he or she was then engaged in doing. So the girls knew it would be easy for them to wish to see Ozma, and from the picture they could quickly learn where she was.

Dorothy advanced to the place where the picture was usually protected by thick satin curtains, and pulled the draperies aside. Then she stared in amazement, while her two friends uttered exclamations of disappointment.

The Magic Picture was gone. Only a blank space on the wall behind the curtains showed where it had formerly hung.

Chapter 2

The TROUBLES of GLINDA the GOOD

That same morning there was great excitement in the castle of the powerful Sorceress of Oz, Glinda the Good. This castle, situated in the Quadling Country, far south of the Emerald City where Ozma ruled, was a splendid structure of exquisite marbles and silver grilles. Here the Sorceress lived, surrounded by a bevy of the most beautiful maidens of Oz, gathered from all the four countries of that fairyland as well as from the magnificent Emerald City itself, which stood in the place where the four countries cornered.

It was considered a great honor to be allowed to serve the good Sorceress, whose arts of magic were used only to benefit the Oz people. Glinda was Ozma's most valued servant, for her knowledge of sorcery was wonderful, and she could accomplish almost anything that her mistress, the lovely girl Ruler of Oz, wished her to.

Of all the magical things which surrounded Glinda in her castle there was none more marvelous than her Great Book of Records. On the pages of this Record Book were constantly being inscribed—day by day and hour by hour—all the important events that happened anywhere in the known world, and they were inscribed in the book at exactly the moment the events happened. Every adventure in the Land of Oz and in the big outside world, and even in places that you and I have never heard of, were recorded accurately in the Great Book, which never made a mistake and stated only the exact truth. For that reason nothing could be concealed from Glinda the Good, who had only to look at the pages of the Great Book of Records to know everything that had taken place. That was one reason she was such a great Sorceress, for the records made her wiser than any other living person.

This wonderful book was placed upon a big gold table that stood in the middle of Glinda's drawing-room. The legs of the table, which were incrusted with precious gems, were firmly fastened to the tiled floor, and the book itself was chained to the table and locked with six stout golden padlocks, the keys to which Glinda carried on a chain that was secured around her own neck.

The pages of the Great Book were larger in size than those of an American newspaper, and although they were exceedingly thin there were so many of them that they made an enormous, bulky volume. With its gold cover and gold clasps the book was so heavy that three men could scarcely have lifted it. Yet this morning, when Glinda entered her drawing-room after breakfast, the good Sorceress was amazed to discover that her Great Book of Records had mysteriously disappeared.

Advancing to the table, she found the chains had been cut with some sharp instrument, and this must have been done while all in the castle slept. Glinda was shocked and grieved. Who could have done this wicked, bold thing? And who could wish to deprive her of her Great Book of Records?

The Sorceress was thoughtful for a time, considering the consequences of her loss. Then she went to her Room of Magic to prepare a charm that would tell her who had stolen the Record Book. But, when she unlocked her cupboards and threw open the doors, all of her magical instruments and rare chemical compounds had been removed from the shelves.

The Sorceress was now both angry and alarmed. She sat down in a chair and tried to think how this extraordinary robbery could have taken place. It was evident that the thief was some person of very great power, or the theft could not have been accomplished without her knowledge. But who, in all the Land of Oz, was powerful and skillful enough to do this awful thing? And who, having the power, could also have an object in defying the wisest and most talented Sorceress the world has ever known?

Glinda thought over the perplexing matter for a full hour, at the end of which time she was still puzzled how to explain it. But although her instruments and chemicals were gone, her *knowledge* of magic had not been stolen, by any means, since no thief, however skillful, can rob one of knowledge, and that is why knowledge is the best and safest treasure to acquire. Glinda believed that when she had time to gather more magical herbs and elixirs and to manufacture more magical instruments she would be able to discover who the robber was, and what had become of her precious Book of Records.

"Whoever has done this," she said to her maidens, "is a very foolish person, for in time he is sure to be found out and will then be severely punished."

She now made a list of the things she needed and dispatched messengers to every part of Oz with instructions to obtain them and bring them to her as soon as possible. And one of her messengers met the little Wizard of Oz, who was seated on the back of the famous live Sawhorse and was clinging to its neck with both his arms, for the Sawhorse was speeding to Glinda's castle with the velocity of the wind, bearing the news that Royal Ozma, Ruler of all the great Land of Oz, had suddenly disappeared and no one in the Emerald City knew what had become of her.

"Also," said the Wizard as he stood before the astonished Sorceress, "Ozma's Magic Picture is gone, so we cannot consult it to discover where she is. So I came to you for assistance as soon as we realized our loss. Let us look in the Great Book of Records."

"Alas," returned the Sorceress sorrowfully, "we cannot do that, for the Great Book of Records has also disappeared!"

····—·◄ Chapter 3 ►·—····

The ROBBERY of CAYKE
the COOKIE COOK

One more important theft was reported in the Land of Oz that eventful morning, but it took place so far from either the Emerald City or the castle of Glinda the Good that none of those persons we have mentioned learned of the robbery until long afterward.

In the far southwestern corner of the Winkie Country is a broad tableland that can be reached only by climbing a steep hill, whichever side one approaches it. On the hillside surrounding this tableland are no paths at all, but there are quantities of bramble bushes with sharp prickers on them, which prevent any of the Oz people who live down below from climbing up to see what is on top. But on top live the Yips, and although the space they occupy is not great in extent the wee country is all their own. The Yips had never—up to the time this story begins—left their broad tableland to go down into the Land of Oz, nor had the Oz people ever climbed up to the country of the Yips.

Living all alone as they did, the Yips had queer ways and notions of their own and did not resemble any other people of the Land of Oz. Their houses were scattered all over the flat surface; not like a city, grouped together, but set wherever their owners' fancy dictated, with fields here, trees there, and odd little paths connecting the houses one with another.

It was here, on the morning when Ozma so strangely disappeared from the Emerald City, that Cayke the Cookie Cook discovered that her diamond-studded gold dishpan had been stolen, and she raised such a hue and cry over her loss and wailed and shrieked so loudly that many of the Yips gathered around her house to inquire what was the matter.

It was a serious thing, in any part of the Land of Oz, to accuse one of stealing, so when the Yips heard Cayke the Cookie Cook declare that her jeweled dishpan had been stolen, they were both humiliated and disturbed and forced Cayke to go with them to the Frogman to see what could be done about it.

I do not suppose you have ever before heard of the Frogman, for like all other dwellers on that tableland he had never been away from it, nor had anyone come up there to see him. The Frogman was, in truth, descended from the common frogs of Oz, and when he was first born he lived in a pool in the Winkie Country and was much like any other frog. Being of an adventurous nature, however, he soon hopped out of his pool and began to travel, when a big bird came along and seized him in its beak and started to fly away with him to its nest. When high in the air the frog wriggled so frantically that he got loose and fell down—down—down into a small hidden pool on the tableland of the Yips. Now that pool, it seems, was unknown to the Yips because it was surrounded by thick bushes and was not near to any dwelling, and it proved to be an enchanted pool, for the frog grew very fast and very big, feeding on the magic skosh which is found nowhere else on earth except in that one pool. And the skosh not only made the frog very big so that when he stood on his hind legs he was as tall as any Yip in the country, but it made him unusually intelligent, so that he soon knew more than the Yips did and was able to reason and to argue very well indeed.

No one could expect a frog with these talents to remain in a hidden pool, so he finally got out of it and mingled with the people of the tableland, who were amazed at his appearance and greatly impressed by his learning. They had never seen a frog before and the frog had never seen a Yip before, but as there were plenty of Yips and only one frog, the frog became the most important. He did not hop any more, but stood upright on his hind legs and dressed himself in fine clothes and sat in chairs and did all the things that people do, so he soon came to be called the Frogman, and that is the only name he has ever had.

After some years had passed, the people came to regard the Frogman as their adviser in all matters that puzzled them. They brought all their difficulties to him, and when he did not know anything he pretended to know it, which seemed to answer just as well. Indeed, the Yips thought the Frogman was much wiser than he really was, and he allowed them to think so, being very proud of his position of authority.

There was another pool on the tableland which was not enchanted but contained good, clear water and was located close to the dwellings. Here the people built the Frogman a house of his own, close to the edge of the pool so that he could take a bath or a swim whenever he wished. He usually swam in the pool in the early morning, before anyone else was up, and during the day he dressed himself in his beautiful clothes and sat in his house and received the visits of all the Yips who came to him to ask his advice.

The Frogman's usual costume consisted of knee-breeches made of yellow satin plush, with trimmings of gold braid and jeweled knee-buckles; a white satin vest with silver buttons in which were set solitaire rubies; a swallow-tailed coat of bright yellow; green stockings and red leather shoes turned up at the toes and having diamond buckles. He wore, when he walked out, a purple silk hat and carried a gold-headed cane. Over his eyes he wore great spectacles with gold rims, not because his eyes were bad but because the spectacles made him look wise, and so distinguished and gorgeous was his appearance that all the Yips were very proud of him.

There was no King or Queen in the Yip Country, so the simple inhabitants naturally came to look upon the Frogman as their leader as well as their counselor in all times of emergency. In his heart the big frog knew he was no wiser than the Yips, but for a frog to know as much as a person was quite remarkable, and the Frogman was shrewd enough to make the people believe he was far more wise than he really was. They never suspected he was a humbug, but listened to his words with great respect and did just what he advised them to do.

Now, when Cayke the Cookie Cook raised such an outcry over the theft of her diamond-studded dishpan, the first thought of the people was to take her to the Frogman and inform him of the loss, thinking that of course he would tell her where to find it.

He listened to the story with his big eyes wide open behind his spectacles, and said in his deep, croaking voice:

"If the dishpan is stolen, somebody must have taken it."

"But who?" asked Cayke anxiously. "Who is the thief?"

"The one who took the dishpan, of course," replied the

Frogman, and hearing this all the Yips nodded their heads gravely and said to one another, "It is absolutely true!"

"But I want my dishpan!" cried Cayke.

"No one can blame you for that wish," remarked the Frogman.

"Then tell me where I may find it," she urged.

The look the Frogman gave her was a very wise look and he rose from his chair and strutted up and down the room with his hands under his coat-tails, in a very pompous and imposing manner. This was the first time so difficult a matter had been brought to him and he wanted time to think. It would never do to let them suspect his ignorance and so he thought very, very hard how best to answer the woman without betraying himself.

"I beg to inform you," said he, "that nothing in the Yip Country has ever been stolen before."

"We know that already," answered Cayke the Cookie Cook, impatiently.

"Therefore," continued the Frogman, "this theft becomes a very important matter."

"Well, where is my dishpan?" demanded the woman.

"It is lost; but it must be found. Unfortunately, we have no policemen or detectives to unravel the mystery, so we must employ other means to regain the lost article. Cayke must first write a Proclamation and tack it to the door of her house, and the Proclamation must read that whoever stole the jeweled dishpan must return it at once."

"But suppose no one returns it," suggested Cayke.

"Then," said the Frogman, "that very fact will be proof that no one has stolen it."

Cayke was not satisfied, but the other Yips seemed to approve the plan highly. They all advised her to do as the Frogman had told her to, so she posted the sign on her door and waited patiently for someone to return the dishpan—which no one ever did.

Again she went, accompanied by a group of her neighbors, to the Frogman, who by this time had given the matter considerable thought. Said he to Cayke, "I am now convinced that no Yip has taken your dishpan, and since it is gone from the Yip Country, I suspect that some stranger came from the world down below us, in the darkness of night when all of us were asleep, and took away your treasure. There can be no other explanation of its disappearance. So, if you wish to recover that golden, diamond-studded dishpan, you must go into the lower world after it."

This was indeed a startling proposition. Cayke and her friends went to the edge of the flat tableland and looked down the steep hillside to the plains below. It was so far to the bottom of the hill that nothing there could be seen very distinctly, and it seemed to the Yips very venturesome, if not dangerous, to go so far from home into an unknown land.

However, Cayke wanted her dishpan very badly, so she

turned to her friends and asked, "Who will go with me?"

No one answered the question, but after a period of silence one of the Yips said, "We know what is here, on the top of this flat hill, and it seems to us a very pleasant place; but what is down below we do not know. The chances are it is not so pleasant, so we had best stay where we are."

"It may be a far better country than this is," suggested the Cookie Cook.

"Maybe, maybe," responded another Yip, "but why take chances? Contentment with one's lot is true wisdom. Perhaps, in some other country, there are better cookies than you cook; but as we have always eaten your cookies, and liked them— except when they are burned on the bottom—we do not long for any better ones."

Cayke might have agreed to this argument had she not been so anxious to find her precious dishpan, but now she exclaimed impatiently, "You are cowards—all of you! If none of you are willing to explore with me the great world beyond this small hill, I will surely go alone."

"That is a wise resolve," declared the Yips, much relieved. "It is your dishpan that is lost, not ours; and, if you are willing to risk your life and liberty to regain it, no one can deny you the privilege."

While they were thus conversing the Frogman joined them and looked down at the plain with his big eyes and seemed unusually thoughtful. In fact, the Frogman was thinking that he'd like to see more of the world. Here in the Yip Country he had become the most important creature of them all and his importance was getting to be a little tame. It would be nice to have other people defer to him and ask his advice and there seemed no reason, so far as he could see, why his fame should not spread throughout all Oz.

He knew nothing of the rest of the world, but it was reasonable to believe that there were more people beyond the mountain where he now lived than there were Yips, and if he went among them he could surprise them with his display of wisdom and make them bow down to him as the Yips did. In other words, the Frogman was ambitious to become still greater than he was, which was impossible if he always remained upon this mountain. He wanted others to see his gorgeous clothes and listen to his solemn sayings, and here was an excuse for him to get away from the Yip Country. So he said to Cayke the Cookie Cook, "*I* will go with you, my good woman," which greatly pleased Cayke because she felt the Frogman could be of much assistance to her in her search.

But now, since the mighty Frogman had decided to undertake the journey, several of the Yips who were young and daring at once made up their minds to go along; so the next morning after breakfast the Frogman and Cayke the Cookie Cook and nine of the Yips started to slide down the side of the mountain. The bramble bushes and cactus plants were very prickly and uncomfortable to the touch, so the Frogman quickly commanded the Yips to go first and break a path, so that when he followed them he would not tear his splendid clothes. Cayke, too, was wearing her best dress and was likewise afraid of the thorns and prickers, so she kept behind the Frogman.

They made rather slow progress and night overtook them before they were halfway down the mountainside, so they found a cave in which they sought shelter until morning. Cayke had brought along a basket full of her famous cookies, so they all had plenty to eat.

On the second day the Yips began to wish they had not embarked on this adventure. They grumbled a good deal at having to cut away the thorns to make the path for the Frogman and the Cookie Cook, for their own clothing suffered many tears, while Cayke and the Frogman traveled safely and in comfort.

"If it is true that anyone came to our country to steal your diamond dishpan," said one of the Yips to Cayke, "it must have been a bird, for no person in the form of a man, woman or child could have climbed through these bushes and back again."

"And, allowing he could have done so," said another Yip, "the diamond-studded gold dishpan would not have repaid him for his troubles and his tribulations."

"For my part," remarked a third Yip, "I would rather go back home and dig and polish some more diamonds, and mine some more gold, and make you another dishpan, than be scratched from head to heel by these dreadful bushes. Even now, if my mother saw me, she would not know I am her son."

Cayke paid no heed to these mutterings, nor did the Frogman. Although their journey was slow it was being made easy for them by the Yips, so they had nothing to complain of and no desire to turn back.

Quite near to the bottom of the great hill they came upon a great gulf, the sides of which were as smooth as glass. The gulf extended a long distance—as far as they could see, in either direction—and although it was not very wide it was far too wide for the Yips to leap across it. And, should they fall into it, it was likely they might never get out again.

"Here our journey ends," said the Yips. "We must go back again."

Cayke the Cookie Cook began to weep.

"I shall never find my pretty dishpan again—and my heart will be broken!" she sobbed.

The Frogman went to the edge of the gulf and with his eye carefully measured the distance to the other side.

"Being a frog," said he, "I can leap, as all frogs do; and, being so big and strong, I am sure I can leap across this gulf with ease. But the rest of you, not being frogs, must return the way you came."

"We will do that with pleasure," cried the Yips, and at once they turned and began to climb up the steep mountain, feeling they had had quite enough of this unsatisfactory adventure. Cayke the Cookie Cook did not go with them, however. She sat on a rock and wept and wailed and was very miserable.

"Well," said the Frogman to her, "I will now bid you good-bye. If I find your diamond-decorated gold dishpan I will promise to see that it is safely returned to you."

"But I prefer to find it myself!" she said. "See here, Frogman, why can't you carry me across the gulf when you leap it? You are big and strong, while I am small and thin."

The Frogman gravely thought over this suggestion. It was a fact that Cayke the Cookie Cook was not a heavy person. Perhaps he could leap the gulf with her on his back.

"If you are willing to risk a fall," said he, "I will make the attempt."

At once she sprang up and grabbed him around his neck with both her arms. That is, she grabbed him where his neck ought to be, for the Frogman had no neck at all. Then he squatted down, as frogs do when they leap, and with his powerful rear legs he made a tremendous jump.

Over the gulf they sailed, with the Cookie Cook on his back, and he had leaped so hard—to make sure of not falling in—that he sailed over a lot of bramble-bushes that grew on the other side and landed in a clear space which was so far beyond the gulf that when they looked back they could not see it at all.

Cayke now got off the Frogman's back and he stood erect

again and carefully brushed the dust from his velvet coat and rearranged his white satin necktie.

"I had no idea I could leap so far," he said wonderingly. "Leaping is one more accomplishment I can now add to the long list of deeds I am able to perform."

"You are certainly fine at leap-frog," said the Cookie Cook admiringly, "but, as you say, you are wonderful in many ways. If we meet with any people down here I am sure they will consider you the greatest and grandest of all living creatures."

"Yes," he replied, "I shall probably astonish strangers, because they have never before had the pleasure of seeing me. Also, they will marvel at my great learning. Every time I open my mouth, Cayke, I am liable to say something important."

"That is true," she agreed, "and it is fortunate your mouth is so very wide and opens so far, for otherwise all the wisdom might not be able to get out of it."

"Perhaps nature made it wide for that very reason," said the Frogman. "But come; let us now go on, for it is getting late and we must find some sort of shelter before night overtakes us."

·—·◄ Chapter 4 ►·—·

AMONG the WINKIES

The settled parts of the Winkie Country are full of happy and contented people who are ruled by a tin Emperor named Nick Chopper, who in turn is a subject of the beautiful girl Ruler, Ozma of Oz. But not all of the Winkie Country is fully settled. At the east, which part lies nearest the Emerald City, there are beautiful farm-houses and roads, but as you travel west, you first come to a branch of the Winkie River, beyond which there is a rough country where few people live, and some of these are quite unknown to the rest of the world. After passing through this rude section of territory, which no one ever visits, you would come to still another branch of the Winkie

River, after crossing which you would find another well-settled part of the Winkie Country, extending westward quite to the Deadly Desert that surrounds all the Land of Oz and separates that favored fairyland from the more common outside world. The Winkies who live in this west section have many tin mines, from which metal they make a great deal of rich jewelry and other articles, all of which are highly esteemed in the Land of Oz because tin is so bright and pretty, and there is not so much of it as there is of gold and silver.

Not all the Winkies are miners, however, for some till the fields and grow grains for food, and it was at one of these far west Winkie farms that the Frogman and Cayke the Cookie Cook first arrived after they had descended from the mountain of the Yips.

"Goodness me!" cried Nellary the Winkie wife, when she saw the strange couple approaching her house. "I have seen many queer creatures in the Land of Oz, but none more queer than this giant frog who dresses like a man and walks on his hind legs. Come here, Wiljon," she called to her husband, who was eating his breakfast, "and take a look at this astonishing freak."

Wiljon the Winkie came to the door and looked out. He was still standing in the doorway when the Frogman approached and said with a haughty croak, "Tell me, my good man, have you seen a diamond-studded gold dishpan?"

"No; nor have I seen a copper-plated lobster," replied Wiljon, in an equally haughty tone.

The Frogman stared at him and said, "Do not be insolent, fellow!"

"No," added Cayke the Cookie Cook hastily, "you must be very polite to the great Frogman, for he is the wisest creature in all the world."

"Who says that?" inquired Wiljon.

"He says so himself," replied Cayke, and the Frogman nodded and strutted up and down, twirling his gold-headed cane very gracefully.

"Does the Scarecrow admit that this overgrown frog is the wisest creature in the world?" asked Wiljon.

"I do not know who the Scarecrow is," answered Cayke the Cookie Cook.

"Well, he lives at the Emerald City, and he is supposed to have the finest brains in all Oz. The Wizard gave them to him, you know."

"Mine grew in my head," said the Frogman pompously, "so I think they must be better than any wizard brains. I am so wise that sometimes my wisdom makes my head ache. I know so much that often I have to forget part of it, since no one creature, however great, is able to contain so much knowledge."

"It must be dreadful to be stuffed full of wisdom," remarked Wiljon reflectively, and eyeing the Frogman with a doubtful look. "It is my good fortune to know very little."

"I hope, however, you know where my jeweled dishpan is," said the Cookie Cook anxiously.

"I do not know even that," returned the Winkie. "We have trouble enough in keeping track of our own dishpans without meddling with the dishpans of strangers."

Finding him so ignorant, the Frogman proposed that they walk on and seek Cayke's dishpan elsewhere. Wiljon the Winkie did not seem greatly impressed by the great Frogman, which seemed to that personage as strange as it was disappointing; but others in this unknown land might prove more respectful.

"I'd like to meet that Wizard of Oz," remarked Cayke as they walked along a path. "If he could give a Scarecrow brains he might be able to find my dishpan."

"Poof!" grunted the Frogman scornfully; "I am greater than any wizard. Depend on *me*. If your dishpan is anywhere in the world I am sure to find it."

"If you do not, my heart will be broken," declared the Cookie Cook in a sorrowful voice.

For a while the Frogman walked on in silence. Then he asked, "Why do you attach so much importance to a dishpan?"

"It is the greatest treasure I possess," replied the woman. "It belonged to my mother and to all my grandmothers, since the beginning of time. It is, I believe, the very oldest thing in all the Yip Country—or was while it was there—and," she added, dropping her voice to an awed whisper, "it has magic powers!"

"In what way?" inquired the Frogman, seeming to be surprised at this statement.

"Whoever has owned that dishpan has been a good cook, for one thing. No one else is able to make such good cookies as I have cooked, as you and all the Yips know. Yet, the very morning after my dishpan was stolen, I tried to make a batch of cookies and they burned up in the oven! I made another batch that proved too tough to eat, and I was so ashamed of them that I buried them in the ground. Even the third batch of cookies, which I brought with me in my basket, were pretty poor stuff and no better than any woman could make who does not own my diamond-studded gold dishpan. In fact, my good Frogman, Cayke the Cookie Cook will never be able to cook good cookies again until her magic dishpan is restored to her."

"In that case," said the Frogman with a sigh, "I suppose we must manage to find it."

Chapter 5

OZMA'S FRIENDS are PERPLEXED

R eally," said Dorothy, looking solemn, "this is very s'prising. We can't even find a shadow of Ozma anywhere in the Em'rald City; and wherever she's gone, she's taken her Magic Picture with her."

She was standing in the courtyard of the palace with Betsy and Trot, while Scraps, the Patchwork Girl, danced around the group, her hair flying in the wind.

"P'raps," said Scraps, still dancing, "someone has stolen Ozma."

"Oh, they'd never dare do that!" exclaimed tiny Trot.

"And stolen the Magic Picture, too, so the thing can't tell where she is," added the Patchwork Girl.

"That's nonsense," said Dorothy. "Why, ev'ryone loves Ozma. There isn't a person in the Land of Oz who would steal a single thing she owns."

"Huh!" replied the Patchwork Girl. "You don't know ev'ry person in the Land of Oz."

"Why don't I?"

"It's a big country," said Scraps. "There are cracks and corners in it that even Ozma doesn't know of."

"The Patchwork Girl's just daffy," declared Betsy.

"No; she's right about that," replied Dorothy thoughtfully. "There are lots of queer people in this fairyland who never come near Ozma or the Em'rald City. I've seen some of 'em myself, girls; but I haven't seen all, of course, and there *might* be some wicked persons left in Oz yet, though I think the wicked witches have all been destroyed."

Just then the Wooden Sawhorse dashed into the courtyard with the Wizard of Oz on his back.

"Have you found Ozma?" cried the Wizard when the Sawhorse stopped beside them.

"Not yet," said Dorothy. "Doesn't Glinda know where she is?"

"No. Glinda's Book of Records and all her magic instruments are gone. Someone must have stolen them."

"Goodness me!" exclaimed Dorothy in alarm. "This is the biggest steal I ever heard of. Who do you think did it, Wizard?"

"I've no idea," he answered. "But I have come to get my own bag of magic tools and carry them to Glinda. She is so much more powerful than I that she may be able to discover the truth by means of my magic, quicker and better than I could myself."

"Hurry, then," said Dorothy, "for we've all gotten terr'bly worried."

The Wizard rushed away to his rooms but presently came back with a long, sad face.

"It's gone!" he said.

"What's gone?" asked Scraps.

"My black bag of magic tools. Someone must have stolen it!"

They looked at one another in amazement.

"This thing is getting desperate," continued the Wizard. "All the magic that belongs to Ozma, or to Glinda, or to me, has been stolen."

"Do you suppose Ozma could have taken them, herself, for some purpose?" asked Betsy.

"No indeed," declared the Wizard. "I suspect some enemy has stolen Ozma and, for fear we would follow and recapture her, has taken all our magic away from us."

"How dreadful!" cried Dorothy. "The idea of anyone wanting to injure our dear Ozma! Can't we do *any*thing to find her, Wizard?"

"I'll ask Glinda. I must go straight back to her and tell her that my magic tools have also disappeared. The good Sorceress will be greatly shocked, I know."

With this, he jumped upon the back of the Sawhorse again, and the quaint steed, which never tired, dashed away at full speed.

The three girls were very much disturbed in mind. Even the Patchwork Girl seemed to realize that a great calamity had overtaken them all. Ozma was a fairy of considerable power, and all the creatures in Oz, as well as the three mortal girls from the outside world, looked upon her as their protector and friend. The idea of their beautiful girl Ruler's being over-powered by an enemy and dragged from her splendid palace a captive was too astonishing for them to comprehend, at first. Yet what other explanation of the mystery could there be?

"Ozma wouldn't go away willingly, without letting us know about it," asserted Dorothy; "and she wouldn't steal Glinda's Great Book of Records, or the Wizard's magic, 'cause she could get them any time just by asking for 'em. I'm sure some wicked person has done all this."

"Someone in the Land of Oz?" asked Trot.

"Of course. No one could get across the Deadly Desert, you know, and no one but an Oz person could know about the Magic Picture and the Book of Records and the Wizard's magic, or where they were kept, and so be able to steal the whole outfit before we could stop 'em. It *must* be someone who lives in the Land of Oz."

"But who—who—who?" asked Scraps. "That's the question. Who?"

"If we knew," replied Dorothy, severely, "we wouldn't be standing here, doing nothing."

Just then two boys entered the courtyard and approached the group of girls. One boy was dressed in the fantastic Munchkin costume—a blue jacket and knickerbockers, blue leather shoes and a blue hat with a high peak and tiny silver bells dangling from its rim—and this was Ojo the Lucky, who had once come from the Munchkin Country of Oz and now lived in the Emerald City. The other boy was an American, from Philadelphia, and had lately found his way to Oz in the company of Trot and Cap'n Bill. His name was Button-Bright; that is, everyone called him by that name and knew no other.

Button-Bright was not quite as big as the Munchkin boy, but he wore the same kind of clothes, only they were of different colors. As the two came up to the girls, arm in arm, Button-Bright remarked, "Hello, Dorothy. They say Ozma is lost."

"*Who* says so?" she asked.

"Ev'rybody's talking about it, in the City," he replied.

"I wonder how the people found it out," Dorothy asked.

"I know," said Ojo. "Jellia Jamb told them. She has been asking everywhere if anyone has seen Ozma."

"That's too bad," observed Dorothy, frowning.

"Why?" asked Button-Bright.

"There wasn't any use making all our people unhappy, till we were dead certain that Ozma can't be found."

"Pshaw," said Button-Bright. "It's nothing to get lost. I've been lost lots of times."

"That's true," admitted Trot, who knew that the boy had a habit of getting lost and then finding himself again; "but it's diff'rent with Ozma. She's the Ruler of all this big fairyland and we're 'fraid that the reason she's lost is because somebody has stolen her away."

"Only wicked people steal," said Ojo. "Do you know of any wicked people in Oz, Dorothy?"

"No," she replied.

"They're here, though," cried Scraps, dancing up to them and then circling around the group. "Ozma's stolen; someone in Oz stole her; only wicked people steal; so someone in Oz is wicked!"

There was no denying the truth of this statement. The faces of all of them were now solemn and sorrowful.

"One thing is sure," said Button-Bright after a time, "if Ozma has been stolen, someone ought to find her and punish the thief."

"There may be a lot of thieves," suggested Trot gravely, "and in this fairy country they don't seem to have any soldiers or policemen."

"There is one soldier," claimed Dorothy. "He has green whiskers and a gun and is a Major-General, but no one is afraid of either his gun or his whiskers, 'cause he's so tender-hearted that he wouldn't hurt a fly."

"Well, a soldier is a soldier," said Betsy, "and perhaps he'd hurt a wicked thief if he wouldn't hurt a fly. Where is he?"

"He went fishing about two months ago and hasn't come back yet," explained Button-Bright.

"Then I can't see that he will be of much use to us in this trouble," sighed little Trot. "But p'raps Ozma, who is a fairy, can get away from the thieves without any help from anyone."

"She *might* be able to," answered Dorothy, reflectively, "but if she had the power to do that, it isn't likely she'd have let herself be stolen. So the thieves must have been even more powerful in magic than our Ozma."

There was no denying this argument and, although they talked the matter over all the rest of that day, they were unable to decide how Ozma had been stolen against her will or who had committed the dreadful deed.

Toward evening the Wizard came back, riding slowly upon the Sawhorse because he felt discouraged and perplexed. Glinda came, later, in her aerial chariot drawn by twenty milk-white swans, and she also seemed worried and unhappy. More of Ozma's friends joined them, and that evening they all had a big talk together.

"I think," said Dorothy, "we ought to start out right away in search of our dear Ozma. It seems cruel for us to live comf'tably in her palace while she is a pris'ner in the power of some wicked enemy."

"Yes," agreed Glinda the Sorceress, "someone ought to search for her. I cannot go myself, because I must work hard in order to create some new instruments of sorcery by means of which I may rescue our fair Ruler. But if you can find her, in the meantime, and let me know who has stolen her, it will enable me to rescue her much more quickly."

"Then we'll start tomorrow morning," decided Dorothy. "Betsy and Trot and I won't waste another minute."

"I'm not sure you girls will make good detectives," remarked the Wizard; "but I'll go with you, to protect you from harm and to give you my advice. All my wizardry, alas, is stolen, so I am now really no more a wizard than any of you; but I will try to protect you from any enemies you may meet."

"What harm could happen to us in Oz?" inquired Trot.

"What harm happened to Ozma?" returned the Wizard. "If there is an Evil Power abroad in our fairyland, which is able to steal not only Ozma and her Magic Picture, but Glinda's Book of Records and all her magic, and my black bag containing all my tricks of wizardry, then that Evil Power may yet cause us considerable injury. Ozma is a fairy, and so is Glinda, so no power can kill or destroy them; but you girls are all mortals, and so are Button-Bright and I, so we must watch out for ourselves."

"Nothing can kill me," said Ojo, the Munchkin boy.

"That is true," replied the Sorceress, "and I think it may be well to divide the searchers into several parties, that they may cover all the land of Oz more quickly. So I will send Ojo and Unc Nunkie and Dr. Pipt into the Munchkin Country, which they are well acquainted with; and I will send the Scarecrow and the Tin Woodman into the Quadling Country, for they are fearless and brave and never tire; and to the Gillikin Country, where many dangers lurk, I will send the Shaggy Man and his brother, with Tik-Tok and Jack Pumpkinhead. Dorothy may make up her own party and travel into the Winkie Country. All of you must inquire everywhere for Ozma and try to discover where she is hidden."

They thought this a very wise plan and adopted it without question. In Ozma's absence Glinda the Good was the most important person in Oz and all were glad to serve under her direction.

Chapter 6

The SEARCH PARTY

Next morning, as soon as the sun was up, Glinda flew back to her castle, stopping on the way to instruct the Scarecrow and the Tin Woodman, who were at that time staying at the college of Professor H. M. Wogglebug, T.E., and taking a course of his Patent Educational Pills. On hearing of Ozma's loss, they started at once for the Quadling Country to search for her.

As soon as Glinda had left the Emerald City, Tik-Tok and the Shaggy Man and Jack Pumpkinhead, who had been present at the conference, began their journey into the Gillikin Country, and an hour later Ojo and Unc Nunkie joined Dr.

Pipt and together they traveled toward the Munchkin Country. When all these searchers were gone, Dorothy and the Wizard completed their own preparations.

The Wizard hitched the Sawhorse to the Red Wagon, which would seat four very comfortably. He wanted Dorothy, Betsy, Trot and the Patchwork Girl to ride in the wagon, but Scraps came up to them mounted upon the Woozy, and the Woozy said he would like to join the party. Now this Woozy was a most peculiar animal, having a square head, square body, square legs and square tail. His skin was very tough and hard, resembling leather, and while his movements were somewhat clumsy, the beast could travel with remarkable swiftness. His square eyes were mild and gentle in expression and he was not especially foolish. The Woozy and the Patchwork Girl were great friends and so the Wizard agreed to let the Woozy go with them.

Another great beast now appeared and asked to go along. This was none other than the famous Cowardly Lion, one of the most interesting creatures in all Oz. No lion that roamed the jungles or plains could compare in size or intelligence with this Cowardly Lion, who—like all animals living in Oz—could talk, and who talked with more shrewdness and wisdom than many of the people did. He said he was cowardly because he always trembled when he faced danger, but he had faced danger many times and never refused to fight when it was necessary. This Lion was a great favorite with Ozma and always guarded her throne on state occasions. He was also an old companion and friend of the Princess Dorothy, so the girl was delighted to have him join the party.

"I'm so nervous over our dear Ozma," said the Cowardly Lion in his deep, rumbling voice, "that it would make me unhappy to remain behind while you are trying to find her. But do not get into any danger, I beg of you, for danger frightens me terribly."

"We'll not get into danger if we can poss'bly help it," promised Dorothy; "but we shall do anything to find Ozma, danger or no danger."

The addition of the Woozy and the Cowardly Lion to the party gave Betsy Bobbin an idea and she ran to the marble stables at the rear of the palace and brought out her mule, Hank by name. Perhaps no mule you ever saw was so lean and bony and altogether plain looking as this Hank, but Betsy loved him dearly because he was faithful and steady and not nearly so stupid as most mules are considered to be. Betsy had a saddle for Hank and declared she would ride on his back, an arrangement approved by the Wizard because it left only four of the party to ride on the seats of the Red Wagon—Dorothy and Button-Bright and Trot and himself.

An old sailor-man, who had one wooden leg, came to see them off and suggested that they put a supply of food and blankets in the Red Wagon, inasmuch as they were uncertain how long they would be gone. This sailor-man was called

Cap'n Bill. He was a former friend and comrade of Trot and had encountered many adventures in company with the little girl. I think he was sorry he could not go with her on this trip, but Glinda the Sorceress had asked Cap'n Bill to remain in the Emerald City and take charge of the royal palace while everyone else was away, and the one-legged sailor had agreed to do so.

They loaded the back end of the Red Wagon with everything they thought they might need, and then they formed a procession and marched from the palace through the Emerald City to the great gates of the wall that surrounded this beautiful capital of the Land of Oz. Crowds of citizens lined the streets to see them pass and to cheer them and wish them success, for all were grieved over Ozma's loss and anxious that she be found again.

First came the Cowardly Lion; then the Patchwork Girl riding upon the Woozy; then Betsy Bobbin on her mule Hank; and finally the Sawhorse drawing the Red Wagon, in which were seated the Wizard and Dorothy and Button-Bright and Trot. No one was obliged to drive the Sawhorse, so there were no reins to his harness; one had only to tell him which way to go, fast or slow, and he understood perfectly.

It was about this time that a shaggy little black dog who had been lying asleep in Dorothy's room in the palace woke up and discovered he was lonesome. Everything seemed very still throughout the great building, and Toto—that was the little dog's name—missed the customary chatter of the three girls. He never paid much attention to what was going on around him and, although he could speak, he seldom said anything; so the little dog did not know about Ozma's loss or that everyone had gone in search of her. But he liked to be with people, and especially with his own mistress, Dorothy, and having yawned and stretched himself and found the door of the room ajar he trotted out into the corridor and went down the stately marble stairs to the hall of the palace, where he met Jellia Jamb.

"Where's Dorothy?" asked Toto.

"She's gone to the Winkie Country," answered the maid.

"When?"

"A little while ago," replied Jellia.

Toto turned and trotted out into the palace garden and down the long driveway until he came to the streets of the Emerald City. Here he paused to listen and, hearing sounds of cheering, he ran swiftly along until he came in sight of the Red Wagon and the Woozy and the Lion and the Mule and all the others. Being a wise little dog, he decided not to show himself to Dorothy just then, lest he be sent back home; but he never lost sight of the party of travelers, all of whom were so eager to get ahead that they never thought to look behind them.

When they came to the gates in the city wall, the Guardian of the Gates came out to throw wide the golden portals and let them pass through.

"Did any strange person come in or out of the city on the

night before last when Ozma was stolen?" asked Dorothy.

"No, indeed, Princess," answered the Guardian of the Gates.

"Of course not," said the Wizard. "Anyone clever enough to steal all the things we have lost would not mind the barrier of a wall like this in the least. I think the thief must have flown through the air, for otherwise he could not have stolen from Ozma's royal palace and Glinda's far-away castle in the same night. Moreover, as there are no airships in Oz and no way for airships from the outside world to get into this country, I believe the thief must have flown from place to place by means of magic arts which neither Glinda nor I understand."

On they went, and before the gates closed behind them, Toto managed to dodge through them. The country surrounding the Emerald City was thickly settled and for a while our friends rode over nicely paved roads which wound through a fertile country dotted with beautiful houses, all built in the quaint Oz fashion. In the course of a few hours, however, they had left the tilled fields and entered the Country of the Winkies, which occupies a quarter of all the territory in the Land of Oz but is not so well known as many other parts of Ozma's fairyland. Long before night the travelers had crossed the Winkie River near to the Scarecrow's Tower (which was now vacant) and had entered the Rolling Prairie where few people live. They asked everyone they met for news of Ozma, but none in this district had seen her or even knew that she had been stolen. And by nightfall they had passed all the farm-houses and were obliged to stop and ask for shelter at the hut of a lonely shepherd. When they halted, Toto was not far behind. The little dog halted, too, and stealing softly around the party, he hid himself behind the hut.

The shepherd was a kindly old man and treated the travelers with much courtesy. He slept out of doors, that night, giving up his hut to the three girls, who made their beds on the floor with the blankets they had brought in the Red Wagon. The Wizard and Button-Bright also slept out of doors, and so did the Cowardly Lion and Hank the Mule. But Scraps and the Sawhorse did not sleep at all, and the Woozy could stay awake for a month at a time, if he wished to, so these three sat in a little group by themselves and talked together all through the night.

In the darkness the Cowardly Lion felt a shaggy little form nestling beside his own, and he said sleepily, "Where did you come from, Toto?"

"From home," said the dog. "If you roll over, roll the other way, so you won't smash me."

"Does Dorothy know you are here?" asked the Lion.

"I believe not," admitted Toto, and he added, a little anxiously, "Do you think, friend Lion, we are now far enough from the Emerald City for me to risk showing myself? Or will Dorothy send me back because I wasn't invited?"

"Only Dorothy can answer that question," said the Lion.

"For my part, Toto, I consider this affair none of my business, so you must act as you think best."

Then the huge beast went to sleep again and Toto snuggled closer to the warm, hairy body and also slept. He was a wise little dog, in his way, and didn't intend to worry when there was something much better to do.

In the morning the Wizard built a fire, over which the girls cooked a very good breakfast.

Suddenly Dorothy discovered Toto sitting quietly before the fire, and the little girl exclaimed, "Goodness me, Toto! Where did *you* come from?"

"From the place you cruelly left me," replied the dog in a reproachful tone.

"I forgot all about you," admitted Dorothy, "and if I hadn't I'd prob'ly left you with Jellia Jamb, seeing this isn't a pleasure trip but stric'ly business. But now that you're here, Toto, I s'pose you'll have to stay with us, unless you'd rather go back again. We may get ourselves into trouble before we're done, Toto."

"Never mind that," said Toto, wagging his tail. "I'm hungry, Dorothy."

"Breakfas'll soon be ready, and then you shall have your share," promised his little mistress, who was really glad to have her dog with her. She and Toto had traveled together before, and she knew he was a good and faithful comrade.

When the food was cooked and served the girls invited the

old shepherd to join them in the morning meal. He willingly consented and while they ate he said to them, "You are now about to pass through a very dangerous country, unless you turn to the north or to the south to escape its perils."

"In that case," said the Cowardly Lion, "let us turn, by all means, for I dread to face dangers of any sort."

"What's the matter with the country ahead of us?" inquired Dorothy.

"Beyond this Rolling Prairie," explained the shepherd, "are the Merry-Go-Round Mountains, set close together and surrounded by deep gulfs, so that no one is able to get past them. Beyond the Merry-Go-Round Mountains it is said the Thistle-Eaters and the Herkus live."

"What are they like?" demanded Dorothy.

"No one knows, for no one has ever passed the Merry-Go-Round Mountains," was the reply; "but it is said that the Thistle-Eaters hitch dragons to their chariots and that the Herkus are waited upon by giants whom they have conquered and made their slaves."

"Who says all that?" asked Betsy.

"It is common report," declared the shepherd. "Everyone believes it."

"I don't see how they know," remarked little Trot, "if no one has been there."

"Perhaps the birds who fly over that country brought the news," suggested Betsy.

"If you escaped those dangers," continued the shepherd, "you might encounter others, still more serious, before you came to the next branch of the Winkie River. It is true that beyond that river there lies a fine country, inhabited by good people, and if you reached there you would have no further trouble. It is between here and the west branch of the Winkie River that all dangers lie, for that is the unknown territory that is inhabited by terrible, lawless people."

"It may be, and it may not be," said the Wizard. "We shall know when we get there."

"Well," persisted the shepherd, "in a fairy country such as ours every undiscovered place is likely to harbor wicked creatures. If they were not wicked, they would discover themselves, and by coming among us submit to Ozma's rule and be good and considerate, as are all the Oz people whom we know."

"That argument," stated the little Wizard, "convinces me that it is our duty to go straight to those unknown places, however dangerous they may be; for it is surely some cruel and wicked person who has stolen our Ozma, and we know it would be folly to search among good people for the culprit. Ozma may not be hidden in the secret places of the Winkie Country, it is true, but it is our duty to travel to every spot, however dangerous, where our beloved Ruler is likely to be imprisoned."

"You're right about that," said Button-Bright approvingly. "Dangers don't hurt us; only things that happen ever hurt anyone, and a danger is a thing that might happen, and might not happen, and sometimes don't amount to shucks. I vote we go ahead and take our chances."

They were all of the same opinion, so they packed up and said good-bye to the friendly shepherd and proceeded on their way.

Chapter 7

The MERRY-GO-ROUND MOUNTAINS

The Rolling Prairie was not difficult to travel over, although it was all up-hill and down-hill, so for a while they made good progress. Not even a shepherd was to be met with now and the farther they advanced the more dreary the landscape became. At noon they stopped for a "picnic luncheon," as Betsy called it, and then they again resumed their journey. All the animals were swift and tireless and even the Cowardly Lion and the Mule found they could keep up with the pace of the Woozy and the Sawhorse.

It was the middle of the afternoon when first they came in

sight of a cluster of low mountains. These were cone-shaped, rising from broad bases to sharp peaks at the tops. From a distance the mountains appeared indistinct and seemed rather small—more like hills than mountains—but as the travelers drew nearer they noted a most unusual circumstance: the hills were all whirling around, some in one direction and some the opposite way.

"I guess those are the Merry-Go-Round Mountains, all right," said Dorothy.

"They must be," said the Wizard.

"They go 'round, sure enough," agreed Trot, "but they don't seem very merry."

There were several rows of these mountains, extending both to the right and to the left, for miles and miles. How many rows there might be, none could tell, but between the first row of peaks could be seen other peaks, all steadily whirling around one way or another. Continuing to ride nearer, our friends watched these hills attentively, until at last, coming close up, they discovered there was a deep but narrow gulf around the edge of each mountain, and that the mountains were set so close together that the outer gulf was continuous and barred farther advance.

At the edge of the gulf they all dismounted and peered over into its depths. There was no telling where the bottom was, if indeed there was any bottom at all. From where they stood it seemed as if the mountains had been set in one great hole in the ground, just close enough together so they would not touch, and that each mountain was supported by a rocky column beneath its base which extended far down in the black pit below. From the land side it seemed impossible to get across the gulf or, succeeding in that, to gain a foothold on any of the whirling mountains.

"This ditch is too wide to jump across," remarked Button-Bright.

"P'raps the Lion could do it," suggested Dorothy.

"What, jump from here to that whirling hill?" cried the Lion indignantly. "I should say not! Even if I landed there, and could hold on, what good would it do? There's another spinning mountain beyond it, and perhaps still another beyond that. I don't believe any living creature could jump from one mountain to another, when both are whirling like tops and in different directions."

"I propose we turn back," said the Wooden Sawhorse with a yawn of his chopped-out mouth as he stared with his knot eyes at the Merry-Go-Round Mountains.

"I agree with you," said the Woozy, wagging his square head.

"We should have taken the shepherd's advice," added Hank the Mule.

The others of the party, however they might be puzzled by the serious problem that confronted them, would not allow themselves to despair.

"If we once get over these mountains," said Button-Bright, "we could probably get along all right."

"True enough," agreed Dorothy. "So we must find some way, of course, to get past these whirligig hills. But how?"

"I wish the Ork was with us," sighed Trot.

"But the Ork isn't here," said the Wizard, "and we must depend upon ourselves to conquer this difficulty. Unfortunately, all my magic has been stolen, otherwise I am sure I could easily get over the mountains."

"Unfortunately," observed the Woozy, "none of us has wings. And we're in a magic country without any magic."

"What is that around your waist, Dorothy?" asked the Wizard.

"That? Oh, that's just the Magic Belt I once captured from the Nome King," she replied.

"A Magic Belt! Why, that's fine. I'm sure a Magic Belt would take you over these hills."

"It might, if I knew how to work it," said the little girl. "Ozma knows a lot of its magic, but I've never found out about it. All I know is that while I am wearing it, nothing can hurt me."

"Try wishing yourself across, and see if it will obey you," suggested the Wizard.

"But what good would that do?" asked Dorothy. "If I got across it wouldn't help the rest of you, and I couldn't go alone among all those giants and dragons while you stayed here."

"True enough," agreed the Wizard, sadly; and then, after looking around the group, he inquired, "What is that on your finger, Trot?"

"A ring. The Mermaids gave it to me," she explained, "and if ever I'm in trouble when I'm on the water I can call the Mermaids and they'll come and help me. But the Mermaids can't help me on the land, you know, 'cause they swim, and—and—they haven't any legs."

"True enough," repeated the Wizard, more sadly.

There was a big, broad-spreading tree near the edge of the gulf and as the sun was hot above them they all gathered under the shade of the tree to study the problem of what to do next.

"If we had a long rope," said Betsy, "we could fasten it to this tree and let the other end of it down into the gulf and all slide down it."

"Well, what then?" asked the Wizard.

"Then, if we could manage to throw the rope up the other side," explained the girl, "we could all climb it and be on the other side of the gulf."

"There are too many 'if's' in that suggestion," remarked the little Wizard. "And you must remember that the other side is nothing but spinning mountains, so we couldn't possibly fasten a rope to them—even if we had one."

"That rope idea isn't half bad, though," said the Patchwork Girl, who had been dancing dangerously near to the edge of the gulf.

"What do you mean?" asked Dorothy.

The Patchwork Girl suddenly stood still and cast her button eyes around the group.

"Ha, I have it!" she exclaimed. "Unharness the Sawhorse, somebody; my fingers are too clumsy."

"Shall we?" asked Button-Bright doubtfully, turning to the others.

"Well, Scraps has a lot of brains, even if she *is* stuffed with cotton," asserted the Wizard. "If her brains can help us out of this trouble, we ought to use them."

So he began unharnessing the Sawhorse, and Button-Bright and Dorothy helped him. When they had removed the harness the Patchwork Girl told them to take it all apart and buckle the straps together, end to end. And, after they had done this, they found they had one very long strap that was stronger than any rope.

"It would reach across the gulf, easily," said the Lion, who with the other animals had sat on his haunches and watched this proceeding. "But I don't see how it could be fastened to one of those dizzy mountains."

Scraps had no such notion as that in her baggy head. She told them to fasten one end of the strap to a stout limb of the tree, pointing to one which extended quite to the edge of the gulf. Button-Bright did that, climbing the tree and then crawling out upon the limb until he was nearly over the gulf. There he managed to fasten the strap, which reached to the ground below, and then he slid down it and was caught by the Wizard, who feared he might fall into the chasm.

Scraps was delighted. She seized the lower end of the strap and, telling them all to get out of her way, she went back as far as the strap would reach and then made a sudden run toward the gulf. Over the edge she swung, clinging to the strap until it had gone as far as its length permitted, when she let go and sailed gracefully through the air until she alighted upon the mountain just in front of them.

Almost instantly, as the great cone continued to whirl, she was sent flying against the next mountain in the rear, and that one had only turned halfway around when Scraps was sent flying to the next mountain behind it. Then her patch-work form disappeared from view entirely and the amazed watchers under the tree wondered what had become of her.

"She's gone, and she can't get back," said the Woozy.

"My, how she bounded from one mountain to another!" exclaimed the Lion.

"That was because they whirl so fast," the Wizard explained. "Scraps had nothing to hold on to and so of course she was tossed from one hill to another. I'm afraid we shall never see the poor Patchwork Girl again."

"*I* shall see her," declared the Woozy. "Scraps is an old friend of mine and, if there are really Thistle-Eaters and Giants on the other side of those tops, she will need someone to protect her. So here I go!"

He seized the dangling strap firmly in his square mouth and in the same way that Scraps had done swung himself over the gulf. He let go the strap at the right moment and fell upon the first whirling mountain. Then he bounded to the next one back of it—not on his feet but "all mixed up," as Trot said—and then he shot across to another mountain, disappearing from view just as the Patchwork Girl had done.

"It seems to work, all right," remarked Button-Bright. "I guess I'll try it."

"Wait a minute," urged the Wizard. "Before any more of us make this desperate leap into the beyond, we must decide whether all will go, or if some of us will remain behind."

"Do you s'pose it hurt them much, to bump against those mountains?" asked Trot.

"I don't s'pose anything could hurt Scraps or the Woozy," said Dorothy, "and nothing can hurt *me*, because I wear the Magic Belt. So, as I'm anxious to find Ozma, I mean to swing myself across, too."

"I'll take my chances," decided Button-Bright.

"I'm sure it will hurt dreadfully, and I'm afraid to do it," said the Lion, who was already trembling; "but I shall do it if Dorothy does."

"Well, that will leave Betsy and the Mule and Trot," said the Wizard; "for of course, I shall go, that I may look after Dorothy. Do you two girls think you can find your way back home again?" he asked, addressing Trot and Betsy.

"I'm not afraid; not much, that is," said Trot. "It looks risky, I know, but I'm sure I can stand it if the others can."

"If it wasn't for leaving Hank," began Betsy in a hesitating voice.

But the Mule interrupted her by saying, "Go ahead if you want to, and I'll come after you. A mule is as brave as a lion any day."

"Braver," said the Lion, "for I'm a coward, friend Hank, and you are not. But of course the Sawhorse—"

"Oh, nothing ever hurts *me*," asserted the Sawhorse calmly. "There's never been any question about *my* going. I can't take the Red Wagon, though."

"No, we must leave the wagon," said the Wizard; "and also we must leave our food and blankets, I fear. But if we can defy these Merry-Go-Round Mountains to stop us we won't mind the sacrifice of some of our comforts."

"No one knows where we're going to land!" remarked the Lion in a voice that sounded as if he were going to cry.

"We may not land at all," replied Hank; "but the best way to find out what will happen to us is to swing across, as Scraps and the Woozy have done."

"I think I shall go last," said the Wizard; "so who wants to go first?"

"I'll go," decided Dorothy.

"No, it's my turn first," said Button-Bright. "Watch me!"

Even as he spoke, the boy seized the strap and after

making a run swung himself across the gulf. Away he went, bumping from hill to hill until he disappeared. They listened intently, but the boy uttered no cry until he had been gone some moments, when they heard a faint "Hullo-a!" as if called from a great distance.

The sound gave them courage, however, and Dorothy picked up Toto and held him fast under one arm while with the other hand she seized the strap and bravely followed after Button-Bright.

When she struck the first whirling mountain, she fell upon it quite softly, but before she had time to think, she flew through the air and lit with a jar on the side of the next mountain. Again she flew, and alighted; and again, and still again, until after five successive bumps she fell sprawling upon a green meadow and was so dazed and bewildered by her bumpy journey across the Merry-Go-Round Mountains that she lay quite still for a time, to collect her thoughts. Toto had escaped from her arms just as she fell, and he now sat beside her panting with excitement.

Then Dorothy realized that someone was helping her to her feet, and here was Button-Bright on one side of her and Scraps on the other, both seeming to be unhurt. The next object her eyes fell upon was the Woozy, squatting upon his square back end and looking at her reflectively, while Toto barked joyously to find his mistress unhurt after her whirl-wind trip.

"Good!" said the Woozy; "here's another and a dog, both

safe and sound. But, my word, Dorothy, you flew some! If you could have seen yourself, you'd have been absolutely astonished."

"They say 'Time flies,'" laughed Button-Bright; "but Time never made a quicker journey than that."

Just then, as Dorothy turned around to look at the whirling mountains, she was in time to see tiny Trot come flying from the nearest hill to fall upon the soft grass not a yard away from where she stood. Trot was so dizzy she couldn't stand, at first, but she wasn't at all hurt and presently Betsy came flying to them and would have bumped into the others had they not retreated in time to avoid her.

Then, in quick succession, came the Lion, Hank and the Sawhorse, bounding from mountain to mountain to fall safely upon the greensward. Only the Wizard was now left behind and they waited so long for him that Dorothy began to be worried. But suddenly he came flying from the nearest mountain and tumbled heels over head beside them. Then they saw that he had wound two of their blankets around his body, to keep the bumps from hurting him, and had fastened the blankets with some of the spare straps from the harness of the Sawhorse.

·——·< Chapter 8 >·——·

The MYSTERIOUS CITY

There they sat upon the grass, their heads still swimming from their dizzy flights, and looked at one another in silent bewilderment. But presently, when assured that no one was injured, they grew more calm and collected and the Lion said with a sigh of relief, "Who would have thought those Merry-Go-Round Mountains were made of rubber?"

"Are they really rubber?" asked Trot.

"They must be," replied the Lion, "for otherwise we would not have bounded so swiftly from one to another without getting hurt."

"That is all guesswork," declared the Wizard, unwinding the blankets from his body, "for none of us stayed long enough on the mountains to discover what they are made of. But where are we?"

"That's guesswork, too," said Scraps. "The shepherd said the Thistle-Eaters live this side of the mountains and are waited on by giants."

"Oh, no," said Dorothy, "it's the Herkus who have giant slaves, and the Thistle-Eaters hitch dragons to their chariots."

"How could they do that?" asked the Woozy. "Dragons have long tails, which would get in the way of the chariot wheels."

"And, if the Herkus have conquered the giants," said Trot, "they must be at least twice the size of giants. P'raps the Herkus are the biggest people in all the world!"

"Perhaps they are," assented the Wizard, in a thoughtful tone of voice. "And perhaps the shepherd didn't know what he was talking about. Let us travel on toward the west and discover for ourselves what the people of this country are like."

It seemed a pleasant enough country, and it was quite still and peaceful when they turned their eyes away from the silently whirling mountains. There were trees here and there and green bushes, while throughout the thick grass were scattered brilliantly colored flowers. About a mile away was a low hill that hid from them all the country beyond it, so they realized they could not tell much about the country until they had crossed the hill.

The Red Wagon having been left behind, it was now necessary to make other arrangements for traveling. The Lion told Dorothy she could ride upon his back, as she had often done before, and the Woozy said he could easily carry both Trot and the Patchwork Girl. Betsy still had her mule, Hank, and Button-Bright and the Wizard could sit together upon the long, thin back of the Sawhorse, but they took care to soften their seat with a pad of blankets before they started. Thus mounted, the adventurers started for the hill, which was reached after a brief journey.

As they mounted the crest and gazed beyond the hill they discovered not far away a walled city, from the towers and spires of which gay banners were flying. It was not a very big city, indeed, but its walls were very high and thick and it appeared that the people who lived there must have feared attack by a powerful enemy, else they would not have surrounded their dwellings with so strong a barrier.

There was no path leading from the mountains to the city, and this proved that the people seldom or never visited the whirling hills; but our friends found the grass soft and agreeable to travel over and with the city before them they could not well lose their way. When they drew nearer to the walls, the breeze carried to their ears the sound of music—dim at first but growing louder as they advanced.

"That doesn't seem like a very terr'ble place," remarked Dorothy.

"Well, it *looks* all right," replied Trot, from her seat on the Woozy, "but looks can't always be trusted."

"*My* looks can," said Scraps. "I *look* patchwork, and I *am* patchwork, and no one but a blind owl could ever doubt that I'm the Patchwork Girl." Saying which she turned a somersault off the Woozy and, alighting on her feet, began wildly dancing about.

"Are owls ever blind?" asked Trot.

"Always, in the daytime," said Button-Bright. "But Scraps can see with her button eyes both day and night. Isn't it queer?"

"It's queer that buttons can see at all," answered Trot; "but—good gracious! what's become of the city?"

"I was going to ask that myself," said Dorothy. "It's gone!"

The animals came to a sudden halt, for the city had really disappeared—walls and all—and before them lay the clear, unbroken sweep of the country.

"Dear me!" exclaimed the Wizard. "This is rather disagreeable. It is annoying to travel almost to a place and then find it is not there."

"Where can it be, then?" asked Dorothy. "It cert'nly was there a minute ago."

"I can hear the music yet," declared Button-Bright, and when they all listened the strains of music could plainly be heard.

"Oh! there's the city—over at the left," called Scraps, and turning their eyes they saw the walls and towers and fluttering banners far to the left of them.

"We must have lost our way," suggested Dorothy.

"Nonsense," said the Lion. "I, and all the other animals, have been tramping straight toward the city ever since we first saw it."

"Then how does it happen—"

"Never mind," interrupted the Wizard, "we are no farther from it than we were before. It is in a different direction, that's all; so let us hurry and get there before it again escapes us."

So on they went, directly toward the city, which seemed only a couple of miles distant; but when they had traveled less than a mile it suddenly disappeared again. Once more they paused, somewhat discouraged, but in a moment the button eyes of Scraps again discovered the city, only this time it was just behind them, in the direction from which they had come.

"Goodness gracious!" cried Dorothy. "There's surely something wrong with that city. Do you s'pose it's on wheels, Wizard?"

"It may not be a city at all," he replied, looking toward it with a speculative glance.

"What *could* it be, then?"

"Just an illusion."

"What's that?" asked Trot.

"Something you think you see and don't see."

"I can't believe that," said Button-Bright. "If we only saw it, we might be mistaken, but if we can see it and hear it, too, it must be there."

"Where?" asked the Patchwork Girl.

"Somewhere near us," he insisted.

"We will have to go back, I suppose," said the Woozy, with a sigh.

So back they turned and headed for the walled city until it disappeared again, only to reappear at the right of them. They were constantly getting nearer to it, however, so they kept their faces turned toward it as it flitted here and there to all points of the compass. Presently the Lion, who was leading the procession, halted abruptly and cried out: "Ouch!"

"What's the matter?" asked Dorothy.

"Ouch—ouch!" repeated the Lion, and leaped backward so suddenly that Dorothy nearly tumbled from his back. At the same time Hank the Mule yelled "Ouch!" almost as loudly as the Lion had done, and he also pranced backward a few paces.

"It's the thistles," said Betsy. "They prick their legs."

Hearing this, all looked down, and sure enough the ground was thick with thistles, which covered the plain from the point where they stood way up to the walls of the mysterious city. No pathways through them could be seen at all; here the soft grass ended and the growth of thistles began.

"They're the prickliest thistles I ever felt," grumbled the Lion. "My legs smart yet from their stings, though I jumped out of them as quick as I could."

"Here is a new difficulty," remarked the Wizard in a grieved tone. "The city has stopped hopping around, it is true;

but how are we to get to it, over this mass of prickers?"

"They can't hurt *me*," said the thick-skinned Woozy, advancing fearlessly and trampling among the thistles.

"Nor me," said the Wooden Sawhorse.

"But the Lion and the Mule cannot stand the prickers," asserted Dorothy, "and we can't leave them behind."

"Must we all go back?" asked Trot.

"Course not!" replied Button-Bright scornfully. "Always, when there's trouble, there's a way out of it, if you can find it."

"I wish the Scarecrow was here," said Scraps, standing on her head on the Woozy's square back. "His splendid brains would soon show us how to conquer this field of thistles."

"What's the matter with *your* brains?" asked the boy.

"Nothing," she said, making a flip-flop into the thistles and dancing among them without feeling their sharp points. "I could tell you in half a minute how to get over the thistles if I wanted to."

"Tell us, Scraps!" begged Dorothy.

"I don't want to wear my brains out with overwork," replied the Patchwork Girl.

"Don't you love Ozma? And don't you want to find her?" asked Betsy reproachfully.

"Yes, indeed," said Scraps, walking on her hands as an acrobat does at the circus.

"Well, we can't find Ozma unless we get past these thistles," declared Dorothy.

Scraps danced around them two or three times, without reply. Then she said, "Don't look at me, you stupid folks. Look at those blankets."

The Wizard's face brightened at once.

"Of course!" he exclaimed. "Why didn't we think of those blankets before?"

"Because you haven't magic brains," laughed Scraps. "Such brains as you have are of the common sort that grow in your heads, like weeds in a garden. I'm sorry for you people who have to be born in order to be alive."

But the Wizard was not listening to her. He quickly removed the blankets from the back of the Sawhorse and spread one of them upon the thistles, just next the grass. The thick cloth rendered the prickers harmless, so the Wizard walked over this first blanket and spread the second one farther on, in the direction of the phantom city.

"These blankets," said he, "are for the Lion and the Mule to walk upon. The Sawhorse and the Woozy can walk on the thistles."

So the Lion and the Mule walked over the first blanket and stood upon the second one until the Wizard had picked up the one they had passed over and spread it in front of them, when they advanced to that one and waited while the one behind them was again spread in front.

"This is slow work," said the Wizard, "but it will get us to the city after a while."

"The city is a good half mile away, yet," announced Button-Bright.

"And this is awful hard work for the Wizard," added Trot.

"Why couldn't the Lion ride on the Woozy's back?" asked Dorothy. "It's a big, flat back, and the Woozy's mighty strong. Perhaps the Lion wouldn't fall off."

"You may try it, if you like," said the Woozy to the Lion. "I can take you to the city in a jiffy and then come back for Hank."

"I'm—I'm afraid," said the Cowardly Lion. He was twice as big as the Woozy.

"Try it," pleaded Dorothy.

"And take a tumble among the thistles?" asked the Lion reproachfully. But when the Woozy came close to him the big beast suddenly bounded upon its back and managed to balance himself there, although forced to hold his four legs so close together that he was in danger of toppling over. The great weight of the monster Lion did not seem to affect the Woozy, who called to his rider: "Hold on tight!" and ran swiftly over the thistles toward the city.

The others stood on the blanket and watched the strange sight anxiously. Of course the Lion couldn't "hold on tight" because there was nothing to hold to, and he swayed from side to side as if likely to fall off any moment. Still, he managed to stick to the Woozy's back until they were close to the walls of the city, when he leaped to the ground. Next moment the Woozy came dashing back at full speed.

"There's a little strip of ground next the wall where there are no thistles," he told them, when he had reached the adventurers once more. "Now, then, friend Hank, see if you can ride as well as the Lion did."

"Take the others first," proposed the Mule. So the Sawhorse and the Woozy made a couple of trips over the thistles to the city walls and carried all the people in safety, Dorothy holding little Toto in her arms. The travelers then sat in a group on a little hillock, just outside the wall, and looked at the great blocks of grey stone and waited for the Woozy to bring Hank to them. The Mule was very awkward and his legs trembled so badly that more than once they thought he would tumble off, but finally he reached them in safety and the entire party was now reunited. More than that, they had reached the city that had eluded them for so long and in so strange a manner.

"The gates must be around the other side," said the Wizard. "Let us follow the curve of the wall until we reach an opening in it."

"Which way?" asked Dorothy.

"We must guess at that," he replied. "Suppose we go to the left? One direction is as good as another."

They formed in marching order and went around the city wall to the left. It wasn't a big city, as I have said, but to go way around it, outside the high wall, was quite a walk, as they became aware. But around it our adventurers went, without finding any sign of a gateway or other opening. When they had returned to the little mound from which they had started, they dismounted from the animals and again seated themselves on the grassy mound.

"It's mighty queer, isn't it?" asked Button-Bright.

"There must be *some* way for the people to get out and in," declared Dorothy. "Do you s'pose they have flying machines, Wizard?"

"No," he replied, "for in that case they would be flying all over the Land of Oz, and we know they have not done that. Flying machines are unknown here. I think it more likely that the people use ladders to get over the walls."

"It would be an awful climb over that high stone wall," said Betsy.

"Stone, is it?" cried Scraps, who was again dancing wildly around, for she never tired and could never keep still for long.

"Course it's stone," answered Betsy scornfully. "Can't you see?"

"Yes," said Scraps, going closer. "I can *see* the wall, but I can't *feel* it." And then, with her arms outstretched, she did a very queer thing. She walked right into the wall and disappeared.

"For goodness sake!" cried Dorothy, amazed, as indeed they all were.

Chapter 9

The HIGH COCO-LORUM of THI

And now the Patchwork Girl came dancing out of the wall again.

"Come on!" she called. "It isn't there. There isn't any wall at all."

"What? No wall?" exclaimed the Wizard.

"Nothing like it," said Scraps. "It's a make-believe. You see it, but it isn't. Come on into the city; we've been wasting time."

With this she danced into the wall again and once more disappeared. Button-Bright, who was rather venturesome, dashed away after her and also became invisible to them. The others followed more cautiously, stretching out their hands to feel the wall and finding, to their astonishment, that they could feel nothing because nothing opposed them. They walked on a few steps and found themselves in the streets of a very beautiful city. Behind them they again saw the wall, grim and forbidding as ever; but now they knew it was merely an illusion, prepared to keep strangers from entering the city.

But the wall was soon forgotten, for in front of them were a number of quaint people who stared at them in amazement, as if wondering where they had come from. Our friends forgot their good manners, for a time, and returned the stares with interest, for so remarkable a people had never before been discovered in all the remarkable Land of Oz.

Their heads were shaped like diamonds and their bodies like hearts. All the hair they had was a little bunch at the tip top of their diamond-shaped heads and their eyes were very large and round and their noses and mouths very small. Their clothing was tight-fitting and of brilliant colors, being handsomely embroidered in quaint designs with gold or silver threads; but on their feet they wore sandals with no stockings whatever. The expression of their faces was pleasant enough, although they now showed surprise at the appearance of strangers so unlike themselves, and our friends thought they seemed quite harmless.

"I beg your pardon," said the Wizard, speaking for his party, "for intruding upon you uninvited, but we are traveling on important business and find it necessary to visit your city.

Will you kindly tell us by what name your city is called?"

They looked at one another uncertainly, each expecting some other to answer. Finally, a short one whose heart-shaped body was very broad replied, "We have no occasion to call our city anything. It is where we live, that is all."

"But by what name do others call your city?" asked the Wizard.

"We know of no others, except yourselves," said the man. And then he inquired, "Were you born with those queer forms you have, or has some cruel magician transformed you to them from your natural shapes?"

"These are our natural shapes," declared the Wizard, "and we consider them very good shapes, too."

The group of inhabitants was constantly being enlarged by others who joined it. All were evidently startled and uneasy at the arrival of strangers.

"Have you a King?" asked Dorothy, who knew it was better to speak with someone in authority. But the man shook his diamond-like head.

"What is a King?" he asked.

"Isn't there anyone who rules over you?" inquired the Wizard.

"No," was the reply, "each of us rules himself; or, at least tries to do so. It is not an easy thing to do, as you probably know."

The Wizard reflected.

"If you have disputes among you," said he after a little thought, "who settles them?"

"The High Coco-Lorum," they answered in a chorus.

"And who is he?"

"The judge who enforces the Laws," said the man who had first spoken.

"Then he is the principal person here?" continued the Wizard.

"Well, I would not say that," returned the man in a puzzled way. "The High Coco-Lorum is a public servant. However, he represents the Laws, which we must all obey."

"I think," said the Wizard, "we ought to see your High Coco-Lorum and talk with him. Our mission here requires us to consult one high in authority, and the High Coco-Lorum ought to be high, whatever else he is."

The inhabitants seemed to consider this proposition reasonable, for they nodded their diamond-shaped heads in approval. So the broad one who had been their spokesman said: "Follow me," and, turning, led the way along one of the streets.

The entire party followed him, the natives falling in behind. The dwellings they passed were quite nicely planned and seemed comfortable and convenient. After leading them a few blocks their conductor stopped before a house which was neither better nor worse than the others. The doorway was shaped to admit the strangely formed bodies of these people, being narrow at the top, broad in the middle and tapering at the bottom. The windows were made in much the same way, giving the house a most peculiar appearance. When their guide opened the gate a music-box concealed in the gatepost began to play, and the sound attracted the attention of the High Coco-Lorum, who appeared at an open window and inquired, "What has happened now?"

But in the same moment his eyes fell upon the strangers and he hastened to open the door and admit them—all but the animals, which were left outside with the throng of natives that had now gathered. For a small city there seemed to be a large number of inhabitants, but they did not try to enter the house and contented themselves with staring curiously at the strange animals. Toto followed Dorothy.

Our friends entered a large room at the front of the house, where the High Coco-Lorum asked them to be seated.

"I hope your mission here is a peaceful one," he said, looking a little worried, "for the Thists are not very good fighters and object to being conquered."

"Are your people called Thists?" asked Dorothy.

"Yes. I thought you knew that. And we call our city Thi."

"Oh!"

"We are Thists because we eat thistles, you know," continued the High Coco-Lorum.

"Do you really eat those prickly things?" inquired Button-Bright wonderingly.

"Why not?" replied the other. "The sharp points of the thistles cannot hurt us, because all our insides are gold-lined."

"Gold-lined!"

"To be sure. Our throats and stomachs are lined with solid gold, and we find the thistles nourishing and good to eat. As a matter of fact, there is nothing else in our country that is fit for food. All around the City of Thi grow countless thistles, and all we need do is to go and gather them. If we wanted anything else to eat, we would have to plant it, and grow it, and harvest it, and that would be a lot of trouble and make us work, which is an occupation we detest."

"But tell me, please," said the Wizard, "how does it happen that your city jumps around so, from one part of the country to another?"

"The city doesn't jump; it doesn't move at all," declared the High Coco-Lorum. "However, I will admit that the land that surrounds it has a trick of turning this way or that; and so, if one is standing upon the plain and facing north, he is likely to find himself suddenly facing west—or east—or south. But once you reach the thistle fields you are on solid ground."

"Ah, I begin to understand," said the Wizard, nodding his head. "But I have another question to ask: How does it happen that the Thists have no King to rule over them?"

"Hush!" whispered the High Coco-Lorum, looking uneasily around to make sure they were not overheard. "In reality, I am the King, but the people don't know it. They think they rule themselves, but the fact is I have everything my own way. No one else knows anything about our Laws, and so I make the Laws to suit myself. If any oppose me, or question my acts, I tell them it's the Law and that settles it. If I called myself King, however, and wore a crown and lived in royal style, the people would not like me, and might do me harm. As the High Coco-Lorum of Thi, I am considered a very agreeable person."

"It seems a very clever arrangement," said the Wizard. "And now, as you are the principal person in Thi, I beg you to tell us if the Royal Ozma is a captive in your city."

"No," answered the diamond-headed man, "we have no captives. No strangers but yourselves are here, and we have never before heard of the Royal Ozma."

"She rules over all of Oz," said Dorothy, "and so she rules your city and you, because you are in the Winkie Country, which is a part of the Land of Oz."

"It may be," returned the High Coco-Lorum, "for we do not study geography and have never inquired whether we live in the Land of Oz or not. And any Ruler who rules us from a distance and unknown to us is welcome to the job. But what has happened to your Royal Ozma?"

"Someone has stolen her," said the Wizard. "Do you happen to have any talented magician among your people—one who is especially clever, you know?"

"No, none especially clever. We do some magic, of course, but it is all of the ordinary kind. I do not think any of us has yet aspired to stealing Rulers, either by magic or otherwise."

"Then we've come a long way for nothing!" exclaimed Trot regretfully.

"But we are going farther than this," asserted the Patchwork Girl, bending her stuffed body backward until her yarn hair touched the floor and then walking around on her hands with her feet in the air.

The High Coco-Lorum watched Scraps admiringly.

"You may go farther on, of course," said he, "but I advise you not to. The Herkus live back of us, beyond the thistles and the twisting lands, and they are not very nice people to meet, I assure you."

"Are they giants?" asked Betsy.

"They are worse than that," was the reply. "They have giants for their slaves and they are so much stronger than giants that the poor slaves dare not rebel, for fear of being torn to pieces."

"How do you know?" asked Scraps.

"Everyone says so," answered the High Coco-Lorum.

"Have you seen the Herkus yourself?" inquired Dorothy.

"No, but what everyone says must be true; otherwise, what would be the use of their saying it?"

"We were told, before we got here, that you people hitch dragons to your chariots," said the little girl.

"So we do," declared the High Coco-Lorum. "And that reminds me that I ought to entertain you, as strangers and my guests, by taking you for a ride around our splendid City of Thi."

He touched a button and a band began to play. At least, they heard the music of a band, but couldn't tell where it came from.

"That tune is the order to my charioteer to bring around my dragon-chariot," said the High Coco-Lorum. "Every time I give an order it is in music, which is a much more pleasant way to address servants than in cold, stern words."

"Does this dragon of yours bite?" asked Button-Bright.

"Mercy no! Do you think I'd risk the safety of my innocent people by using a biting dragon to draw my chariot? I'm proud to say that my dragon is harmless—unless his steering gear breaks—and he was manufactured at the famous dragon-factory in this City of Thi. Here he comes and you may examine him for yourselves."

They heard a low rumble and a shrill squeaking sound and, going out to the front of the house, they saw coming around the corner a car drawn by a gorgeous jeweled dragon, which moved its head to right and left and flashed its eyes like headlights of an automobile and uttered a growling noise as it slowly moved toward them.

When it stopped before the High Coco-Lorum's house, Toto barked sharply at the sprawling beast, but even tiny Trot could see that the dragon was not alive. Its scales were of gold and each one was set with sparkling jewels, while it walked in such a stiff, regular manner that it could be nothing else than a machine. The chariot that trailed behind it was likewise of gold and jewels, and when they entered it they found there were no seats. Everyone was supposed to stand up while riding.

The charioteer was a little diamond-headed fellow who straddled the neck of the dragon and moved the levers that made it go.

"This," said the High Coco-Lorum, pompously, "is a wonderful invention. We are all very proud of our auto-dragons, many of which are in use by our wealthy inhabitants. Start the thing going, charioteer!"

The charioteer did not move.

"You forgot to order him in music," suggested Dorothy.

"Ah, so I did." He touched a button and a music-box in the dragon's head began to play a tune. At once the little charioteer pulled over a lever and the dragon began to move—very slowly and groaning dismally as it drew the clumsy chariot after it. Toto trotted between the wheels. The Sawhorse, the Mule, the Lion and the Woozy followed after and had no trouble in keeping up with the machine; indeed, they had to go slow to keep from running into it. When the wheels turned, another music-box concealed somewhere under the chariot played a lively march tune which was in striking contrast with the dragging movement of the strange vehicle, and Button-Bright decided that the music he had heard when they first sighted this city was nothing else than a chariot plodding its weary way through the streets.

All the travelers from the Emerald City thought this ride the most uninteresting and dreary they had ever experienced, but the High Coco-Lorum seemed to think it was grand. He pointed out the different buildings and parks and fountains, in much the same way that the conductor of an American "sightseeing wagon" does, and being guests they were obliged to submit to the ordeal. But they became a little worried when their host told them he had ordered a banquet prepared for them in the City Hall.

"What are we going to eat?" asked Button-Bright suspiciously.

"Thistles," was the reply. "Fine, fresh thistles, gathered this very day."

Scraps laughed, for she never ate anything, but Dorothy said in a protesting voice, "*Our* insides are not lined with gold, you know."

"How sad!" exclaimed the High Coco-Lorum; and then he added, as an afterthought, "But we can have the thistles boiled, if you prefer."

"I'm 'fraid they wouldn't taste good, even then," said little Trot. "Haven't you anything else to eat?"

The High Coco-Lorum shook his diamond-shaped head.

"Nothing that I know of," said he. "But why should we have anything else, when we have so many thistles? However, if you can't eat what we eat, don't eat anything. We shall not be offended and the banquet will be just as merry and delightful."

Knowing his companions were all hungry, the Wizard said, "I trust you will excuse us from the banquet, sir, which will be merry enough without us, although it is given in our honor. For, as Ozma is not in your city, we must leave here at once and seek her elsewhere."

"Sure we must!" agreed Dorothy, and she whispered to Betsy and Trot: "I'd rather starve somewhere else than in this city, and—who knows?—we may run across somebody who eats reg'lar food and will give us some."

So, when the ride was finished, in spite of the protests of the High Coco-Lorum they insisted on continuing their journey.

"It will soon be dark," he objected.

"We don't mind the darkness," replied the Wizard.

"Some wandering Herku may get you."

"Do you think the Herkus would hurt us?" asked Dorothy.

"I cannot say, not having had the honor of their acquaintance. But they are said to be so strong that, if they had any other place to stand upon, they could lift the world."

"All of them together?" asked Button-Bright wonderingly.

"Any one of them could do it," said the High Coco-Lorum.

"Have you heard of any magicians being among them?" asked the Wizard, knowing that only a magician could have stolen Ozma in the way she had been stolen.

"I am told it is quite a magical country," declared the High Coco-Lorum, "and magic is usually performed by magicians.

But I have never heard that they have any invention or sorcery to equal our wonderful auto-dragons."

They thanked him for his courtesy and, mounting their own animals, rode to the farther side of the city and right through the Wall of Illusion out into the open country.

"I'm glad we got away so easily," said Betsy. "I didn't like those queer-shaped people."

"Nor did I," agreed Dorothy. "It seems dreadful to be lined with sheets of pure gold and have nothing to eat but thistles."

"They seemed happy and contented, though," remarked the little Wizard, "and those who are contented have nothing to regret and nothing more to wish for."

Chapter 10

TOTO LOSES SOMETHING

For a while the travelers were constantly losing their direction, for beyond the thistle fields they again found themselves upon the turning-lands, which swung them around one way and then another. But by keeping the City of Thi constantly behind them the adventurers finally passed the treacherous turning-lands and came upon a stony country where no grass grew at all. There were plenty of bushes, however, and although it was now almost dark the girls discovered some delicious yellow berries growing upon the bushes, one taste of which set them all to picking as many as they could find. The berries relieved their pangs of hunger, for a time, and as it now became too dark to see anything they camped where they were.

The three girls lay down upon one of the blankets—all in a row—and then the Wizard covered them with the other blanket and tucked them in. Button-Bright crawled under the shelter of some bushes and was asleep in half a minute. The Wizard sat down with his back to a big stone and looked at the stars in the sky and thought gravely upon the dangerous adventure they had undertaken, wondering if they would ever be able to find their beloved Ozma again. The animals lay in a group by themselves, a little distance from the others.

"I've lost my growl!" said Toto, who had been very silent and sober all that day. "What do you suppose has become of it?"

"If you had asked me to keep track of your growl, I might be able to tell you," remarked the Lion sleepily. "But frankly, Toto, I supposed you were taking care of it yourself."

"It's an awful thing to lose one's growl," said Toto, wagging his tail disconsolately. "What if you lost your roar, Lion? Wouldn't you feel terrible?"

"My roar," replied the Lion, "is the fiercest thing about me. I depend on it to frighten my enemies so badly that they won't dare to fight me."

"Once," said the Mule, "I lost my bray, so that I couldn't call to Betsy to let her know I was hungry. That was before I could talk, you know, for I had not yet come into the Land of Oz, and I found it was certainly very uncomfortable not to be able to make a noise."

"You make enough noise now," declared Toto. "But none of you have answered my question: Where is my growl?"

"You may search *me*," said the Woozy. "I don't care for such things, myself."

"You snore terribly," asserted Toto.

"It may be," said the Woozy. "What one does when asleep one is not accountable for. I wish you would wake me up, sometime when I'm snoring, and let me hear the sound. Then I can judge whether it is terrible or delightful."

"It isn't pleasant, I assure you," said the Lion, yawning.

"To me it seems wholly unnecessary," declared Hank the Mule.

"You ought to break yourself of the habit," said the Sawhorse. "You never hear me snore, because I never sleep. I don't even whinny as those puffy meat horses do. I wish that whoever stole Toto's growl had taken the Mule's bray and the Lion's roar and the Woozy's snore at the same time."

"Do you think, then, that my growl was stolen?"

"You have never lost it before, have you?" inquired the Sawhorse.

"Only once, when I had a sore throat from barking too long at the moon."

"Is your throat sore now?" asked the Woozy.

"No," replied the dog.

"I can't understand," said Hank, "why dogs bark at the moon. They can't scare the moon, and the moon doesn't pay any attention to the bark. So why do dogs do it?"

"Were you ever a dog?" asked Toto.

"No indeed," replied Hank. "I am thankful to say I was created a mule—the most beautiful of all beasts—and have always remained one."

The Woozy sat upon his square haunches to examine Hank with care.

"Beauty," he said, "must be a matter of taste. I don't say your judgment is bad, friend Hank, or that you are so vulgar as to be conceited. But if you admire big waggly ears and a tail like a paint-brush, and hoofs big enough for an elephant, and a long neck and a body so skinny that one can count the ribs with one eye shut—if that's your idea of beauty, Hank—then either you or I must be much mistaken."

"You're full of edges," sneered the Mule. "If I were square, as you are, I suppose you'd think me lovely."

"Outwardly, dear Hank, I would," replied the Woozy. "But to be really lovely one must be beautiful without and within."

The Mule couldn't deny this statement, so he gave a disgusted grunt and rolled over so that his back was toward the Woozy. But the Lion, regarding the two calmly with his great yellow eyes, said to the dog, "My dear Toto, our friends have taught us a lesson in humility. If the Woozy and the Mule are indeed beautiful creatures, as they seem to think, you and I must be decidedly ugly."

"Not to ourselves," protested Toto, who was a shrewd little

dog. "You and I, Lion, are fine specimens of our own races. I am a fine dog, and you are a fine lion. Only in point of comparison, one with another, can we be properly judged, so I will leave it to the poor old Sawhorse to decide which is the most beautiful animal among us all. The Sawhorse is wood, so he won't be prejudiced and will speak the truth."

"I surely will," responded the Sawhorse, wagging his ears, which were chips set in his wooden head. "Are you all agreed to accept my judgment?"

"We are!" they declared, each one hopeful.

"Then," said the Sawhorse, "I must point out to you the fact that you are all meat creatures, who tire unless they sleep, and starve unless they eat, and suffer from thirst unless they drink. Such animals must be very imperfect, and imperfect creatures cannot be beautiful. Now, *I* am made of wood."

"You surely have a wooden head," said the Mule.

"Yes, and a wooden body and wooden legs—which are as swift as the wind and as tireless. I've heard Dorothy say that 'handsome is as handsome does,' and I surely perform my duties in a handsome manner. Therefore, if you wish my honest judgment, I will confess that among us all I am the most beautiful."

The Mule snorted and the Woozy laughed; Toto had lost his growl and could only look scornfully at the Sawhorse, who stood in his place unmoved. But the Lion stretched himself and yawned, saying quietly, "Were we all like the Sawhorse, we would all be Sawhorses, which would be too many of the kind; were we all like Hank, we would be a herd of mules; if like Toto, we would be a pack of dogs; should we all become the shape of the Woozy, he would no longer be remarkable for his unusual appearance. Finally, were you all like me, I would consider you so common that I would not care to associate with you. To be individual, my friends, to be different from others, is the only way to become distinguished from the common herd. Let us be glad, therefore, that we differ from one another in form and in disposition. Variety is the spice of life and we are various enough to enjoy one another's society; so let us be content."

"There is some truth in that speech," remarked Toto reflectively. "But how about my lost growl?"

"The growl is of importance only to you," responded the Lion, "so it is your business to worry over the loss, not ours. If you love us, do not afflict your burdens on us; be unhappy all by yourself."

"If the same person stole my growl who stole Ozma," said the little dog, "I hope we shall find him very soon and punish him as he deserves. He must be the most cruel person in all the world, for to prevent a dog from growling when it is his nature to growl is just as wicked, in my opinion, as stealing all the magic in Oz."

Chapter 11

BUTTON-BRIGHT LOSES HIMSELF

The Patchwork Girl, who never slept and who could see very well in the dark, had wandered among the rocks and bushes all night long, with the result that she was able to tell some good news the next morning.

"Over the crest of the hill before us," she said, "is a big grove of trees of many kinds on which all sorts of fruits grow. If you will go there you will find a nice breakfast awaiting you."

This made them eager to start, so as soon as the blankets were folded and strapped to the back of the Sawhorse, they all took their places on the animals and set out for the big grove Scraps had told them of.

As soon as they got over the brow of the hill they discovered it to be a really immense orchard, extending for miles to the right and left of them. As their way led straight through the trees they hurried forward as fast as possible.

The first trees they came to bore quinces, which they did not like. Then there were rows of citron trees and then crab apples and afterward limes and lemons. But beyond these they found a grove of big golden oranges, juicy and sweet, and the fruit hung low on the branches, so they could pluck it easily.

They helped themselves freely and all ate oranges as they continued on their way. Then, a little farther along, they came to some trees bearing fine red apples, which they also feasted on, and the Wizard stopped here long enough to tie a lot of the apples in one end of a blanket.

"We do not know what will happen to us after we leave this delightful orchard," he said, "so I think it wise to carry a supply of apples with us. We can't starve as long as we have apples, you know."

Scraps wasn't riding the Woozy just now. She loved to climb the trees and swing herself by the branches from one tree to another. Some of the choicest fruit was gathered by the Patchwork Girl from the very highest limbs and tossed down to the others.

Suddenly Trot asked: "Where's Button-Bright?" and when

the others looked for him they found the boy had disappeared.

"Dear me!" cried Dorothy. "I guess he's lost again, and that will mean our waiting here until we can find him."

"It's a good place to wait," suggested Betsy, who had found a plum tree and was eating some of its fruit.

"How can you wait here, and find Button-Bright, at one and the same time?" inquired the Patchwork Girl, hanging by her toes on a limb just over the heads of the three mortal girls.

"Perhaps he'll come back here," answered Dorothy.

"If he tries that, he'll prob'ly lose his way," said Trot. "I've known him to do that lots of times. It's losing his way that gets him lost."

"Very true," said the Wizard. "So all the rest of you must stay here while I go look for the boy."

"Won't *you* get lost, too?" asked Betsy.

"I hope not, my dear."

"Let *me* go," said Scraps, dropping lightly to the ground. "I can't get lost, and I'm more likely to find Button-Bright than any of you."

Without waiting for permission she darted away through the trees and soon disappeared from their view.

"Dorothy," said Toto, squatting beside his little mistress, "I've lost my growl."

"How did that happen?" she asked.

"I don't know," replied Toto. "Yesterday morning the

Woozy nearly stepped on me and I tried to growl at him and found I couldn't growl a bit."

"Can you bark?" inquired Dorothy.

"Oh, yes, indeed!"

"Then never mind the growl," said she.

"But what will I do when I get home to the Glass Cat and the Pink Kitten?" asked the little dog in an anxious tone.

"They won't mind, if you can't growl at them, I'm sure," said Dorothy. "I'm sorry for you, of course, Toto, for it's just those things we can't do that we want to do most of all; but before we get back, you may find your growl again."

"Do you think the person who stole Ozma stole my growl?"

Dorothy smiled.

"Perhaps, Toto."

"Then he's a scoundrel!" cried the little dog.

"Anyone who would steal Ozma is as bad as bad can be," agreed Dorothy, "and when we remember that our dear friend, the lovely Ruler of Oz, is lost, we ought not to worry over just a growl."

Toto was not entirely satisfied with this remark, for the more he thought upon his lost growl the more important his misfortune became. When no one was looking he went away among the trees and tried his best to growl—even a little bit—but could not manage to do so. All he could do was bark, and a bark cannot take the place of a growl, so he sadly returned to the others.

Now, Button-Bright had no idea that he was lost at first. He had merely wandered from tree to tree, seeking the finest fruit, until he discovered he was alone in the great orchard. But that didn't worry him just then and seeing some apricot trees farther on he went to them; then he discovered some cherry trees; just beyond these were some tangerines.

"We've found 'most ev'ry kind of fruit but peaches," he said to himself, "so I guess there are peaches here, too, if I can find the trees."

He searched here and there, paying no attention to his way, until he found that the trees surrounding him bore only nuts. He put some walnuts in his pockets and kept on searching and at last—right among the nut trees—he came upon one solitary peach tree. It was a graceful, beautiful tree, but although it was thickly leaved it bore no fruit except one large, splendid peach, rosy-cheeked and fuzzy and just right to eat.

Button-Bright had some trouble getting that lonesome peach, for it hung far out of reach; but he climbed the tree nimbly and crept out on the branch on which it grew and after several trials, during which he was in danger of falling, he finally managed to pick it. Then he got back to the ground and decided the fruit was well worth his trouble. It was delightfully fragrant and when he bit into it he found it the most delicious morsel he had ever tasted.

"I really ought to divide it with Trot and Dorothy and

Betsy," he said; "but p'rhaps there are plenty more in some other part of the orchard."

In his heart he doubted this statement, for this was a solitary peach tree, while all the other fruits grew upon many trees set close to one another; but that one luscious bite made him unable to resist eating the rest of it and soon the peach was all gone except the pit.

Button-Bright was about to throw this peach-pit away when he noticed that it was of pure gold. Of course this surprised him, but so many things in the Land of Oz were surprising that he did not give much thought to the golden peach-pit. He put it in his pocket, however, to show to the girls, and five minutes afterward had forgotten all about it.

For now he realized that he was far separated from his companions, and knowing that this would worry them and delay their journey, he began to shout as loud as he could. His voice did not penetrate very far among all those trees, and after shouting a dozen times and getting no answer, he sat down on the ground and said, "Well, I'm lost again. It's too bad, but I don't see how it can be helped."

As he leaned his back against a tree he looked up and saw a Bluefinch fly down from the sky and alight upon a branch just before him. The bird looked and looked at him. First it looked with one bright eye and then turned its head and looked at him with the other eye. Then, fluttering its wings a little, it said, "Oho! So you've eaten the enchanted peach, have you?"

"Was it enchanted?" asked Button-Bright.

"Of course," replied the Bluefinch. "Ugu the Shoemaker did that."

"But why? And how was it enchanted? And what will happen to one who eats it?" questioned the boy.

"Ask Ugu the Shoemaker; he knows," said the bird, preening its feathers with its bill.

"And who is Ugu the Shoemaker?"

"The one who enchanted the peach, and placed it here—in the exact center of the Great Orchard—so no one would ever find it. We birds didn't dare to eat it; we are too wise for that. But you are Button-Bright, from the Emerald City, and you—*you*—YOU ate the enchanted peach! You must explain to Ugu the Shoemaker why you did that."

And then, before the boy could ask any more questions, the bird flew away and left him alone.

Button-Bright was not much worried to find that the peach he had eaten was enchanted. It certainly had tasted very good, and his stomach didn't ache a bit. So again he began to reflect upon the best way to rejoin his friends.

"Whichever direction I follow is likely to be the wrong one," he said to himself, "so I'd better stay just where I am and let *them* find *me*—if they can."

A White Rabbit came hopping through the orchard and paused a little way off to look at him.

"Don't be afraid," said Button-Bright. "I won't hurt you."

"Oh, I'm not afraid for myself," returned the White Rabbit. "It's you I'm worried about."

"Yes; I'm lost," said the boy.

"I fear you are, indeed," answered the Rabbit. "Why on earth did you eat the enchanted peach?"

The boy looked at the excited little animal thoughtfully.

"There were two reasons," he explained. "One reason was that I like peaches, and the other reason was that I didn't know it was enchanted."

"That won't save you from Ugu the Shoemaker," declared the White Rabbit, and it scurried away before the boy could ask any more questions.

"Rabbits and birds," he thought, "are timid creatures and seem afraid of this shoemaker—whoever he may be. If there was another peach half as good as that other, I'd eat it in spite of a dozen enchantments or a hundred shoemakers!"

Just then Scraps came dancing along and saw him sitting at the foot of the tree.

"Oh, here you are!" she said. "Up to your old tricks, eh? Don't you know it's impolite to get lost and keep everybody waiting for you? Come along, and I'll lead you back to Dorothy and the others."

Button-Bright rose slowly to accompany her.

"That wasn't much of a loss," he said cheerfully. "I haven't been gone half a day, so there's no harm done."

Dorothy, however, when the boy rejoined the party, gave him a good scolding.

"When we're doing such an important thing as searching for Ozma," said she, "it's naughty for you to wander away and keep us from getting on. S'pose she's a pris'ner—in a dungeon cell!—do you want to keep our dear Ozma there any longer than we can help?"

"If she's in a dungeon cell, how are you going to get her out?" inquired the boy.

"Never you mind; we'll leave that to the Wizard; he's sure to find a way."

The Wizard said nothing, for he realized that without his magic tools he could do no more than any other person. But there was no use reminding his companions of that fact; it might discourage them.

"The important thing just now," he remarked, "is to find Ozma; and, as our party is again happily reunited, I propose we move on."

As they came to the edge of the Great Orchard the sun was setting and they knew it would soon be dark. So it was decided to camp under the trees, as another broad plain was before them. The Wizard spread the blankets on a bed of soft leaves and presently all of them except Scraps and the Sawhorse were fast asleep. Toto snuggled close to his friend the Lion, and the Woozy snored so loudly that the Patchwork Girl covered his square head with her apron to deaden the sound.

Chapter 12

The CZAROVER of HERKU

Trot wakened just as the sun rose and, slipping out of the blankets, went to the edge of the Great Orchard and looked across the plain. Something glittered in the far distance.

"That looks like another city," she said half aloud.

"And another city it is," declared Scraps, who had crept to Trot's side unheard, for her stuffed feet made no sound. "The Sawhorse and I made a journey in the dark, while you were all asleep, and we found over there a bigger city than Thi. There's a wall around it, too, but it has gates and plenty of pathways."

"Did you get in?" asked Trot.

"No, for the gates were locked and the wall was a real wall.

So we came back here again. It isn't far to the city. We can reach it in two hours after you've had your breakfasts."

Trot went back and, finding the other girls now awake, told them what Scraps had said. So they hurriedly ate some fruit—there were plenty of plums and fijoas in this part of the orchard—and then they mounted the animals and set out upon the journey to the strange city. Hank the Mule had breakfasted on grass and the Lion had stolen away and found a breakfast to his liking; he never told what it was, but Dorothy hoped the little rabbits and the field mice had kept out of his way. She warned Toto not to chase birds and gave the dog some apple, with which he was quite content. The Woozy was as fond of fruit as of any other food, except honey, and the Sawhorse never ate at all.

Except for their worry over Ozma they were all in good spirits as they proceeded swiftly over the plain. Toto still worried over his lost growl, but like a wise little dog kept his worry to himself. Before long the city grew nearer and they could examine it with interest.

In outward appearance the place was more imposing than Thi, and it was a square city, with a square, four-sided wall around it and on each side was a square gate of burnished copper. Everything about the city looked solid and substantial; there were no banners flying, and the towers that rose above the city wall seemed bare of any ornament whatever.

A path led from the fruit orchard directly to one of the city gates, showing that the inhabitants preferred fruit to thistles. Our friends followed this path to the gate, which they found fast shut. But the Wizard advanced and pounded upon it with his fist, saying in a loud voice: "Open!"

At once there rose above the great wall a row of immense heads, all of which looked down at them as if to see who was intruding. The size of these heads was astonishing and our friends at once realized that they belonged to giants, who were standing within the city. All had thick, bushy hair and whiskers, on some the hair being white and on others black or red or yellow, while the hair of a few was just turning grey, showing that the giants were of all ages. However fierce the heads might seem the eyes were mild in expression, as if the creatures had been long subdued, and their faces expressed patience rather than ferocity.

"What's wanted?" asked one old giant in a low, grumbling voice.

"We are strangers and we wish to enter the city," replied the Wizard.

"Do you come in war or peace?" asked another.

"In peace, of course," retorted the Wizard, and he added impatiently: "Do we look like an army of conquest?"

"No," said the first giant who had spoken, "you look like innocent tramps; but you never can tell by appearances. Wait here until we report to our masters. No one can enter here without the permission of Vig, the Czarover."

"Who's that?" inquired Dorothy. But the heads had all bobbed down and disappeared behind the wall, so there was no answer.

They waited a long time before the gate rolled back with a rumbling sound and a loud voice cried: "Enter!" But they lost no time in taking advantage of the invitation.

On either side of the broad street that led into the city from the gate stood a row of huge giants—twenty of them on a side and all standing so close together that their elbows touched. They wore uniforms of blue and yellow and were armed with clubs as big around as tree-trunks. Each giant had around his neck a broad band of gold, riveted on, to show he was a slave.

As our friends entered, riding upon the Lion, the Woozy, the Sawhorse and the Mule, the giants half turned and walked in two files on either side of them, as if escorting them on their way. It looked to Dorothy as if all her party had been made prisoners, for even mounted on their animals their heads scarcely reached to the knees of the marching giants. The girls and Button-Bright were anxious to know what sort of a city they had entered, and what the people were like who had made these powerful creatures their slaves. Through the legs of the giants, as they walked, Dorothy could see rows of houses on each side of the street and throngs of people standing on the sidewalks; but the people were of ordinary size and the only remarkable thing about them was the fact that they were dreadfully lean and thin. Between their skin and their bones there seemed to be little or no flesh, and they were mostly stoop-shouldered and weary looking, even to the little children.

More and more Dorothy wondered how and why the great giants had ever submitted to become slaves of such skinny, languid masters, but there was no chance to question anyone until they arrived at a big palace located in the heart of the city. Here the giants formed lines to the entrance and stood still while our friends rode into the courtyard of the palace. Then the gates closed behind them, and before them was a skinny little man who bowed low and said in a sad voice, "If you will be so obliging as to dismount, it will give me pleasure to lead you into the presence of the World's Most Mighty Ruler, Vig the Czarover."

"I don't believe it!" said Dorothy indignantly.

"What don't you believe?" asked the man.

"I don't believe your Czarover can hold a candle to our Ozma."

"He wouldn't hold a candle under any circumstances, or to any living person," replied the man very seriously, "for he has slaves to do such things and the Mighty Vig is too dignified to do anything that others can do for him. He even obliges a slave to sneeze for him, if ever he catches cold. However, if you dare to face our powerful Ruler, follow me."

"We dare anything," said the Wizard, "so go ahead."

Through several marble corridors having lofty ceilings

they passed, finding each corridor and doorway guarded by servants; but these servants of the palace were of the people and not giants, and they were so thin that they almost resembled skeletons. Finally they entered a great circular room with a high domed ceiling where the Czarover sat on a throne cut from a solid block of white marble and decorated with purple silk hangings and gold tassels.

The Ruler of these people was combing his eyebrows when our friends entered the throne-room and stood before him, but he put the comb in his pocket and examined the strangers with evident curiosity. Then he said, "Dear me, what a surprise! You have really shocked me. For no outsider has ever before come to our City of Herku, and I cannot imagine why *you* have ventured to do so."

"We are looking for Ozma, the Supreme Ruler of the Land of Oz," replied the Wizard.

"Do you see her anywhere around here?" asked the Czarover.

"Not yet, your Majesty; but perhaps you may tell us where she is."

"No; I have my hands full keeping track of my own people. I find them hard to manage because they are so tremendously strong."

"They don't look very strong," said Dorothy. "It seems as if a good wind would blow 'em way out of the city, if it wasn't for the wall."

"Just so—just so," admitted the Czarover. "They really look that way, don't they? But you must never trust to appearances, which have a way of fooling one. Perhaps you noticed that I prevented you from meeting any of my people. I protected you with my giants while you were on the way from the gates to my palace, so that not a Herku got near you."

"Are your people so dangerous, then?" asked the Wizard.

"To strangers, yes; but only because they are so friendly. For, if they shake hands with you, they are likely to break your arms or crush your fingers to a jelly."

"Why?" asked Button-Bright.

"Because we are the strongest people in all the world."

"Pshaw!" exclaimed the boy; "that's bragging. You prob'ly don't know how strong other people are. Why, once I knew a man in Philadelphi' who could bend iron bars with just his hands!"

"But—mercy me!—it's no trick to bend iron bars," said his Majesty. "Tell me, could this man crush a block of stone with his bare hands?"

"No one could do that," declared the boy.

"If I had a block of stone I'd show you," said the Czarover, looking around the room. "Ah, here is my throne. The back is too high, anyhow, so I'll just break off a piece of that."

He rose to his feet and tottered in an uncertain way around the throne. Then he took hold of the back and broke off a piece of marble over a foot thick.

"This," said he, coming back to his seat, "is very solid marble and much harder than ordinary stone. Yet I can crumble it easily with my fingers—a proof that I am very strong."

Even as he spoke he began breaking off chunks of marble and crumbling them as one would a bit of earth. The Wizard was so astonished that he took a piece in his own hands and tested it, finding it very hard indeed.

Just then one of the giant servants entered and exclaimed, "Oh, your Majesty, the cook has burned the soup! What shall we do?"

"How dare you interrupt me?" asked the Czarover, and grasping the immense giant by one of his legs he raised him in the air and threw him headfirst out of an open window.

"Now, tell me," he said, turning to Button-Bright, "could your man in Philadelphia crumble marble in his fingers?"

"I guess not," said Button-Bright, much impressed by the skinny monarch's strength.

"What makes you so strong?" inquired Dorothy.

"It's the zosozo," he explained, "which is an invention of my own. I and all my people eat zosozo, and it gives us tremendous strength. Would you like to eat some?"

"No, thank you," replied the girl. "I—I don't want to get so thin."

"Well, of course one can't have strength and flesh at the same time," said the Czarover. "Zosozo is pure energy, and it's the only compound of its sort in existence. I never allow our giants to have it, you know, or they would soon become our masters, since they are bigger that we; so I keep all the stuff locked up in my private laboratory. Once a year I feed a teaspoonful of it to each of my people—men, women and children—so every one of them is nearly as strong as I am. Wouldn't *you* like a dose, sir?" he asked, turning to the Wizard.

"Well," said the Wizard, "if you would give me a little zosozo in a bottle, I'd like to take it with me on my travels. It might come in handy, on occasion."

"To be sure. I'll give you enough for six doses," promised the Czarover. "But don't take more than a teaspoonful at a time. Once Ugu the Shoemaker took two teaspoonsful, and it made him so strong that when he leaned against the city wall he pushed it over, and we had to build it up again."

"Who is Ugu the Shoemaker?" asked Button-Bright curiously, for he now remembered that the bird and the rabbit had claimed Ugu the Shoemaker had enchanted the peach he had eaten.

"Why, Ugu is a great magician, who used to live here. But he's gone away now," replied the Czarover.

"Where has he gone?" asked the Wizard quickly.

"I am told he lives in a wickerwork castle in the mountains to the west of here. You see, Ugu became such a powerful magician that he didn't care to live in our city any longer, for fear we would discover some of his secrets. So he went to the mountains and built himself a splendid wicker castle, which is so strong that even I and my people could not batter it down, and there he lives all by himself."

"This is good news," declared the Wizard, "for I think this is just the magician we are searching for. But why is he called Ugu the Shoemaker?"

"Once he was a very common citizen here and made shoes for a living," replied the monarch of Herku. "But he was descended from the greatest wizard and sorcerer who ever lived—in this or in any other country—and one day Ugu the Shoemaker discovered all the magical books and recipes of his famous great-grandfather, which had been hidden away in the attic of his house. So he began to study the papers and books and to practice magic, and in time he became so skillful that, as I said, he scorned our city and built a solitary castle for himself."

"Do you think," asked Dorothy anxiously, "that Ugu the Shoemaker would be wicked enough to steal our Ozma of Oz?"

"And the Magic Picture?" asked Trot.

"And the Great Book of Records of Glinda the Good?" asked Betsy.

"And my own magic tools?" asked the Wizard.

"Well," replied the Czarover, "I won't say that Ugu is wicked, exactly, but he is very ambitious to become the most powerful magician in the world, and so I suppose he would not be too proud to steal any magic things that belonged to anybody else—if he could manage to do so."

"But how about Ozma? Why would he wish to steal *her*?" questioned Dorothy.

"Don't ask me, my dear. Ugu doesn't tell me why he does things, I assure you."

"Then we must go and ask him ourselves," declared the little girl.

"I wouldn't do that, if I were you," advised the Czarover, looking first at the three girls and then at the boy and the little Wizard and finally at the stuffed Patchwork Girl. "If Ugu has really stolen your Ozma, he will probably keep her a prisoner, in spite of all your threats or entreaties. And, with all his magical knowledge, he would be a dangerous person to attack. Therefore, if you are wise, you will go home again and find a new Ruler for the Emerald City and the Land of Oz. But perhaps it isn't Ugu the Shoemaker who has stolen your Ozma."

"The only way to settle that question," replied the Wizard, "is to go to Ugu's castle and see if Ozma is there. If she is, we will report the matter to the great Sorceress, Glinda the Good, and I'm pretty sure she will find a way to rescue our darling Ruler from the Shoemaker."

"Well, do as you please," said the Czarover. "But, if you are all transformed into hummingbirds or caterpillars, don't blame me for not warning you."

They stayed the rest of that day in the City of Herku and were fed at the royal table of the Czarover and given sleeping rooms in his palace. The strong monarch treated them very nicely and gave the Wizard a little golden vial of zosozo, to use if ever he or any of his party wished to acquire great strength.

Even at the last the Czarover tried to persuade them not to go near Ugu the Shoemaker, but they were resolved on the venture and the next morning bade the friendly monarch a cordial good-bye and, mounting upon their animals, left the Herkus and the City of Herku and headed for the mountains that lay to the west.

Chapter 13

The TRUTH POND

It seems a long time since we have heard anything of the Frogman and Cayke the Cookie Cook, who had left the Yip Country in search of the diamond-studded dishpan which had been mysteriously stolen the same night that Ozma had disappeared from the Emerald City. But you must remember that while the Frogman and the Cookie Cook were preparing to descend from their mountain-top, and even while on their way to the farm-house of Wiljon the Winkie, Dorothy and the Wizard and their friends were encountering the adventures we have just related.

So it was that on the very morning when the travelers from the Emerald City bade farewell to the Czarover of the City of

Herku, Cayke and the Frogman awoke in a grove in which they had passed the night sleeping on beds of leaves. There were plenty of farm-houses in the neighborhood, but no one seemed to welcome the puffy, haughty Frogman or the little dried-up Cookie Cook, and so they slept comfortably enough underneath the trees of the grove.

The Frogman wakened first, on this morning, and after going to the tree where Cayke slept and finding her still wrapped in slumber, he decided to take a little walk and seek some breakfast. Coming to the edge of the grove he observed, half a mile away, a pretty yellow house that was surrounded by a yellow picket fence, so he walked toward this house and on entering the yard found a Winkie woman picking up sticks with which to build a fire to cook her morning meal.

"For goodness sakes!" she exclaimed on seeing the Frogman, "what are you doing out of your frog-pond?"

"I am traveling in search of a jeweled gold dishpan, my good woman," he replied, with an air of great dignity.

"You won't find it here, then," said she. "Our dishpans are tin, and they're good enough for anybody. So go back to your pond and leave me alone."

She spoke rather crossly and with a lack of respect that greatly annoyed the Frogman.

"Allow me to tell you, madam," said he, "that although I am a frog I am the Greatest and Wisest Frog in all the world. I may add that I possess much more wisdom than any Winkie—

man or woman—in this land. Wherever I go, people fall on their knees before me and render homage to the Great Frogman! No one else knows so much as I; no one else is so grand—so magnificent!"

"If you know so much," she retorted, "why don't you know where your dishpan is, instead of chasing around the country after it?"

"Presently," he answered, "I am going where it is; but just now I am traveling and have had no breakfast. Therefore I honor you by asking you for something to eat."

"Oho! the Great Frogman is hungry as any tramp, is he? Then pick up these sticks and help me to build the fire," said the woman contemptuously.

"Me! The Great Frogman pick up sticks?" he exclaimed in horror. "In the Yip Country, where I am more honored and powerful than any King could be, people weep with joy when I ask them to feed me."

"Then that's the place to go for your breakfast," declared the woman.

"I fear you do not realize my importance," urged the Frogman. "Exceeding wisdom renders me superior to menial duties."

"It's a great wonder to me," remarked the woman, carrying her sticks to the house, "that your wisdom doesn't inform you that you'll get no breakfast here," and she went in and slammed the door behind her.

The Frogman felt he had been insulted, so he gave a loud croak of indignation and turned away. After going a short distance he came upon a faint path which led across a meadow in the direction of a grove of pretty trees, and thinking this circle of evergreens must surround a house—where perhaps he would be kindly received—he decided to follow the path. And by and by he came to the trees, which were set close together, and pushing aside some branches he found no house inside the circle, but instead a very beautiful pond of clear water.

Now the Frogman, although he was so big and so well educated and now aped the ways and customs of human beings, was still a frog. As he gazed at this solitary, deserted pond, his love for water returned to him with irresistible force.

"If I cannot get a breakfast I may at least have a fine swim," said he, and pushing his way between the trees he reached the bank. There he took off his fine clothing, laying his shiny purple hat and his gold-headed cane beside it. A moment later he sprang with one leap into the water and dived to the very bottom of the pond.

The water was deliciously cool and grateful to his thick, rough skin, and the Frogman swam around the pond several times before he stopped to rest. Then he floated upon the surface and examined the pond with some curiosity. The bottom and sides were all lined with glossy tiles of a light pink color; just one place in the bottom, where the water bubbled up from a hidden spring, had been left free. On the banks the green grass grew to the edge of the pink tiling.

And now, as the Frogman examined the place, he found that on one side of the pool, just above the water line, had been set a golden plate on which some words were deeply engraved. He swam toward this plate and on reaching it read the following inscription:

This is
THE TRUTH POND
Whoever bathes in this

water must always

afterward tell
THE TRUTH.

This statement startled the Frogman. It even worried him, so that he leaped upon the bank and hurriedly began to dress himself.

"A great misfortune has befallen me," he told himself, "for hereafter I cannot tell people I am wise, since it is not the truth. The truth is that my boasted wisdom is all a sham, assumed by me to deceive people and make them defer to me. In truth, no living creature can know much more than his fellows, for one may know one thing, and another know another thing, so that wisdom is evenly scattered throughout the world. But—ah me!—what a terrible fate will now be mine. Even Cayke the Cookie Cook will soon discover that my knowledge is no greater than her own; for having bathed in the enchanted water of the Truth Pond, I can no longer deceive her or tell a lie."

More humbled than he had been for many years, the Frogman went back to the grove where he had left Cayke and found the woman now awake and washing her face in a tiny brook.

"Where has Your Honor been?" she asked.

"To a farm-house to ask for something to eat," said he, "but the woman refused me."

"How dreadful!" she exclaimed. "But never mind; there are other houses where the people will be glad to feed the Wisest Creature in all the World."

"Do you mean yourself?" he asked.

"No, I mean you."

The Frogman felt strongly impelled to tell the truth, but struggled hard against it. His reason told him there was no use in letting Cayke know he was not wise, for then she would lose much respect for him, but each time he opened his mouth to speak he realized he was about to tell the truth and shut it again as quickly as possible. He tried to talk about something else, but the words necessary to undeceive the woman would force themselves to his lips in spite of all his struggles. Finally, knowing that he must either remain dumb or let the truth prevail, he gave a low groan of despair and said, "Cayke, I am *not* the Wisest Creature in all the World; I am not wise at all."

"Oh, you must be!" she protested. "You told me so your-self, only last evening."

"Then last evening I failed to tell you the truth," he admit-ted, looking very shamefaced, for a frog. "I am sorry I told you this lie, my good Cayke; but, if you must know the truth, the whole truth and nothing but the truth, I am not really as wise as you are."

The Cookie Cook was greatly shocked to hear this, for it shattered one of her most pleasing illusions. She looked at the gorgeously dressed Frogman in amazement.

"What has caused you to change your mind so suddenly?" she inquired.

"I have bathed in the Truth Pond," he said, "and who-ever bathes in that water is ever afterward obliged to tell the truth."

"You were foolish to do that," declared the woman. "It is often very embarrassing to tell the truth. I'm glad *I* didn't bathe in that dreadful water!"

The Frogman looked at his companion thoughtfully.

"Cayke," said he, "I want you to go to the Truth Pond and take a bath in its water. For, if we are to travel together and encounter unknown adventures, it would not be fair that I alone must always tell you the truth, while you could tell me whatever you pleased. If we both dip in the enchanted water there will be no chance in the future of our deceiving one another."

"No," she asserted, shaking her head positively, "I won't do it, Your Honor. For, if I told you the truth, I'm sure you wouldn't like me. No Truth Pond for me. I'll be just as I am, an honest woman who can say what she wants to without hurting anyone's feelings."

With this decision the Frogman was forced to be content, although he was sorry the Cookie Cook would not listen to his advice.

Chapter 14

The UNHAPPY FERRYMAN

Leaving the grove where they had slept, the Frogman and the Cookie Cook turned to the east to seek another house and after a short walk came to one where the people received them very politely. The children stared rather hard at the big, pompous Frogman, but the woman of the house, when Cayke asked for something to eat, at once brought them food and said they were welcome to it.

"Few people in need of help pass this way," she remarked, "for the Winkies are all prosperous and love to stay in their own homes. But perhaps you are not a Winkie," she added.

"No," said Cayke, "I am a Yip, and my home is on a high mountain at the southeast of your country."

"And the Frogman—is he, also, a Yip?"

"I do not know what he is, other than a very remarkable and highly educated creature," replied the Cookie Cook. "But he has lived many years among the Yips, who have found him so wise and intelligent that they always go to him for advice."

"May I ask why you have left your home, and where you are going?" said the Winkie woman.

Then Cayke told her of the diamond-studded gold dishpan and how it had been mysteriously stolen from her house, after which she had discovered that she could no longer cook good cookies. So she had resolved to search until she found her dishpan again, because a Cookie Cook who cannot cook good cookies is not of much use. The Frogman, who had wanted to see more of the world, had accompanied her to assist in the search. When the woman had listened to this story she asked, "Then you have no idea as yet who has stolen your dishpan?"

"I only know it must have been some mischievous fairy, or a magician, or some such powerful person, because none other could have climbed the steep mountain to the Yip Country. And who else could have carried away my beautiful magic dishpan without being seen?"

The woman thought about this during the time that Cayke and the Frogman ate their breakfast. When they had finished, she said, "Where are you going next?"

"We have not decided," answered the Cookie Cook.

"Our plan," explained the Frogman, in his important way, "is to travel from place to place until we learn where the thief is located, and then to force him to return the dishpan to its proper owner."

"The plan is all right," agreed the woman, "but it may take you a long time before you succeed, your method being sort of haphazard and indefinite. However, I advise you to travel toward the east."

"Why?" asked the Frogman.

"Because if you went west you would soon come to the desert, and also because in this part of the Winkie Country no one steals, so your time here would be wasted. But toward the east, beyond the river, live many strange people whose honesty I would not vouch for. Moreover, if you journey far enough east and cross the river for a second time, you will come to the Emerald City, where there is much magic and sorcery. The Emerald City is ruled by a dear little girl called Ozma, who also rules the Emperor of the Winkies and all the Land of Oz. So, as Ozma is a fairy, she may be able to tell you just who has taken your precious dishpan. Provided, of course, you do not find it before you reach her."

"This seems to me to be excellent advice," said the Frogman, and Cayke agreed with him.

"The most sensible thing for you to do," continued the woman, "would be to return to your home and use another dishpan, learning to cook cookies as other people cook cookies, without the aid of magic. But, if you cannot be happy without the magic dishpan you have lost, you are likely to learn more about it in the Emerald City than at any other place in Oz."

They thanked the good woman and on leaving her house faced the east and continued in that direction all the way. Toward evening they came to the west branch of the Winkie River and there, on the river bank, found a ferryman who lived all alone in a little yellow house.

This ferryman was a Winkie with a very small head and a very large body. He was sitting in his doorway as the travelers approached him and did not even turn his head to look at them.

"Good evening," said the Frogman.

The ferryman made no reply.

"We would like some supper and the privilege of sleeping in your house until morning," continued the Frogman. "At daybreak we would like some breakfast and then we would like to have you row us across the river."

The ferryman neither moved nor spoke. He sat in his doorway and looked straight ahead.

"I think he must be deaf and dumb," Cayke whispered to her companion. Then she stood directly in front of the ferryman and putting her mouth close to his ear she yelled as loudly as she could, "Good evening!"

The ferryman scowled.

"Why do you yell at me, woman?" he asked.

"Can you hear what I say?" she asked in her ordinary tone of voice.

"Of course," replied the man.

"Then why didn't you answer the Frogman?"

"Because," said the ferryman; "I don't understand the frog language."

"He speaks the same words that I do and in the same way," declared Cayke.

"Perhaps," replied the ferryman, "but to me his voice sounded like a frog's croak. I know that in the Land of Oz animals can speak our language, and so can the birds and bugs and fishes; but in *my* ears, they sound merely like growls and chirps and croaks."

"Why is that?" asked the Cookie Cook in surprise.

"Once, many years ago, I cut the tail off a fox which had taunted me; and I stole some birds' eggs from a nest to make an omelet with, and also I pulled a fish from the river and left it lying on the bank to gasp for lack of water until it died. I don't know why I did those wicked things, but I did them. So the Emperor of the Winkies—who is the Tin Woodman and has a very tender tin heart—punished me by denying me any communication with beasts, birds or fishes. I cannot understand them when they speak to me, although I know that other people can do so, nor can the creatures understand a word I say to them. Every time I meet one of them I am reminded of my former cruelty, and it makes me very unhappy."

"Really," said Cayke, "I'm sorry for you, although the Tin Woodman is not to blame for punishing you."

"What is he mumbling about?" asked the Frogman.

"He is talking to me, but you don't understand him," she replied. And then she told him of the ferryman's punishment and afterward explained to the ferryman that they wanted to stay all night with him and be fed.

He gave them some fruit and bread, which was the only sort of food he had, and he allowed Cayke to sleep in a room of his cottage. But the Frogman he refused to admit to his house, saying that the frog's presence made him miserable and unhappy. At no time would he look directly at the Frogman, or even toward him, fearing he would shed tears if he did so; so the big frog slept on the river bank, where he could hear little frogs croaking in the river all the night through. But that did not keep him awake; it merely soothed him to slumber, for he realized how much superior he was to them.

Just as the sun was rising on a new day the ferryman rowed the two travelers across the river—keeping his back to the Frogman all the way—and then Cayke thanked him and bade him good-bye and the ferryman rowed home again.

On this side of the river there were no paths at all, so it was evident they had reached a part of the country little frequented by travelers. There was a marsh at the south of them, sandhills at the north and a growth of scrubby underbrush leading toward a forest at the east. So the east was really the least difficult way to go and that direction was the one they had determined to follow.

Now the Frogman, although he wore green patent-leather shoes with ruby buttons, had very large and flat feet, and when he tramped through the scrub his weight crushed down the underbrush and made a path for Cayke to follow him. Therefore they soon reached the forest, where the tall trees were set far apart but were so leafy that they shaded all the spaces between them with their branches.

"There are no bushes here," said Cayke, much pleased, "so we can now travel faster and with more comfort."

···—···◄ Chapter 15 ►···—···

The BIG LAVENDER BEAR

It was a pleasant place to wander in and the two travelers were proceeding at a brisk pace when suddenly a voice shouted, "Halt!"

They looked around in surprise, seeing at first no one at all. Then from behind a tree there stepped a brown fuzzy bear, whose head came about as high as Cayke's waist— and Cayke was a small woman. The bear was chubby as well as fuzzy; his body was even puffy, while his legs and arms seemed jointed at the knees and elbows and fastened to his body by pins or rivets. His ears were round in shape and stuck out in a comical way, while his round black eyes were bright and sparkling as beads. Over his shoulder the little brown bear bore a gun with a tin barrel. The barrel had a cork in the end of it and a string was attached to the cork and to the handle of the gun.

Both the Frogman and Cayke gazed hard at this curious bear, standing silent for some time. But finally the Frogman recovered from his surprise and remarked, "It seems to me that you are stuffed with sawdust and ought not to be alive."

"That's all you know about it," answered the little Brown Bear in a squeaky voice. "I am stuffed with a very good quality of curled hair and my skin is the best plush that was ever made. As for my being alive, that is my own affair and cannot concern you at all—except that it gives me the privilege to say you are my prisoners."

"Prisoners! Why do you speak such nonsense?" asked the Frogman angrily. "Do you think we are afraid of a toy bear with a toy gun?"

"You ought to be," was the confident reply, "for I am merely the sentry guarding the way to Bear Center, which is a city containing hundreds of my race, who are ruled by a very powerful sorcerer known as the Lavender Bear. He ought to be a purple color, you know, seeing he is a King, but he's only light lavender, which is, of course, second-cousin to royal purple. So unless you come with me peaceably, as my prisoners, I shall fire my gun and bring a hundred bears—of all sizes and colors—to capture you."

"Why do you wish to capture us?" inquired the Frogman, who had listened to his speech with much astonishment.

L. Frank Baum

"I don't wish to, as a matter of fact," replied the little Brown Bear, "but it is my duty to, because you are now trespassing on the domain of his Majesty the King of Bear Center. Also I will admit that things are rather quiet in our city, just now, and the excitement of your capture, followed by your trial and execution, should afford us much entertainment."

"We defy you!" said the Frogman.

"Oh, no; don't do that," pleaded Cayke, speaking to her companion. "He says his King is a sorcerer, so perhaps it is he or one of his bears who ventured to steal my jeweled dishpan. Let us go to the City of the Bears and discover if my dishpan is there."

"I must now register one more charge against you," remarked the little Brown Bear, with evident satisfaction. "You have just accused us of stealing, and that is such a dreadful thing to say that I am quite sure our noble King will command you to be executed."

"But how could you execute us?" inquired the Cookie Cook.

"I've no idea. But our King is a wonderful inventor and there is no doubt he can find a proper way to destroy you. So, tell me, are you going to struggle, or will you go peaceably to meet your doom?"

It was all so ridiculous that Cayke laughed aloud and even the Frogman's wide mouth curled in a smile. Neither was a bit afraid to go to the Bear City and it seemed to both that there was a possibility they might discover the missing dishpan. So

the Frogman said, "Lead the way, little Bear, and we will follow without a struggle."

"That's very sensible of you; very sensible, indeed!" declared
the Brown Bear. "So, for-ward—*march!*" and with the command
he turned around and began to waddle along a path that led
between the trees.

Cayke and the Frogman, as they followed their conductor,
could scarce forbear laughing at his stiff, awkward manner of
walking and, although he moved his stuffy legs fast, his steps were
so short that they had to go slowly in order not to run into him.
But after a time they reached a large, circular space in the center
of the forest, which was clear of any stumps or underbrush. The
ground was covered by a soft grey moss, pleasant to tread upon.
All the trees surrounding this space seemed to be hollow and had
round holes in their trunks, set a little way above the ground,
but otherwise there was nothing unusual about the place and
nothing, in the opinion of the prisoners, to indicate a settlement.
But the little Brown Bear said in a proud and impressive voice
(although it still squeaked), "This is the wonderful city known to
fame as Bear Center!"

"But there are no houses; there are no bears living here at
all!" exclaimed Cayke.

"Oh, indeed!" retorted their captor and raising his gun he
pulled the trigger. The cork flew out of the tin barrel with a
loud "pop!" and at once from every hole in every tree within
view of the clearing appeared the head of a bear. They were of

many colors and of many sizes, but all were made in the same manner as the bear who had met and captured them.

At first a chorus of growls arose and then a sharp voice cried: "What has happened, Corporal Waddle?"

"Captives, your Majesty!" answered the Brown Bear. "Intruders upon our domain and slanderers of our good name."

"Ah, that's important," answered the voice.

Then from out of the hollow trees tumbled a whole regiment of stuffed bears, some carrying tin swords, some popguns and others long spears with gay ribbons tied to the handles. There were hundreds of them, altogether, and they quietly formed a circle around the Frogman and the Cookie Cook but kept at a distance and left a large space for the prisoners to stand in.

Presently this circle parted and into the center of it stalked a huge toy bear of a lovely lavender color. He walked upon his hind legs, as did all the others, and on his head he wore a tin crown set with diamonds and amethysts, while in one paw he carried a short wand of some glittering metal that resembled silver but wasn't.

"His Majesty the King!" shouted Corporal Waddle, and all the bears bowed low. Some bowed so low that they lost their balance and toppled over, but they soon scrambled up again, and the Lavender King squatted on his haunches before the prisoners and gazed at them steadily with his bright pink eyes.

Chapter 16

The LITTLE PINK BEAR

One Person and one Freak," said the big Lavender Bear, when he had carefully examined the strangers.

"I am sorry to hear you call poor Cayke the Cookie Cook a Freak," remonstrated the Frogman.

"She is the Person," asserted the King. "Unless I am mistaken, it is you who are the Freak."

The Frogman was silent, for he could not truthfully deny it.

"Why have you dared intrude in my forest?" demanded the Bear King.

"We didn't know it *was* your forest," said Cayke, "and we are on our way to the far east, where the Emerald City is."

"Ah, it's a long way from here to the Emerald City," remarked the King. "It is so far away, indeed, that no bear among us has even been there. But what errand requires you to travel such a distance?"

"Someone has stolen my diamond-studded gold dishpan," explained Cayke; "and, as I cannot be happy without it, I have decided to search the world over until I find it again. The Frogman, who is very learned and wonderfully wise, has come with me to give me his assistance. Isn't it kind of him?"

The King looked at the Frogman.

"What makes you so wonderfully wise?" he asked.

"I'm not," was the candid reply. "The Cookie Cook, and some others in the Yip Country, think because I am a big frog and talk and act like a man, that I must be very wise. I have learned more than a frog usually knows, it is true, but I am not yet so wise as I hope to become at some future time."

The King nodded, and when he did so, something squeaked in his chest.

"Did your Majesty speak?" asked Cayke.

"Not just then," answered the Lavender Bear, seeming to be somewhat embarrassed. "I am so built, you must know, that when anything pushes against my chest, as my chin accidentally did just then, I make that silly noise. In this city it isn't considered good manners to notice. But I like your Frogman. He is honest and truthful, which is more than can be said of many others. As for your late lamented dishpan, I'll show it to you."

With this he waved three times the metal wand which he held in his paw and instantly there appeared upon the ground, midway between the King and Cayke, a big round pan made of beaten gold. Around the top edge was a row of small diamonds; around the center of the pan was another row of larger diamonds; and at the bottom was a row of exceedingly large and brilliant diamonds. In fact, they all sparkled magnificently and the pan was so big and broad that it took a lot of diamonds to go around it three times.

Cayke stared so hard that her eyes seemed about to pop out of her head.

"O-o-o-oh!" she exclaimed, drawing a deep breath of delight.

"Is this your dishpan?" inquired the King.

"It is—it is!" cried the Cookie Cook, and rushing forward she fell on her knees and threw her arms around the precious pan. But her arms came together without meeting any resistance at all. Cayke tried to seize the edge, but found nothing to grasp. The pan was surely there, she thought, for she could see it plainly; but it was not solid; she could not feel it at all. With a moan of astonishment and despair, she raised her head to look at the Bear King, who was watching her actions curiously. Then she turned to the pan again, only to find it had completely disappeared.

"Poor creature!" murmured the King pityingly. "You must have thought, for the moment, that you had actually recovered your dishpan. But what you saw was merely the image of it, conjured up by means of my magic. It is a pretty dishpan, indeed, though rather big and awkward to handle. I hope you will some day find it."

Cayke was grievously disappointed. She began to cry, wiping her eyes on her apron. The King turned to the throng of toy bears surrounding him and asked, "Has any of you ever seen this golden dishpan before?"

"No," they answered in a chorus.

The King seemed to reflect. Presently he inquired, "Where is the little Pink Bear?"

"At home, your Majesty," was the reply.

"Fetch him here," commanded the King.

Several of the bears waddled over to one of the trees and pulled from its hollow a tiny pink bear, smaller than any of the others. A big white bear carried the pink one in his arms and set it down beside the King, arranging the joints of its legs so that it would stand upright.

This Pink Bear seemed lifeless until the King turned a crank which protruded from its side, when the little creature turned its head stiffly from side to side and said in a small shrill voice, "Hurrah for the King of Bear Center!"

"Very good," said the big Lavender Bear; "he seems to be working very well today. Tell me, my Pink Pinkerton, what has become of this lady's jeweled dishpan?"

"U—u—u," said the Pink Bear, and then stopped short.

The King turned the crank again.

"U-g-u the Shoemaker has it," said the Pink Bear.

"Who is Ugu the Shoemaker?" demanded the King, again turning the crank.

"A magician who lives on a mountain in a wickerwork castle," was the reply.

"Where is the mountain?" was the next question.

"Nineteen miles and three furlongs from Bear Center to the northeast."

"And is the dishpan still at the castle of Ugu the Shoemaker?" asked the King.

"It is."

The King turned to Cayke.

"You may rely on this information," said he. "The Pink Bear can tell us anything we wish to know, and his words are always words of truth."

"Is he alive?" asked the Frogman, much interested in the Pink Bear.

"Something animates him—when you turn his crank," replied the King. "I do not know if it is life, or what it is, or how it happens that the little Pink Bear can answer correctly every question put to him. We discovered his talent a long time ago and whenever we wish to know anything—which is not very often— we ask the Pink Bear. There is no doubt whatever, madam, that Ugu the Magician has your dishpan, and if you dare to go to him you may be able to recover it. But of that I am not certain."

"Can't the Pink Bear tell?" asked Cayke anxiously.

"No, for that is in the future. He can tell anything that *has* happened, but nothing that is going to happen. Don't ask me why, for I don't know."

"Well," said the Cookie Cook after a little thought, "I mean to go to this magician, anyhow, and tell him I want my dishpan. I wish I knew what Ugu the Shoemaker is like."

"Then I'll show him to you," promised the King. "But do not be frightened; it won't be Ugu, remember, but only his image."

With this he waved his metal wand again and in the circle suddenly appeared a thin little man, very old and skinny, who was seated on a wicker stool before a wicker table. On the table lay a Great Book with gold clasps. The Book was open and the man was reading in it. He wore great spectacles, which were fastened before his eyes by means of a ribbon that passed around his head and was tied in a bow at the back. His hair was very thin and white; his skin, which clung fast to his bones, was brown and seared with furrows; he had a big, fat nose and little eyes set close together.

On no account was Ugu the Shoemaker a pleasant person to gaze at. As his image appeared before them, all were silent and intent until Corporal Waddle, the Brown Bear, became nervous and pulled the trigger of his gun. Instantly the cork flew out of the tin barrel with a loud "pop!" that made them all jump. And, at this sound, the image of the magician vanished.

"So! *That's* the thief, is it?" said Cayke, in an angry voice. "I should think he'd be ashamed of himself for stealing a poor woman's diamond dishpan! But I mean to face him in his wicker castle and force him to return my property."

"To me," said the Bear King, reflectively, "he looked like a dangerous person. I hope he won't be so unkind as to argue the matter with you."

The Frogman was much disturbed by the vision of Ugu the Shoemaker, and Cayke's determination to go to the magician filled her companion with misgivings. But he would not break his pledged word to assist the Cookie Cook and after breathing a deep sigh of resignation he asked the King, "Will your Majesty lend us this Pink Bear who answers questions that we may take him with us on our journey? He would be very useful to us, and we will promise to bring him safely back to you."

The King did not reply at once; he seemed to be thinking.

"*Please* let us take the Pink Bear," begged Cayke. "I'm sure he would be a great help to us."

"The Pink Bear," said the King, "is the best bit of magic I possess, and there is not another like him in the world. I do not care to let him out of my sight; nor do I wish to disappoint you; so I believe I will make the journey in your company and carry my Pink Bear with me. He can walk, when you wind the other side of him, but so slowly and awkwardly that he would delay you. But if I go along I can carry him in my arms, so I will join your party. Whenever you are ready to start, let me know."

"But—your Majesty!" exclaimed Corporal Waddle in protest, "I hope you do not intend to let these prisoners escape without punishment."

"Of what crime do you accuse them?" inquired the King.

"Why, they trespassed on your domain, for one thing," said the Brown Bear.

"We didn't know it was private property, your Majesty," said the Cookie Cook.

"And they asked if any of us had stolen the dishpan!" continued Corporal Waddle indignantly. "That is the same thing as calling us thieves and robbers and bandits and brigands, is it not?"

"Every person has the right to ask questions," said the Frogman.

"But the Corporal is quite correct," declared the Lavender Bear. "I condemn you both to death, the execution to take place ten years from this hour."

"But we belong in the Land of Oz, where no one ever dies," Cayke reminded him.

"Very true," said the King. "I condemn you to death merely as a matter of form. It sounds quite terrible, and in ten years we shall have forgotten all about it. Are you ready to start for the wicker castle of Ugu the Shoemaker?"

"Quite ready, your Majesty."

"But who will rule in your place, while you are gone?" asked a big Yellow Bear.

"I myself will rule while I am gone," was the reply. "A King isn't required to stay at home forever, and if he takes a notion to travel, whose business is it but his own? All I ask is that you bears behave yourselves while I am away. If any of you is naughty, I'll send him to some girl or boy in America to play with."

This dreadful threat made all the toy bears look solemn. They assured the King, in a chorus of growls, that they would be good. Then the big Lavender Bear picked up the little Pink Bear and after tucking it carefully under one arm he said, "Good-bye till I come back!" and waddled along the path that led through the forest. The Frogman and Cayke the Cookie Cook also said good-bye to the bears and then followed after the King, much to the regret of the little Brown Bear, who pulled the trigger of his gun and popped the cork as a parting salute.

Chapter 17

The MEETING

While the Frogman and his party were advancing from the west, Dorothy and her party were advancing from the east, and so it happened that on the following night they all camped at a little hill that was only a few miles from the wicker castle of Ugu the Shoemaker. But the two parties did not see one another that night, for one camped on one side of the hill while the other camped on the opposite side. But the next morning the Frogman thought he would climb the hill and see what was on top of it, and at the same time Scraps, the Patchwork Girl, also decided to climb the hill to find if the wicker castle was visible from its top. So she stuck her head over an edge just as the Frogman's head appeared over another edge and both, being surprised, kept still while they took a good look at one another.

Scraps recovered from her astonishment first and bounding upward she turned a somersault and landed sitting down and facing the big Frogman, who slowly advanced and sat opposite her.

"Well met, Stranger!" cried the Patchwork Girl, with a whoop of laughter. "You are quite the funniest individual I have seen in all my travels."

"Do you suppose I can be any funnier than you?" asked the Frogman, gazing at her in wonder.

"I'm not funny to myself, you know," returned Scraps. "I wish I were. And perhaps you are so used to your own absurd shape that you do not laugh whenever you see your reflection in a pool, or in a mirror."

"No," said the Frogman gravely, "I do not. I used to be proud of my great size and vain of my culture and education, but since I bathed in the Truth Pond, I sometimes think it is not right that I should be different from all other frogs."

"Right or wrong," said the Patchwork Girl, "to be different is to be distinguished. Now, in my case, I'm just like all other Patchwork Girls because I'm the only one there is. But, tell me, where did you come from?"

"The Yip Country," said he.

"Is that in the Land of Oz?"

"Of course," replied the Frogman.

"And do you know that your Ruler, Ozma of Oz, has been stolen?"

"I was not aware that I had a Ruler, so of course I couldn't know that she was stolen."

"Well, you have. All the people of Oz," explained Scraps, "are ruled by Ozma, whether they know it or not. And she has been stolen. Aren't you angry? Aren't you indignant? Your Ruler, whom you didn't know you had, has positively been stolen!"

"That is queer," remarked the Frogman thoughtfully. "Stealing is a thing practically unknown in Oz, yet this Ozma has been taken and a friend of mine has also had her dishpan stolen. With her I have traveled all the way from the Yip Country in order to recover it."

"I don't see any connection between a Royal Ruler of Oz and a dishpan!" declared Scraps.

"They've both been stolen, haven't they?"

"True. But why can't your friend wash her dishes in another dishpan?" asked Scraps.

"Why can't you use another Royal Ruler? I suppose you prefer the one who is lost, and my friend wants her own dishpan, which is made of gold and studded with diamonds and has magic powers."

"Magic, eh?" exclaimed Scraps. "*There* is a link that connects the two steals, anyhow, for it seems that all the magic in the Land of Oz was stolen at the same time, whether it was in the Emerald City or in Glinda's castle or in the Yip Country. Seems mighty strange and mysterious, doesn't it?"

"It used to seem that way to me," admitted the Frogman, "but we have now discovered who took our dishpan. It was Ugu the Shoemaker."

"Ugu? Good gracious! That's the same magician we think has stolen Ozma. We are now on our way to the castle of this Shoemaker."

"So are we," said the Frogman.

"Then follow me, quick! And let me introduce you to Dorothy and the other girls and to the Wizard of Oz and all the rest of us."

She sprang up and seized his coat-sleeve, dragging him off the hilltop and down the other side from that whence he had come. And at the foot of the hill the Frogman was astonished to find the three girls and the Wizard and Button-Bright, who were surrounded by a Wooden Sawhorse, a lean Mule, a square Woozy and a Cowardly Lion. A little black dog ran up and smelled at the Frogman, but couldn't growl at him.

"I've discovered another party that has been robbed," shouted Scraps as she joined them. "This is their leader and they're all going to Ugu's castle to fight the wicked Shoemaker!"

They regarded the Frogman with much curiosity and interest and, finding all eyes fixed upon him, the newcomer arranged his necktie and smoothed his beautiful vest and swung his gold-headed cane like a regular dandy. The big spectacles over his eyes quite altered his froglike countenance and gave him a learned and impressive look. Used as she was to seeing strange creatures in the Land of Oz, Dorothy was amazed at discovering the Frogman. So were all her companions. Toto wanted to growl at him, but couldn't, and he didn't dare bark. The Sawhorse snorted rather contemptuously, but the Lion whispered to the wooden steed: "Bear with this strange creature, my friend, and remember he is no more extraordinary than you are. Indeed, it is more natural for a frog to be big than for a Sawhorse to be alive."

On being questioned, the Frogman told them the whole story of the loss of Cayke's highly prized dishpan and their adventures in search of it. When he came to tell of the Lavender Bear King and of the little Pink Bear who could tell anything you wanted to know, his hearers became eager to see such interesting animals.

"It will be best," said the Wizard, "to unite our two parties and share our fortunes together, for we are all bound on the same errand and as one band we may more easily defy this shoemaker magician than if separate. Let us be allies."

"I will ask my friends about that," replied the Frogman, and he climbed over the hill to find Cayke and the toy bears. The Patchwork Girl accompanied him and when they came upon the Cookie Cook and the Lavender Bear and the Pink

Bear it was hard to tell which of the lot was the most surprised.

"Mercy me!" cried Cayke, addressing the Patchwork Girl. "However did you come alive?"

Scraps stared at the bears.

"Mercy me!" she echoed, "You are stuffed, as I am, with cotton, and yet you appear to be living. That makes me feel ashamed, for I have prided myself on being the only live cotton-stuffed person in Oz."

"Perhaps you are," returned the Lavender Bear, "for I am stuffed with extra-quality curled hair, and so is the little Pink Bear."

"You have relieved my mind of a great anxiety," declared the Patchwork Girl, now speaking more cheerfully. "The Scarecrow is stuffed with straw, and you with hair, so I am still the Original and Only Cotton-Stuffed!"

"I hope I am too polite to criticize cotton, as compared with curled hair," said the King, "especially as you seem satisfied with it."

Then the Frogman told of his interview with the party from the Emerald City and added that the Wizard of Oz had invited the bears and Cayke and himself to travel in company with them to the castle of Ugu the Shoemaker. Cayke was much pleased, but the Bear King looked solemn. He set the little Pink Bear on his lap and turned the crank in its side and asked, "Is it safe for us to associate with those people from the Emerald City?"

And the Pink Bear at once replied:

"Safe for you and safe for me;
Perhaps no others safe will be."

"That 'perhaps' need not worry us," said the King; "so let us join the others and offer them our protection."

Even the Lavender Bear was astonished, however, when on climbing over the hill he found on the other side the group of queer animals and the people from the Emerald City. The bears and Cayke were received very cordially, although Button-Bright was cross when they wouldn't let him play with the little Pink Bear. The three girls greatly admired the toy bears, and especially the pink one, which they longed to hold.

"You see," explained the Lavender King, in denying them this privilege, "he's a very valuable bear, because his magic is a correct guide on all occasions, and especially if one is in difficulties. It was the Pink Bear who told us that Ugu the Shoemaker had stolen the Cookie Cook's dishpan."

"And the King's magic is just as wonderful," added Cayke, "because it showed us the Magician himself."

"What did he look like?" inquired Dorothy.

"He was dreadful!"

"He was sitting at a table and examining an immense Book which had three golden clasps," remarked the King.

"Why, that must have been Glinda's Great Book of

Records!" exclaimed Dorothy. "If it is, it proves that Ugu the Shoemaker stole Ozma, and with her all the magic in the Emerald City."

"And my dishpan," said Cayke.

And the Wizard added, "It also proves that he is following our adventures in the Book of Records, and therefore knows that we are seeking him and that we are determined to find him and reach Ozma at all hazards."

"If we can," added the Woozy, but everybody frowned at him.

The Wizard's statement was so true that the faces around him were very serious until the Patchwork Girl broke into a peal of laughter.

"Wouldn't it be a rich joke if he made prisoners of *us*, too?" she said.

"No one but a crazy Patchwork Girl would consider *that* a joke," grumbled Button-Bright.

And then the Lavender Bear King asked, "Would you like to see this magical shoemaker?"

"Wouldn't he know it?" Dorothy inquired.

"No, I think not."

Then the King waved his metal wand and before them appeared a room in the wicker castle of Ugu. On the wall of the room hung Ozma's Magic Picture, and seated before it was the Magician. They could see the Picture as well as he could, because it faced them, and in the Picture was the hillside where they were now sitting, all their forms being reproduced in miniature. And, curiously enough, within the scene of the Picture was the scene they were now beholding, so they knew that the Magician was at this moment watching them in the Picture, and also that he saw himself and the room he was in become visible to the people on the hillside. Therefore he knew very well that they were watching him while he was watching them.

In proof of this, Ugu sprang from his seat and turned a scowling face in their direction; but now he could not see the travelers who were seeking him, although they could still see him. His actions were so distinct, indeed, that it seemed he was actually before them.

"It is only a ghost," said the Bear King. "It isn't real at all, except that it shows us Ugu just as he looks and tells us truly just what he is doing."

"I don't see anything of my lost growl, though," said Toto, as if to himself.

Then the vision faded away and they could see nothing but the grass and trees and bushes around them.

Chapter 18

The CONFERENCE

N ow, then," said the Wizard, "let us talk this matter over and decide what to do when we get to Ugu's wicker castle. There can be no doubt that the Shoemaker is a powerful Magician, and his powers have been increased a hundred-fold since he secured the Great Book of Records, the Magic Picture, all of Glinda's recipes for sorcery, and my own black bag—which was full of tools of wizardry. The man who could rob us of those things, and the man with all their powers at his command, is one who may prove somewhat difficult to conquer; therefore we should plan our actions well before we venture too near to his castle."

"I didn't see Ozma in the Magic Picture," said Trot. "What do you suppose Ugu has done with her?"

"Couldn't the little Pink Bear tell us what he did with Ozma?" asked Button-Bright.

"To be sure," replied the Lavender King; "I'll ask him."

So he turned the crank in the little Pink Bear's side and inquired: "Did Ugu the Shoemaker steal Ozma of Oz?"

"Yes," answered the little Pink Bear.

"Then what did he do with her?" asked the King.

"Shut her up in a dark place," answered the Little Pink Bear.

"Oh, that must be a dungeon cell!" cried Dorothy, horrified. "How dreadful!"

"Well, we must get her out of it," said the Wizard. "That is what we came for and of course we must rescue Ozma. But—how?"

Each one looked at some other one for an answer and all shook their heads in a grave and dismal manner. All but Scraps, who danced around them gleefully.

"You're afraid," said the Patchwork Girl, "because so many things can hurt your meat bodies. Why don't you give it up and go home? How can you fight a great magician when you have nothing to fight with?"

Dorothy looked at her reflectively.

"Scraps," said she, "you know that Ugu couldn't hurt you, a bit, whatever he did; nor could he hurt *me*, 'cause I wear the

Nome King's Magic Belt. S'pose just we two go on together, and leave the others here to wait for us."

"No, no!" said the Wizard positively. "That won't do at all. Ozma is more powerful than either of you, yet she could not defeat the wicked Ugu, who has shut her up in a dungeon. We must go to the Shoemaker in one mighty band, for only in union is there strength."

"That is excellent advice," said the Lavender Bear approvingly.

"But what can we do, when we get to Ugu?" inquired the Cookie Cook anxiously.

"Do not expect a prompt answer to that important question," replied the Wizard, "for we must first plan our line of conduct. Ugu knows, of course, that we are after him, for he has seen our approach in the Magic Picture, and he has read of all we have done up to the present moment in the Great Book of Records. Therefore we cannot expect to take him by surprise."

"Don't you suppose Ugu would listen to reason?" asked Betsy. "If we explained to him how wicked he has been, don't you think he'd let poor Ozma go?"

"And give me back my dishpan?" added the Cookie Cook eagerly.

"Yes, yes; won't he say he's sorry and get on his knees and beg our pardon?" cried Scraps, turning a flip-flop to show her scorn of the suggestion. "When Ugu the Shoemaker does that, please knock at the front door and let me know."

The Wizard sighed and rubbed his bald head with a puzzled air.

"I'm quite sure Ugu will not be polite to us," said he, "so we must conquer this cruel magician by force, much as we dislike to be rude to anyone. But none of you has yet suggested a way to do that. Couldn't the little Pink Bear tell us how?" he asked, turning to the Bear King.

"No, for that is something that is *going* to happen," replied the Lavender Bear. "He can only tell us what already *has* happened."

Again they were grave and thoughtful. But after a time Betsy said in a hesitating voice: "Hank is a great fighter; perhaps *he* could conquer the magician."

The Mule turned his head to look reproachfully at his old friend, the young girl.

"Who can fight against magic?" he asked.

"The Cowardly Lion could," said Dorothy.

The Lion, who was lying with his front legs spread out, his chin on his paws, raised his shaggy head.

"I can fight when I'm not afraid," said he calmly; "but the mere mention of a fight sets me to trembling."

"Ugu's magic couldn't hurt the Sawhorse," suggested tiny Trot.

"And the Sawhorse couldn't hurt the Magician," declared that wooden animal.

"For my part," said Toto, "I am helpless, having lost my growl."

"Then," said Cayke the Cookie Cook, "we must depend upon the Frogman. His marvelous wisdom will surely inform him how to conquer the wicked Magician and restore to me my dishpan."

All eyes were now turned questioningly upon the Frogman. Finding himself the center of observation, he swung his gold-headed cane, adjusted his big spectacles, and after swelling out his chest, sighed and said in a modest tone of voice:

"Respect for truth obliges me to confess that Cayke is mistaken in regard to my superior wisdom. I am not very wise. Neither have I had any practical experience in conquering magicians. But let us consider this case. What is Ugu, and what is a magician? Ugu is a renegade shoemaker and a magician is an ordinary man who, having learned how to do magical tricks, considers himself above his fellows. In this case, the Shoemaker has been naughty enough to steal a lot of magical tools and things that did not belong to him, and he is more wicked to steal than to be a magician. Yet, with all the arts at his command, Ugu is still a man, and surely there are ways in which a man may be conquered. How, do you say, how? Allow me to state that I don't know. In my judgment we cannot decide how best to act until we get to Ugu's castle. So let us go to it and take a look at it. After that we may discover an idea that will guide us to victory."

"That may not be a wise speech, but it sounds good," said Dorothy approvingly. "Ugu the Shoemaker is not only a common man, but he's a wicked man and a cruel man and deserves to be conquered. We mustn't have any mercy on him till Ozma is set free. So let's go to his castle, as the Frogman says, and see what the place looks like."

No one offered any objection to this plan and so it was adopted. They broke camp and were about to start on the journey to Ugu's castle when they discovered that Button-Bright was lost again. The girls and the Wizard shouted his name and the Lion roared and the Donkey brayed and the Frogman croaked and the Big Lavender Bear growled (to the envy of Toto, who couldn't growl but barked his loudest) yet none of them could make Button-Bright hear. So, after vainly searching for the boy a full hour, they formed a procession and proceeded in the direction of the wicker castle of Ugu the Shoemaker.

"Button-Bright's always getting lost," said Dorothy. "And if he wasn't always getting found again, I'd prob'ly worry. He may have gone ahead of us, and he may have gone back; but, wherever he is, we'll find him sometime and somewhere, I'm almost sure."

Chapter 19

UGU the SHOEMAKER

A curious thing about Ugu the Shoemaker was that he didn't suspect, in the least, that he was wicked. He wanted to be powerful and great and he hoped to make himself master of all the Land of Oz, that he might compel everyone in that fairy country to obey him. His ambition blinded him to the rights of others and he imagined anyone else would act just as he did if anyone else happened to be as clever as himself.

When he inhabited his little shoemaking shop in the City of Herku he had been discontented, for a shoemaker is not looked upon with high respect and Ugu knew that his ancestors had been famous magicians for many centuries past and therefore his family was above the ordinary. Even his father practiced magic, when Ugu was a boy; but his father had wandered away from Herku and had never come back again. So, when Ugu grew up, he was forced to make shoes for a living, knowing nothing of the magic of his forefathers. But one day, in searching through the attic of his house, he discovered all the books of magical recipes and many magical instruments which had formerly been in use in his family. From that day he stopped making shoes and began to study magic. Finally he aspired to become the greatest magician in Oz, and for days and weeks and months he thought on a plan to render all the other sorcerers and wizards, as well as those with fairy powers, helpless to oppose him.

From the books of his ancestors he learned the following facts:

(1) That Ozma of Oz was the fairy Ruler of the Emerald City and the Land of Oz, and that she could not be destroyed by any magic ever devised. Also, by means of her Magic Picture she would be able to discover anyone who approached her royal palace with the idea of conquering it.

(2) That Glinda the Good was the most powerful Sorceress in Oz, among her other magical possessions being the Great Book of Records, which told her all that happened anywhere in the world. This Book of Records was very dangerous to Ugu's plans and Glinda was in the service of Ozma and

would use her arts of sorcery to protect the girl Ruler.

(3) That the Wizard of Oz, who lived in Ozma's palace, had been taught much powerful magic by Glinda and had a bag of magic tools with which he might be able to conquer the Shoemaker.

(4) That there existed in Oz—in the Yip Country—a jeweled dishpan made of gold, which dishpan possessed marvelous powers of magic. At a magic word, which Ugu learned from the book, the dishpan would grow large enough for a man to sit inside it. Then, when he grasped both the golden handles, the dishpan would transport him in an instant to any place he wished to go within the borders of the Land of Oz.

No one now living, except Ugu, knew of the powers of this Magic Dishpan; so, after long study, the shoemaker decided that if he could manage to secure the dishpan he could, by its means, rob Ozma and Glinda and the Wizard of Oz of all their magic, thus becoming himself the most powerful person in all the land.

His first act was to go away from the City of Herku and build for himself the wicker castle in the hills. Here he carried his books and instruments of magic and here for a full year he diligently practiced all the magical arts learned from his ancestors. At the end of that time he could do a good many wonderful things.

Then, when all his preparations were made, he set out for the Yip Country and climbing the steep mountain at night he entered the house of Cayke the Cookie Cook and stole her diamond-studded gold dishpan while all the Yips were asleep. Taking his prize outside, he set the pan upon the ground and uttered the required magic word. Instantly the dishpan grew as large as a big washtub and Ugu seated himself in it and grasped the two handles. Then he wished himself in the great drawing-room of Glinda the Good.

He was there in a flash. First he took the Great Book of Records and put it in the dishpan. Then he went to Glinda's laboratory and took all her rare chemical compounds and her instruments of sorcery, placing these also in the dishpan which he caused to grow large enough to hold them. Next he seated himself amongst the treasures he had stolen and wished himself in the room in Ozma's palace which the Wizard occupied and where he kept his bag of magic tools. This bag Ugu added to his plunder and then wished himself in the apartments of Ozma.

Here he first took the Magic Picture from the wall and then seized all the other magical things which Ozma possessed. Having placed these in the dishpan, he was about to climb in himself when he looked up and saw Ozma standing beside him. Her fairy instinct had warned her that danger was threatening her, so the beautiful girl Ruler rose from her couch and leaving her bedchamber at once confronted the thief.

Ugu had to think quickly, for he realized that if he permitted Ozma to rouse the inmates of her palace all his plans and his present successes were likely to come to naught. So he threw a scarf over the girl's head, so she could not scream, and pushed her into the dishpan and tied her fast, so she could not move. Then he climbed in beside her and wished himself in his own wicker castle. The Magic Dishpan was there in an instant, with all its contents, and Ugu rubbed his hands together in triumphant joy as he realized that he now possessed all the important magic in the Land of Oz and could force all the inhabitants of that fairyland to do as he willed.

So quickly had his journey been accomplished that before daylight the robber magician had locked Ozma in a room, making her a prisoner, and had unpacked and arranged all his stolen goods. The next day he placed the Book of Records on his table and hung the Magic Picture on his wall and put away in his cupboards and drawers all the elixirs and magic compounds he had stolen. The magical instruments he polished and arranged, and this was fascinating work and made him very happy. The only thing that bothered him was Ozma. By turns the imprisoned Ruler wept and scolded the Shoemaker, haughtily threatening him with dire punishment for the wicked deeds he had done. Ugu became somewhat afraid of his fairy prisoner, in spite of the fact that he believed he had robbed her of all her powers; so he performed an enchantment that quickly disposed of her and placed her out of his sight and hearing. After that, being occupied with other things, he soon forgot her.

But now, when he looked into the Magic Picture and read the Great Book of Records, the Shoemaker learned that his wickedness was not to go unchallenged. Two important expeditions had set out to find him and force him to give up his stolen property. One was the party headed by the Wizard and Dorothy, while the other consisted of Cayke and the Frogman. Others were also searching, but not in the right places. These two groups, however, were headed straight for the wicker castle and so Ugu began to plan how best to meet them and to defeat their efforts to conquer him.

Chapter 20

MORE SURPRISES

All that first day after the union of the two parties our friends marched steadily toward the wicker castle of Ugu the Shoemaker. When night came they camped in a little grove and passed a pleasant evening together, although some of them were worried because Button-Bright was still lost.

"Perhaps," said Toto, as the animals lay grouped together for the night, "this Shoemaker who stole my growl, and who stole Ozma, has also stolen Button-Bright."

"How do you know that the Shoemaker stole your growl?" demanded the Woozy.

"He has stolen about everything else of value in Oz, hasn't he?" replied the dog.

"He has stolen everything he wants, perhaps," agreed the Lion; "but what could anyone want with your growl?"

"Well," said the dog, wagging his tail slowly, "my recollection is that it was a wonderful growl, soft and low and—and—"

"And ragged at the edges," said the Sawhorse.

"So," continued Toto, "if that magician hadn't any growl of his own, he might have wanted mine and stolen it."

"And, if he has, he will soon wish he hadn't," remarked the Mule. "Also, if he has stolen Button-Bright he will be sorry."

"Don't you like Button-Bright, then?" asked the Lion in surprise.

"It isn't a question of liking him," replied the Mule. "It's a question of watching him and looking after him. Any boy who causes his friends so much worry isn't worth having around. *I* never get lost."

"If you did," said Toto, "no one would worry a bit. I think Button-Bright is a very lucky boy, because he always gets found."

"See here," said the Lion, "this chatter is keeping us all awake, and tomorrow is likely to be a busy day. Go to sleep and forget your quarrels."

"Friend Lion," retorted the dog, "if I hadn't lost my growl you would hear it now. I have as much right to talk as you have to sleep."

The Lion sighed.

"If only you had lost your voice, when you lost your growl," said he, "you would be a more agreeable companion."

But they quieted down, after that, and soon the entire camp was wrapped in slumber.

Next morning they made an early start but had hardly proceeded on their way an hour when, on climbing a slight elevation, they beheld in the distance a low mountain, on top of which stood Ugu's wicker castle. It was a good-sized building and rather pretty because the sides, roofs and domes were all of wicker closely woven, as it is in fine baskets.

"I wonder if it is strong?" said Dorothy musingly, as she eyed the queer castle.

"I suppose it is, since a magician built it," answered the Wizard. "With magic to protect it, even a paper castle might be as strong as if made of stone. This Ugu must be a man of ideas, because he does things in a different way from other people."

"Yes; no one else would steal our dear Ozma," sighed tiny Trot.

"I wonder if Ozma is there?" said Betsy, indicating the castle with a nod of her head.

"Where else could she be?" asked Scraps.

"S'pose we ask the Pink Bear," suggested Dorothy.

That seemed a good idea, so they halted the procession and the Bear King held the little Pink Bear on his lap and turned the crank in its side and asked: "Where is Ozma of Oz?"

And the little Pink Bear answered: "She is in a hole in the ground, a half mile away at your left."

"Good gracious!" cried Dorothy. "Then she is not in Ugu's castle at all."

"It is lucky we asked that question," said the Wizard; "for, if we can find Ozma and rescue her, there will be no need for us to fight that wicked and dangerous magician."

"Indeed!" said Cayke. "Then what about my dishpan?"

The Wizard looked puzzled at her tone of remonstrance, so she added, "Didn't you people from the Emerald City promise that we would all stick together, and that you would help me to get my dishpan if I would help you to get your Ozma? And didn't I bring to you the little Pink Bear, which has told you where Ozma is hidden?"

"She's right," said Dorothy to the Wizard. "We must do as we agreed."

"Well, first of all, let us go and rescue Ozma," proposed the Wizard. "Then our beloved Ruler may be able to advise us how to conquer Ugu the Shoemaker."

So they turned to the left and marched for half a mile until they came to a small but deep hole in the ground. At once all rushed to the brim to peer into the hole, but instead of finding there Princess Ozma of Oz, all that they saw was Button-Bright, who was lying asleep on the bottom.

Their cries soon wakened the boy, who sat up and rubbed his eyes. When he recognized his friends he smiled sweetly, saying: "Found again!"

"Where is Ozma?" inquired Dorothy anxiously.

"I don't know," answered Button-Bright from the depths of the hole. "I got lost, yesterday, as you may remember, and in the night, while I was wandering around in the moonlight, trying to find my way back to you, I suddenly fell into this hole."

"And wasn't Ozma in it then?"

"There was no one in it but me, and I was sorry it wasn't entirely empty. The sides are so steep I can't climb out, so there was nothing to be done but sleep until someone found me. Thank you for coming. If you'll please let down a rope I'll empty this hole in a hurry."

"How strange!" said Dorothy, greatly disappointed. "It's evident the Pink Bear didn't tell us the truth."

"He never makes a mistake," declared the Lavender Bear King, in a tone that showed his feelings were hurt. And then he turned the crank of the little Pink Bear again and asked: "Is this the hole that Ozma of Oz is in?"

"Yes," answered the Pink Bear.

"That settles it," said the King, positively. "Your Ozma is in this hole in the ground."

"Don't be silly," returned Dorothy impatiently. "Even your beady eyes can see there is no one in the hole but Button-Bright."

"Perhaps Button-Bright is Ozma," suggested the King.

"And perhaps he isn't! Ozma is a girl, and Button-Bright is a boy."

"Your Pink Bear must be out of order," said the Wizard; "for, this time at least, his machinery has caused him to make an untrue statement."

The Bear King was so angry at this remark that he turned away, holding the Pink Bear in his paws, and refused to discuss the matter in any further way.

"At any rate," said the Frogman, "the Pink Bear has led us to your boy friend and so enabled you to rescue him."

Scraps was leaning so far over the hole, trying to find Ozma in it, that suddenly she lost her balance and pitched in head foremost. She fell upon Button-Bright and tumbled him over, but he was not hurt by her soft stuffed body and only laughed at the mishap. The Wizard buckled some straps together and let one end of them down into the hole, and soon both Scraps and the boy had climbed up and were standing safely beside the others.

They looked once more for Ozma, but the hole was now absolutely vacant. It was a round hole, so from the top they could plainly see every part of it. Before they left the place Dorothy went to the Bear King and said, "I'm sorry we couldn't believe what the little Pink Bear said, 'cause we don't want to make you feel bad by doubting him. There must be a mistake, somewhere, and we prob'ly don't understand just what the little

Pink Bear means. Will you let me ask him one more question?"

The Lavender Bear King was a good-natured bear, considering how he was made and stuffed and jointed, so he accepted Dorothy's apology and turned the crank and allowed the little girl to question his wee Pink Bear.

"Is Ozma *really* in this hole?" asked Dorothy.

"No," said the little Pink Bear.

This surprised everybody. Even the Bear King was now puzzled by the contradictory statements of his oracle.

"Where *is* she?" asked the King.

"Here, among you," answered the little Pink Bear.

"Well," said Dorothy, "this beats me, entirely! I guess the little Pink Bear has gone crazy."

"Perhaps," called Scraps, who was rapidly turning "cartwheels" all around the perplexed group, "Ozma is invisible."

"Of course!" cried Betsy. "That would account for it."

"Well, I've noticed that people can speak, even when they've been made invisible," said the Wizard. And then he looked all around him and said in a solemn voice: "Ozma, are you here?"

There was no reply. Dorothy asked the question, too, and so did Button-Bright and Trot and Betsy; but none received any reply at all.

"It's strange—it's terrible strange!" muttered Cayke the Cookie Cook. "I was sure that the little Pink Bear always tells the truth."

"I still believe in his honesty," said the Frogman, and this tribute so pleased the Bear King that he gave these last speakers grateful looks, but still gazed sourly on the others.

"Come to think of it," remarked the Wizard, "Ozma couldn't be invisible, for she is a fairy and fairies cannot be made invisible against their will. Of course she could be imprisoned by the magician, or even enchanted, or transformed, in spite of her fairy powers; but Ugu could not render her invisible by any magic at his command."

"I wonder if she's been transformed into Button-Bright?" said Dorothy nervously. Then she looked steadily at the boy and asked: "Are you Ozma? Tell me truly!"

Button-Bright laughed.

"You're getting rattled, Dorothy," he replied. "Nothing ever enchants *me*. If I were Ozma, do you think I'd have tumbled into that hole?"

"Anyhow," said the Wizard, "Ozma would never try to deceive her friends, or prevent them from recognizing her, in whatever form she happened to be. The puzzle is still a puzzle, so let us go on to the wicker castle and question the magician himself. Since it was he who stole our Ozma, Ugu is the one who must tell us where to find her."

Chapter 21

MAGIC AGAINST MAGIC

The Wizard's advice was good, so again they started in the direction of the low mountain on the crest of which the wicker castle had been built. They had been gradually advancing up-hill, so now the elevation seemed to them more like a round knoll than a mountain-top. However, the sides of the knoll were sloping and covered with green grass, so there was a stiff climb before them yet.

Undaunted, they plodded on and had almost reached the knoll when they suddenly observed that it was surrounded by a circle of flame. At first the flames barely rose above the ground, but presently they grew higher and higher until a circle of

flaming tongues of fire taller than any of their heads quite surrounded the hill on which the wicker castle stood. When they
approached the flames the heat was so intense that it drove
them back again.

"This will never do for me!" exclaimed the Patchwork Girl.
"I catch fire very easily."

"It won't do for me, either," grumbled the Sawhorse,
prancing to the rear.

"I also strongly object to fire," said the Bear King, following the Sawhorse to a safe distance and hugging the little Pink
Bear with his paws.

"I suppose the foolish Shoemaker imagines these blazes
will stop us," remarked the Wizard, with a smile of scorn for
Ugu. "But I am able to inform you that this is merely a simple
magic trick which the robber stole from Glinda the Good, and
by good fortune I know how to destroy these flames, as well as
how to produce them. Will some one of you kindly give me a
match?"

You may be sure the girls carried no matches, nor did the
Frogman or Cayke or any of the animals. But Button-Bright,
after searching carefully through his pockets, which contained
all sorts of useful and useless things, finally produced a match
and handed it to the Wizard, who tied it to the end of a branch
which he tore from a small tree growing near them. Then the
little Wizard carefully lighted the match and running forward
thrust it into the nearest flame. Instantly the circle of fire

began to die away and soon vanished completely, leaving the way clear for them to proceed.

"That was funny!" laughed Button-Bright.

"Yes," agreed the Wizard, "it seems odd that a little match could destroy such a great circle of fire, but when Glinda invented this trick she believed no one would ever think of a match being a remedy for fire. I suppose even Ugu doesn't know how we managed to quench the flames of his barrier, for only Glinda and I know the secret. Glinda's Book of Magic, which Ugu stole, told how to make the flames, but not how to put them out."

They now formed in marching order and proceeded to advance up the slope of the hill; but had not gone far when before them rose a wall of steel, the surface of which was thickly covered with sharp, gleaming points resembling daggers. The wall completely surrounded the wicker castle and its sharp points prevented anyone from climbing it. Even the Patchwork Girl might be ripped to pieces if she dared attempt it.

"Ah!" exclaimed the Wizard cheerfully, "Ugu is now using one of my own tricks against me. But this is more serious than the Barrier of Fire, because the only way to destroy the wall is to get on the other side of it."

"How can that be done?" asked Dorothy.

The Wizard looked thoughtfully around his little party and his face grew troubled.

"It's a pretty high wall," he sadly remarked. "I'm pretty sure the Cowardly Lion could not leap over it."

"I'm sure of that, too!" said the Lion with a shudder of fear. "If I foolishly tried such a leap I would be caught on those dreadful spikes."

"I think I could do it, sir," said the Frogman, with a bow to the Wizard. "It is an up-hill jump, as well as being a high jump, but I'm considered something of a jumper by my friends in the Yip Country and I believe a good strong leap will carry me to the other side."

"I'm sure it would," agreed the Cookie Cook.

"Leaping, you know, is a froglike accomplishment," continued the Frogman, modestly, "but please tell me what I am to do when I reach the other side of the wall."

"You're a brave creature," said the Wizard admiringly. "Has anyone a pin?"

Betsy had one, which she gave him.

"All you need do," said the Wizard to the Frogman, giving him the pin, "is to stick this into the other side of the wall."

"But the wall is of steel!" exclaimed the big frog.

"I know; at least, it *seems* to be steel; but do as I tell you. Stick the pin into the wall and it will disappear."

The Frogman took off his handsome coat and carefully folded it and laid it on the grass. Then he removed his hat and laid it, together with his gold-headed cane, beside the coat. He then went back a way and made three powerful leaps, in rapid succession. The first two leaps took him to the wall and the third leap carried him well over it, to the amazement of all. For a short time he disappeared from their view, but when he had obeyed the Wizard's injunction and had thrust the pin into the wall, the huge barrier vanished and showed them the form of the Frogman, who now went to where his coat lay and put it on again.

"We thank you very much," said the delighted Wizard. "That was the most wonderful leap I ever saw and it has saved us from defeat by our enemy. Let us now hurry on to the castle before Ugu the Shoemaker thinks up some other means to stop us."

"We must have surprised him, so far," declared Dorothy.

"Yes, indeed. The fellow knows a lot of magic—all of our tricks and some of his own," replied the Wizard. "So, if he is half as clever as he ought to be, we shall have trouble with him yet."

He had scarcely spoken these words when out from the gates of the wicker castle marched a regiment of soldiers, clad in gay uniforms and all bearing long, pointed spears and sharp battle-axes. These soldiers were girls, and the uniforms were short skirts of yellow and black satin, golden shoes, bands of gold across their foreheads and necklaces of glittering jewels. Their jackets were scarlet, braided with silver cords. There were hundreds of these girl-soldiers, and they were more terrible than beautiful, being strong and fierce in appearance.

They formed a circle all around the castle and faced outward, their spears pointed toward the invaders and their battle-axes held over their shoulders, ready to strike.

Of course our friends halted at once, for they had not expected this dreadful array of soldiery. The Wizard seemed puzzled and his companions exchanged discouraged looks.

"I'd no idea Ugu had such an army as that," said Dorothy. "The castle doesn't look big enough to hold them all."

"It isn't," declared the Wizard.

"But they all marched out of it."

"They seemed to; but I don't believe it is a real army at all. If Ugu the Shoemaker had so many people living with him, I'm sure the Czarover of Herku would have mentioned the fact to us."

"They're only girls!" laughed Scraps.

"Girls are the fiercest soldiers of all," declared the Frog-man. "They are more brave than men and they have better nerves. That is probably why the magician uses them for soldiers and has sent them to oppose us."

No one argued this statement, for all were staring hard at the line of soldiers, which now, having taken a defiant position, remained motionless.

"Here is a trick of magic new to me," admitted the Wizard, after a time. "I do not believe the army is real, but the spears may be sharp enough to prick us, nevertheless, so we must be cautious. Let us take time to consider how to meet this difficulty."

While they were thinking it over Scraps danced closer to the line of girl soldiers. Her button eyes sometimes saw more than did the natural eyes of her comrades and so, after staring hard at the magician's army, she boldly advanced and danced right through the threatening line! On the other side she waved her stuffed arms and called out, "Come on, folks. The spears can't hurt you."

"Ah!" said the Wizard, gaily, "an optical illusion, as I thought. Let us all follow the Patchwork Girl."

The three little girls were somewhat nervous in attempting to brave the spears and battle-axes, but after the others had safely passed the line they ventured to follow. And when all had passed through the ranks of the girl army, the army itself magically disappeared from view.

All this time our friends had been getting farther up the hill and nearer to the wicker castle. Now, continuing their advance, they expected something else to oppose their way, but to their astonishment nothing happened and presently they arrived at the wicker gates, which stood wide open, and boldly entered the domain of Ugu the Shoemaker.

—··< Chapter 22 >··—

In the WICKER CASTLE

No sooner were the Wizard of Oz and his followers well within the castle entrance when the big gates swung to with a clang and heavy bars dropped across them. They looked at one another uneasily, but no one cared to speak of the incident. If they were indeed prisoners in the wicker castle it was evident they must find a way to escape, but their first duty was to attend to the errand on which they had come and seek the Royal Ozma, whom they believed to be a prisoner of the magician, and rescue her.

They found they had entered a square courtyard, from which an entrance led into the main building of the castle. No person had appeared to greet them, so far, although a gaudy peacock perched upon the wall, cackled with laughter and said in its sharp, shrill voice: "Poor fools! Poor fools!"

"I hope the peacock is mistaken," remarked the Frogman, but no one else paid any attention to the bird. They were a little awed by the stillness and loneliness of the place.

As they entered the doors of the castle, which stood invitingly open, these also closed behind them and huge bolts shot into place. The animals had all accompanied the party into the castle, because they felt it would be dangerous for them to separate. They were forced to follow a zigzag passage, turning this way and that, until finally they entered a great central hall, circular in form and with a high dome from which was suspended an enormous chandelier.

The Wizard went first, and Dorothy, Betsy and Trot followed him, Toto keeping at the heels of his little mistress. Then came the Lion, the Woozy and the Sawhorse; then Cayke the Cookie Cook and Button-Bright; then the Lavender Bear carrying the Pink Bear; and finally the Frogman and the Patchwork Girl, with Hank the Mule tagging behind. So it was the Wizard who caught the first glimpse of the big domed hall, but the others quickly followed and gathered in a wondering group just within the entrance.

Upon a raised platform at one side was a heavy table on which lay Glinda's Great Book of Records; but the platform was firmly fastened to the floor and the table was fastened to the platform and the Book was chained fast to the table—just as it had been when it was kept in Glinda's palace. On the wall over the table hung Ozma's Magic Picture. On a row of shelves at the opposite side of the hall stood all the chemicals and essences of magic and all the magical instruments that had been stolen from Glinda and Ozma and the Wizard, with glass doors covering the shelves so that no one could get at them.

And in a far corner sat Ugu the Shoemaker, his feet lazily extended, his skinny hands clasped behind his head. He was leaning back at his ease and calmly smoking a long pipe. Around the magician was a sort of cage, seemingly made of golden bars set wide apart, and at his feet—also within the cage—reposed the long-sought diamond-studded dishpan of Cayke the Cookie Cook.

Princess Ozma of Oz was nowhere to be seen.

"Well, well," said Ugu, when the invaders had stood in silence for a moment, staring about them. "This visit is an unexpected pleasure, I assure you. I knew you were coming and I know why you are here. You are not welcome, for I cannot use any of you to my advantage, but as you have insisted on coming I hope you will make the afternoon call as brief as possible. It won't take long to transact your business with me. You will ask me for Ozma, and my reply will be that you may find her—if you can."

"Sir," answered the Wizard, in a tone of rebuke, "you are a

very wicked and cruel person. I suppose you imagine, because you have stolen this poor woman's dishpan and all the best magic in Oz, that you are more powerful than we are and will be able to triumph over us."

"Yes," said Ugu the Shoemaker, slowly filling his pipe with fresh tobacco from a silver bowl that stood beside him, "that is exactly what I imagine. It will do you no good to demand from me the girl who was formerly the Ruler of Oz, because I will not tell you where I have hidden her—and you can't guess in a thousand years. Neither will I restore to you any of the magic I have captured. I am not so foolish. But bear this in mind: I mean to be the Ruler of Oz myself, hereafter, so I advise you to be careful how you address your future Monarch."

"Ozma is still Ruler of Oz, wherever you may have hidden her," declared the Wizard. "And bear this in mind, miserable Shoemaker: We intend to find her and to rescue her, in time, but our first duty and pleasure will be to conquer you and then punish you for your misdeeds."

"Very well; go ahead and conquer," said Ugu. "I'd really like to see how you can do it."

Now, although the little Wizard had spoken so boldly, he had at the moment no idea how they might conquer the magician. He had that morning given the Frogman, at his request, a dose of zosozo from his bottle, and the Frogman had promised to fight a good fight if it was necessary; but the Wizard knew that strength alone could not avail against magical arts.

The toy Bear King seemed to have some pretty good magic, however, and the Wizard depended to an extent on that. But something ought to be done right away, and the Wizard didn't know what it was.

While he considered this perplexing question and the others stood looking at him as their leader, a queer thing happened. The floor of the great circular hall, on which they were standing, suddenly began to tip. Instead of being flat and level it became a slant, and the slant grew steeper and steeper until none of the party could manage to stand upon it. Presently they all slid down to the wall, which was now under them, and then it became evident that the whole vast room was slowly turning upside down! Only Ugu the Shoemaker, kept in place by the bars of his golden cage, remained in his former position, and the wicked magician seemed to enjoy the surprise of his victims immensely.

First, they all slid down to the wall back of them, but as the room continued to turn over they next slid down the wall and found themselves at the bottom of the great dome, bumping against the big chandelier which, like everything else, was now upside-down.

The turning movement now stopped and the room became stationary. Looking far up, they saw Ugu suspended in his cage at the very top, which had once been the floor.

"Ah," said he, grinning down at them, "the way to conquer is to act, and he who acts promptly is sure to win. This makes a very good prison, from which I am sure you cannot escape. Please amuse yourselves in any way you like, but I must beg you to excuse me, as I have business in another part of my castle."

Saying this, he opened a trap door in the floor of his cage (which was now over his head) and climbed through it and disappeared from their view. The diamond dishpan still remained in the cage, but the bars kept it from falling down on their heads.

"Well, I declare," said the Patchwork Girl, seizing one of the bars of the chandelier and swinging from it, "we must peg one for the Shoemaker, for he has trapped us very cleverly."

"Get off my foot, please," said the Lion to the Sawhorse.

"And oblige me, Mr. Mule," remarked the Woozy, "by taking your tail out of my left eye."

"It's rather crowded down here," explained Dorothy, "because the dome is rounding and we have all slid into the middle of it. But let us keep as quiet as possible until we can think what's best to be done."

"Dear, dear!" wailed Cayke; "I wish I had my darling dishpan," and she held her arms longingly toward it.

"I wish I had the magic on those shelves up there," sighed the Wizard.

"Don't you s'pose we could get to it?" asked Trot anxiously.

"We'd have to fly," laughed the Patchwork Girl.

But the Wizard took the suggestion seriously, and so did

the Frogman. They talked it over and soon planned an attempt to reach the shelves where the magical instruments were. First the Frogman lay against the rounding dome and braced his foot on the stem of the chandelier; then the Wizard climbed over him and lay on the dome with his feet on the Frogman's shoulders; the Cookie Cook came next; then Button-Bright climbed to the woman's shoulders; then Dorothy climbed up, and Betsy and Trot, and finally the Patchwork Girl, and all their lengths made a long line that reached far up the dome but not far enough for Scraps to touch the shelves.

"Wait a minute; perhaps I can reach the magic," called the Bear King, and began scrambling up the bodies of the others. But when he came to the Cookie Cook his soft paws tickled her side so that she squirmed and upset the whole line. Down they came, tumbling in a heap against the animals, and although no one was much hurt it was a bad mix-up and the Frogman, who was at the bottom, almost lost his temper before he could get on his feet again.

Cayke positively refused to try what she called "the pyramid act" again, and as the Wizard was now convinced they could not reach the magic tools in that manner, the attempt was abandoned. "But *something* must be done," said the Wizard, and then he turned to the Lavender Bear and asked: "Cannot your Majesty's magic help us to escape from here?"

"My magic powers are limited," was the reply. "When I was stuffed, the fairies stood by and slyly dropped some magic into my stuffing. Therefore I can do any of the magic that's inside me, but nothing else. You, however, are a wizard, and a wizard should be able to do anything."

"Your Majesty forgets that my tools of magic have been stolen," said the Wizard sadly, "and a wizard without tools is as helpless as a carpenter without a hammer or saw."

"Don't give up," pleaded Button-Bright, "'cause if we can't get out of this queer prison, we'll all starve to death."

"Not I!" laughed the Patchwork Girl, now standing on top of the chandelier, at the place that was meant to be the bottom of it.

"Don't talk of such dreadful things," said Trot, shuddering. "We came here to capture the Shoemaker, didn't we?"

"Yes, and to save Ozma," said Betsy.

"And here we are, captured ourselves, and my darling dishpan up there in plain sight!" wailed the Cookie Cook, wiping her eyes on the tail of the Frogman's coat.

"Hush!" called the Lion, with a low, deep growl. "Give the Wizard time to think."

"He has plenty of time," said Scraps. "What he needs is the Scarecrow's brains."

After all, it was little Dorothy who came to their rescue, and her ability to save them was almost as much a surprise to the girl as it was to her friends. Dorothy had been secretly testing the powers of her Magic Belt, which she had once captured from the Nome King, and experimenting with it in various ways, ever since she had started on this eventful journey. At different times she had stolen away from the others of her party and in solitude had tried to find out what the Magic Belt could do and what it could not do. There were a lot of things it could not do, she discovered, but she learned some things about the Belt which even her girl friends did not suspect she knew.

For one thing, she had remembered that when the Nome King owned it the Magic Belt used to perform transformations, and by thinking hard she had finally recalled the way in which such transformations had been accomplished. Better than this, however, was the discovery that the Magic Belt would grant its wearer one wish a day. All she need do was close her right eye and wiggle her left toe and then draw a long breath and make her wish. Yesterday she had wished in secret for a box of caramels, and instantly found the box beside her. Today she had saved her daily wish in case she might need it in an emergency, and the time had now come when she must use the wish to enable her to escape with her friends from the prison in which Ugu had caught them.

So, without telling anyone what she intended to do—for she had only used the wish once and could not be certain how powerful the Magic Belt might be—Dorothy closed her right eye and wiggled her left big toe and drew a long breath and wished with all her might. The next moment the room began to revolve again, as slowly as before, and by degrees they all

slid to the side wall and down the wall to the floor—all but
Scraps, who was so astonished that she still clung to the chandelier. When the big hall was in its proper position again and
the others stood firmly upon the floor of it, they looked far
up the dome and saw the Patchwork girl swinging from the
chandelier.

"Good gracious!" cried Dorothy. "How ever will you get
down?"

"Won't the room keep turning?" asked Scraps.

"I hope not. I believe it has stopped for good," said Princess
Dorothy.

"Then stand from under, so you won't get hurt!" shouted
the Patchwork Girl, and as soon as they had obeyed this
request she let go the chandelier and came tumbling down
heels over head and twisting and turning in a very exciting
manner. Plump! She fell on the tiled floor, and they ran to her
and rolled her and patted her into shape again.

Chapter 23

The DEFIANCE of UGU the SHOEMAKER

The delay caused by Scraps had prevented anyone from running to the shelves to secure the magic instruments so badly needed. Even Cayke neglected to get her diamond-studded dishpan because she was watching the Patchwork Girl. And now the magician had opened his trap door and appeared in his golden cage again, frowning angrily because his prisoners had been able to turn their upside-down prison right side up.

"Which of you has dared defy my magic?" he shouted in a terrible voice.

"It was I," answered Dorothy calmly.

"Then I shall destroy you, for you are only an Earth girl and no fairy," he said, and began to mumble some magic words.

Dorothy now realized that Ugu must be treated as an enemy, so she advanced toward the corner in which he sat, saying as she went, "I am not afraid of you, Mr. Shoemaker, and I think you'll be sorry, pretty soon, that you're such a bad man. You can't destroy me and I won't destroy you, but I'm going to punish you for your wickedness."

Ugu laughed a laugh that was not nice to hear, and then he waved his hand. Dorothy was halfway across the room when suddenly a wall of glass rose before her and stopped her progress. Through the glass she could see the magician sneering at her because she was a weak little girl, and this provoked her. Although the glass wall obliged her to halt, she instantly pressed both hands to her Magic Belt and cried in a loud voice: "Ugu the Shoemaker, by the magic virtues of the Magic Belt, I command you to become a dove!"

The magician instantly realized he was being enchanted, for he could feel his form changing. He struggled desperately against the enchantment, mumbling magic words and making magic passes with his hands. And in one way he succeeded in defeating Dorothy's purpose, for while his form soon changed to that of a grey dove, the dove was of an enormous size—bigger even than Ugu had been as a man—and this feat he had been able to accomplish before his powers of magic wholly deserted him.

And the dove was not gentle, as doves usually are, for Ugu was terribly enraged at the little girl's success. His books had told him nothing of the Nome King's Magic Belt, the Country of the Nomes being outside the Land of Oz. He knew, however, that he was likely to be conquered unless he made a fierce fight, so he spread his wings and rose in the air and flew directly toward Dorothy. The Wall of Glass had disappeared the instant Ugu became transformed.

Dorothy had meant to command the Belt to transform the magician into a Dove of Peace, but in her excitement she forgot to say more than "dove," and now Ugu was not a Dove of Peace by any means, but rather a spiteful Dove of War. His size made his sharp beak and claws very dangerous, but Dorothy was not afraid when he came darting toward her with his talons outstretched and his sword-like beak open. She knew the Magic Belt would protect its wearer from harm.

But the Frogman did not know that fact and became alarmed at the little girl's seeming danger. So he gave a sudden leap and leaped full upon the back of the great dove.

Then began a desperate struggle. The dove was as strong as Ugu had been, and in size it was considerably bigger than the Frogman. But the Frogman had eaten the zosozo, and it had made him fully as strong as Ugu the Dove. At the first leap he bore the dove to the floor, but the giant bird got free and began to bite and claw the Frogman, beating him down with its great wings whenever he attempted to rise. The thick, tough skin of the big frog was not easily damaged, but Dorothy feared for her champion and by again using the transformation power of the Magic Belt she made the dove grow small, until it was no larger than a canary bird.

Ugu had not lost his knowledge of magic when he lost his shape as a man, and he now realized it was hopeless to oppose the power of the Magic Belt and knew that his only hope of escape lay in instant action. So he quickly flew into the golden jeweled dishpan he had stolen from Cayke the Cookie Cook and, as birds can talk as well as beasts or men in the Fairyland of Oz, he muttered the magic word that was required and wished himself in the Country of the Quadlings—which was as far away from the wicker castle as he believed he could get.

Our friends did not know, of course, what Ugu was about to do. They saw the dishpan tremble an instant and then disappear, the dove disappearing with it, and although they waited expectantly for some minutes for the magician's return, Ugu did not come back again.

"Seems to me," said the Wizard in a cheerful voice, "that we have conquered the wicked magician more quickly than we expected to."

"Don't say 'we'—Dorothy did it!" cried the Patchwork Girl, turning three somersaults in succession and then walking around on her hands. "Hurrah for Dorothy!"

"I thought you said you did not know how to use the magic of the Nome King's Belt," said the Wizard to Dorothy.

"I didn't know at that time," she replied, "but afterward I remembered how the Nome King once used the Magic Belt to enchant people and transform 'em into ornaments and all sorts of things; so I tried some enchantments in secret, and after a while I transformed the Sawhorse into a potato-masher and back again, and the Cowardly Lion into a pussycat and back again, and then I knew the thing would work all right."

"When did you perform those enchantments?" asked the Wizard, much surprised.

"One night when all the rest of you were asleep but Scraps, and she had gone chasing moonbeams."

"Well," remarked the Wizard, "your discovery has certainly saved us a lot of trouble, and we must all thank the Frogman, too, for making such a good fight. The dove's shape had Ugu's evil disposition inside it, and that made the monster bird dangerous."

The Frogman was looking sad because the bird's talons had torn his pretty clothes, but he bowed with much dignity at this well-deserved praise. Cayke, however, had squatted on the floor and was sobbing bitterly.

"My precious dishpan is gone!" she wailed. "Gone, just as I had found it again!"

"Never mind," said Trot, trying to comfort her, "it's sure to be *some*where, so we'll cert'nly run across it some day."

"Yes, indeed," added Betsy; "now that we have Ozma's Magic Picture, we can tell just where the Dove went with your dishpan." They all approached the Magic Picture, and Dorothy wished it to show the enchanted form of Ugu the Shoemaker, wherever it might be. At once there appeared in the frame of the Picture a scene in the far Quadling Country, where the Dove was perched disconsolately on the limb of a tree and the jeweled dishpan lay on the ground just underneath the limb.

"But where is the place—how far or how near?" asked Cayke anxiously.

"The Book of Records will tell us that," answered the Wizard. So they looked in the Great Book and read the following:

> "Ugu the Magician, being transformed into a dove by Princess Dorothy of Oz, has used the magic of the golden dishpan to carry him instantly to the northeast corner of the Quadling Country."

"That's all right," said Dorothy. "Don't worry, Cayke, for the Scarecrow and the Tin Woodman are in that part of the country, looking for Ozma, and they'll surely find your dishpan."

"Good gracious!" exclaimed Button-Bright. "We've forgot all about Ozma. Let's find out where the magician hid her."

Back to the Magic Picture they trooped, but when they wished to see Ozma, wherever she might be hidden, only a round black spot appeared in the center of the canvas.

"I don't see how *that* can be Ozma!" said Dorothy, much puzzled.

"It seems to be the best the Magic Picture can do, however," said the Wizard, no less surprised. "If it's an enchantment, looks as if the magician had transformed Ozma into a chunk of pitch."

Chapter 24

The LITTLE PINK BEAR
SPEAKS TRULY

For several minutes they all stood staring at the black spot on the canvas of the Magic Picture, wondering what it could mean.

"P'r'aps we'd better ask the little Pink Bear about Ozma," suggested Trot.

"Pshaw!" said Button-Bright. "*He* don't know anything."

"He never makes a mistake," declared the King.

"He did once, surely," said Betsy. "But perhaps he wouldn't make a mistake again."

"He won't have the chance," grumbled the Bear King.

"We might hear what he has to say," said Dorothy. "It

won't do any harm to ask the Pink Bear where Ozma is."

"I will not have him questioned," declared the King, in a surly voice. "I do not intend to allow my little Pink Bear to be again insulted by your foolish doubts. He never makes a mistake."

"Didn't he say Ozma was in that hole in the ground?" asked Betsy.

"He did; and I am certain she was there," replied the Lavender Bear.

Scraps laughed jeeringly and the others saw there was no use arguing with the stubborn Bear King, who seemed to have absolute faith in his Pink Bear. The Wizard, who knew that magical things can usually be depended upon, and that the little Pink Bear was able to answer questions by some remarkable power of magic, thought it wise to apologize to the Lavender Bear for the unbelief of his friends, at the same time urging the King to consent to question the Pink Bear once more. Cayke and the Frogman also pleaded with the big Bear, who finally agreed, although rather ungraciously, to put the little Bear's wisdom to the test once more. So he sat the little one on his knee and turned the crank and the Wizard himself asked the questions in a very respectful tone of voice.

"Where is Ozma?" was his first query.

"Here, in this room," answered the little Pink Bear.

They all looked around the room, but of course did not see her.

"In what part of the room is she?" was the Wizard's next question.

"In Button-Bright's pocket," said the little Pink Bear.

This reply amazed them all, you may be sure, and although the three girls smiled and Scraps yelled: "Hoo-ray!" in derision, the Wizard turned to consider the matter with grave thoughtfulness.

"In which one of Button-Bright's pockets is Ozma?" he presently inquired.

"In the lefthand jacket-pocket," said the little Pink Bear.

"The pink one has gone crazy!" exclaimed Button-Bright, staring hard at the little bear on the big bear's knee.

"I am not so sure of that," declared the Wizard. "If Ozma proves to be really in your pocket, then the little Pink Bear spoke truly when he said Ozma was in that hole in the ground. For at that time you were also in the hole, and after we had pulled you out of it the little Pink Bear said Ozma was not in the hole."

"He never makes a mistake," asserted the Bear King, stoutly.

"Empty that pocket, Button-Bright, and let's see what's in it," requested Dorothy.

So Button-Bright laid the contents of his left jacket-pocket on the table. These proved to be a peg-top, a bunch of string, a small rubber ball and a golden peach-pit.

"What's this?" asked the Wizard, picking up the peach-pit and examining it closely.

"Oh," said the boy, "I saved that to show to the girls, and

then forgot all about it. It came out of a lonesome peach that I found in the orchard back yonder, and which I ate while I was lost. It looks like gold, and I never saw a peach-pit like it before."

"Nor I," said the Wizard, "and that makes it seem suspicious."

All heads were bent over the golden peach-pit. The Wizard turned it over several times and then took out his pocket-knife and pried the pit open.

As the two halves fell apart a pink, cloud-like haze came pouring from the golden peach-pit, almost filling the big room, and from the haze a form took shape and settled beside them. Then, as the haze faded away, a sweet voice said: "Thank you, my friends!" and there before them stood their lovely girl Ruler, Ozma of Oz.

With a cry of delight Dorothy rushed forward and embraced her. Scraps turned gleeful flip-flops all around the room. Button-Bright gave a low whistle of astonishment. The Frogman took off his tall hat and bowed low before the beautiful girl who had been freed from her enchantment in so startling a manner.

For a time no sound was heard beyond the low murmur of delight that came from the amazed group, but presently the growl of the big Lavender Bear grew louder, and he said in a tone of triumph: "He never makes a mistake!"

Chapter 25

OZMA of OZ

"It's funny," said Toto, standing before his friend the Lion and wagging his tail, "but I've found my growl at last! I am positive, now, that it was the cruel magician who stole it."

"Let's hear your growl," requested the Lion.

"Gr-r-r-r-r!" said Toto.

"That is fine," declared the big beast. "It isn't as loud or as deep as the growl of the big Lavender Bear, but it is a very respectable growl for a small dog. Where did you find it, Toto?"

"I was smelling in the corner yonder," said Toto, "when suddenly a mouse ran out—and I growled!"

The others were all busy congratulating Ozma, who was

very happy at being released from the confinement of the golden peach-pit, where the magician had placed her with the notion that she never could be found or liberated.

"And only to think," cried Dorothy, "that Button-Bright has been carrying you in his pocket all this time, and we never knew it!"

"The little Pink Bear told you," said the Bear King, "but you wouldn't believe him."

"Never mind, my dears," said Ozma graciously; "all is well that ends well, and you couldn't be expected to know I was inside the peach-pit. Indeed, I feared I would remain a captive much longer than I did, for Ugu is a bold and clever magician and he had hidden me very securely."

"You were in a fine peach," said Button-Bright; "the best I ever ate."

"The magician was foolish to make the peach so tempting," remarked the Wizard; "but Ozma would lend beauty to any transformation."

"How did you manage to conquer Ugu the Shoemaker?" inquired the girl Ruler of Oz.

Dorothy started to tell the story and Trot helped her, and Button-Bright wanted to relate it in his own way, and the Wizard tried to make it clear to Ozma, and Betsy had to remind them of important things they left out, and all together there was such a chatter that it was a wonder that Ozma understood any of it. But she listened patiently, with a smile on her lovely face at their eagerness, and presently had gleaned all the details of their adventures.

Ozma thanked the Frogman very earnestly for his assistance and she advised Cayke the Cookie Cook to dry her weeping eyes, for she promised to take her to the Emerald City and see that her cherished dishpan was restored to her. Then the beautiful Ruler took a chain of emeralds from around her own neck and placed it around the neck of the little Pink Bear.

"Your wise answers to the questions of my friends," said she, "helped them to rescue me. Therefore I am deeply grateful to you and to your noble King."

The bead eyes of the little Pink Bear stared unresponsive to this praise until the big Lavender Bear turned the crank in its side, when it said in its squeaky voice: "I thank your Majesty."

"For my part," returned the Bear King, "I realize that you were well worth saving, Miss Ozma, and so I am much pleased that we could be of service to you. By means of my Magic Wand I have been creating exact images of your Emerald City and your royal palace, and I must confess that they are more attractive than any places I have ever seen—not excepting Bear Center."

"I would like to entertain you in my palace," returned Ozma, sweetly, "and you are welcome to return with me and to make me a long visit, if your bear subjects can spare you from your own kingdom."

"As for that," answered the King, "my kingdom causes me little worry, and I often find it somewhat tame and uninteresting. Therefore I am glad to accept your kind invitation. Corporal Waddle may be trusted to care for my bears in my absence."

"And you'll bring the little Pink Bear?" asked Dorothy eagerly.

"Of course, my dear; I would not willingly part with him."

They remained in the wicker castle for three days, carefully packing all the magical things that had been stolen by Ugu and also taking whatever in the way of magic the shoemaker had inherited from his ancestors.

"For," said Ozma, "I have forbidden any of my subjects except Glinda the Good and the Wizard of Oz to practice magical arts, because they cannot be trusted to do good and not harm. Therefore Ugu must never again be permitted to work magic of any sort."

"Well," remarked Dorothy cheerfully, "a dove can't do much in the way of magic, anyhow, and I'm going to keep Ugu in the form of a dove until he reforms and becomes a good and honest shoemaker."

When everything was packed and loaded on the backs of the animals, they set out for the river, taking a more direct route than that by which Cayke and the Frogman had come. In this way they avoided the Cities of Thi and Herku and Bear Center and after a pleasant journey reached the Winkie River and found a jolly ferryman who had a fine, big boat and was willing to carry the entire party by water to a place quite near to the Emerald City.

The river had many windings and many branches, and the journey did not end in a day, but finally the boat floated into a pretty lake which was but a short distance from Ozma's home. Here the jolly ferryman was rewarded for his labors and then the entire party set out in a grand procession to march to the Emerald City.

News that the Royal Ozma had been found spread quickly throughout the neighborhood and both sides of the road soon became lined with loyal subjects of the beautiful and beloved Ruler. Therefore Ozma's ears heard little but cheers and her eyes beheld little else than waving handkerchiefs and banners during all the triumphal march from the lake to the city's gates.

And there she met a still greater concourse, for all the inhabitants of the Emerald City turned out to welcome her return and several bands played gay music and all the houses were decorated with flags and bunting and never before were the people so joyous and happy as at this moment when they welcomed home their girl Ruler. For she had been lost and was now found again, and surely that was cause for rejoicing.

Glinda was at the royal palace to meet the returning party and the good Sorceress was indeed glad to have her Great Book of Records returned to her, as well as all the precious collection of magic instruments and elixirs and chemicals that had been stolen from her castle. Cap'n Bill and the Wizard at once hung the Magic Picture upon the wall of Ozma's boudoir and the Wizard was so light-hearted that he did several tricks with the tools in his black bag to amuse his companions and prove that once again he was a powerful wizard.

For a whole week there was feasting and merriment and all sorts of joyous festivities at the palace, in honor of Ozma's safe return. The Lavender Bear and the little Pink Bear received much attention and were honored by all, much to the Bear King's satisfaction. The Frogman speedily became a favorite at the Emerald City and the Shaggy Man and Tik-Tok and Jack Pumpkinhead, who had now returned from their search, were very polite to the big frog and made him feel quite at home. Even the Cookie Cook, because she was quite a stranger and Ozma's guest, was shown as much deference as if she had been a Queen.

"All the same, your Majesty," said Cayke to Ozma, day after day, with tiresome repetition, "I hope you will soon find my jeweled dishpan, for never can I be quite happy without it."

·——·••◄ Chapter 26 ►••·——··

DOROTHY FORGIVES

he grey dove which had once been Ugu the Shoemaker sat on its tree in the far Quadling Country and moped, chirping dismally and brooding over its misfortunes. After a time, the Scarecrow and the Tin Woodman came along and sat beneath the tree, paying no heed to the mutterings of the grey dove.

The Tin Woodman took a small oilcan from his tin pocket and carefully oiled his tin joints with it. While he was thus engaged, the Scarecrow remarked, "I feel much better, dear comrade, since we found that heap of nice clean straw and you stuffed me anew with it."

"And I feel much better now that my joints are oiled," returned the Tin Woodman, with a sigh of pleasure. "You and I, friend Scarecrow, are much more easily cared for than those clumsy meat people, who spend half their time dressing in fine clothes and who must live in splendid dwellings in order to be contented and happy. You and I do not eat, and so we are spared the dreadful bother of getting three meals a day. Nor do we waste half our lives in sleep, a condition that causes the meat people to lose all consciousness and become as thoughtless and helpless as logs of wood."

"You speak truly," responded the Scarecrow, tucking some wisps of straw into his breast with his padded fingers. "I often feel sorry for the meat people, many of whom are my friends. Even the beasts are happier than they, for they require less to make them content. And the birds are the luckiest creatures of all, for they can fly swiftly where they will and find a home at any place they care to perch; their food consists of seeds and grains they gather from the fields and their drink is a sip of water from some running brook. If I could not be a Scarecrow—or a Tin Woodman—my next choice would be to live as a bird does."

The grey dove had listened carefully to this speech and seemed to find comfort in it, for it hushed its moaning. And just then the Tin Woodman discovered Cayke's dishpan, which was on the ground quite near to him.

"Here is a rather pretty utensil," he said, taking it in his tin hand to examine it, "but I would not care to own it. Whoever fashioned it of gold and covered it with diamonds did not add to its usefulness, nor do I consider it as beautiful as the bright dishpans of tin one usually sees. No yellow color is ever so handsome as the silver sheen of tin," and he turned to look at his tin legs and body with approval.

"I cannot quite agree with you there," replied the Scarecrow. "My straw stuffing has a light yellow color, and it is not only pretty to look at but it crunkles most delightfully when I move."

"Let us admit that all colors are good in their proper places," said the Tin Woodman, who was too kind-hearted to quarrel; "but you must agree with me that a dishpan that is yellow is unnatural. What shall we do with this one, which we have just found?"

"Let us carry it back to the Emerald City," suggested the Scarecrow. "Some of our friends might like to have it for a foot-bath, and in using it that way, its golden color and sparkling ornaments would not injure its usefulness."

So they went away and took the jeweled dishpan with them. And, after wandering through the country for a day or so longer, they learned the news that Ozma had been found. Therefore they straightway returned to the Emerald City and presented the dishpan to Princess Ozma as a token of their joy that she had been restored to them.

Ozma promptly gave the diamond-studded gold dishpan

to Cayke the Cookie Cook, who was so delighted at regaining her lost treasure that she danced up and down in glee and then threw her skinny arms around Ozma's neck and kissed her gratefully. Cayke's mission was now successfully accomplished, but she was having such a good time at the Emerald City that she seemed in no hurry to go back to the Country of the Yips.

It was several weeks after the dishpan had been restored to the Cookie Cook when one day, as Dorothy was seated in the royal gardens with Trot and Betsy beside her, a grey dove came flying down and alighted at the girl's feet.

"I am Ugu the Shoemaker," said the dove in a soft, mourning voice, "and I have come to ask you to forgive me for the great wrong I did in stealing Ozma and the magic that belonged to her and to others."

"Are you sorry, then?" asked Dorothy, looking hard at the bird.

"I am *very* sorry," declared Ugu. "I've been thinking over my misdeeds for a long time, for doves have little else to do but think, and I'm surprised that I was such a wicked man and had so little regard for the rights of others. I am now convinced that even had I succeeded in making myself Ruler of all Oz I should not have been happy, for many days of quiet thought have shown me that only those things one acquires honestly are able to render one content."

"I guess that's so," said Trot.

"Anyhow," said Betsy, "the bad man seems truly sorry, and if he has now become a good and honest man, we ought to forgive him."

"I fear I cannot become a good *man* again," said Ugu, "for the transformation I am under will always keep me in the form of a dove. But, with the kind forgiveness of my former enemies, I hope to become a very good dove, and highly respected."

"Wait here till I run for my Magic Belt," said Dorothy, "and I'll transform you back to your reg'lar shape in a jiffy."

"No—don't do that!" pleaded the dove, fluttering its wings in an excited way. "I only want your forgiveness; I don't want to be a man again. As Ugu the Shoemaker I was skinny and old and unlovely; as a dove I am quite pretty to look at. As a man I was ambitious and cruel, while as a dove I can be content with my lot and happy in my simple life. I have learned to love the free and independent life of a bird and I'd rather not change back."

"Just as you like, Ugu," said Dorothy, resuming her seat. "Perhaps you are right, for you're certainly a better dove than you were a man, and if you should ever backslide, an' feel wicked again, you couldn't do much harm as a grey dove."

"Then you forgive me for all the trouble I caused you?" he asked earnestly.

"Of course; anyone who's sorry just *has* to be forgiven."

"Thank you," said the grey dove, and flew away again.

The
Tin
Woodman
of
OZ

This book is dedicated
to the son of my son,
Frank Alden Baum

To My Readers

I know that some of you have been waiting for this story of the Tin Woodman, because many of my correspondents have asked me, time and again, what ever became of the "pretty Munchkin girl" whom Nick Chopper was engaged to marry before the Wicked Witch enchanted his axe and he traded his flesh for tin. I, too, have wondered what became of her, but until Woot the Wanderer interested himself in the matter the Tin Woodman knew no more than we did. However, he found her, after many thrilling adventures, as you will discover when you have read this story.

I am delighted at the continued interest of both young and old in the Oz stories. A learned college professor recently wrote me to ask: "For readers of what age are your books intended?" It puzzled me to answer that properly, until I had looked over some of the letters I have received. One says: "I'm a little boy five years old, and I just love your Oz stories. My sister, who is writing this for me, reads me the Oz books, but I wish I could read them myself." Another letter says: "I'm a great girl thirteen years old, so you'll be surprised when I tell you I am not too old yet for the Oz stories." Here's another letter: "Since I was a young girl I've never missed getting a Baum book for Christmas. I'm married, now, but am as eager to get and read the Oz stories as ever." And still another writes: "My good wife and I, both more than seventy years of age, believe that we find more real enjoyment in your Oz books than in any other books we read." Considering these statements, I wrote the college professor that my books are intended for all those whose hearts are young, no matter what their ages may be.

I think I am justified in promising that there will be some astonishing revelations about The Magic of Oz in my book for 1919.

Always your loving and grateful friend,

L. Frank Baum, Royal Historian of Oz

"Ozcot" at Hollywood in California, 1918

Chapter 1

WOOT the WANDERER

The Tin Woodman sat on his glittering tin throne in the handsome tin hall of his splendid tin castle in the Winkie Country of the Land of Oz. Beside him, in a chair of woven straw, sat his best friend, the Scarecrow of Oz. At times they spoke to one another of curious things they had seen and strange adventures they had known since first they two had met and become comrades. But at times they were silent, for these things had been talked over many times between them, and they found themselves contented in merely being together, speaking now and then a brief sentence to prove they were wide awake and attentive. But then, these two quaint persons never slept. Why should they sleep, when they never tired?

And now, as the brilliant sun sank low over the Winkie Country of Oz, tinting the glistening tin towers and tin minarets of the tin castle with glorious sunset hues, there approached along a winding pathway Woot the Wanderer, who met at the castle entrance a Winkie servant.

The servants of the Tin Woodman all wore tin helmets and tin breastplates and uniforms covered with tiny tin discs sewed closely together on silver cloth, so that their bodies sparkled as beautifully as did the tin castle—and almost as beautifully as did the Tin Woodman himself.

Woot the Wanderer looked at the man servant—all bright and glittering—and at the magnificent castle—all bright and glittering—and as he looked his eyes grew big with wonder. For Woot was not very big and not very old and, wanderer though he was, this proved the most gorgeous sight that had ever met his boyish gaze.

"Who lives here?" he asked.

"The Emperor of the Winkies, who is the famous Tin Woodman of Oz," replied the servant, who had been trained to treat all strangers with courtesy.

"A Tin Woodman? How queer!" exclaimed the little wanderer.

"Well, perhaps our Emperor is queer," admitted the servant; "but he is a kind master and as honest and true as good tin can make him; so we, who gladly serve him, are apt to forget that he is not like other people."

"May I see him?" asked Woot the Wanderer, after a moment's thought.

"If it please you to wait a moment, I will go and ask him," said the servant, and then he went into the hall where the Tin Woodman sat with his friend the Scarecrow. Both were glad to learn that a stranger had arrived at the castle, for this would give them something new to talk about, so the servant was asked to admit the boy at once.

By the time Woot the Wanderer had passed through the grand corridors—all lined with ornamental tin—and under stately tin archways and through the many tin rooms all set with beautiful tin furniture, his eyes had grown bigger than ever and his whole little body thrilled with amazement. But, astonished though he was, he was able to make a polite bow before the throne and to say in a respectful voice: "I salute your Illustrious Majesty and offer you my humble services."

"Very good!" answered the Tin Woodman in his accustomed cheerful manner. "Tell me who you are, and whence you come."

"I am known as Woot the Wanderer," answered the boy, "and I have come, through many travels and by roundabout ways, from my former home in a far corner of the Gillikin Country of Oz."

"To wander from one's home," remarked the Scarecrow,

"is to encounter dangers and hardships, especially if one is made of meat and bone. Had you no friends in that corner of the Gillikin Country? Was it not homelike and comfortable?"

To hear a man stuffed with straw speak, and speak so well, quite startled Woot, and perhaps he stared a bit rudely at the Scarecrow. But after a moment he replied:

"I had home and friends, your Honorable Strawness, but they were so quiet and happy and comfortable that I found them dismally stupid. Nothing in that corner of Oz interested me, but I believed that in other parts of the country I would find strange people and see new sights, and so I set out upon my wandering journey. I have been a wanderer for nearly a full year, and now my wanderings have brought me to this splendid castle."

"I suppose," said the Tin Woodman, "that in this year you have seen so much that you have become very wise."

"No," replied Woot, thoughtfully, "I am not at all wise, I beg to assure your Majesty. The more I wander the less I find that I know, for in the Land of Oz much wisdom and many things may be learned."

"To learn is simple. Don't you ask questions?" inquired the Scarecrow.

"Yes; I ask as many questions as I dare; but some people refuse to answer questions."

"That is not kind of them," declared the Tin Woodman. "If one does not ask for information he seldom receives it; so

I, for my part, make it a rule to answer any civil question that is asked me."

"So do I," added the Scarecrow, nodding.

"I am glad to hear this," said the Wanderer, "for it makes me bold to ask for something to eat."

"Bless the boy!" cried the Emperor of the Winkies; "how careless of me not to remember that wanderers are usually hungry. I will have food brought you at once."

Saying this he blew upon a tin whistle that was suspended from his tin neck, and at the summons a servant appeared and bowed low. The Tin Woodman ordered food for the stranger, and in a few minutes the servant brought in a tin tray heaped with a choice array of good things to eat, all neatly displayed on tin dishes that were polished till they shone like mirrors. The tray was set upon a tin table drawn before the throne, and the servant placed a tin chair before the table for the boy to seat himself.

"Eat, friend Wanderer," said the Emperor cordially, "and I trust the feast will be to your liking. I, myself, do not eat, being made in such manner that I require no food to keep me alive. Neither does my friend the Scarecrow. But all my Winkie people eat, being formed of flesh, as you are, and so my tin cupboard is never bare, and strangers are always welcome to whatever it contains."

The boy ate in silence for a time, being really hungry, but after his appetite was somewhat satisfied, he said:

"How happened your Majesty to be made of tin, and still be alive?"

"That," replied the tin man, "is a long story."

"The longer the better," said the boy. "Won't you please tell me the story?"

"If you desire it," promised the Tin Woodman, leaning back in his tin throne and crossing his tin legs. "I haven't related my history in a long while, because everyone here knows it nearly as well as I do. But you, being a stranger, are no doubt curious to learn how I became so beautiful and prosperous, so I will recite for your benefit my strange adventures."

"Thank you," said Woot the Wanderer, still eating.

"I was not always made of tin," began the Emperor, "for in the beginning I was a man of flesh and bone and blood and lived in the Munchkin Country of Oz. There I was, by trade, a woodchopper, and contributed my share to the comfort of the Oz people by chopping up the trees of the forest to make firewood, with which the women would cook their meals while the children warmed themselves about the fires. For my home I had a little hut by the edge of the forest, and my life was one of much content until I fell in love with a beautiful Munchkin girl who lived not far away."

"What was the Munchkin girl's name?" asked Woot.

"Nimmie Amee. This girl, so fair that the sunsets blushed when their rays fell upon her, lived with a powerful witch who wore silver shoes and who had made the poor child her slave.

Nimmie Amee was obliged to work from morning till night for the old Witch of the East, scrubbing and sweeping her hut and cooking her meals and washing her dishes. She had to cut firewood, too, until I found her one day in the forest and fell in love with her. After that, I always brought plenty of firewood to Nimmie Amee and we became very friendly. Finally I asked her to marry me, and she agreed to do so, but the Witch happened to overhear our conversation and it made her very angry, for she did not wish her slave to be taken away from her. The Witch commanded me never to come near Nimmie Amee again, but I told her I was my own master and would do as I pleased, not realizing that this was a careless way to speak to a Witch.

"The next day, as I was cutting wood in the forest, the cruel Witch enchanted my axe, so that it slipped and cut off my right leg."

"How dreadful!" cried Woot the Wanderer.

"Yes, it was a seeming misfortune," agreed the Tin Man, "for a one-legged woodchopper is of little use in his trade. But I would not allow the Witch to conquer me so easily. I knew a very skillful mechanic at the other side of the forest, who was my friend, so I hopped on one leg to him and asked him to help me. He soon made me a new leg out of tin and fastened it cleverly to my meat body. It had joints at the knee and at the ankle and was almost as comfortable as the leg I had lost."

"Your friend must have been a wonderful workman!" exclaimed Woot.

"He was, indeed," admitted the Emperor. "He was a tin-smith by trade and could make anything out of tin. When I returned to Nimmie Amee, the girl was delighted and threw her arms around my neck and kissed me, declaring she was proud of me. The Witch saw the kiss and was more angry than before. When I went to work in the forest, next day, my axe, being still enchanted, slipped and cut off my other leg. Again I hopped—on my tin leg—to my friend the tinsmith, who kindly made me another tin leg and fastened it to my body. So I returned joyfully to Nimmie Amee, who was much pleased with my glittering legs and promised that when we were wed she would always keep them oiled and polished. But the Witch was more furious than ever, and as soon as I raised my axe to chop, it twisted around and cut off one of my arms. The tin-smith made me a tin arm and I was not much worried, because Nimmie Amee declared she still loved me."

Chapter 2

The HEART of the TIN WOODMAN

The Emperor of the Winkies paused in his story to reach for an oil-can, with which he carefully oiled the joints in his tin throat, for his voice had begun to squeak a little. Woot the Wanderer, having satisfied his hunger, watched this oiling process with much curiosity, but begged the Tin Man to go on with his tale.

"The Witch with the Silver Shoes hated me for having defied her," resumed the Emperor, his voice now sounding clear as a bell, "and she insisted that Nimmie Amee should never marry me. Therefore she made the enchanted axe cut off my other arm, and the tinsmith also replaced that member with tin, including these finely-jointed hands that you see me using. But, alas! after that, the axe, still enchanted by the cruel Witch, cut my body in two, so that I fell to the ground. Then the Witch, who was watching from a near-by bush, rushed up and seized the axe and chopped my body into several small pieces, after which, thinking that at last she had destroyed me, she ran away laughing in wicked glee.

"But Nimmie Amee found me. She picked up my arms and legs and head, and made a bundle of them and carried them to the tinsmith, who set to work and made me a fine body of pure tin. When he had joined the arms and legs to the body, and set my head in the tin collar, I was a much better man than ever, for my body could not ache or pain me, and I was so beautiful and bright that I had no need of clothing. Clothing is always a nuisance, because it soils and tears and has to be replaced; but my tin body only needs to be oiled and polished.

"Nimmie Amee still declared she would marry me, as she still loved me in spite of the Witch's evil deeds. The girl declared I would make the brightest husband in all the world, which was quite true. However, the Wicked Witch was not yet defeated. When I returned to my work the axe slipped and cut off my head, which was the only meat part of me then remaining. Moreover, the old woman grabbed up my severed head and carried it away with her and hid it. But Nimmie Amee came into the forest and found me wandering around helplessly, because I could not see where to go, and she led me to my friend the tinsmith. The faithful fellow at once set to work to make me a tin head, and he had just completed it when Nimmie Amee came running up with my old head, which she had stolen from the Witch. But, on reflection, I considered the tin head far superior to the meat one—I am wearing it yet, so you can see its beauty and grace of outline—and the girl agreed with me that a man all made of tin was far more perfect than one formed of different materials. The tinsmith was as proud of his workmanship as I was, and for three whole days, all admired me and praised my beauty.

"Being now completely formed of tin, I had no more fear of the Wicked Witch, for she was powerless to injure me. Nimmie Amee said we must be married at once, for then she could come to my cottage and live with me and keep me bright and sparkling.

"'I am sure, my dear Nick,' said the brave and beautiful girl—my name was then Nick Chopper, you should be told— 'that you will make the best husband any girl could have. I shall not be obliged to cook for you, for now you do not eat; I shall not have to make your bed, for tin does not tire or require sleep; when we go to a dance, you will not get weary before the music stops and say you want to go home. All day long, while you are chopping wood in the forest, I shall be able to amuse myself in my own way—a privilege few wives enjoy. There is no temper in your new head, so you will not get angry with me. Finally, I shall take pride in being the wife of the only live Tin

Woodman in all the world!' Which shows that Nimmie Amee was as wise as she was brave and beautiful."

"I think she was a very nice girl," said Woot the Wanderer. "But, tell me, please, why were you not killed when you were chopped to pieces?"

"In the Land of Oz," replied the Emperor, "no one can ever be killed. A man with a wooden leg or a tin leg is still the same man; and, as I lost parts of my meat body by degrees, I always remained the same person as in the beginning, even though in the end I was all tin and no meat."

"I see," said the boy, thoughtfully. "And did you marry Nimmie Amee?"

"No," answered the Tin Woodman, "I did not. She said she still loved me, but I found that I no longer loved her. My tin body contained no heart, and without a heart no one can love. So the Wicked Witch conquered in the end, and when I left the Munchkin Country of Oz, the poor girl was still the slave of the Witch and had to do her bidding day and night."

"Where did you go?" asked Woot.

"Well, I first started out to find a heart, so I could love Nimmie Amee again; but hearts are more scarce than one would think. One day, in a big forest that was strange to me, my joints suddenly became rusted, because I had forgotten to oil them. There I stood, unable to move hand or foot. And there I continued to stand—while days came and went—until Dorothy and the Scarecrow came along and rescued me. They oiled my joints and set me free, and I've taken good care never to rust again."

"Who was this Dorothy?" questioned the Wanderer.

"A little girl who happened to be in a house when it was carried by a cyclone all the way from Kansas to the Land of Oz. When the house fell, in the Munchkin Country, it fortunately landed on the Wicked Witch and smashed her flat. It was a big house, and I think the Witch is under it yet."

"No," said the Scarecrow, correcting him, "Dorothy says the Witch turned to dust, and the wind scattered the dust in every direction."

"Well," continued the Tin Woodman, "after meeting the Scarecrow and Dorothy, I went with them to the Emerald City, where the Wizard of Oz gave me a heart. But the Wizard's stock of hearts was low, and he gave me a Kind Heart instead of a Loving Heart, so that I could not love Nimmie Amee any more than I did when I was heartless."

"Couldn't the Wizard give you a heart that was both Kind and Loving?" asked the boy.

"No; that was what I asked for, but he said he was so short on hearts, just then, that there was but one in stock, and I could take that or none at all. So I accepted it, and I must say that for its kind it is a very good heart indeed."

"It seems to me," said Woot, musingly, "that the Wizard fooled you. It can't be a very Kind Heart, you know."

"Why not?" demanded the Emperor.

"Because it was unkind of you to desert the girl who loved you, and who had been faithful and true to you when you were in trouble. Had the heart the Wizard gave you been a Kind Heart, you would have gone back home and made the beautiful Munchkin girl your wife, and then brought her here to be an Empress and live in your splendid tin castle."

The Tin Woodman was so surprised at this frank speech that for a time he did nothing but stare hard at the boy Wanderer. But the Scarecrow wagged his stuffed head and said in a positive tone:

"This boy is right. I've often wondered, myself, why you didn't go back and find that poor Munchkin girl."

Then the Tin Woodman stared hard at his friend the Scarecrow. But finally he said in a serious tone of voice:

"I must admit that never before have I thought of such a thing as finding Nimmie Amee and making her Empress of the Winkies. But it is surely not too late, even now, to do this, for the girl must still be living in the Munchkin Country. And, since this strange Wanderer has reminded me of Nimmie Amee, I believe it is my duty to set out and find her. Surely it is not the girl's fault that I no longer love her, and so, if I can make her happy, it is proper that I should do so, and in this way reward her for her faithfulness."

"Quite right, my friend!" agreed the Scarecrow.

"Will you accompany me on this errand?" asked the Tin Emperor.

"Of course," said the Scarecrow.

"And will you take me along?" pleaded Woot the Wanderer in an eager voice.

"To be sure," said the Tin Woodman, "if you care to join our party. It was you who first told me it was my duty to find and marry Nimmie Amee, and I'd like you to know that Nick Chopper, the Tin Emperor of the Winkies, is a man who never shirks his duty, once it is pointed out to him."

"It ought to be a pleasure, as well as a duty, if the girl is so beautiful," said Woot, well pleased with the idea of the adventure.

"Beautiful things may be admired, if not loved," asserted the Tin Man. "Flowers are beautiful, for instance, but we are not inclined to marry them. Duty, on the contrary, is a bugle call to action, whether you are inclined to act, or not. In this case, I obey the bugle call of duty."

"When shall we start?" inquired the Scarecrow, who was always glad to embark upon a new adventure. "I don't hear any bugle, but when do we go?"

"As soon as we can get ready," answered the Emperor. "I'll call my servants at once and order them to make preparations for our journey."

···—··◄ Chapter 3 ►··—··

ROUNDABOUT

Woot the Wanderer slept that night in the tin castle of the Emperor of the Winkies and found his tin bed quite comfortable. Early the next morning he rose and took a walk through the gardens, where there were tin fountains and beds of curious tin flowers, and where tin birds perched upon the branches of tin trees and sang songs that sounded like the notes of tin whistles. All these wonders had been made by the clever Winkie tinsmiths, who wound the birds up every morning so that they would move about and sing.

After breakfast the boy went into the Throne Room, where the Emperor was having his tin joints carefully oiled by a servant, while other servants were stuffing sweet, fresh straw into the body of the Scarecrow.

Woot watched this operation with much interest, for the Scarecrow's body was only a suit of clothes filled with straw. The coat was buttoned tight to keep the packed straw from falling out and a rope was tied around the waist to hold it in shape and prevent the straw from sagging down. The Scarecrow's head was a gunnysack filled with bran, on which the eyes, nose and mouth had been painted. His hands were white cotton gloves stuffed with fine straw. Woot noticed that even when carefully stuffed and patted into shape, the straw man was awkward in his movements and decidedly wobbly on his feet, so the boy wondered if the Scarecrow would be able to travel with them all the way to the forests of the Munchkin Country of Oz.

The preparations made for this important journey were very simple. A knapsack was filled with food and given Woot the Wanderer to carry upon his back, for the food was for his use alone. The Tin Woodman shouldered an axe which was sharp and brightly polished, and the Scarecrow put the Emperor's oil-can in his pocket, that he might oil his friend's joints should they need it.

"Who will govern the Winkie Country during your absence?" asked the boy.

"Why, the Country will run itself," answered the Emperor. "As a matter of fact, my people do not need an Emperor, for

Ozma of Oz watches over the welfare of all her subjects, including the Winkies. Like a good many kings and emperors, I have a grand title, but very little real power, which allows me time to amuse myself in my own way. The people of Oz have but one Law to obey, which is: 'Behave Yourself,' so it is easy for them to abide by this Law, and you'll notice they behave very well. But it is time for us to be off, and I am eager to start because I suppose that that poor Munchkin girl is anxiously awaiting my coming."

"She's waited a long time already, seems to me," remarked the Scarecrow, as they left the grounds of the castle and followed a path that led eastward.

"True," replied the Tin Woodman; "but I've noticed that the last end of a wait, however long it has been, is the hardest to endure; so I must try to make Nimmie Amee happy as soon as possible."

"Ah; that proves you have a Kind Heart," remarked the Scarecrow, approvingly.

"It's too bad he hasn't a Loving Heart," said Woot. "This Tin Man is going to marry a nice girl through kindness, and not because he loves her, and somehow that doesn't seem quite right."

"Even so, I am not sure it isn't best for the girl," said the Scarecrow, who seemed very intelligent for a straw man, "for a loving husband is not always kind, while a kind husband is sure to make any girl content."

"Nimmie Amee will become an Empress!" announced the Tin Woodman, proudly. "I shall have a tin gown made for her, with tin ruffles and tucks on it, and she shall have tin slippers, and tin earrings and bracelets, and wear a tin crown on her head. I am sure that will delight Nimmie Amee, for all girls are fond of finery."

"Are we going to the Munchkin Country by way of the Emerald City?" inquired the Scarecrow, who looked upon the Tin Woodman as the leader of the party.

"I think not," was the reply. "We are engaged upon a rather delicate adventure, for we are seeking a girl who fears her former lover has forgotten her. It will be rather hard for me, you must admit, when I confess to Nimmie Amee that I have come to marry her because it is my duty to do so, and therefore the fewer witnesses there are to our meeting the better for both of us. After I have found Nimmie Amee and she has managed to control her joy at our reunion, I shall take her to the Emerald City and introduce her to Ozma and Dorothy, and to Betsy Bobbin and Tiny Trot, and all our other friends; but, if I remember rightly, poor Nimmie Amee has a sharp tongue when angry, and she may be a trifle angry with me, at first, because I have been so long in coming to her."

"I can understand that," said Woot gravely. "But how can we get to that part of the Munchkin Country where you once lived without passing through the Emerald City?"

"Why, that is easy," the Tin Man assured him.

"I have a map of Oz in my pocket," persisted the boy, "and it shows that the Winkie Country, where we now are, is at the west of Oz, and the Munchkin Country at the east, while directly between them lies the Emerald City."

"True enough; but we shall go toward the north, first of all, into the Gillikin Country, and so pass around the Emerald City," explained the Tin Woodman.

"That may prove a dangerous journey," replied the boy. "I used to live in one of the top corners of the Gillikin Country, near to Oogaboo, and I have been told that in this northland country are many people whom it is not pleasant to meet. I was very careful to avoid them during my journey south."

"A Wanderer should have no fear," observed the Scarecrow, who was wobbling along in a funny, haphazard manner, but keeping pace with his friends.

"Fear does not make one a coward," returned Woot, growing a little red in the face, "but I believe it is more easy to avoid danger than to overcome it. The safest way is the best way, even for one who is brave and determined."

"Do not worry, for we shall not go far to the north," said the Emperor. "My one idea is to avoid the Emerald City without going out of our way more than is necessary. Once around the Emerald City we will turn south into the Munchkin Country, where the Scarecrow and I are well acquainted and have many friends."

"I have traveled some in the Gillikin Country," remarked

the Scarecrow, "and while I must say I have met some strange people there at times, I have never yet been harmed by them."

"Well, it's all the same to me," said Woot, with assumed carelessness. "Dangers, when they cannot be avoided, are often quite interesting, and I am willing to go wherever you two venture to go."

So they left the path they had been following and began to travel toward the northeast, and all that day they were in the pleasant Winkie Country, and all the people they met saluted the Emperor with great respect and wished him good luck on his journey. At night they stopped at a house where they were well entertained and where Woot was given a comfortable bed to sleep in.

"Were the Scarecrow and I alone," said the Tin Woodman, "we would travel by night as well as by day; but with a meat person in our party, we must halt at night to permit him to rest."

"Meat tires, after a day's travel," added the Scarecrow, "while straw and tin never tire at all. Which proves," said he, "that we are somewhat superior to people made in the common way."

Woot could not deny that he was tired, and he slept soundly until morning, when he was given a good breakfast, smoking hot.

"You two miss a great deal by not eating," he said to his companions.

"It is true," responded the Scarecrow. "We miss suffering from hunger, when food cannot be had, and we miss a stomach-ache, now and then."

As he said this, the Scarecrow glanced at the Tin Wood-man, who nodded his assent.

All that second day they traveled steadily, entertaining one another the while with stories of adventures they had for-merly met and listening to the Scarecrow recite poetry. He had learned a great many poems from Professor Wogglebug and loved to repeat them whenever anybody would listen to him. Of course Woot and the Tin Woodman now listened, because they could not do otherwise—unless they rudely ran away from their stuffed comrade.

One of the Scarecrow's recitations was like this:

"What sound is so sweet
As the straw from the wheat
When it crunkles so tender and low?
It is yellow and bright,
So it gives me delight
To crunkle wherever I go.

"Sweet, fresh, golden Straw!
There is surely no flaw
In a stuffing so clean and compact.
It creaks when I walk,

And it thrills when I talk,
And its fragrance is fine, for a fact.

"To cut me don't hurt,
For I've no blood to squirt,
And I therefore can suffer no pain;
The straw that I use
Doesn't lump up or bruise,
Though it's pounded again and again!

"I know it is said
That my beautiful head
Has brains of mixed wheat-straw and bran,
But my thoughts are so good
I'd not change, if I could,
For the brains of a common meat man.

"Content with my lot,
I'm glad that I'm not
Like others I meet day by day;
If my insides get musty,
Or mussed-up, or dusty,
I get newly stuffed right away."

Chapter 4

The LOONS of LOONVILLE

oward evening, the travelers found there was no longer a path to guide them, and the purple hues of the grass and trees warned them that they were now in the Country of the Gillikins, where strange peoples dwelt in places that were quite unknown to the other inhabitants of Oz. The fields were wild and uncultivated and there were no houses of any sort to be seen. But our friends kept on walking even after the sun went down, hoping to find a good place for Woot the Wanderer to sleep; but when it grew quite dark and the boy was weary with his long walk, they halted right in the middle of a field and allowed Woot to get his supper from the food he carried in his knapsack. Then the Scarecrow laid himself down, so that Woot could use his stuffed body as a pillow, and the Tin Woodman stood up beside them all night, so the dampness of the ground might not rust his joints or dull his brilliant polish. Whenever the dew settled on his body he carefully wiped it off with a cloth, and so in the morning the Emperor shone as brightly as ever in the rays of the rising sun.

They wakened the boy at daybreak, the Scarecrow saying to him:

"We have discovered something queer, and therefore we must counsel together what to do about it."

"What have you discovered?" asked Woot, rubbing the sleep from his eyes with his knuckles and giving three wide yawns to prove he was fully awake.

"A Sign," said the Tin Woodman. "A Sign, and another path."

"What does the Sign say?" inquired the boy.

"It says that 'All Strangers are Warned not to Follow this Path to Loonville,'" answered the Scarecrow, who could read very well when his eyes had been freshly painted.

"In that case," said the boy, opening his knapsack to get some breakfast, "let us travel in some other direction."

But this did not seem to please either of his companions.

"I'd like to see what Loonville looks like," remarked the Tin Woodman.

"When one travels, it is foolish to miss any interesting sight," added the Scarecrow.

"But a warning means danger," protested Woot the Wanderer, "and I believe it sensible to keep out of danger whenever we can."

They made no reply to this speech for a while. Then said the Scarecrow:

"I have escaped so many dangers, during my lifetime, that I am not much afraid of anything that can happen."

"Nor am I!" exclaimed the Tin Woodman, swinging his glittering axe around his tin head, in a series of circles. "Few things can injure tin, and my axe is a powerful weapon to use against a foe. But our boy friend," he continued, looking solemnly at Woot, "might perhaps be injured if the people of Loonville are really dangerous; so I propose he waits here while you and I, Friend Scarecrow, visit the forbidden City of Loonville."

"Don't worry about me," advised Woot, calmly. "Wherever you wish to go, I will go, and share your dangers. During my wanderings I have found it more wise to keep out of danger than to venture in, but at that time I was alone, and now I have two powerful friends to protect me."

So, when he had finished his breakfast, they all set out along the path that led to Loonville.

"It is a place I have never heard of before," remarked the Scarecrow, as they approached a dense forest. "The inhabitants may be people, of some sort, or they may be animals, but whatever they prove to be, we will have an interesting story to relate to Dorothy and Ozma on our return."

The path led into the forest, but the big trees grew so closely together and the vines and underbrush were so thick and matted that they had to clear a path at each step in order to proceed. In one or two places the Tin Man, who went first to clear the way, cut the branches with a blow of his axe. Woot followed next, and last of the three came the Scarecrow, who could not have kept the path at all had not his comrades broken the way for his straw-stuffed body.

Presently the Tin Woodman pushed his way through some heavy underbrush, and almost tumbled headlong into a vast cleared space in the forest. The clearing was circular, big and roomy, yet the top branches of the tall trees reached over and formed a complete dome or roof for it. Strangely enough, it was not dark in this immense natural chamber in the woodland, for the place glowed with a soft, white light that seemed to come from some unseen source.

In the chamber were grouped dozens of queer creatures, and these so astonished the Tin Man that Woot had to push his metal body aside, that he might see, too. And the Scarecrow pushed Woot aside, so that the three travelers stood in a row, staring with all their eyes.

The creatures they beheld were round and ball-like; round in body, round in legs and arms, round in hands and feet and round of head. The only exception to the roundness was a slight hollow on the top of each head, making it saucer-shaped instead of dome-shaped. They wore no clothes on their puffy bodies, nor had they any hair. Their skins were all of a light grey color, and their eyes were mere purple spots. Their noses were as puffy as the rest of them.

"Are they rubber, do you think?" asked the Scarecrow, who noticed that the creatures bounded, as they moved, and seemed almost as light as air.

"It is difficult to tell what they are," answered Woot, "they seem to be covered with warts."

The Loons—for so these folks were called—had been doing many things, some playing together, some working at tasks and some gathered in groups to talk; but at the sound of strange voices, which echoed rather loudly through the clearing, all turned in the direction of the intruders. Then, in a body, they all rushed forward, running and bounding with tremendous speed.

The Tin Woodman was so surprised by this sudden dash that he had no time to raise his axe before the Loons were on them. The creatures swung their puffy hands, which looked like boxing-gloves, and pounded the three travelers as hard as they could, on all sides. The blows were quite soft and did not hurt our friends at all, but the onslaught quite bewildered them, so that in a brief period all three were knocked over and fell flat upon the ground. Once down, many of the Loons held them, to prevent their getting up again, while others wound long tendrils of vines about them, binding their arms and legs to their bodies and so rendering them helpless.

"Aha!" cried the biggest Loon of all; "we've got 'em safe; so let's carry 'em to King Bal and have 'em tried, and condemned and perforated!"

They had to drag their captives to the center of the domed chamber, for their weight, as compared with that of the Loons, prevented their being carried. Even the Scarecrow was much heavier than the puffy Loons. But finally the party halted before a raised platform, on which stood a sort of throne, consisting of a big, wide chair with a string tied to one arm of it. This string led upward to the roof of the dome.

Arranged before the platform, the prisoners were allowed to sit up, facing the empty throne.

"Good!" said the big Loon who had commanded the party. "Now to get King Bal to judge these terrible creatures we have so bravely captured."

As he spoke he took hold of the string and began to pull as hard as he could. One or two of the others helped him and pretty soon, as they drew in the cord, the leaves above them parted and a Loon appeared at the other end of the string. It didn't take long to draw him down to the throne, where he seated himself and was tied in, so he wouldn't float upward again.

"Hello," said the King, blinking his purple eyes at his followers; "what's up now!"

"Strangers, your Majesty—strangers and captives," replied the big Loon, pompously.

"Dear me! I see 'em. I see 'em very plainly," exclaimed the King, his purple eyes bulging out as he looked at the three prisoners. "What curious animals! Are they dangerous, do you think, my good Panta?"

"I'm 'fraid so, your Majesty. Of course, they may not be dangerous, but we mustn't take chances. Enough accidents happen to us poor Loons as it is, and my advice is to condemn and perforate 'em as quickly as possible."

"Keep your advice to yourself," said the monarch, in a peeved tone. "Who's King here, anyhow? You or Me?"

"We made you our King because you have less common sense than the rest of us," answered Panta Loon, indignantly. "I could have been King myself, had I wanted to, but I didn't care for the hard work and responsibility."

As he said this, the big Loon strutted back and forth in the space between the throne of King Bal and the prisoners, and the other Loons seemed much impressed by his defiance. But suddenly there came a sharp report and Panta Loon instantly disappeared, to the great astonishment of the Scarecrow, the Tin Woodman and Woot the Wanderer, who saw on the spot where the big fellow had stood a little heap of flabby, wrinkled skin that looked like a collapsed rubber balloon.

"There!" exclaimed the King; "I expected that would happen. The conceited rascal wanted to puff himself up until he was bigger than the rest of you, and this is the result of his folly. Get the pump working, some of you, and blow him up again."

"We will have to mend the puncture first, your Majesty," suggested one of the Loons, and the prisoners noticed that none of them seemed surprised or shocked at the sad accident to Panta.

"All right," grumbled the King. "Fetch Til to mend him."

One or two ran away and presently returned, followed by a lady Loon wearing huge, puffed-up rubber skirts. Also she had a purple feather fastened to a wart on the top of her head, and around her waist was a sash of fibre-like vines, dried and tough, that looked like strings.

"Get to work, Til," commanded King Bal. "Panta has just exploded."

The lady Loon picked up the bunch of skin and examined it carefully until she discovered a hole in one foot. Then she pulled a strand of string from her sash, and drawing the edges of the hole together, she tied them fast with the string, thus making one of those curious warts which the strangers had noticed on so many Loons. Having done this, Til Loon tossed the bit of skin to the other Loons and was about to go away when she noticed the prisoners and stopped to inspect them.

"Dear me!" said Til; "what dreadful creatures. Where did they come from?"

"We captured them," replied one of the Loons.

"And what are we going to do with them?" inquired the girl Loon.

"Perhaps we'll condemn 'em and puncture 'em," answered the King.

"Well," said she, still eyeing the captives "I'm not sure they'll puncture. Let's try it, and see."

One of the Loons ran to the forest's edge and quickly returned with a long, sharp thorn. He glanced at the King, who nodded his head in assent, and then he rushed forward and stuck the thorn into the leg of the Scarecrow. The Scarecrow merely smiled and said nothing, for the thorn didn't hurt him at all.

Then the Loon tried to prick the Tin Woodman's leg, but the tin only blunted the point of the thorn.

"Just as I thought," said Til, blinking her purple eyes and shaking her puffy head; but just then the Loon stuck the thorn into the leg of Woot the Wanderer, and while it had been blunted somewhat, it was still sharp enough to hurt.

"Ouch!" yelled Woot, and kicked out his leg with so much energy that the frail bonds that tied him burst apart. His foot caught the Loon—who was leaning over him—full on his puffy stomach, and sent him shooting up into the air. When he was high over their heads he exploded with a loud "pop" and his skin fell to the ground.

"I really believe," said the King, rolling his spot-like eyes in a frightened way, "that Panta was right in claiming these prisoners are dangerous. Is the pump ready?"

Some of the Loons had wheeled a big machine in front of the throne and now took Panta's skin and began to pump air into it. Slowly it swelled out until the King cried "Stop!"

"No, no!" yelled Panta, "I'm not big enough yet."

"You're as big as you're going to be," declared the King. "Before you exploded you were bigger than the rest of us, and that caused you to be proud and overbearing. Now you're a little smaller than the rest, and you will last longer and be more humble."

"Pump me up—pump me up!" wailed Panta "If you don't you'll break my heart."

"If we do we'll break your skin," replied the King.

So the Loons stopped pumping air into Panta, and pushed him away from the pump. He was certainly more humble than before his accident, for he crept into the background and said nothing more.

"Now pump up the other one," ordered the King. Til had already mended him, and the Loons set to work to pump him full of air.

During these last few moments none had paid much attention to the prisoners, so Woot, finding his legs free, crept over to the Tin Woodman and rubbed the bonds that were still around his arms and body against the sharp edge of the axe, which quickly cut them.

The boy was now free, and the thorn which the Loon had stuck into his leg was lying unnoticed on the ground, where the creature had dropped it when he exploded. Woot leaned forward and picked up the thorn, and while the Loons were busy watching the pump, the boy sprang to his feet and suddenly rushed upon the group.

"Pop"—"pop"—"pop!" went three of the Loons, when the Wanderer pricked them with his thorn, and at the sounds the others looked around and saw their danger. With yells of fear they bounded away in all directions, scattering about the clearing, with Woot the Wanderer in full chase. While they could run much faster than the boy, they often stumbled and fell, or got in one another's way, so he managed to catch several and prick them with his thorn.

It astonished him to see how easily the Loons exploded. When the air was let out of them they were quite helpless. Til Loon was one of those who ran against his thorn and many others suffered the same fate. The creatures could not escape from the enclosure, but in their fright many bounded upward and caught branches of the trees, and then climbed out of reach of the dreaded thorn.

Woot was getting pretty tired chasing them, so he stopped and came over, panting, to where his friends were sitting, still bound.

"Very well done, my Wanderer," said the Tin Woodman. "It is evident that we need fear these puffed-up creatures no longer, so be kind enough to unfasten our bonds and we will proceed upon our journey."

Woot untied the bonds of the Scarecrow and helped him to his feet. Then he freed the Tin Woodman, who got up without help. Looking around them, they saw that the only Loon now remaining within reach was Bal Loon, the King, who had remained seated in his throne, watching the punishment of his people with a bewildered look in his purple eyes.

"Shall I puncture the King?" the boy asked his companions.

King Bal must have overheard the question, for he fumbled with the cord that fastened him to the throne and managed to release it. Then he floated upward until he reached the leafy dome, and parting the branches he disappeared from sight. But the string that was tied to his body was still connected with the arm of the throne, and they knew they could pull his Majesty down again, if they wanted to.

"Let him alone," suggested the Scarecrow. "He seems a good enough King for his peculiar people, and after we are gone, the Loons will have something of a job to pump up all those whom Woot has punctured."

"Every one of them ought to be exploded," declared Woot, who was angry because his leg still hurt him.

"No," said the Tin Woodman, "that would not be just fair. They were quite right to capture us, because we had no business to intrude here, having been warned to keep away from Loonville. This is their country, not ours, and since the poor things can't get out of the clearing, they can harm no one save those who venture here out of curiosity, as we did."

"Well said, my friend," agreed the Scarecrow. "We really had no right to disturb their peace and comfort; so let us go away."

They easily found the place where they had forced their way into the enclosure, so the Tin Woodman pushed aside the underbrush and started first along the path. The Scarecrow followed next and last came Woot, who looked back and saw that the Loons were still clinging to their perches on the trees and watching their former captives with frightened eyes.

"I guess they're glad to see the last of us," remarked the boy, and laughing at the happy ending of the adventure, he followed his comrades along the path.

Chapter 5

MRS. YOOP, the GIANTESS

When they had reached the end of the path, where they had first seen the warning sign, they set off across the country in an easterly direction. Before long they reached Rolling Lands, which were a succession of hills and valleys where constant climbs and descents were required, and their journey now became tedious, because on climbing each hill, they found before them nothing in the valley below it—except grass, or weeds or stones.

Up and down they went for hours, with nothing to relieve the monotony of the landscape, until finally, when they had topped a higher hill than usual, they discovered a cup-shaped valley before them in the center of which stood an enormous castle, built of purple stone. The castle was high and broad and long, but had no turrets and towers. So far as they could see, there was but one small window and one big door on each side of the great building.

"This is strange!" mused the Scarecrow. "I'd no idea such a big castle existed in this Gillikin Country. I wonder who lives here?"

"It seems to me, from this distance," remarked the Tin Woodman, "that it's the biggest castle I ever saw. It is really too big for any use, and no one could open or shut those big doors without a stepladder."

"Perhaps, if we go nearer, we shall find out whether anybody lives there or not," suggested Woot. "Looks to me as if nobody lived there."

On they went, and when they reached the center of the valley, where the great stone castle stood, it was beginning to grow dark. So they hesitated as to what to do.

"If friendly people happen to live here," said Woot. "I shall be glad of a bed; but should enemies occupy the place, I prefer to sleep upon the ground."

"And if no one at all lives here," added the Scarecrow, "we can enter, and take possession, and make ourselves at home."

While speaking he went nearer to one of the great doors, which was three times as high and broad as any he had ever seen in a house before, and then he discovered, engraved in big letters upon a stone over the doorway, the words:

YOOP CASTLE

"Oho!" he exclaimed; "I know the place now. This was probably the home of Mr. Yoop, a terrible giant whom I have seen confined in a cage, a long way from here. Therefore this castle is likely to be empty and we may use it in any way we please."

"Yes, yes," said the Tin Emperor, nodding; "I also remember Mr. Yoop. But how are we to get into his deserted castle? The latch of the door is so far above our heads that none of us can reach it."

They considered this problem for a while, and then Woot said to the Tin Man:

"If I stand upon your shoulders, I think I can unlatch the door."

"Climb up, then," was the reply, and when the boy was perched upon the tin shoulders of Nick Chopper, he was just able to reach the latch and raise it.

At once the door swung open, its great hinges making a groaning sound as if in protest, so Woot leaped down and followed his companions into a big, bare hallway. Scarcely were the three inside, however, when they heard the door slam shut behind them, and this astonished them because no one had touched it. It had closed of its own accord, as if by magic. Moreover, the latch was on the outside, and the thought occurred to each one of them that they were now prisoners in this unknown castle.

"However," mumbled the Scarecrow, "we are not to blame for what cannot be helped; so let us push bravely ahead and see what may be seen."

It was quite dark in the hallway, now that the outside door was shut, so as they stumbled along a stone passage they kept close together, not knowing what danger was likely to befall them.

Suddenly a soft glow enveloped them. It grew brighter, until they could see their surroundings distinctly. They had reached the end of the passage and before them was another huge door. This noiselessly swung open before them, without the help of anyone, and through the doorway they observed a big chamber, the walls of which were lined with plates of pure gold, highly polished.

This room was also lighted, although they could discover no lamps, and in the center of it was a great table at which sat an immense woman. She was clad in silver robes embroidered with gay floral designs, and wore over this splendid raiment a short apron of elaborate lace-work. Such an apron was no protection, and was not in keeping with the handsome gown, but the huge woman wore it, nevertheless. The table at which she sat was spread with a white cloth and had golden dishes upon it, so the travelers saw that they had surprised the Giantess while she was eating her supper.

She had her back toward them and did not even turn around, but taking a biscuit from a dish she began to butter it and said in a voice that was big and deep but not especially unpleasant:

"Why don't you come in and allow the door to shut? You're causing a draught, and I shall catch cold and sneeze. When I sneeze, I get cross, and when I get cross I'm liable to do something wicked. Come in, you foolish strangers; come in!"

Being thus urged, they entered the room and approached the table, until they stood where they faced the great Giantess. She continued eating, but smiled in a curious way as she looked at them. Woot noticed that the door had closed silently after they had entered, and that didn't please him at all.

"Well," said the Giantess, "what excuse have you to offer?"

"We didn't know anyone lived here, Madam," explained the Scarecrow; "so, being travelers and strangers in these parts, and wishing to find a place for our boy friend to sleep, we ventured to enter your castle."

"You knew it was private property, I suppose?" said she, buttering another biscuit.

"We saw the words, 'Yoop Castle,' over the door, but we knew that Mr. Yoop is a prisoner in a cage in a far-off part of the Land of Oz, so we decided there was no one now at home and that we might use the castle for the night."

"I see," remarked the Giantess, nodding her head and smiling again in that curious way—a way that made Woot shudder. "You didn't know that Mr. Yoop was married, or that after he was cruelly captured his wife still lived in his castle and ran it to suit herself."

"Who captured Mr. Yoop?" asked Woot, looking gravely at the big woman.

"Wicked enemies. People who selfishly objected to Yoop's taking their cows and sheep for his food. I must admit, however, that Yoop had a bad temper, and had the habit of knocking over a few houses, now and then, when he was angry. So one day the little folks came in a great crowd and captured Mr. Yoop, and carried him away to a cage somewhere in the mountains. I don't know where it is, and I don't care, for my husband treated me badly at times, forgetting the respect a giant owes to a giantess. Often he kicked me on my shins, when I wouldn't wait on him. So I'm glad he is gone."

"It's a wonder the people didn't capture you, too," remarked Woot.

"Well, I was too clever for them," said she, giving a sudden laugh that caused such a breeze that the wobbly Scarecrow was almost blown off his feet and had to grab his friend Nick Chopper to steady himself. "I saw the people coming," continued Mrs. Yoop, "and knowing they meant mischief I transformed myself into a mouse and hid in a cupboard. After they had gone away, carrying my shin-kicking husband with them, I transformed myself back to my former shape again, and here I've lived in peace and comfort ever since."

"Are you a Witch, then?" inquired Woot.

"Well, not exactly a Witch," she replied, "but I'm an Artist in Transformations. In other words, I'm more of a Yookoohoo than a Witch, and of course you know that the Yookoohoos are the cleverest magic-workers in the world."

The travelers were silent for a time, uneasily considering this statement and the effect it might have on their future. No doubt the Giantess had wilfully made them her prisoners; yet she spoke so cheerfully, in her big voice, that until now they had not been alarmed in the least.

By and by the Scarecrow, whose mixed brains had been working steadily, asked the woman:

"Are we to consider you our friend, Mrs. Yoop, or do you intend to be our enemy?"

"I never have friends," she said in a matter-of-fact tone, "because friends get too familiar and always forget to mind their own business. But I am not your enemy; not yet, anyhow. Indeed, I'm glad you've come, for my life here is rather lonely. I've had no one to talk to since I transformed Polychrome, the Daughter of the Rainbow, into a canary-bird."

"How did you manage to do that?" asked the Tin Woodman, in amazement. "Polychrome is a powerful fairy!"

"She was," said the Giantess; "but now she's a canary-bird. One day after a rain, Polychrome danced off the Rainbow and fell asleep on a little mound in this valley, not far from my castle. The sun came out and drove the Rainbow away, and before Poly wakened, I stole out and transformed her into a canary-bird in a gold cage studded with diamonds. The cage was so she couldn't fly away. I expected she'd sing and talk and we'd have good times together; but she has proved no company for me at all. Ever since the moment of her transformation, she has refused to speak a single word."

"Where is she now?" inquired Woot, who had heard tales of lovely Polychrome and was much interested in her.

"The cage is hanging up in my bedroom," said the Giantess, eating another biscuit.

The travelers were now more uneasy and suspicious of the Giantess than before. If Polychrome, the Rainbow's Daughter, who was a real fairy, had been transformed and enslaved by this huge woman, who claimed to be a Yookoohoo, what was liable to happen to them? Said the Scarecrow, twisting his stuffed head around in Mrs. Yoop's direction:

"Do you know, Ma'am, who we are?"

"Of course," said she; "a straw man, a tin man and a boy."

"We are very important people," declared the Tin Woodman.

"All the better," she replied. "I shall enjoy your society the more on that account. For I mean to keep you here as long as I live, to amuse me when I get lonely. And," she added slowly, "in this Valley no one ever dies."

They didn't like this speech at all, so the Scarecrow frowned in a way that made Mrs. Yoop smile, while the Tin Woodman looked so fierce that Mrs. Yoop laughed. The Scarecrow suspected she was going to laugh, so he slipped behind his friends to escape the wind from her breath. From this safe position he said warningly:

"We have powerful friends who will soon come to rescue us."

"Let them come," she returned, with an accent of scorn. "When they get here they will find neither a boy, nor a tin man, nor a scarecrow, for tomorrow morning I intend to transform you all into other shapes, so that you cannot be recognized."

This threat filled them with dismay. The good-natured Giantess was more terrible than they had imagined. She could smile and wear pretty clothes and at the same time be even more cruel than her wicked husband had been.

Both the Scarecrow and the Tin Woodman tried to think of some way to escape from the castle before morning, but she seemed to read their thoughts and shook her head.

"Don't worry your poor brains," said she. "You can't escape me, however hard you try. But why should you wish to escape? I shall give you new forms that are much better than the ones you now have. Be contented with your fate, for discontent leads to unhappiness, and unhappiness, in any form, is the greatest evil that can befall you."

"What forms do you intend to give us?" asked Woot earnestly.

"I haven't decided, as yet. I'll dream over it tonight, so

in the morning I shall have made up my mind how to transform you. Perhaps you'd prefer to choose your own transformations?"

"No," said Woot, "I prefer to remain as I am."

"That's funny," she retorted. "You are little, and you're
weak; as you are, you're not much account, anyhow. The best
thing about you is that you're alive, for I shall be able to make
of you some sort of live creature which will be a great improvement on your present form."

She took another biscuit from a plate and dipped it in a
pot of honey and calmly began eating it.

The Scarecrow watched her thoughtfully.

"There are no fields of grain in your Valley," said he;
"where, then, did you get the flour to make your biscuits?"

"Mercy me! do you think I'd bother to make biscuits out of
flour?" she replied. "That is altogether too tedious a process
for a Yookoohoo. I set some traps this afternoon and caught a
lot of field-mice, but as I do not like to eat mice, I transformed
them into hot biscuits for my supper. The honey in this pot
was once a wasp's nest, but since being transformed it has
become sweet and delicious. All I need do, when I wish to eat,
is to take something I don't care to keep, and transform it into
any sort of food I like, and eat it. Are you hungry?"

"I don't eat, thank you," said the Scarecrow.

"Nor do I," said the Tin Woodman.

"I have still a little natural food in my knapsack," said

Woot the Wanderer, "and I'd rather eat that than any wasp's nest."

"Every one to his taste," said the Giantess carelessly, and having now finished her supper she rose to her feet, clapped her hands together, and the supper table at once disappeared.

Chapter 6

The MAGIC of a YOOKOOHOO

Woot had seen very little of magic during his wanderings, while the Scarecrow and the Tin Woodman had seen a great deal of many sorts in their lives, yet all three were greatly impressed by Mrs. Yoop's powers. She did not affect any mysterious airs or indulge in chants or mystic rites, as most witches do, nor was the Giantess old and ugly or disagreeable in face or manner. Nevertheless, she frightened her prisoners more than any witch could have done.

"Please be seated," she said to them, as she sat herself down in a great arm-chair and spread her beautiful embroidered skirts for them to admire. But all the chairs in the room were so high that our friends could not climb to the seats of them. Mrs. Yoop observed this and waved her hand, when instantly a golden ladder appeared leaning against a chair opposite her own.

"Climb up," said she, and they obeyed, the Tin Man and the boy assisting the more clumsy Scarecrow. When they were all seated in a row on the cushion of the chair, the Giantess continued: "Now tell me how you happened to travel in this direction, and where you came from and what your errand is."

So the Tin Woodman told her all about Nimmie Amee, and how he had decided to find her and marry her, although he had no Loving Heart. The story seemed to amuse the big woman, who then began to ask the Scarecrow questions and for the first time in her life heard of Ozma of Oz, and of Dorothy and Jack Pumpkinhead and Dr. Pipt and Tik-Tok and many other Oz people who are well known in the Emerald City. Also Woot had to tell his story, which was very simple and did not take long. The Giantess laughed heartily when the boy related their adventure at Loonville, but said she knew nothing of the Loons because she never left her Valley.

"There are wicked people who would like to capture me, as they did my giant husband, Mr. Yoop," said she; "so I stay at home and mind my own business."

"If Ozma knew that you dared to work magic without her consent, she would punish you severely," declared the Scarecrow, "for this castle is in the Land of Oz, and no persons in the Land of Oz are permitted to work magic except Glinda the Good and the little Wizard who lives with Ozma in the Emerald City."

"That for your Ozma!" exclaimed the Giantess, snapping her fingers in derision. "What do I care for a girl whom I have never seen and who has never seen me?"

"But Ozma is a fairy," said the Tin Woodman, "and therefore she is very powerful. Also, we are under Ozma's protection, and to injure us in any way would make her extremely angry."

"What I do here, in my own private castle in this secluded Valley—where no one comes but fools like you—can never be known to your fairy Ozma," returned the Giantess. "Do not seek to frighten me from my purpose, and do not allow yourselves to be frightened, for it is best to meet bravely what cannot be avoided. I am now going to bed, and in the morning I will give you all new forms, such as will be more interesting to me than the ones you now wear. Good night, and pleasant dreams."

Saying this, Mrs. Yoop rose from her chair and walked through a doorway into another room. So heavy was the tread of the Giantess that even the walls of the big stone castle trembled as she stepped. She closed the door of her bedroom behind her, and then suddenly the light went out and the three prisoners found themselves in total darkness.

The Tin Woodman and the Scarecrow didn't mind the

dark at all, but Woot the Wanderer felt worried to be left in this strange place in this strange manner, without being able to see any danger that might threaten.

"The big woman might have given me a bed, anyhow," he said to his companions, and scarcely had he spoken when he felt something press against his legs, which were then dangling from the seat of the chair. Leaning down, he put out his hand and found that a bedstead had appeared, with mattress, sheets and covers, all complete. He lost no time in slipping down upon the bed and was soon fast asleep.

During the night the Scarecrow and the Emperor talked in low tones together, and they got out of the chair and moved all about the room, feeling for some hidden spring that might open a door or window and permit them to escape.

Morning found them still unsuccessful in the quest and as soon as it was daylight Woot's bed suddenly disappeared, and he dropped to the floor with a thump that quickly wakened him. And after a time the Giantess came from her bedroom, wearing another dress that was quite as elaborate as the one in which she had been attired the evening before, and also wearing the pretty lace apron. Having seated herself in a chair, she said:

"I'm hungry; so I'll have breakfast at once."

She clapped her hands together and instantly the table appeared before her, spread with snowy linen and laden with golden dishes. But there was no food upon the table, nor anything else except a pitcher of water, a bundle of weeds and a handful of pebbles. But the Giantess poured some water into her coffee-pot, patted it once or twice with her hand, and then poured out a cupful of steaming hot coffee.

"Would you like some?" she asked Woot.

He was suspicious of magic coffee, but it smelled so good that he could not resist it; so he answered: "If you please, Madam."

The Giantess poured out another cup and set it on the floor for Woot. It was as big as a tub, and the golden spoon in the saucer beside the cup was so heavy the boy could scarcely lift it. But Woot managed to get a sip of the coffee and found it delicious.

Mrs. Yoop next transformed the weeds into a dish of oatmeal, which she ate with good appetite.

"Now, then," said she, picking up the pebbles. "I'm wondering whether I shall have fish-balls or lamb-chops to complete my meal. Which would you prefer, Woot the Wanderer?"

"If you please, I'll eat the food in my knapsack," answered the boy. "Your magic food might taste good, but I'm afraid of it."

The woman laughed at his fears and transformed the pebbles into fish-balls.

"I suppose you think that after you had eaten this food it would turn to stones again and make you sick," she remarked; "but that would be impossible. Nothing I transform ever gets back to its former shape again, so these fish-balls can never more be pebbles. That is why I have to be careful of my transformations," she added, busily eating while she talked, "for while I can change forms at will I can never change them back again—which proves that even the powers of a clever Yookoohoo are limited. When I have transformed you three people, you must always wear the shapes that I have given you."

"Then please don't transform us," begged Woot, "for we are quite satisfied to remain as we are."

"I am not expecting to satisfy you, but intend to please myself," she declared, "and my pleasure is to give you new shapes. For, if by chance your friends came in search of you, not one of them would be able to recognize you."

Her tone was so positive that they knew it would be useless to protest. The woman was not unpleasant to look at; her face was not cruel; her voice was big but gracious in tone; but her words showed that she possessed a merciless heart and no pleadings would alter her wicked purpose.

Mrs. Yoop took ample time to finish her breakfast and the prisoners had no desire to hurry her, but finally the meal was concluded and she folded her napkin and made the table disappear by clapping her hands together. Then she turned to her captives and said:

"The next thing on the programme is to change your forms."

"Have you decided what forms to give us?" asked the Scarecrow, uneasily.

"Yes; I dreamed it all out while I was asleep. This Tin Man seems a very solemn person"—indeed, the Tin Woodman was looking solemn, just then, for he was greatly disturbed—"so I shall change him into an Owl."

All she did was to point one finger at him as she spoke, but immediately the form of the Tin Woodman began to change and in a few seconds Nick Chopper, the Emperor of the Winkies, had been transformed into an Owl, with eyes as big as saucers and a hooked beak and strong claws. But he was still tin. He was a Tin Owl, with tin legs and beak and eyes and feathers. When he flew to the back of a chair and perched upon it, his tin feathers rattled against one another with a tinny clatter.

The Giantess seemed much amused by the Tin Owl's appearance, for her laugh was big and jolly.

"You're not liable to get lost," said she, "for your wings and feathers will make a racket wherever you go. And, on my word, a Tin Owl is so rare and pretty that it is an improvement on the ordinary bird. I did not intend to make you tin, but I forgot to wish you to be meat. However, tin you were, and tin you are, and as it's too late to change you, that settles it."

Until now the Scarecrow had rather doubted the possibility of Mrs. Yoop's being able to transform him, or his friend the Tin Woodman, for they were not made as ordinary people are. He had worried more over what might happen to Woot than to himself, but now he began to worry about himself.

"Madam," he said hastily, "I consider this action very impolite. It may even be called rude, considering we are your guests."

"You are not guests, for I did not invite you here," she replied.

"Perhaps not; but we craved hospitality. We threw ourselves upon your mercy, so to speak, and we now find you have no mercy. Therefore, if you will excuse the expression, I must say it is downright wicked to take our proper forms away from us and give us others that we do not care for."

"Are you trying to make me angry?" she asked, frowning.

"By no means," said the Scarecrow; "I'm just trying to make you act more ladylike."

"Oh, indeed! In my opinion, Mr. Scarecrow, you are now acting like a bear—so a Bear you shall be!"

Again the dreadful finger pointed, this time in the Scarecrow's direction, and at once his form began to change. In a few seconds he had become a small Brown Bear, but he was stuffed with straw as he had been before, and when the little Brown Bear shuffled across the floor he was just as wobbly as the Scarecrow had been and moved just as awkwardly.

Woot was amazed, but he was also thoroughly frightened.

"Did it hurt?" he asked the little Brown Bear.

"No, of course not," growled the Scarecrow in the Bear's

form; "but I don't like walking on four legs; it's undignified."

"Consider my humiliation!" chirped the Tin Owl, trying to settle its tin feathers smoothly with its tin beak. "And I can't see very well, either. The light seems to hurt my eyes."

"That's because you are an Owl," said Woot. "I think you will see better in the dark."

"Well," remarked the Giantess, "I'm very well pleased with these new forms, for my part, and I'm sure you will like them better when you get used to them. So now," she added, turning to the boy, "it is your turn."

"Don't you think you'd better leave me as I am?" asked Woot in a trembling voice.

"No," she replied, "I'm going to make a Monkey of you. I love monkeys—they're so cute!—and I think a Green Monkey will be lots of fun and amuse me when I am sad."

Woot shivered, for again the terrible magic finger pointed, and pointed directly his way. He felt himself changing; not so very much, however, and it didn't hurt him a bit. He looked down at his limbs and body and found that his clothes were gone and his skin covered with a fine, silk-like green fur. His hands and feet were now those of a monkey. He realized he really was a monkey, and his first feeling was one of anger. He began to chatter as monkeys do. He bounded to the seat of a giant chair, and then to its back and with a wild leap sprang upon the laughing Giantess. His idea was to seize her hair and pull it out by the roots, and so have revenge for her wicked transformations. But she raised her hand and said:

"Gently, my dear Monkey—gently! You're not angry; you're happy as can be!"

Woot stopped short. No; he wasn't a bit angry now; he felt as good-humored and gay as ever he did when a boy. Instead of pulling Mrs. Yoop's hair, he perched on her shoulder and smoothed her soft cheek with his hairy paw. In return, she smiled at the funny green animal and patted his head.

"Very good," said the Giantess. "Let us all become friends and be happy together. How is my Tin Owl feeling?"

"Quite comfortable," said the Owl. "I don't like it, to be sure, but I'm not going to allow my new form to make me unhappy. But, tell me, please: what is a Tin Owl good for?"

"You are only good to make me laugh," replied the Giantess.

"Will a stuffed Bear also make you laugh?" inquired the Scarecrow, sitting back on his haunches to look up at her.

"Of course," declared the Giantess; "and I have added a little magic to your transformations to make you all contented with wearing your new forms. I'm sorry I didn't think to do that when I transformed Polychrome into a Canary-Bird. But perhaps, when she sees how cheerful you are, she will cease to be silent and sullen and take to singing. I will go get the bird and let you see her."

With this, Mrs. Yoop went into the next room and soon returned bearing a golden cage in which sat upon a swinging perch a lovely yellow Canary.

"Polychrome," said the Giantess, "permit me to introduce to you a Green Monkey, which used to be a boy called Woot the Wanderer, and a Tin Owl, which used to be a Tin Woodman named Nick Chopper, and a straw-stuffed little Brown Bear which used to be a live Scarecrow."

"We already know one another," declared the Scarecrow. "The bird is Polychrome, the Rainbow's Daughter, and she and I used to be good friends."

"Are you really my old friend, the Scarecrow?" asked the bird, in a sweet, low voice.

"There!" cried Mrs. Yoop; "that's the first time she has spoken since she was transformed."

"I am really your old friend," answered the Scarecrow; "but you must pardon me for appearing just now in this brutal form."

"I am a bird, as you are, dear Poly," said the Tin Woodman; "but, alas! a Tin Owl is not as beautiful as a Canary-Bird."

"How dreadful it all is!" sighed the Canary. "Couldn't you manage to escape from this terrible Yookoohoo?"

"No," answered the Scarecrow, "we tried to escape, but failed. She first made us her prisoners and then transformed us. But how did she manage to get you, Polychrome?"

"I was asleep, and she took unfair advantage of me," answered the bird sadly. "Had I been awake, I could easily have protected myself."

"Tell me," said the Green Monkey earnestly, as he came close to the cage, "what must we do, Daughter of the Rainbow, to escape from these transformations? Can't you help us, being a Fairy?"

"At present I am powerless to help even myself," replied the Canary.

"That's the exact truth!" exclaimed the Giantess, who seemed pleased to hear the bird talk, even though it complained; "you are all helpless and in my power, so you may as well make up your minds to accept your fate and be content. Remember that you are transformed for good, since no magic on earth can break your enchantments. I am now going out for my morning walk, for each day after breakfast I walk sixteen times around my castle for exercise. Amuse yourselves while I am gone, and when I return I hope to find you all reconciled and happy."

So the Giantess walked to the door by which our friends had entered the great hall and spoke one word: "Open!" Then the door swung open and after Mrs. Yoop had passed out it closed again with a snap as its powerful bolts shot into place. The Green Monkey had rushed toward the opening, hoping to escape, but he was too late and only got a bump on his nose as the door slammed shut.

Chapter 7

The LACE APRON

Now," said the Canary, in a tone more brisk than before, "we may talk together more freely, as Mrs. Yoop cannot hear us. Perhaps we can figure out a way to escape."

"Open!" said Woot the Monkey, still facing the door; but his command had no effect and he slowly rejoined the others.

"You cannot open any door or window in this enchanted castle unless you are wearing the Magic Apron," said the Canary.

"What Magic Apron do you mean?" asked the Tin Owl, in a curious voice.

"The lace one, which the Giantess always wears. I have been her prisoner, in this cage, for several weeks, and she hangs my cage in her bedroom every night, so that she can keep her eye on me," explained Polychrome the Canary. "Therefore I have discovered that it is the Magic Apron that opens the doors and windows, and nothing else can move them. When she goes to bed, Mrs. Yoop hangs her apron on the bedpost, and one morning she forgot to put it on when she commanded the door to open, and the door would not move. So then she put on the lace apron and the door obeyed her. That was how I learned the magic power of the apron."

"I see—I see!" said the little Brown Bear, wagging his stuffed head. "Then, if we could get the apron from Mrs. Yoop, we could open the doors and escape from our prison."

"That is true, and it is the plan I was about to suggest," replied Polychrome the Canary-Bird. "However, I don't believe the Owl could steal the apron, or even the Bear, but perhaps the Monkey could hide in her room at night and get the apron while she is asleep."

"I'll try it!" cried Woot the Monkey. "I'll try it this very night, if I can manage to steal into her bedroom."

"You mustn't think about it, though," warned the bird, "for she can read your thoughts whenever she cares to do so. And do not forget, before you escape, to take me with you. Once I am out of the power of the Giantess, I may discover a way to save us all."

"We won't forget our fairy friend," promised the boy; "but perhaps you can tell me how to get into the bedroom."

"No," declared Polychrome, "I cannot advise you as to that. You must watch for a chance, and slip in when Mrs. Yoop isn't looking."

They talked it over for a while longer and then Mrs. Yoop returned. When she entered, the door opened suddenly, at her command, and closed as soon as her huge form had passed through the doorway. During that day she entered her bedroom several times, on one errand or another, but always she commanded the door to close behind her and her prisoners found not the slightest chance to leave the big hall in which they were confined.

The Green Monkey thought it would be wise to make a friend of the big woman, so as to gain her confidence, so he sat on the back of her chair and chattered to her while she mended her stockings and sewed silver buttons on some golden shoes that were as big as row-boats. This pleased the Giantess and she would pause at times to pat the Monkey's head. The little Brown Bear curled up in a corner and lay still all day. The Owl and the Canary found they could converse together in the bird language, which neither the Giantess nor the Bear nor the Monkey could understand; so at times they twittered away to each other and passed the long, dreary day quite cheerfully.

After dinner Mrs. Yoop took a big fiddle from a big cupboard and played such loud and dreadful music that her prisoners were all thankful when at last she stopped and said she was going to bed.

After cautioning the Monkey and Bear and Owl to behave themselves during the night, she picked up the cage containing the Canary and, going to the door of her bedroom, commanded it to open. Just then, however, she remembered she had left her fiddle lying upon a table, so she went back for it and put it away in the cupboard, and while her back was turned the Green Monkey slipped through the open door into her bedroom and hid underneath the bed. The Giantess, being sleepy, did not notice this, and entering her room she made the door close behind her and then hung the bird-cage on a peg by the window. Then she began to undress, first taking off the lace apron and laying it over the bedpost, where it was within easy reach of her hand.

As soon as Mrs. Yoop was in bed the lights all went out, and Woot the Monkey crouched under the bed and waited patiently until he heard the Giantess snoring. Then he crept out and in the dark felt around until he got hold of the apron, which he at once tied around his own waist.

Next, Woot tried to find the Canary, and there was just enough moonlight showing through the window to enable him to see where the cage hung; but it was out of his reach. At first he was tempted to leave Polychrome and escape with his other friends, but remembering his promise to the Rainbow's Daughter, Woot tried to think how to save her.

A chair stood near the window, and this—showing dimly in the moonlight—gave him an idea. By pushing against it with all his might, he found he could move the giant chair a few inches at a time. So he pushed and pushed until the chair was beneath the bird-cage, and then he sprang noiselessly upon the seat—for his monkey form enabled him to jump higher than he could do as a boy—and from there to the back of the chair, and so managed to reach the cage and take it off the peg. Then down he sprang to the floor and made his way to the door.

"Open!" he commanded, and at once the door obeyed and swung open. But his voice wakened Mrs. Yoop, who gave a wild cry and sprang out of bed with one bound. The Green Monkey dashed through the doorway, carrying the cage with him, and before the Giantess could reach the door it slammed shut and imprisoned her in her own bed-chamber!

The noise she made, pounding upon the door, and her yells of anger and dreadful threats of vengeance, filled all our friends with terror, and Woot the Monkey was so excited that in the dark he could not find the outer door of the hall. But the Tin Owl could see very nicely in the dark, so he guided his friends to the right place and when all were grouped before the door Woot commanded it to open. The Magic Apron proved as powerful as when it had been worn by the Giantess, so a moment later they had rushed through the passage and were standing in the fresh night air outside the castle, free to go wherever they willed.

Chapter 8

The MENACE of the FOREST

Quick!" cried Polychrome the Canary; "we must hurry, or Mrs. Yoop may find some way to recapture us, even now. Let us get out of her Valley as soon as possible."

So they set off toward the east, moving as swiftly as they could, and for a long time they could hear the yells and struggles of the imprisoned Giantess. The Green Monkey could run over the ground very swiftly, and he carried with him the bird-cage containing Polychrome the Rainbow's Daughter. Also the Tin Owl could skip and fly along at a good rate of speed, his feathers rattling against one another with a tinkling sound as he moved. But the little Brown Bear, being

stuffed with straw, was a clumsy traveler and the others had
to wait for him to follow.

However, they were not very long in reaching the ridge
that led out of Mrs. Yoop's Valley, and when they had passed
this ridge and descended into the next valley they stopped to
rest, for the Green Monkey was tired.

"I believe we are safe, now," said Polychrome, when her
cage was set down and the others had all gathered around it,
"for Mrs. Yoop dares not go outside of her own Valley, for fear
of being captured by her enemies. So we may take our time to
consider what to do next."

"I'm afraid poor Mrs. Yoop will starve to death, if no one
lets her out of her bedroom," said Woot, who had a heart as
kind as that of the Tin Woodman. "We've taken her Magic
Apron away, and now the doors will never open."

"Don't worry about that," advised Polychrome. "Mrs. Yoop
has plenty of magic left to console her."

"Are you sure of that?" asked the Green Monkey.

"Yes, for I've been watching her for weeks," said the
Canary. "She has six magic hairpins, which she wears in her
hair, and a magic ring which she wears on her thumb and
which is invisible to all eyes except those of a fairy, and magic
bracelets on both her ankles. So I am positive that she will
manage to find a way out of her prison."

"She might transform the door into an archway," suggested the little Brown Bear.

"That would be easy for her," said the Tin Owl; "but I'm glad she was too angry to think of that before we got out of her Valley."

"Well, we have escaped the big woman, to be sure," remarked the Green Monkey, "but we still wear the awful forms the cruel Yookoohoo gave us. How are we going to get rid of these shapes, and become ourselves again?"

None could answer that question. They sat around the cage, brooding over the problem, until the Monkey fell asleep. Seeing this, the Canary tucked her head under her wing and also slept, and the Tin Owl and the Brown Bear did not disturb them until morning came and it was broad daylight.

"I'm hungry," said Woot, when he wakened, for his knapsack of food had been left behind at the castle.

"Then let us travel on until we can find something for you to eat," returned the Scarecrow Bear.

"There is no use in your lugging my cage any farther," declared the Canary. "Let me out, and throw the cage away. Then I can fly with you and find my own breakfast of seeds. Also I can search for water, and tell you where to find it."

So the Green Monkey unfastened the door of the golden cage and the Canary hopped out. At first she flew high in the air and made great circles overhead, but after a time she returned and perched beside them.

"At the east, in the direction we were following," announced the Canary, "there is a fine forest, with a brook running through it. In the forest there may be fruits or nuts growing, or berry bushes at its edge, so let us go that way."

They agreed to this and promptly set off, this time moving more deliberately. The Tin Owl, which had guided their way during the night, now found the sunshine very trying to his big eyes, so he shut them tight and perched upon the back of the little Brown Bear, which carried the Owl's weight with ease. The Canary sometimes perched upon the Green Monkey's shoulder and sometimes fluttered on ahead of the party, and in this manner they traveled in good spirits across that valley and into the next one to the east of it.

This they found to be an immense hollow, shaped like a saucer, and on its farther edge appeared the forest which Polychrome had seen from the sky.

"Come to think of it," said the Tin Owl, waking up and blinking comically at his friends, "there's no object, now, in our traveling to the Munchkin Country. My idea in going there was to marry Nimmie Amee, but however much the Munchkin girl may have loved a Tin Woodman, I cannot reasonably expect her to marry a Tin Owl."

"There is some truth in that, my friend," remarked the Brown Bear. "And to think that I, who was considered the handsomest Scarecrow in the world, am now condemned to be a scrubby, no-account beast, whose only redeeming feature is that he is stuffed with straw!"

"Consider my case, please," said Woot. "The cruel Giantess has made a Monkey of a Boy, and that is the most dreadful deed of all!"

"Your color is rather pretty," said the Brown Bear, eyeing Woot critically. "I have never seen a pea-green monkey before, and it strikes me you are quite gorgeous."

"It isn't so bad to be a bird," asserted the Canary, fluttering from one to another with a free and graceful motion, "but I long to enjoy my own shape again."

"As Polychrome, you were the loveliest maiden I have ever seen—except, of course, Ozma," said the Tin Owl; "so the Giantess did well to transform you into the loveliest of all birds, if you were to be transformed at all. But tell me, since you are a fairy, and have a fairy wisdom: do you think we shall be able to break these enchantments?"

"Queer things happen in the Land of Oz," replied the Canary, again perching on the Green Monkey's shoulder and turning one bright eye thoughtfully toward her questioner. "Mrs. Yoop has declared that none of her transformations can ever be changed, even by herself, but I believe that if we could get to Glinda, the Good Sorceress, she might find a way to restore us to our natural shapes. Glinda, as you know, is the most powerful Sorceress in the world, and there are few things she cannot do if she tries."

"In that case," said the little Brown Bear, "let us return southward and try to get to Glinda's castle. It lies in the Quadling Country, you know, so it is a good way from here."

"First, however, let us visit the forest and search for something to eat," pleaded Woot. So they continued on to the edge of the forest, which consisted of many tall and beautiful trees. They discovered no fruit trees, at first, so the Green Monkey pushed on into the forest depths and the others followed close behind him.

They were traveling quietly along, under the shade of the trees, when suddenly an enormous jaguar leaped upon them from a limb and with one blow of his paw sent the little Brown Bear tumbling over and over until he was stopped by a tree-trunk. Instantly they all took alarm. The Tin Owl shrieked: "Hoot—hoot!" and flew straight up to the branch of a tall tree, although he could scarcely see where he was going. The Canary swiftly darted to a place beside the Owl, and the Green Monkey sprang up, caught a limb, and soon scrambled to a high perch of safety.

The Jaguar crouched low and with hungry eyes regarded the little Brown Bear, which slowly got upon its feet and asked reproachfully:

"For goodness' sake, Beast, what were you trying to do?"

"Trying to get my breakfast," answered the Jaguar with a snarl, "and I believe I've succeeded. You ought to make a delicious meal—unless you happen to be old and tough."

"I'm worse than that, considered as a breakfast," said the Bear, "for I'm only a skin stuffed with straw, and therefore not fit to eat."

"Indeed!" cried the Jaguar, in a disappointed voice; "then you must be a magic Bear, or enchanted, and I must seek my breakfast from among your companions."

With this he raised his lean head to look up at the Tin Owl and the Canary and the Monkey, and he lashed his tail upon the ground and growled as fiercely as any jaguar could.

"My friends are enchanted, also," said the little Brown Bear.

"All of them?" asked the Jaguar.

"Yes. The Owl is tin, so you couldn't possibly eat him. The Canary is a fairy—Polychrome, the Daughter of the Rainbow—and you never could catch her because she can easily fly out of your reach."

"There still remains the Green Monkey," remarked the Jaguar hungrily. "He is neither made of tin nor stuffed with straw, nor can he fly. I'm pretty good at climbing trees, myself, so I think I'll capture the Monkey and eat him for my breakfast."

Woot the Monkey, hearing this speech from his perch on the tree, became much frightened, for he knew the nature of jaguars and realized they could climb trees and leap from limb to limb with the agility of cats. So he at once began to scamper through the forest as fast as he could go, catching at a branch with his long monkey arms and swinging his green body through space to grasp another branch in a neighboring tree, and so on, while the Jaguar followed him from below, his eyes fixed steadfastly on his prey. But presently Woot got his feet tangled in the Lace Apron, which he was still wearing, and that tripped him in his flight and made him fall to the ground, where the Jaguar placed one huge paw upon him and said grimly:

"I've got you, now!"

The fact that the Apron had tripped him made Woot remember its magic powers, and in his terror he cried out: "Open!" without stopping to consider how this command might save him. But, at the word, the earth opened at the exact spot where he lay under the Jaguar's paw, and his body sank downward, the earth closing over it again. The last thing Woot the Monkey saw, as he glanced upward, was the Jaguar peering into the hole in astonishment.

"He's gone!" cried the beast, with a long-drawn sigh of disappointment; "he's gone, and now I shall have no breakfast."

The clatter of the Tin Owl's wings sounded above him, and the little Brown Bear came trotting up and asked:

"Where is the monkey? Have you eaten him so quickly?"

"No, indeed," answered the Jaguar. "He disappeared into the earth before I could take one bite of him!"

And now the Canary perched upon a stump, a little way from the forest beast, and said:

"I am glad our friend has escaped you; but, as it is natural for a hungry beast to wish his breakfast, I will try to give you one."

"Thank you," replied the Jaguar. "You're rather small for a full meal, but it's kind of you to sacrifice yourself to my appetite."

"Oh, I don't intend to be eaten, I assure you," said the Canary, "but as I am a fairy I know something of magic, and though I am now transformed into a bird's shape, I am sure I can conjure up a breakfast that will satisfy you."

"If you can work magic, why don't you break the enchantment you are under and return to your proper form?" inquired the beast doubtingly.

"I haven't the power to do that," answered the Canary, "for Mrs. Yoop, the Giantess who transformed me, used a peculiar form of Yookoohoo magic that is unknown to me. However, she could not deprive me of my own fairy knowledge, so I will try to get you a breakfast."

"Do you think a magic breakfast would taste good, or relieve the pangs of hunger I now suffer?" asked the Jaguar.

"I am sure it would. What would you like to eat?"

"Give me a couple of fat rabbits," said the beast.

"Rabbits! No, indeed. I'd not allow you to eat the dear little things," declared Polychrome the Canary.

"Well, three or four squirrels, then," pleaded the Jaguar.

"Do you think me so cruel?" demanded the Canary, indignantly. "The squirrels are my especial friends."

"How about a plump owl?" asked the beast. "Not a tin one, you know, but a real meat owl."

"Neither beast nor bird shall you have," said Polychrome in a positive voice.

"Give me a fish, then; there's a river a little way off," proposed the Jaguar.

"No living thing shall be sacrificed to feed you," returned the Canary.

"Then what in the world do you expect me to eat?" said the Jaguar in a scornful tone.

"How would mush-and-milk do?" asked the Canary.

The Jaguar snarled in derision and lashed his tail against the ground angrily.

"Give him some scrambled eggs on toast, Poly," suggested the Bear Scarecrow. "He ought to like that."

"I will," responded the Canary, and fluttering her wings she made a flight of three circles around the stump. Then she flew up to a tree and the Bear and the Owl and the Jaguar saw that upon the stump had appeared a great green leaf upon which was a large portion of scrambled eggs on toast, smoking hot.

"There!" said the Bear; "eat your breakfast, friend Jaguar, and be content."

The Jaguar crept closer to the stump and sniffed the fragrance of the scrambled eggs. They smelled so good that he tasted them, and they tasted so good that he ate the strange meal in a hurry, proving he had been really hungry.

"I prefer rabbits," he muttered, licking his chops, "but I

must admit the magic breakfast has filled my stomach full, and brought me comfort. So I'm much obliged for the kindness, little Fairy, and I'll now leave you in peace."

Saying this, he plunged into the thick underbrush and soon disappeared, although they could hear his great body crashing through the bushes until he was far distant.

"That was a good way to get rid of the savage beast, Poly," said the Tin Woodman to the Canary; "but I'm surprised that you didn't give our friend Woot a magic breakfast, when you knew he was hungry."

"The reason for that," answered Polychrome, "was that my mind was so intent on other things that I quite forgot my power to produce food by magic. But where is the monkey boy?"

"Gone!" said the Scarecrow Bear, solemnly. "The earth has swallowed him up."

Chapter 9

The QUARRELSOME DRAGONS

The Green Monkey sank gently into the earth for a little way and then tumbled swiftly through space, landing on a rocky floor with a thump that astonished him. Then he sat up, found that no bones were broken, and gazed around him.

He seemed to be in a big underground cave, which was dimly lighted by dozens of big round discs that looked like moons. They were not moons, however, as Woot discovered when he had examined the place more carefully. They were eyes. The eyes were in the heads of enormous beasts whose bodies trailed far behind them. Each beast was bigger than an elephant, and three times as long, and there were a dozen or more of the creatures scattered here and there about the cavern. On their bodies were big scales, as round as pie-plates, which were beautifully tinted in shades of green, purple and orange. On the ends of their long tails were clusters of jewels. Around the great, moon-like eyes were circles of diamonds which sparkled in the subdued light that glowed from the eyes.

Woot saw that the creatures had wide mouths and rows of terrible teeth and, from tales he had heard of such beings, he knew he had fallen into a cavern inhabited by the great Dragons that had been driven from the surface of the earth and were only allowed to come out once in a hundred years to search for food. Of course he had never seen Dragons before, yet there was no mistaking them, for they were unlike any other living creatures.

Woot sat upon the floor where he had fallen, staring around, and the owners of the big eyes returned his look, silently and motionless. Finally one of the Dragons which was farthest away from him asked, in a deep, grave voice:

"What was that?"

And the greatest Dragon of all, who was just in front of the Green Monkey, answered in a still deeper voice:

"It is some foolish animal from Outside."

"Is it good to eat?" inquired a smaller Dragon beside the great one. "I'm hungry."

"Hungry!" exclaimed all the Dragons, in a reproachful chorus; and then the great one said chidingly: "Tut-tut, my son! You've no reason to be hungry at this time."

"Why not?" asked the little Dragon. "I haven't eaten anything in eleven years."

"Eleven years is nothing," remarked another Dragon, sleepily opening and closing his eyes; "I haven't feasted for eighty-seven years, and I dare not get hungry for a dozen or so years to come. Children who eat between meals should be broken of the habit."

"All I had, eleven years ago, was a rhinoceros, and that's not a full meal at all," grumbled the young one. "And, before that, I had waited sixty-two years to be fed; so it's no wonder I'm hungry."

"How old are you now?" asked Woot, forgetting his own dangerous position in his interest in the conversation.

"Why, I'm—I'm—How old am I, Father?" asked the little Dragon.

"Goodness gracious! what a child to ask questions. Do you want to keep me thinking all the time? Don't you know that thinking is very bad for Dragons?" returned the big one, impatiently.

"How old am I, Father?" persisted the small Dragon.

"About six hundred and thirty, I believe. Ask your mother."

"No; don't!" said an old Dragon in the background; "haven't I enough worries, what with being wakened in the middle of a nap, without being obliged to keep track of my children's ages?"

"You've been fast asleep for over sixty years, Mother," said the child Dragon. "How long a nap do you wish?"

"I should have slept forty years longer. And this strange little green beast should be punished for falling into our cavern and disturbing us."

"I didn't know you were here, and I didn't know I was going to fall in," explained Woot.

"Nevertheless, here you are," said the great Dragon, "and you have carelessly wakened our entire tribe; so it stands to reason you must be punished."

"In what way?" inquired the Green Monkey, trembling a little.

"Give me time and I'll think of a way. You're in no hurry, are you?" asked the great Dragon.

"No, indeed," cried Woot. "Take your time. I'd much rather you'd all go to sleep again, and punish me when you wake up in a hundred years or so."

"Let me eat him!" pleaded the littlest Dragon.

"He is too small," said the father. "To eat this one Green Monkey would only serve to make you hungry for more, and there are no more."

"Quit this chatter and let me get to sleep," protested another Dragon, yawning in a fearful manner, for when he opened his mouth a sheet of flame leaped forth from it and made Woot jump back to get out of its way.

In his jump he bumped against the nose of a Dragon behind

him, which opened its mouth to growl and shot another sheet of flame at him. The flame was bright, but not very hot, yet Woot screamed with terror and sprang forward with a great bound. This time he landed on the paw of the great Chief Dragon, who angrily raised his other front paw and struck the Green Monkey a fierce blow. Woot went sailing through the air and fell sprawling upon the rocky floor far beyond the place where the Dragon Tribe was grouped.

All the great beasts were now thoroughly wakened and aroused, and they blamed the monkey for disturbing their quiet. The littlest Dragon darted after Woot and the others turned their unwieldy bodies in his direction and followed, flashing from their eyes and mouths flames which lighted up the entire cavern.

Woot almost gave himself up for lost, at that moment, but he scrambled to his feet and dashed away to the farthest end of the cave, the Dragons following more leisurely because they were too clumsy to move fast. Perhaps they thought there was no need of haste, as the monkey could not escape from the cave. But, away up at the end of the place, the cavern floor was heaped with tumbled rocks, so Woot, with an agility born of fear, climbed from rock to rock until he found himself crouched against the cavern roof. There he waited, for he could go no farther, while on over the tumbled rocks slowly crept the Dragons—the littlest one coming first because he was hungry as well as angry.

The beasts had almost reached him when Woot, remembering his lace apron—now sadly torn and soiled—recovered his wits and shouted: "Open!" At the cry a hole appeared in the roof of the cavern, just over his head, and through it the sunlight streamed full upon the Green Monkey.

The Dragons paused, astonished at the magic and blinking at the sunlight, and this gave Woot time to climb through the opening. As soon as he reached the surface of the earth the hole closed again, and the boy monkey realized, with a thrill of joy, that he had seen the last of the dangerous Dragon family.

He sat upon the ground, still panting hard from his exertions, when the bushes before him parted and his former enemy, the Jaguar, appeared.

"Don't run," said the woodland beast, as Woot sprang up; "you are perfectly safe, so far as I am concerned, for since you so mysteriously disappeared I have had my breakfast. I am now on my way home to sleep the rest of the day."

"Oh, indeed!" returned the Green Monkey, in a tone both sorry and startled. "Which of my friends did you manage to eat?"

"None of them," returned the Jaguar, with a sly grin. "I had a dish of magic scrambled eggs—on toast—and it wasn't a bad feast, at all. There isn't room in me for even you, and I don't regret it because I judge, from your green color, that you are not ripe, and would make an indifferent meal. We jaguars have to be careful of our digestions. Farewell, Friend Monkey. Follow the path I made through the bushes and you will find your friends."

With this the Jaguar marched on his way and Woot took his advice and followed the trail he had made until he came to the place where the little Brown Bear, and the Tin Owl, and the Canary were conferring together and wondering what had become of their comrade, the Green Monkey.

Chapter 10

TOMMY KWIKSTEP

ur best plan," said the Scarecrow Bear, when the Green Monkey had related the story of his adventure with the Dragons, "is to get out of this Gillikin Country as soon as we can and try to find our way to the castle of Glinda, the Good Sorceress. There are too many dangers lurking here to suit me, and Glinda may be able to restore us to our proper forms."

"If we turn south now," the Tin Owl replied, "we might go straight into the Emerald City. That's a place I wish to avoid, for I'd hate to have my friends see me in this sad plight," and he blinked his eyes and fluttered his tin wings mournfully.

"But I am certain we have passed beyond Emerald City,"

the Canary assured him, sailing lightly around their heads. "So, should we turn south from here, we would pass into the Munchkin Country, and continuing south we would reach the Quadling Country where Glinda's castle is located."

"Well, since you're sure of that, let's start right away," proposed the Bear. "It's a long journey, at the best, and I'm getting tired of walking on four legs."

"I thought you never tired, being stuffed with straw," said Woot.

"I mean that it annoys me, to be obliged to go on all fours, when two legs are my proper walking equipment," replied the Scarecrow. "I consider it beneath my dignity. In other words, my remarkable brains can tire, through humiliation, although my body cannot tire."

"That is one of the penalties of having brains," remarked the Tin Owl with a sigh. "I have had no brains since I was a man of meat, and so I never worry. Nevertheless, I prefer my former manly form to this owl's shape and would be glad to break Mrs. Yoop's enchantment as soon as possible. I am so noisy, just now, that I disturb myself," and he fluttered his wings with a clatter that echoed throughout the forest.

So, being all of one mind, they turned southward, traveling steadily on until the woods were left behind and the landscape turned from purple tints to blue tints, which assured them they had entered the Country of the Munchkins.

"Now I feel myself more safe," said the Scarecrow Bear.

"I know this country pretty well, having been made here by a Munchkin farmer and having wandered over these lovely blue lands many times. Seems to me, indeed, that I even remember that group of three tall trees ahead of us; and, if I do, we are not far from the home of my friend Jinjur."

"Who is Jinjur?" asked Woot, the Green Monkey.

"Haven't you heard of Jinjur?" exclaimed the Scarecrow, in surprise.

"No," said Woot. "Is Jinjur a man, a woman, a beast or a bird?"

"Jinjur is a girl," explained the Scarecrow Bear. "She's a fine girl, too, although a bit restless and liable to get excited. Once, a long time ago, she raised an army of girls and called herself 'General Jinjur.' With her army she captured the Emerald City, and drove me out of it, because I insisted that an army in Oz was highly improper. But Ozma punished the rash girl, and afterward Jinjur and I became fast friends. Now Jinjur lives peacefully on a farm, near here, and raises fields of cream-puffs, chocolate-caramels and macaroons. They say she's a pretty good farmer, and in addition to that she's an artist, and paints pictures so perfect that one can scarcely tell them from nature. She often repaints my face for me, when it gets worn or mussy, and the lovely expression I wore when the Giantess transformed me was painted by Jinjur only a month or so ago."

"It was certainly a pleasant expression," agreed Woot.

"Jinjur can paint anything," continued the Scarecrow Bear, with enthusiasm, as they walked along together. "Once, when I came to her house, my straw was old and crumpled, so that my body sagged dreadfully. I needed new straw to replace the old, but Jinjur had no straw on all her ranch and I was really unable to travel farther until I had been restuffed. When I explained this to Jinjur, the girl at once painted a straw-stack which was so natural that I went to it and secured enough straw to fill all my body. It was a good quality of straw, too, and lasted me a long time."

This seemed very wonderful to Woot, who knew that such a thing could never happen in any place but a fairy country like Oz.

The Munchkin Country was much nicer than the Gillikin Country, and all the fields were separated by blue fences, with grassy lanes and paths of blue ground, and the land seemed well cultivated. They were on a little hill looking down upon this favored country, but had not quite reached the settled parts, when on turning a bend in the path they were halted by a form that barred their way.

A more curious creature they had seldom seen, even in the Land of Oz, where curious creatures abound. It had the head of a young man—evidently a Munchkin—with a pleasant face and hair neatly combed. But the body was very long, for it had twenty legs—ten legs on each side—and this caused the body to stretch out and lie in a horizontal position, so that all the legs could touch the ground and stand firm. From the shoulders extended two small arms; at least, they seemed small beside so many legs.

This odd creature was dressed in the regulation clothing of the Munchkin people, a dark blue coat neatly fitting the long body and each pair of legs having a pair of sky-blue trousers, with blue-tinted stockings and blue leather shoes turned up at the pointed toes.

"I wonder who you are?" said Polychrome the Canary, fluttering above the strange creature, who had probably been asleep on the path.

"I sometimes wonder, myself, who I am," replied the many-legged young man; "but, in reality, I am Tommy Kwikstep, and I live in a hollow tree that fell to the ground with age. I have polished the inside of it, and made a door at each end, and that's a very comfortable residence for me because it just fits my shape."

"How did you happen to have such a shape?" asked the Scarecrow Bear, sitting on his haunches and regarding Tommy Kwikstep with a serious look. "Is the shape natural?"

"No; it was wished on me," replied Tommy, with a sigh. "I used to be very active and loved to run errands for anyone who needed my services. That was how I got my name of Tommy Kwikstep. I could run an errand more quickly than any other boy, and so I was very proud of myself. One day, however, I met an old lady who was a fairy, or a witch, or something of the sort, and she said if I would run an errand for her—to carry some magic medicine to another old woman—she would grant me just one Wish, whatever the Wish happened to be. Of course I consented and, taking the medicine, I hurried away. It was a long distance, mostly up-hill, and my legs began to grow weary. Without thinking what I was doing I said aloud: 'Dear me; I wish I had twenty legs!' and in an instant I became the unusual creature you see beside you. Twenty legs! Twenty on one man! You may count them, if you doubt my word."

"You've got 'em, all right," said Woot the Monkey, who had already counted them.

"After I had delivered the magic medicine to the old woman, I returned and tried to find the witch, or fairy, or whatever she was, who had given me the unlucky wish, so she could take it away again. I've been searching for her ever since, but never can I find her," continued poor Tommy Kwikstep, sadly.

"I suppose," said the Tin Owl, blinking at him, "you can travel very fast, with those twenty legs."

"At first I was able to," was the reply; "but I traveled so much, searching for the fairy, or witch, or whatever she was, that I soon got corns on my toes. Now, a corn on one toe is not so bad, but when you have a hundred toes—as I have—and get corns on most of them, it is far from pleasant. Instead of running, I now painfully crawl, and although I try not to be discouraged I do hope I shall find that witch or fairy, or whatever she was, before long."

"I hope so, too," said the Scarecrow. "But, after all, you have the pleasure of knowing you are unusual, and therefore remarkable among the people of Oz. To be just like other persons is small credit to one, while to be unlike others is a mark of distinction."

"That sounds very pretty," returned Tommy Kwikstep, "but if you had to put on ten pair of trousers every morning, and tie up twenty shoes, you would prefer not to be so distinguished."

"Was the witch, or fairy, or whatever she was, an old person, with wrinkled skin and half her teeth gone?" inquired the Tin Owl.

"No," said Tommy Kwikstep.

"Then she wasn't Old Mombi," remarked the transformed Emperor.

"I'm not interested in who it wasn't, so much as I am in who it was," said the twenty-legged young man. "And, whatever or whomsoever she was, she has managed to keep out of my way."

"If you found her, do you suppose she'd change you back into a two-legged boy?" asked Woot.

"Perhaps so, if I could run another errand for her and so earn another wish."

"Would you really like to be as you were before?" asked Polychrome the Canary, perching upon the Green Monkey's shoulder to observe Tommy Kwikstep more attentively.

"I would, indeed," was the earnest reply.

"Then I will see what I can do for you," promised the Rainbow's Daughter, and flying to the ground she took a small twig in her bill and with it made several mystic figures on each side of Tommy Kwikstep.

"Are you a witch, or fairy, or something of the sort?" he asked as he watched her wonderingly.

The Canary made no answer, for she was busy, but the Scarecrow Bear replied: "Yes; she's something of the sort, and a bird of a magician."

The twenty-legged boy's transformation happened so queerly that they were all surprised at its method. First, Tommy Kwikstep's last two legs disappeared; then the next two, and the next, and as each pair of legs vanished his body shortened. All this while Polychrome was running around him and chirping mystical words, and when all the young man's legs had disappeared but two he noticed that the Canary was still busy and cried out in alarm:

"Stop—stop! Leave me two of my legs, or I shall be worse off than before."

"I know," said the Canary. "I'm only removing with my magic the corns from your last ten toes."

"Thank you for being so thoughtful," he said gratefully, and now they noticed that Tommy Kwikstep was quite a nice looking young fellow.

"What will you do now?" asked Woot the Monkey.

"First," he answered, "I must deliver a note which I've carried in my pocket ever since the witch, or fairy, or whatever she was, granted my foolish wish. And I am resolved never to speak again without taking time to think carefully on what I am going to say, for I realize that speech without thought is dangerous. And after I've delivered the note, I shall run errands again for anyone who needs my services."

So he thanked Polychrome again and started away in a different direction from their own, and that was the last they saw of Tommy Kwikstep.

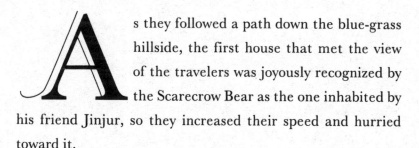

·····—·◄ Chapter 11 ►··—··

JINJUR'S RANCH

As they followed a path down the blue-grass hillside, the first house that met the view of the travelers was joyously recognized by the Scarecrow Bear as the one inhabited by his friend Jinjur, so they increased their speed and hurried toward it.

On reaching the place, however, they found the house deserted. The front door stood open, but no one was inside. In the garden surrounding the house were neat rows of bushes bearing cream-puffs and macaroons, some of which were still green, but others ripe and ready to eat. Farther back were fields of caramels, and all the land seemed well cultivated and carefully tended. They looked through the fields for the girl farmer, but she was nowhere to be seen.

"Well," finally remarked the little Brown Bear, "let us go into the house and make ourselves at home. That will be sure to please my friend Jinjur, who happens to be away from home just now. When she returns, she will be greatly surprised."

"Would she care if I ate some of those ripe cream-puffs?" asked the Green Monkey.

"No, indeed; Jinjur is very generous. Help yourself to all you want," said the Scarecrow Bear.

So Woot gathered a lot of the cream-puffs that were golden yellow and filled with a sweet, creamy substance, and ate until his hunger was satisfied. Then he entered the house with his friends and sat in a rocking-chair—just as he was accustomed to do when a boy. The Canary perched herself upon the mantel and daintily plumed her feathers; the Tin Owl sat on the back of another chair; the Scarecrow squatted on his hairy haunches in the middle of the room.

"I believe I remember the girl Jinjur," remarked the Canary, in her sweet voice. "She cannot help us very much, except to direct us on our way to Glinda's castle, for she does not understand magic. But she's a good girl, honest and sensible, and I'll be glad to see her."

"All our troubles," said the Owl with a deep sigh, "arose from my foolish resolve to seek Nimmie Amee and make her Empress of the Winkies, and while I wish to reproach no one,

I must say that it was Woot the Wanderer who put the notion into my head."

"Well, for my part, I am glad he did," responded the Canary. "Your journey resulted in saving me from the Giantess, and had you not traveled to the Yoop Valley, I would still be Mrs. Yoop's prisoner. It is much nicer to be free, even though I still bear the enchanted form of a Canary-Bird."

"Do you think we shall ever be able to get our proper forms back again?" asked the Green Monkey earnestly.

Polychrome did not make reply at once to this important question, but after a period of thoughtfulness she said:

"I have been taught to believe that there is an antidote for every magic charm, yet Mrs. Yoop insists that no power can alter her transformations. I realize that my own fairy magic cannot do it, although I have thought that we Sky Fairies have more power than is accorded to Earth Fairies. The Yookoohoo magic is admitted to be very strange in its workings and different from the magic usually practiced, but perhaps Glinda or Ozma may understand it better than I. In them lies our only hope. Unless they can help us, we must remain forever as we are."

"A Canary-Bird on a Rainbow wouldn't be so bad," asserted the Tin Owl, winking and blinking with his round tin eyes, "so if you can manage to find your Rainbow again you need have little to worry about."

"That's nonsense, Friend Chopper," exclaimed Woot. "I

know just how Polychrome feels. A beautiful girl is much superior to a little yellow bird, and a boy—such as I was—far better than a Green Monkey. Neither of us can be happy again unless we recover our rightful forms."

"I feel the same way," announced the stuffed Bear. "What do you suppose my friend the Patchwork Girl would think of me, if she saw me wearing this beastly shape?"

"She'd laugh till she cried," admitted the Tin Owl. "For my part, I'll have to give up the notion of marrying Nimmie Amee, but I'll try not to let that make me unhappy. If it's my duty, I'd like to do my duty, but if magic prevents my getting married I'll flutter along all by myself and be just as contented."

Their serious misfortunes made them all silent for a time, and as their thoughts were busy in dwelling upon the evils with which fate had burdened them, none noticed that Jinjur had suddenly appeared in the doorway and was looking at them in astonishment. The next moment her astonishment changed to anger, for there, in her best rocking-chair, sat a Green Monkey. A great shiny Owl perched upon another chair and a Brown Bear squatted upon her parlor rug. Jinjur did not notice the Canary, but she caught up a broomstick and dashed into the room, shouting as she came:

"Get out of here, you wild creatures! How dare you enter my house?"

With a blow of her broom she knocked the Brown Bear over,

and the Tin Owl tried to fly out of her reach and made a great clatter with his tin wings. The Green Monkey was so startled by the sudden attack that he sprang into the fireplace—where there was fortunately no fire—and tried to escape by climbing up the chimney. But he found the opening too small, and so was forced to drop down again. Then he crouched trembling in the fireplace, his pretty green hair all blackened with soot and covered with ashes. From this position Woot watched to see what would happen next.

"Stop, Jinjur—stop!" cried the Brown Bear, when the broom again threatened him. "Don't you know me? I'm your old friend the Scarecrow?"

"You're trying to deceive me, you naughty beast! I can see plainly that you are a bear, and a mighty poor specimen of a bear, too," retorted the girl.

"That's because I'm not properly stuffed," he assured her. "When Mrs. Yoop transformed me, she didn't realize I should have more stuffing."

"Who is Mrs. Yoop?" inquired Jinjur, pausing with the broom still upraised.

"A Giantess in the Gillikin Country."

"Oh; I begin to understand. And Mrs. Yoop transformed you? You are really the famous Scarecrow of Oz."

"I was, Jinjur. Just now I'm as you see me—a miserable little Brown Bear with a poor quality of stuffing. That Tin Owl is none other than our dear Tin Woodman—Nick Chopper, the Emperor of the Winkies—while this Green Monkey is a nice little boy we recently became acquainted with, Woot the Wanderer."

"And I," said the Canary, flying close to Jinjur, "am Polychrome, the Daughter of the Rainbow, in the form of a bird."

"Goodness me!" cried Jinjur, amazed; "that Giantess must be a powerful Sorceress, and as wicked as she is powerful."

"She's a Yookoohoo," said Polychrome. "Fortunately, we managed to escape from her castle, and we are now on our way to Glinda the Good to see if she possesses the power to restore us to our former shapes."

"Then I must beg your pardons; all of you must forgive me," said Jinjur, putting away the broom. "I took you to be a lot of wild, unmannerly animals, as was quite natural. You are very welcome to my home and I'm sorry I haven't the power to help you out of your troubles. Please use my house and all that I have, as if it were your own."

At this declaration of peace, the Bear got upon his feet and the Owl resumed his perch upon the chair and the Monkey crept out of the fireplace. Jinjur looked at Woot critically, and scowled.

"For a Green Monkey," said she, "you're the blackest creature I ever saw. And you'll get my nice clean room all dirty with soot and ashes. Whatever possessed you to jump up the chimney?"

"I—I was scared," explained Woot, somewhat ashamed.

"Well, you need renovating, and that's what will happen to you, right away. Come with me!" she commanded.

"What are you going to do?" asked Woot.

"Give you a good scrubbing," said Jinjur.

Now, neither boys nor monkeys relish being scrubbed, so Woot shrank away from the energetic girl, trembling fearfully. But Jinjur grabbed him by his paw and dragged him out to the back yard, where, in spite of his whines and struggles, she plunged him into a tub of cold water and began to scrub him with a stiff brush and a cake of yellow soap.

This was the hardest trial that Woot had endured since he became a monkey, but no protest had any influence with Jinjur, who lathered and scrubbed him in a business-like manner and afterward dried him with a coarse towel.

The Bear and the Owl gravely watched this operation and nodded approval when Woot's silky green fur shone clear and bright in the afternoon sun. The Canary seemed much amused and laughed a silvery ripple of laughter as she said:

"Very well done, my good Jinjur; I admire your energy and judgment. But I had no idea a monkey could look so comical as this monkey did while he was being bathed."

"I'm not a monkey!" declared Woot, resentfully; "I'm just a boy in a monkey's shape, that's all."

"If you can explain to me the difference," said Jinjur, "I'll agree not to wash you again—that is, unless you foolishly get into the fireplace. All persons are usually judged by the shapes in which they appear to the eyes of others. Look at me, Woot; what am I?"

Woot looked at her.

"You're as pretty a girl as I've ever seen," he replied.

Jinjur frowned. That is, she tried hard to frown.

"Come out into the garden with me," she said, "and I'll give you some of the most delicious caramels you ever ate. They're a new variety, that no one can grow but me, and they have a heliotrope flavor."

Chapter 12

OZMA and DOROTHY

In her magnificent palace in the Emerald City, the beautiful girl Ruler of all the wonderful Land of Oz sat in her dainty boudoir with her friend Princess Dorothy beside her. Ozma was studying a roll of manuscript which she had taken from the Royal Library, while Dorothy worked at her embroidery and at times stooped to pat a shaggy little black dog that lay at her feet. The little dog's name was Toto, and he was Dorothy's faithful companion.

To judge Ozma of Oz by the standards of our world, you would think her very young—perhaps fourteen or fifteen years of age—yet for years she had ruled the Land of Oz and had never seemed a bit older. Dorothy appeared much younger than Ozma. She had been a little girl when first she came to the Land of Oz, and she was a little girl still, and would never seem to be a day older while she lived in this wonderful fairyland.

Oz was not always a fairyland, I am told. Once it was much like other lands, except it was shut in by a dreadful desert of sandy wastes that lay all around it, thus preventing its people from all contact with the rest of the world. Seeing this isolation, the fairy band of Queen Lurline, passing over Oz while on a journey, enchanted the country and so made it a fairyland. And Queen Lurline left one of her fairies to rule this enchanted Land of Oz, and then passed on and forgot all about it.

From that moment no one in Oz ever died. Those who were old remained old; those who were young and strong did not change as years passed them by; the children remained children always, and played and romped to their hearts' content, while all the babies lived in their cradles and were tenderly cared for and never grew up. So people in Oz stopped counting how old they were in years, for years made no difference in their appearance and could not alter their station. They did not get sick, so there were no doctors among them. Accidents might happen to some, on rare occasions, it is true, and while no one could die naturally, as other people do, it was possible that one might be totally destroyed. Such incidents, however, were very unusual, and so seldom was there anything to worry over that the Oz people were as happy and contented as can be.

Another strange thing about this fairy Land of Oz was that whoever managed to enter it from the outside world came under the magic spell of the place and did not change in appearance as long as they lived there. So Dorothy, who now lived with Ozma, seemed just the same sweet little girl she had been when first she came to this delightful fairyland.

Perhaps all parts of Oz might not be called truly delightful, but it was surely delightful in the neighborhood of the Emerald City, where Ozma reigned. Her loving influence was felt for many miles around, but there were places in the mountains of the Gillikin Country, and the forests of the Quadling Country, and perhaps in far-away parts of the Munchkin and Winkie Countries, where the inhabitants were somewhat rude and uncivilized and had not yet come under the spell of Ozma's wise and kindly rule. Also, when Oz first became a fairyland, it harbored several witches and magicians and sorcerers and necromancers, who were scattered in various parts, but most of these had been deprived of their magic powers, and Ozma had issued a royal edict forbidding anyone in her dominions to work magic except Glinda the Good and the Wizard of Oz. Ozma herself, being a real fairy, knew a lot of magic, but she only used it to benefit her subjects.

This little explanation will help you to understand better the story you are reaching, but most of it is already known to those who are familiar with the Oz people whose adventures they have followed in other Oz books.

Ozma and Dorothy were fast friends and were much together. Everyone in Oz loved Dorothy almost as well as they did their lovely Ruler, for the little Kansas girl's good fortune had not spoiled her or rendered her at all vain. She was just the same brave and true and adventurous child as before she lived in a royal palace and became the chum of the fairy Ozma.

In the room in which the two sat—which was one of Ozma's private suite of apartments—hung the famous Magic Picture. This was the source of constant interest to little Dorothy. One had but to stand before it and wish to see what any person was doing, and at once a scene would flash upon the magic canvas which showed exactly where that person was, and like our own moving pictures would reproduce the actions of that person as long as you cared to watch them. So today, when Dorothy tired of her embroidery, she drew the curtains from before the Magic Picture and wished to see what her friend Button-Bright was doing. Button-Bright, she saw, was playing ball with Ojo, the Munchkin boy, so Dorothy next wished to see what her Aunt Em was doing. The picture showed Aunt Em quietly engaged in darning socks for Uncle Henry, so Dorothy wished to see what her old friend the Tin Woodman was doing.

The Tin Woodman was then just leaving his tin castle in the company of the Scarecrow and Woot the Wanderer.

Dorothy had never seen this boy before, so she wondered who he was. Also she was curious to know where the three were going, for she noticed Woot's knapsack and guessed they had started on a long journey. She asked Ozma about it, but Ozma did not know.

That afternoon Dorothy again saw the travelers in the Magic Picture, but they were merely tramping through the country and Dorothy was not much interested in them. A couple of days later, however, the girl, being again with Ozma, wished to see her friends, the Scarecrow and the Tin Woodman, in the Magic Picture, and on this occasion found them in the great castle of Mrs. Yoop, the Giantess, who was at the time about to transform them. Both Dorothy and Ozma now became greatly interested and watched the transformations with indignation and horror.

"What a wicked Giantess!" exclaimed Dorothy.

"Yes," answered Ozma, "she must be punished for this cruelty to our friends, and to the poor boy who is with them."

After this they followed the adventure of the little Brown Bear and the Tin Owl and the Green Monkey with breathless interest, and were delighted when they escaped from Mrs. Yoop. They did not know, then, who the Canary was, but realized it must be the transformation of some person of consequence, whom the Giantess had also enchanted.

When, finally, the day came when the adventurers headed south into the Munchkin Country, Dorothy asked anxiously:

"Can't something be done for them, Ozma? Can't you change 'em back into their own shapes? They've suffered enough from these dreadful transformations, seems to me."

"I've been studying ways to help them, ever since they were transformed," replied Ozma. "Mrs. Yoop is now the only Yookoohoo in my dominions, and the Yookoohoo magic is very peculiar and hard for others to understand, yet I am resolved to make the attempt to break these enchantments. I may not succeed, but I shall do the best I can. From the directions our friends are taking, I believe they are going to pass by Jinjur's Ranch, so if we start now we may meet them there. Would you like to go with me, Dorothy?"

"Of course," answered the little girl; "I wouldn't miss it for anything."

"Then order the Red Wagon," said Ozma of Oz, "and we will start at once."

Dorothy ran to do as she was bid, while Ozma went to her Magic Room to make ready the things she believed she would need. In half an hour the Red Wagon stood before the grand entrance of the palace, and before it was hitched the Wooden Sawhorse, which was Ozma's favorite steed.

This Sawhorse, while made of wood, was very much alive and could travel swiftly and without tiring. To keep the ends of his wooden legs from wearing down short, Ozma had shod the Sawhorse with plates of pure gold. His harness was studded with brilliant emeralds and other jewels and so, while he

himself was not at all handsome, his outfit made a splendid
appearance.

Since the Sawhorse could understand her spoken words,
Ozma used no reins to guide him. She merely told him where
to go. When she came from the palace with Dorothy, they both
climbed into the Red Wagon and then the little dog, Toto, ran
up and asked:

"Are you going to leave me behind, Dorothy?"

Dorothy looked at Ozma, who smiled in return and said:

"Toto may go with us, if you wish him to."

So Dorothy lifted the little dog into the wagon, for, while
he could run fast, he could not keep up with the speed of the
wonderful Sawhorse.

Away they went, over hills and through meadows, covering
the ground with astonishing speed. It is not surprising, therefore, that the Red Wagon arrived before Jinjur's house just as
that energetic young lady had finished scrubbing the Green
Monkey and was about to lead him to the caramel patch.

⊶————◅ Chapter 13 ▸∙∙—————∙∙

The RESTORATION

The Tin Owl gave a hoot of delight when he saw the Red Wagon draw up before Jinjur's house, and the Brown Bear grunted and growled with glee and trotted toward Ozma as fast as he could wobble. As for the Canary, it flew swiftly to Dorothy's shoulder and perched there, saying in her ear:

"Thank goodness you have come to our rescue!"

"But who are you?" asked Dorothy.

"Don't you know?" returned the Canary.

"No; for the first time we noticed you in the Magic Picture, you were just a bird, as you are now. But we've guessed that the giant woman had transformed you, as she did the others."

"Yes; I'm Polychrome, the Rainbow's Daughter," announced the Canary.

"Goodness me!" cried Dorothy. "How dreadful."

"Well, I make a rather pretty bird, I think," returned Polychrome, "but of course I'm anxious to resume my own shape and get back upon my rainbow."

"Ozma will help you, I'm sure," said Dorothy. "How does it feel, Scarecrow, to be a Bear?" she asked, addressing her old friend.

"I don't like it," declared the Scarecrow Bear. "This brutal form is quite beneath the dignity of a wholesome straw man."

"And think of me," said the Owl, perching upon the dashboard of the Red Wagon with much noisy clattering of his tin feathers. "Don't I look horrid, Dorothy, with eyes several sizes too big for my body, and so weak that I ought to wear spectacles?"

"Well," said Dorothy critically, as she looked him over, "you're nothing to brag of, I must confess. But Ozma will soon fix you up again."

The Green Monkey had hung back, bashful at meeting two lovely girls while in the form of a beast; but Jinjur now took his hand and led him forward while she introduced him to Ozma, and Woot managed to make a low bow, not really ungraceful, before her girlish Majesty, the Ruler of Oz.

"You have all been forced to endure a sad experience," said Ozma, "and so I am anxious to do all in my power to break Mrs. Yoop's enchantments. But first tell me how you happened to stray into that lonely Valley where Yoop Castle stands."

Between them they related the object of their journey, the Scarecrow Bear telling of the Tin Woodman's resolve to find Nimmie Amee and marry her, as a just reward for her loyalty to him. Woot told of their adventures with the Loons of Loonville, and the Tin Owl described the manner in which they had been captured and transformed by the Giantess. Then Polychrome related her story, and when all had been told, and Dorothy had several times reproved Toto for growling at the Tin Owl, Ozma remained thoughtful for a while, pondering upon what she had heard. Finally she looked up, and with one of her delightful smiles, said to the anxious group:

"I am not sure my magic will be able to restore every one of you, because your transformations are of such a strange and unusual character. Indeed, Mrs. Yoop was quite justified in believing no power could alter her enchantments. However, I am sure I can restore the Scarecrow to his original shape. He was stuffed with straw from the beginning, and even the Yookoohoo magic could not alter that. The Giantess was merely able to make a bear's shape of a man's shape, but the bear is stuffed with straw, just as the man was. So I feel confident I can make a man of the bear again."

"Hurrah!" cried the Brown Bear, and tried clumsily to dance a jig of delight.

"As for the Tin Woodman, his case is much the same," resumed Ozma, still smiling. "The power of the Giantess could not make him anything but a tin creature, whatever shape she transformed him into, so it will not be impossible to restore him to his manly form. Anyhow, I shall test my magic at once, and see if it will do what I have promised."

She drew from her bosom a small silver Wand and, making passes with the Wand over the head of the Bear, she succeeded in the brief space of a moment in breaking his enchantment. The original Scarecrow of Oz again stood before them, well stuffed with straw and with his features nicely painted upon the bag which formed his head.

The Scarecrow was greatly delighted, as you may suppose, and he strutted proudly around while the powerful fairy, Ozma of Oz, broke the enchantment that had transformed the Tin Woodman and made a Tin Owl into a Tin Man again.

"Now, then," chirped the Canary, eagerly; "I'm next, Ozma!"

"But your case is different," replied Ozma, no longer smiling but wearing a grave expression on her sweet face. "I shall have to experiment on you, Polychrome, and I may fail in all my attempts."

She then tried two or three different methods of magic, hoping one of them would succeed in breaking Polychrome's enchantment, but still the Rainbow's Daughter remained a Canary-Bird. Finally, however, she experimented in another

way. She transformed the Canary into a Dove, and then transformed the Dove into a Speckled Hen, and then changed the
Speckled Hen into a Rabbit, and then the Rabbit into a Fawn.
And at the last, after mixing several powders and sprinkling
them upon the Fawn, the Yookoohoo enchantment was suddenly broken and before them stood one of the daintiest and
loveliest creatures in any fairyland in the world. Polychrome
was as sweet and merry in disposition as she was beautiful, and
when she danced and capered around in delight, her beautiful
hair floated around her like a golden mist and her many-hued
raiment, as soft as cobwebs, reminded one of drifting clouds
in a summer sky.

Woot was so awed by the entrancing sight of this exquisite Sky Fairy that he quite forgot his own sad plight until
be noticed Ozma gazing upon him with an intent expression
that denoted sympathy and sorrow. Dorothy whispered in her
friend's ear, but the Ruler of Oz shook her head sadly.

Jinjur, noticing this and understanding Ozma's looks, took
the paw of the Green Monkey in her own hand and patted it
softly.

"Never mind," she said to him. "You are a very beautiful
color, and a monkey can climb better than a boy and do a lot
of other things no boy can ever do."

"What's the matter?" asked Woot, a sinking feeling at his
heart. "Is Ozma's magic all used up?"

Ozma herself answered him.

"Your form of enchantment, my poor boy," she said pityingly, "is different from that of the others. Indeed, it is a form that is impossible to alter by any magic known to fairies or Yookoohoos. The wicked Giantess was well aware, when she gave you the form of a Green Monkey, that the Green Monkey must exist in the Land of Oz for all future time."

Woot drew a long sigh.

"Well, that's pretty hard luck," he said bravely, "but if it can't be helped I must endure it; that's all. I don't like being a monkey, but what's the use of kicking against my fate?"

They were all very sorry for him, and Dorothy anxiously asked Ozma:

"Couldn't Glinda save him?"

"No," was the reply. "Glinda's power in transformations is no greater than my own. Before I left my palace I went to my Magic Room and studied Woot's case very carefully. I found that no power can do away with the Green Monkey. He might transfer, or exchange his form with some other person, it is true; but the Green Monkey we cannot get rid of by any magic arts known to science."

"But—see here," said the Scarecrow, who had listened intently to this explanation, "why not put the monkey's form on some one else?"

"Who would agree to make the change?" asked Ozma. "If by force we caused anyone else to become a Green Monkey, we would be as cruel and wicked as Mrs. Yoop. And what good would an exchange do?" she continued. "Suppose, for instance, we worked the enchantment, and made Toto into a Green Monkey. At the same moment Woot would become a little dog."

"Leave me out of your magic, please," said Toto, with a reproachful growl. "I wouldn't become a Green Monkey for anything."

"And I wouldn't become a dog," said Woot. "A green monkey is much better than a dog, it seems to me."

"That is only a matter of opinion," answered Toto.

"Now, here's another idea," said the Scarecrow. "My brains are working finely today, you must admit. Why not transform Toto into Woot the Wanderer, and then have them exchange forms? The dog would become a green monkey and the monkey would have his own natural shape again."

"To be sure!" cried Jinjur. "That's a fine idea."

"Leave me out of it," said Toto. "I won't do it."

"Wouldn't you be willing to become a green monkey— see what a pretty color it is—so that this poor boy could be restored to his own shape?" asked Jinjur, pleadingly.

"No," said Toto.

"I don't like that plan the least bit," declared Dorothy, "for then I wouldn't have any little dog."

"But you'd have a green monkey in his place," persisted Jinjur, who liked Woot and wanted to help him.

"I don't want a green monkey," said Dorothy positively.

"Don't speak of this again, I beg of you," said Woot. "This is my own misfortune and I would rather suffer it alone than deprive Princess Dorothy of her dog, or deprive the dog of his proper shape. And perhaps even her Majesty, Ozma of Oz, might not be able to transform anyone else into the shape of Woot the Wanderer."

"Yes; I believe I might do that," Ozma returned; "but Woot is quite right; we are not justified in inflicting upon anyone—man or dog—the form of a green monkey. Also it is certain that in order to relieve the boy of the form he now wears, we must give it to someone else, who would be forced to wear it always."

"I wonder," said Dorothy, thoughtfully, "if we couldn't find someone in the Land of Oz who would be willing to become a green monkey? Seems to me a monkey is active and spry, and he can climb trees and do a lot of clever things, and green isn't a bad color for a monkey—it makes him unusual."

"I wouldn't ask anyone to take this dreadful form," said Woot; "it wouldn't be right, you know. I've been a monkey for some time, now, and I don't like it. It makes me ashamed to be a beast of this sort when by right of birth I'm a boy; so I'm sure it would be wicked to ask anyone else to take my place."

They were all silent, for they knew he spoke the truth. Dorothy was almost ready to cry with pity and Ozma's sweet face was sad and disturbed. The Scarecrow rubbed and patted his stuffed head to try to make it think better, while the Tin Woodman went into the house and began to oil his tin joints so that the sorrow of his friends might not cause him to weep. Weeping is liable to rust tin, and the Emperor prided himself upon his highly polished body—now doubly dear to him because for a time he had been deprived of it.

Polychrome had danced down the garden paths and back again a dozen times, for she was seldom still a moment, yet she had heard Ozma's speech and understood very well Woot's unfortunate position. But the Rainbow's Daughter, even while dancing, could think and reason very clearly, and suddenly she solved the problem in the nicest possible way. Coming close to Ozma, she said:

"Your Majesty, all this trouble was caused by the wickedness of Mrs. Yoop, the Giantess. Yet even now that cruel woman is living in her secluded castle, enjoying the thought that she has put this terrible enchantment on Woot the Wanderer. Even now she is laughing at our despair because we can find no way to get rid of the green monkey. Very well, we do not wish to get rid of it. Let the woman who created the form wear it herself, as a just punishment for her wickedness. I am sure your fairy power can give to Mrs. Yoop the form of Woot the Wanderer—even at this distance from her—and then it will be possible to exchange the two forms. Mrs. Yoop will become the Green Monkey, and Woot will recover his own form again."

Ozma's face brightened as she listened to this clever proposal.

"Thank you, Polychrome," said she. "The task you propose is not so easy as you suppose, but I will make the attempt, and perhaps I may succeed."

—··◄ Chapter 14 ►··—··

The GREEN MONKEY

They now entered the house, and as an interested group, watched Jinjur, at Ozma's command, build a fire and put a kettle of water over to boil. The Ruler of Oz stood before the fire silent and grave, while the others, realizing that an important ceremony of magic was about to be performed, stood quietly in the background so as not to interrupt Ozma's proceedings. Only Polychrome kept going in and coming out, humming softly to herself as she danced, for the Rainbow's Daughter could not keep still for long, and the four walls of a room always made her nervous and ill at ease. She moved so noiselessly, however, that her movements were like the shifting of sunbeams and did not annoy anyone.

When the water in the kettle bubbled, Ozma drew from her bosom two tiny packets containing powders. These powders she threw into the kettle and after briskly stirring the contents with a branch from a macaroon bush, Ozma poured the mystic broth upon a broad platter which Jinjur had placed upon the table. As the broth cooled it became as silver, reflecting all objects from its smooth surface like a mirror.

While her companions gathered around the table, eagerly attentive—and Dorothy even held little Toto in her arms that he might see—Ozma waved her wand over the mirror-like surface. At once it reflected the interior of Yoop Castle, and in the big hall sat Mrs. Yoop, in her best embroidered silken robes, engaged in weaving a new lace apron to replace the one she had lost.

The Giantess seemed rather uneasy, as if she had a faint idea that someone was spying upon her, for she kept looking behind her and this way and that, as though expecting danger from an unknown source. Perhaps some Yookoohoo instinct warned her. Woot saw that she had escaped from her room by some of the magical means at her disposal, after her prisoners had escaped her. She was now occupying the big hall of her castle as she used to do. Also Woot thought, from the cruel expression on the face of the Giantess, that she was planning revenge on them, as soon as her new magic apron was finished.

But Ozma was now making passes over the platter with

her silver Wand, and presently the form of the Giantess began to shrink in size and to change its shape. And now, in her place sat the form of Woot the Wanderer, and as if suddenly realizing her transformation Mrs. Yoop threw down her work and rushed to a looking-glass that stood against the wall of her room. When she saw the boy's form reflected as her own, she grew violently angry and dashed her head against the mirror, smashing it to atoms.

Just then Ozma was busy with her magic Wand, making strange figures, and she had also placed her left hand firmly upon the shoulder of the Green Monkey. So now, as all eyes were turned upon the platter, the form of Mrs. Yoop gradually changed again. She was slowly transformed into the Green Monkey, and at the same time Woot slowly regained his natural form.

It was quite a surprise to them all when they raised their eyes from the platter and saw Woot the Wanderer standing beside Ozma. And, when they glanced at the platter again, it reflected nothing more than the walls of the room in Jinjur's house in which they stood. The magic ceremonial was ended, and Ozma of Oz had triumphed over the wicked Giantess.

"What will become of her, I wonder?" said Dorothy, as she drew a long breath.

"She will always remain a Green Monkey," replied Ozma, "and in that form she will be unable to perform any magical arts whatsoever. She need not be unhappy, however, and as she lives all alone in her castle she probably won't mind the transformation very much after she gets used to it."

"Anyhow, it serves her right," declared Dorothy, and all agreed with her.

"But," said the kind hearted Tin Woodman, "I'm afraid the Green Monkey will starve, for Mrs. Yoop used to get her food by magic, and now that the magic is taken away from her, what can she eat?"

"Why, she'll eat what other monkeys do," returned the Scarecrow. "Even in the form of a Green Monkey, she's a very clever person, and I'm sure her wits will show her how to get plenty to eat."

"Don't worry about her," advised Dorothy. "She didn't worry about you, and her condition is no worse than the condition she imposed on poor Woot. She can't starve to death in the Land of Oz, that's certain, and if she gets hungry at times it's no more than the wicked thing deserves. Let's forget Mrs. Yoop; for, in spite of her being a Yookoohoo, our fairy friends have broken all of her transformations."

Chapter 15

The MAN of TIN

Ozma and Dorothy were quite pleased with Woot the Wanderer, whom they found modest and intelligent and very well mannered. The boy was truly grateful for his release from the cruel enchantment, and he promised to love, revere and defend the girl Ruler of Oz forever afterward, as a faithful subject.

"You may visit me at my palace, if you wish," said Ozma, "where I will be glad to introduce you to two other nice boys, Ojo the Munchkin and Button-Bright."

"Thank your Majesty," replied Woot, and then he turned to the Tin Woodman and inquired: "What are your further plans, Mr. Emperor? Will you still seek Nimmie Amee and marry her, or will you abandon the quest and return to the Emerald City and your own castle?"

The Tin Woodman, now as highly polished and well-oiled as ever, reflected a while on this question and then answered:

"Well, I see no reason why I should not find Nimmie Amee. We are now in the Munchkin Country, where we are perfectly safe, and if it was right for me, before our enchantment, to marry Nimmie Amee and make her Empress of the Winkies, it must be right now, when the enchantment has been broken and I am once more myself. Am I correct, friend Scarecrow?"

"You are, indeed," answered the Scarecrow. "No one can oppose such logic."

"But I'm afraid you don't love Nimmie Amee," suggested Dorothy.

"That is just because I can't love anyone," replied the Tin Woodman. "But, if I cannot love my wife, I can at least be kind to her, and all husbands are not able to do that."

"Do you s'pose Nimmie Amee still loves you, after all these years?" asked Dorothy.

"I'm quite sure of it, and that is why I am going to her to make her happy. Woot the Wanderer thinks I ought to reward her for being faithful to me after my meat body was chopped to pieces and I became tin. What do you think, Ozma?"

Ozma smiled as she said:

"I do not know your Nimmie Amee, and so I cannot tell

what she most needs to make her happy. But there is no harm in your going to her and asking her if she still wishes to marry you. If she does, we will give you a grand wedding at the Emerald City and, afterward, as Empress of the Winkies, Nimmie Amee would become one of the most important ladies in all Oz."

So it was decided that the Tin Woodman would continue his journey, and that the Scarecrow and Woot the Wanderer should accompany him, as before. Polychrome also decided to join their party, somewhat to the surprise of all.

"I hate to be cooped up in a palace," she said to Ozma, "and of course the first time I meet my Rainbow I shall return to my own dear home in the skies, where my fairy sisters are even now awaiting me and my father is cross because I get lost so often. But I can find my Rainbow just as quickly while traveling in the Munchkin Country as I could if living in the Emerald City—or any other place in Oz—so I shall go with the Tin Woodman and help him woo Nimmie Amee."

Dorothy wanted to go, too, but as the Tin Woodman did not invite her to join his party, she felt she might be intruding if she asked to be taken. She hinted, but she found he didn't take the hint. It is quite a delicate matter for one to ask a girl to marry him, however much she loves him, and perhaps the Tin Woodman did not desire to have too many looking on when he found his old sweetheart, Nimmie Amee. So Dorothy contented herself with the thought that she would help Ozma prepare a splendid wedding feast, to be followed by a round of parties and festivities when the Emperor of the Winkies reached the Emerald City with his bride.

Ozma offered to take them all in the Red Wagon to a place as near to the great Munchkin forest as a wagon could get. The Red Wagon was big enough to seat them all, and so, bidding good-bye to Jinjur, who gave Woot a basket of ripe cream-puffs and caramels to take with him, Ozma commanded the Wooden Sawhorse to start, and the strange creature moved swiftly over the lanes and presently came to the road of yellow bricks. This road led straight to a dense forest, where the path was too narrow for the Red Wagon to proceed farther, so here the party separated.

Ozma and Dorothy and Toto returned to the Emerald City, after wishing their friends a safe and successful journey, while the Tin Woodman, the Scarecrow, Woot the Wanderer and Polychrome, the Rainbow's Daughter, prepared to push their way through the thick forest. However, these forest paths were well known to the Tin Man and the Scarecrow, who felt quite at home among the trees.

"I was born in this grand forest," said Nick Chopper, the tin Emperor, speaking proudly, "and it was here that the Witch enchanted my axe and I lost different parts of my meat body until I became all tin. Here, also—for it is a big forest—Nimmie Amee lived with the Wicked Witch, and at the other edge of the trees stands the cottage of my friend Ku-Klip, the famous tinsmith who made my present beautiful form."

"He must be a clever workman," declared Woot, admiringly.

"He is simply wonderful," declared the Tin Woodman.

"I shall be glad to make his acquaintance," said Woot.

"If you wish to meet with real cleverness," remarked the Scarecrow, "you should visit the Munchkin farmer who first made me. I won't say that my friend the Emperor isn't all right for a tin man, but any judge of beauty can understand that a Scarecrow is far more artistic and refined."

"You are too soft and flimsy," said the Tin Woodman.

"You are too hard and stiff," said the Scarecrow, and this was as near to quarreling as the two friends ever came. Polychrome laughed at them both, as well she might, and Woot hastened to change the subject.

At night they all camped underneath the trees. The boy ate cream-puffs for supper and offered Polychrome some, but she preferred other food and at daybreak sipped the dew that was clustered thick on the forest flowers. Then they tramped onward again, and presently the Scarecrow paused and said:

"It was on this very spot that Dorothy and I first met the Tin Woodman, who was rusted so badly that none of his joints would move. But after we had oiled him up, he was as good as new and accompanied us to the Emerald City."

"Ah, that was a sad experience," asserted the Tin Woodman soberly. "I was caught in a rainstorm while chopping down a tree for exercise, and before I realized it, I was firmly rusted in every joint. There I stood, axe in hand, but unable to move, for days and weeks and months! Indeed, I have never known exactly how long the time was; but finally along came Dorothy and I was saved. See! This is the very tree I was chopping at the time I rusted."

"You cannot be far from your old home, in that case," said Woot.

"No; my little cabin stands not a great way off, but there is no occasion for us to visit it. Our errand is with Nimmie Amee, and her house is somewhat farther away, to the left of us."

"Didn't you say she lives with a Wicked Witch, who makes her a slave?" asked the boy.

"She did, but she doesn't," was the reply. "I am told the Witch was destroyed when Dorothy's house fell on her, so now Nimmie Amee must live all alone. I haven't seen her, of course, since the Witch was crushed, for at that time I was standing rusted in the forest and had been there a long time, but the poor girl must have felt very happy to be free from her cruel mistress."

"Well," said the Scarecrow, "let's travel on and find Nimmie Amee. Lead on, your Majesty, since you know the way, and we will follow."

So the Tin Woodman took a path that led through the thickest part of the forest, and they followed it for some time. The light was dim here, because vines and bushes and leafy foliage were all about them, and often the Tin Man had to push aside the branches that obstructed their way, or cut them off with his axe. After they had proceeded some distance, the Emperor suddenly stopped short and exclaimed: "Good gracious!"

The Scarecrow, who was next, first bumped into his friend and then peered around his tin body, and said in a tone of wonder:

"Well, I declare!"

Woot the Wanderer pushed forward to see what was the matter, and cried out in astonishment: "For goodness' sake!"

Then the three stood motionless, staring hard, until Polychrome's merry laughter rang out behind them and aroused them from their stupor.

In the path before them stood a tin man who was the exact duplicate of the Tin Woodman. He was of the same size, he was jointed in the same manner, and he was made of shining tin from top to toe. But he stood immovable, with his tin jaws half parted and his tin eyes turned upward. In one of his hands was held a long, gleaming sword. Yes, there was the difference, the only thing that distinguished him from the Emperor of the Winkies. This tin man bore a sword, while the Tin Woodman bore an axe.

"It's a dream; it must be a dream!" gasped Woot.

"That's it, of course," said the Scarecrow; "there couldn't be two Tin Woodmen."

"No," agreed Polychrome, dancing nearer to the stranger, "this one is a Tin Soldier. Don't you see his sword?"

The Tin Woodman cautiously put out one tin hand and felt of his double's arm. Then he said in a voice that trembled with emotion:

"Who are you, friend?"

There was no reply.

"Can't you see he's rusted, just as you were once?" asked Polychrome, laughing again. "Here, Nick Chopper, lend me your oil-can a minute!"

The Tin Woodman silently handed her his oil-can, without which he never traveled, and Polychrome first oiled the stranger's tin jaws and then worked them gently to and fro until the Tin Soldier said:

"That's enough. Thank you. I can now talk. But please oil my other joints."

Woot seized the oil-can and did this, but all the others helped wiggle the soldier's joints as soon as they were oiled, until they moved freely.

The Tin Soldier seemed highly pleased at his release. He strutted up and down the path, saying in a high, thin voice:

"The Soldier is a splendid man
When marching on parade,
And when he meets the enemy
He never is afraid.

He rights the wrongs of nations,
His country's flag defends,
The foe he'll fight with great delight,
But seldom fights his friends."

·——·•‹ Chapter 16 ›•·——·•

Captain Fyter

re you really a soldier?" asked Woot, when they had all watched this strange tin person parade up and down the path and proudly flourish his sword.

"I was a soldier," was the reply, "but I've been a prisoner to Mr. Rust so long that I don't know exactly what I am."

"But—dear me!" cried the Tin Woodman, sadly perplexed; "how came you to be made of tin?"

"That," answered the Soldier, "is a sad, sad story. I was in love with a beautiful Munchkin girl, who lived with a Wicked Witch. The Witch did not wish me to marry the girl, so she enchanted my sword, which began hacking me to pieces.

When I lost my legs I went to the tinsmith, Ku-Klip, and he made me some tin legs. When I lost my arms, Ku-Klip made me tin arms, and when I lost my head he made me this fine one out of tin. It was the same way with my body, and finally I was all tin. But I was not unhappy, for Ku-Klip made a good job of me, having had experience in making another tin man before me."

"Yes," observed the Tin Woodman, "it was Ku-Klip who made me. But, tell me, what was the name of the Munchkin girl you were in love with?"

"She is called Nimmie Amee," said the Tin Soldier.

Hearing this, they were all so astonished that they were silent for a time, regarding the stranger with wondering looks. Finally the Tin Woodman ventured to ask:

"And did Nimmie Amee return your love?"

"Not at first," admitted the Soldier. "When first I marched into the forest and met her, she was weeping over the loss of her former sweetheart, a woodman whose name was Nick Chopper."

"That is me," said the Tin Woodman.

"She told me he was nicer than a soldier, because he was all made of tin and shone beautifully in the sun. She said a tin man appealed to her artistic instincts more than an ordinary meat man, as I was then. But I did not despair, because her tin sweetheart had disappeared, and could not be found. And finally Nimmie Amee permitted me to call upon her and we became friends. It was then that the Wicked Witch discovered me and became furiously angry when I said I wanted to marry the girl. She enchanted my sword, as I said, and then my troubles began. When I got my tin legs, Nimmie Amee began to take an interest in me; when I got my tin arms, she began to like me better than ever, and when I was all made of tin, she said I looked like her dear Nick Chopper and she would be willing to marry me.

"The day of our wedding was set, and it turned out to be a rainy day. Nevertheless I started out to get Nimmie Amee, because the Witch had been absent for some time, and we meant to elope before she got back. As I traveled the forest paths the rain wetted my joints, but I paid no attention to this because my thoughts were all on my wedding with beautiful Nimmie Amee and I could think of nothing else until suddenly my legs stopped moving. Then my arms rusted at the joints and I became frightened and cried for help, for now I was unable to oil myself. No one heard my calls and before long my jaws rusted, and I was unable to utter another sound. So I stood helpless in this spot, hoping some wanderer would come my way and save me. But this forest path is seldom used, and I have been standing here so long that I have lost all track of time. In my mind I composed poetry and sang songs, but not a sound have I been able to utter. But this desperate condition has now been relieved by your coming my way and I must thank you for my rescue."

"This is wonderful!" said the Scarecrow, heaving a stuffy, long sigh. "I think Ku-Klip was wrong to make two tin men, just alike, and the strangest thing of all is that both you tin men fell in love with the same girl."

"As for that," returned the Soldier, seriously, "I must admit I lost my ability to love when I lost my meat heart. Ku-Klip gave me a tin heart, to be sure, but it doesn't love anything, as far as I can discover, and merely rattles against my tin ribs, which makes me wish I had no heart at all."

"Yet, in spite of this condition, you were going to marry Nimmie Amee?"

"Well, you see I had promised to marry her, and I am an honest man and always try to keep my promises. I didn't like to disappoint the poor girl, who had been disappointed by one tin man already."

"That was not my fault," declared the Emperor of the Winkies, and then he related how he, also, had rusted in the forest and after a long time had been rescued by Dorothy and the Scarecrow and had traveled with them to the Emerald City in search of a heart that could love.

"If you have found such a heart, sir," said the Soldier, "I will gladly allow you to marry Nimmie Amee in my place."

"If she loves you best, sir," answered the Woodman, "I shall not interfere with your wedding her. For, to be quite frank with you, I cannot yet love Nimmie Amee as I did before I became tin."

"Still, one of you ought to marry the poor girl," remarked Woot; "and, if she likes tin men, there is not much choice between you. Why don't you draw lots for her?"

"That wouldn't be right," said the Scarecrow.

"The girl should be permitted to choose her own husband," asserted Polychrome. "You should both go to her and allow her to take her choice. Then she will surely be happy."

"That, to me, seems a very fair arrangement," said the Tin Soldier.

"I agree to it," said the Tin Woodman, shaking the hand of his twin to show the matter was settled. "May I ask your name, sir?" he continued.

"Before I was so cut up," replied the other, "I was known as Captain Fyter, but afterward I was merely called 'The Tin Soldier.'"

"Well, Captain, if you are agreeable, let us now go to Nimmie Amee's house and let her choose between us."

"Very well; and if we meet the Witch, we will both fight her—you with your axe and I with my sword."

"The Witch is destroyed," announced the Scarecrow, and as they walked away he told the Tin Soldier of much that had happened in the Land of Oz since he had stood rusted in the forest.

"I must have stood there longer than I had imagined," he said thoughtfully.

...——·‹ ℂhapter 17 ›···——··

The WORKSHOP of KU-KLIP

It was not more than a two hours' journey to the house where Nimmie Amee had lived, but when our travelers arrived there they found the place deserted. The door was partly off its hinges, the roof had fallen in at the rear and the interior of the cottage was thick with dust. Not only was the place vacant, but it was evident that no one had lived there for a long time.

"I suppose," said the Scarecrow, as they all stood looking wonderingly at the ruined house, "that after the Wicked Witch was destroyed, Nimmie Amee became lonely and went somewhere else to live."

"One could scarcely expect a young girl to live all alone in a forest," added Woot. "She would want company, of course, and so I believe she has gone where other people live."

"And perhaps she is still crying her poor little heart out because no tin man comes to marry her," suggested Polychrome.

"Well, in that case, it is the clear duty of you two tin persons to seek Nimmie Amee until you find her," declared the Scarecrow.

"I do not know where to look for the girl," said the Tin Soldier, "for I am almost a stranger to this part of the country."

"I was born here," said the Tin Woodman, "but the forest has few inhabitants except the wild beasts. I cannot think of anyone living near here with whom Nimmie Amee might care to live."

"Why not go to Ku-Klip and ask him what has become of the girl?" proposed Polychrome.

That struck them all as being a good suggestion, so once more they started to tramp through the forest, taking the direct path to Ku-Klip's house, for both the tin twins knew the way, having followed it many times.

Ku-Klip lived at the far edge of the great forest, his house facing the broad plains of the Munchkin Country that lay to the eastward. But, when they came to this residence by the forest's edge, the tinsmith was not at home.

It was a pretty place, all painted dark blue with trimmings of lighter blue. There was a neat blue fence around the yard and several blue benches had been placed underneath the shady blue trees which marked the line between forest and plain. There was a blue lawn before the house, which was a good sized building. Ku-Klip lived in the front part of the house and had his work-shop in the back part, where he had also built a lean-to addition, in order to give him more room.

Although they found the tinsmith absent on their arrival, there was smoke coming out of his chimney, which proved that he would soon return.

"And perhaps Nimmie Amee will be with him," said the Scarecrow in a cheerful voice.

While they waited, the Tin Woodman went to the door of the workshop and, finding it unlocked, entered and looked curiously around the room where he had been made.

"It seems almost like home to me," he told his friends, who had followed him in. "The first time I came here I had lost a leg, so I had to carry it in my hand while I hopped on the other leg all the way from the place in the forest where the enchanted axe cut me. I remember that old Ku-Klip carefully put my meat leg into a barrel—I think that is the same barrel, still standing in the corner yonder—and then at once he began to make a tin leg for me. He worked fast and with skill, and I was much interested in the job."

"My experience was much the same," said the Tin Soldier. "I used to bring all the parts of me, which the enchanted sword had cut away, here to the tinsmith, and Ku-Klip would put them into the barrel."

"I wonder," said Woot, "if those cast-off parts of you two unfortunates are still in that barrel in the corner?"

"I suppose so," replied the Tin Woodman. "In the Land of Oz no part of a living creature can ever be destroyed."

"If that is true, how was that Wicked Witch destroyed?" inquired Woot.

"Why, she was very old and was all dried up and withered before Oz became a fairyland," explained the Scarecrow. "Only her magic arts had kept her alive so long, and when Dorothy's house fell upon her she just turned to dust, and was blown away and scattered by the wind. I do not think, however, that the parts cut away from these two young men could ever be entirely destroyed and, if they are still in those barrels, they are likely to be just the same as when the enchanted axe or sword severed them."

"It doesn't matter, however," said the Tin Woodman; "our tin bodies are more brilliant and durable, and quite satisfy us."

"Yes, the tin bodies are best," agreed the Tin Soldier. "Nothing can hurt them."

"Unless they get dented or rusted," said Woot, but both the tin men frowned on him.

Scraps of tin, of all shapes and sizes, lay scattered around the workshop. Also there were hammers and anvils and soldering irons and a charcoal furnace and many other tools such as a tinsmith works with. Against two of the side walls had been built stout work-benches and in the center of the room was a long table. At the end of the shop, which adjoined the dwelling, were several cupboards.

After examining the interior of the workshop until his curiosity was satisfied, Woot said:

"I think I will go outside until Ku-Klip comes. It does not seem quite proper for us to take possession of his house while he is absent."

"That is true," agreed the Scarecrow, and they were all about to leave the room when the Tin Woodman said: "Wait a minute," and they halted in obedience to the command.

····◄ Chapter 18 ►····

The TIN WOODMAN
TALKS to HIMSELF

The Tin Woodman had just noticed the cupboards and was curious to know what they contained, so he went to one of them and opened the door. There were shelves inside, and upon one of the shelves which was about on a level with his tin chin the Emperor discovered a Head—it looked like a doll's head, only it was larger, and he soon saw it was the Head of some person. It was facing the Tin Woodman and as the cupboard door swung back, the eyes of the Head slowly opened and looked at him. The Tin Woodman was not at all surprised, for in the Land of Oz one runs into magic at every turn.

"Dear me!" said the Tin Woodman, staring hard. "It seems as if I had met you, somewhere, before. Good morning, sir!"

"You have the advantage of me," replied the Head. "I never saw you before in my life."

"Still, your face is very familiar," persisted the Tin Woodman. "Pardon me, but may I ask if you—eh—eh—if you ever had a Body?"

"Yes, at one time," answered the Head, "but that is so long ago I can't remember it. Did you think," with a pleasant smile, "that I was born just as I am? That a Head would be created without a Body?"

"No, of course not," said the other. "But how came you to lose your Body?"

"Well, I can't recollect the details; you'll have to ask Ku-Klip about it," returned the Head. "For, curious as it may seem to you, my memory is not good since my separation from the rest of me. I still possess my brains and my intellect is as good as ever, but my memory of some of the events I formerly experienced is quite hazy."

"How long have you been in this cupboard?" asked the Emperor.

"I don't know."

"Haven't you a name?"

"Oh, yes," said the Head; "I used to be called Nick Chopper, when I was a woodman and cut down trees for a living."

"Good gracious!" cried the Tin Woodman in astonishment.

"If you are Nick Chopper's Head, then you are Me—or I'm You—or—or—What relation are we, anyhow?"

"Don't ask me," replied the Head. "For my part, I'm not anxious to claim relationship with any common, manufactured article, like you. You may be all right in your class, but your class isn't my class. You're tin."

The poor Emperor felt so bewildered that for a time he could only stare at his old Head in silence. Then he said:

"I must admit that I wasn't at all bad looking before I became tin. You're almost handsome—for meat. If your hair was combed, you'd be quite attractive."

"How do you expect me to comb my hair without help?" demanded the Head, indignantly. "I used to keep it smooth and neat, when I had arms, but after I was removed from the rest of me, my hair got mussed, and old Ku-Klip never has combed it for me."

"I'll speak to him about it," said the Tin Woodman. "Do you remember loving a pretty Munchkin girl named Nimmie Amee?"

"No," answered the Head. "That is a foolish question. The heart in my body—when I had a body—might have loved someone, for all I know, but a head isn't made to love; it's made to think."

"Oh; do you think, then?"

"I used to think."

"You must have been shut up in this cupboard for years

and years. What have you thought about, in all that time?"

"Nothing. That's another foolish question. A little reflection will convince you that I have had nothing to think about, except the boards on the inside of the cupboard door, and it didn't take me long to think of everything about those boards that could be thought of. Then, of course, I quit thinking."

"And are you happy?"

"Happy? What's that?"

"Don't you know what happiness is?" inquired the Tin Woodman.

"I haven't the faintest idea whether it's round or square, or black or white, or what it is. And, if you will pardon my lack of interest in it, I will say that I don't care."

The Tin Woodman was much puzzled by these answers. His traveling companions had grouped themselves at his back, and had fixed their eyes on the Head and listened to the conversation with much interest, but until now, they had not interrupted because they thought the Tin Woodman had the best right to talk to his own head and renew acquaintance with it.

But now the Tin Soldier remarked:

"I wonder if my old head happens to be in any of these cupboards," and he proceeded to open all the cupboard doors. But no other head was to be found on any of the shelves.

"Oh, well; never mind," said Woot the Wanderer; "I can't imagine what anyone wants of a cast-off head, anyhow."

"I can understand the Soldier's interest," asserted Polychrome, dancing around the grimy workshop until her draperies formed a cloud around her dainty form. "For sentimental reasons a man might like to see his old head once more, just as one likes to revisit an old home."

"And then to kiss it good-bye," added the Scarecrow.

"I hope that tin thing won't try to kiss me good-bye!" exclaimed the Tin Woodman's former head. "And I don't see what right you folks have to disturb my peace and comfort, either."

"You belong to me," the Tin Woodman declared.

"I do not!"

"You and I are one."

"We've been parted," asserted the Head. "It would be unnatural for me to have any interest in a man made of tin. Please close the door and leave me alone."

"I did not think that my old head could be so disagreeable," said the Emperor. "I—I'm quite ashamed of myself; meaning you."

"You ought to be glad that I've enough sense to know what my rights are," retorted the Head. "In this cupboard I am leading a simple life, peaceful and dignified, and when a mob of people in whom I am not interested disturb me, they are the disagreeable ones; not I."

With a sigh the Tin Woodman closed and latched the cupboard door and turned away.

"Well," said the Tin Soldier, "if my old head would have treated me as coldly and in so unfriendly a manner as your old head has treated you, friend Chopper, I'm glad I could not find it."

"Yes; I'm rather surprised at my head, myself," replied the Tin Woodman, thoughtfully. "I thought I had a more pleasant disposition when I was made of meat."

But just then old Ku-Klip the Tinsmith arrived, and he seemed surprised to find so many visitors. Ku-Klip was a stout man and a short man. He had his sleeves rolled above his elbows, showing muscular arms, and he wore a leathern apron that covered all the front of him, and was so long that Woot was surprised he didn't step on it and trip whenever he walked. And Ku-Klip had a grey beard that was almost as long as his apron, and his head was bald on top and his ears stuck out from his head like two fans. Over his eyes, which were bright and twinkling, he wore big spectacles. It was easy to see that the tinsmith was a kind hearted man, as well as a merry and agreeable one.

"Oh-ho!" he cried in a joyous bass voice; "here are both my tin men come to visit me, and they and their friends are welcome indeed. I'm very proud of you two characters, I assure you, for you are so perfect that you are proof that I'm a good workman. Sit down. Sit down, all of you—if you can find anything to sit on—and tell me why you are here."

So they found seats and told him all of their adventures

that they thought he would like to know. Ku-Klip was glad to learn that Nick Chopper, the Tin Woodman, was now Emperor of the Winkies and a friend of Ozma of Oz, and the tinsmith was also interested in the Scarecrow and Polychrome.

He turned the straw man around, examining him curiously, and patted him on all sides, and then said:

"You are certainly wonderful, but I think you would be more durable and steady on your legs if you were made of tin. Would you like me to—"

"No, indeed!" interrupted the Scarecrow hastily; "I like myself better as I am."

But to Polychrome the tinsmith said:

"Nothing could improve you, my dear, for you are the most beautiful maiden I have ever seen. It is pure happiness just to look at you."

"That is praise, indeed, from so skillful a workman," returned the Rainbow's Daughter, laughing and dancing in and out the room.

"Then it must be this boy you wish me to help," said Ku-Klip, looking at Woot.

"No," said Woot, "we are not here to seek your skill, but have merely come to you for information."

Then, between them, they related their search for Nimmie Amee, whom the Tin Woodman explained he had resolved to marry, yet who had promised to become the bride of the Tin Soldier before he unfortunately became rusted. And when the story was told, they asked Ku-Klip if he knew what had become of Nimmie Amee.

"Not exactly," replied the old man, "but I know that she wept bitterly when the Tin Soldier did not come to marry her, as he had promised to do. The old Witch was so provoked at the girl's tears that she beat Nimmie Amee with her crooked stick and then hobbled away to gather some magic herbs, with which she intended to transform the girl into an old hag, so that no one would again love her or care to marry her. It was while she was away on this errand that Dorothy's house fell on the Wicked Witch, and she turned to dust and blew away. When I heard this good news, I sent Nimmie Amee to find the Silver Shoes which the Witch had worn, but Dorothy had taken them with her to the Emerald City."

"Yes, we know all about those Silver Shoes," said the Scarecrow.

"Well," continued Ku-Klip, "after that, Nimmie Amee decided to go away from the forest and live with some people she was acquainted with who had a house on Mount Munch. I have never seen the girl since."

"Do you know the name of the people on Mount Munch, with whom she went to live?" asked the Tin Woodman.

"No, Nimmie Amee did not mention her friend's name, and I did not ask her. She took with her all that she could carry of the goods that were in the Witch's house, and she told me I could have the rest. But when I went there I found nothing worth taking except some magic powders that I did not know how to use, and a bottle of Magic Glue."

"What is Magic Glue?" asked Woot.

"It is a magic preparation with which to mend people when they cut themselves. One time, long ago, I cut off one of my fingers by accident, and I carried it to the Witch, who took down her bottle and glued it on again for me. See!" showing them his finger, "it is as good as ever it was. No one else that I ever heard of had this Magic Glue, and of course when Nick Chopper cut himself to pieces with his enchanted axe and Captain Fyter cut himself to pieces with his enchanted sword, the Witch would not mend them, or allow me to glue them together, because she had herself wickedly enchanted the axe and sword. Nothing remained but for me to make them new parts out of tin; but, as you see, tin answered the purpose very well, and I am sure their tin bodies are a great improvement on their meat bodies."

"Very true," said the Tin Soldier.

"I quite agree with you," said the Tin Woodman. "I happened to find my old head in your cupboard, a while ago, and certainly it is not as desirable a head as the tin one I now wear."

"By the way," said the Tin Soldier, "what ever became of my old head, Ku-Klip?"

"And of the different parts of our bodies?" added the Tin Woodman.

"Let me think a minute," replied Ku-Klip. "If I remember right, you two boys used to bring me most of your parts, when they were cut off, and I saved them in that barrel in the corner. You must not have brought me all the parts, for when I made Chopfyt I had hard work finding enough pieces to complete the job. I finally had to finish him with one arm."

"Who is Chopfyt?" inquired Woot.

"Oh, haven't I told you about Chopfyt?" exclaimed Ku-Klip. "Of course not! And he's quite a curiosity, too. You'll be interested in hearing about Chopfyt. This is how he happened:

"One day, after the Witch had been destroyed and Nimmie Amee had gone to live with her friends on Mount Munch, I was looking around the shop for something and came upon the bottle of Magic Glue which I had brought from the old Witch's house. It occurred to me to piece together the odds and ends of you two people, which of course were just as good as ever, and see if I couldn't make a man out of them. If I succeeded, I would have an assistant to help me with my work, and I thought it would be a clever idea to put to some practical use the scraps of Nick Chopper and Captain Fyter. There were two perfectly good heads in my cupboard, and a lot of feet and legs and parts of bodies in the barrel, so I set to work to see what I could do.

"First, I pieced together a body, gluing it with the Witch's Magic Glue, which worked perfectly. That was the hardest part of my job, however, because the bodies didn't match up well and some parts were missing. But by using a piece of Captain Fyter here and a piece of Nick Chopper there, I finally got together a very decent body, with heart and all the trimmings complete."

"Whose heart did you use in making the body?" asked the Tin Woodman anxiously.

"I can't tell, for the parts had no tags on them and one heart looks much like another. After the body was completed, I glued two fine legs and feet onto it. One leg was Nick Chopper's and one was Captain Fyter's and, finding one leg longer than the other, I trimmed it down to make them match. I was much disappointed to find that I had but one arm. There was an extra leg in the barrel, but I could find only one arm. Having glued this onto the body, I was ready for the head, and I had some difficulty in making up my mind which head to use. Finally I shut my eyes and reached out my hand toward the cupboard shelf, and the first head I touched I glued upon my new man."

"It was mine!" declared the Tin Soldier, gloomily.

"No, it was mine," asserted Ku-Klip, "for I had given you another in exchange for it—the beautiful tin head you now wear. When the glue had dried, my man was quite an interesting fellow. I named him Chopfyt, using a part of Nick Chopper's name and a part of Captain Fyter's name, because he was a mixture of both your cast-off parts. Chopfyt was interesting, as I said, but he did not prove a very agreeable companion. He complained bitterly because I had given him but one arm—as if it were my fault!—and he grumbled because the suit of blue Munchkin clothes, which I got for him from a neighbor, did not fit him perfectly."

"Ah, that was because he was wearing my old head," remarked the Tin Soldier. "I remember that head used to be very particular about its clothes."

"As an assistant," the old tinsmith continued, "Chopfyt was not a success. He was awkward with tools and was always hungry. He demanded something to eat six or eight times a day, so I wondered if I had fitted his insides properly. Indeed, Chopfyt ate so much that little food was left for myself; so, when he proposed, one day, to go out into the world and seek adventures, I was delighted to be rid of him. I even made him a tin arm to take the place of the missing one, and that pleased him very much, so that we parted good friends."

"What became of Chopfyt after that?" the Scarecrow inquired.

"I never heard. He started off toward the east, into the plains of the Munchkin Country, and that was the last I ever saw of him."

"It seems to me," said the Tin Woodman reflectively, "that you did wrong in making a man out of our cast-off parts. It is evident that Chopfyt could, with justice, claim relationship with both of us."

"Don't worry about that," advised Ku-Klip cheerfully; "it

is not likely that you will ever meet the fellow. And, if you should meet him, he doesn't know who he is made of, for I never told him the secret of his manufacture. Indeed, you are the only ones who know of it, and you may keep the secret to yourselves, if you wish to."

"Never mind Chopfyt," said the Scarecrow. "Our business now is to find poor Nimmie Amee and let her choose her tin husband. To do that, it seems, from the information Ku-Klip has given us, we must travel to Mount Munch."

"If that's the programme, let us start at once," suggested Woot.

So they all went outside, where they found Polychrome dancing about among the trees and talking with the birds and laughing as merrily as if she had not lost her Rainbow and so been separated from all her fairy sisters.

They told her they were going to Mount Munch, and she replied:

"Very well; I am as likely to find my Rainbow there as here, and any other place is as likely as there. It all depends on the weather. Do you think it looks like rain?"

They shook their heads, and Polychrome laughed again and danced on after them when they resumed their journey.

⸱⸺⸱◃ Chapter 19 ▹⸱⸺⸱⸱

The INVISIBLE COUNTRY

They were proceeding so easily and comfortably on their way to Mount Munch that Woot said in a serious tone of voice:

"I'm afraid something is going to happen."

"Why?" asked Polychrome, dancing around the group of travelers.

"Because," said the boy, thoughtfully, "I've noticed that when we have the least reason for getting into trouble, something is sure to go wrong. Just now the weather is delightful; the grass is beautifully blue and quite soft to our feet; the mountain we are seeking shows clearly in the distance and there is no reason anything should happen to delay us in getting there. Our troubles all seem to be over, and—well, that's why I'm afraid," he added, with a sigh.

"Dear me!" remarked the Scarecrow, "what unhappy thoughts you have, to be sure. This is proof that born brains cannot equal manufactured brains, for my brains dwell only on facts and never borrow trouble. When there is occasion for my brains to think, they think, but I would be ashamed of my brains if they kept shooting out thoughts that were merely fears and imaginings, such as do no good, but are likely to do harm."

"For my part," said the Tin Woodman, "I do not think at all, but allow my velvet heart to guide me at all times."

"The tinsmith filled my hollow head with scraps and clippings of tin," said the Soldier, "and he told me they would do nicely for brains, but when I begin to think, the tin scraps rattle around and get so mixed that I'm soon bewildered. So I try not to think. My tin heart is almost as useless to me, for it is hard and cold, so I'm sure the red velvet heart of my friend Nick Chopper is a better guide."

"Thoughtless people are not unusual," observed the Scarecrow, "but I consider them more fortunate than those who have useless or wicked thoughts and do not try to curb them. Your oil can, friend Woodman, is filled with oil, but you only apply the oil to your joints, drop by drop, as you need it, and do not keep spilling it where it will do no good. Thoughts should be restrained in the same way as your oil, and only applied when necessary, and for a good purpose. If used carefully, thoughts are good things to have."

Polychrome laughed at him, for the Rainbow's Daughter knew more about thoughts than the Scarecrow did. But the others were solemn, feeling they had been rebuked, and tramped on in silence.

Suddenly Woot, who was in the lead, looked around and found that all his comrades had mysteriously disappeared. But where could they have gone to? The broad plain was all about him and there were neither trees nor bushes that could hide even a rabbit, nor any hole for one to fall into. Yet there he stood, alone.

Surprise had caused him to halt, and with a thoughtful and puzzled expression on his face he looked down at his feet. It startled him anew to discover that he had no feet. He reached out his hands, but he could not see them. He could feel his hands and arms and body; he stamped his feet on the grass and knew they were there, but in some strange way they had become invisible.

While Woot stood, wondering, a crash of metal sounded in his ears and he heard two heavy bodies tumble to the earth just beside him.

"Good gracious!" exclaimed the voice of the Tin Woodman.

"Mercy me!" cried the voice of the Tin Soldier.

"Why didn't you look where you were going?" asked the Tin Woodman reproachfully.

"I did, but I couldn't see you," said the Tin Soldier. "Something has happened to my tin eyes. I can't see you, even now, nor can I see anyone else!"

"It's the same way with me," admitted the Tin Woodman.

Woot couldn't see either of them, although he heard them plainly, and just then something smashed against him unexpectedly and knocked him over; but it was only the straw-stuffed body of the Scarecrow that fell upon him and while he could not see the Scarecrow he managed to push him off and rose to his feet just as Polychrome whirled against him and made him tumble again.

Sitting upon the ground, the boy asked:

"Can you see us, Poly?"

"No, indeed," answered the Rainbow's Daughter; "we've all become invisible."

"How did it happen, do you suppose?" inquired the Scarecrow, lying where he had fallen.

"We have met with no enemy," answered Polychrome, "so it must be that this part of the country has the magic quality of making people invisible—even fairies falling under the charm. We can see the grass, and the flowers, and the stretch of plain before us, and we can still see Mount Munch in the distance; but we cannot see ourselves or one another."

"Well, what are we to do about it?" demanded Woot.

"I think this magic affects only a small part of the plain," replied Polychrome; "perhaps there is only a streak of the country where an enchantment makes people become invisible. So, if we get together and hold hands, we can travel toward Mount Munch until the enchanted streak is passed."

"All right," said Woot, jumping up, "give me your hand, Polychrome. Where are you?"

"Here," she answered. "Whistle, Woot, and keep whistling until I come to you."

So Woot whistled, and presently Polychrome found him and grasped his hand.

"Someone must help me up," said the Scarecrow, lying near them; so they found the straw man and sat him upon his feet, after which he held fast to Polychrome's other hand.

Nick Chopper and the Tin Soldier had managed to scramble up without assistance, but it was awkward for them and the Tin Woodman said:

"I don't seem to stand straight, somehow. But my joints all work, so I guess I can walk."

Guided by his voice, they reached his side, where Woot grasped his tin fingers so they might keep together.

The Tin Soldier was standing nearby and the Scarecrow soon touched him and took hold of his arm.

"I hope you're not wobbly," said the straw man, "for if two of us walk unsteadily we will be sure to fall."

"I'm not wobbly," the Tin Soldier assured him, "but I'm

certain that one of my legs is shorter than the other. I can't see it, to tell what's gone wrong, but I'll limp on with the rest of you until we are out of this enchanted territory."

They now formed a line, holding hands, and turning their faces toward Mount Munch resumed their journey. They had not gone far, however, when a terrible growl saluted their ears. The sound seemed to come from a place just in front of them, so they halted abruptly and remained silent, listening with all their ears.

"I smell straw!" cried a hoarse, harsh voice, with more growls and snarls. "I smell straw, and I'm a Hip-po-gy-raf who loves straw and eats all he can find. I want to eat this straw! Where is it? Where is it?"

The Scarecrow, hearing this, trembled but kept silent. All the others were silent, too, hoping that the invisible beast would be unable to find them. But the creature sniffed the odor of the straw and drew nearer and nearer to them until he reached the Tin Woodman, on one end of the line. It was a big beast and it smelled of the Tin Woodman and grated two rows of enormous teeth against the Emperor's tin body.

"Bah! that's not straw," said the harsh voice, and the beast advanced along the line to Woot.

"Meat! Pooh, you're no good! I can't eat meat," grumbled the beast, and passed on to Polychrome.

"Sweetmeats and perfume—cobwebs and dew! Nothing to eat in a fairy like you," said the creature.

Now, the Scarecrow was next to Polychrome in the line, and he realized if the beast devoured his straw he would be helpless for a long time, because the last farm-house was far behind them and only grass covered the vast expanse of plain. So in his fright he let go of Polychrome's hand and put the hand of the Tin Soldier in that of the Rainbow's Daughter. Then he slipped back of the line and went to the other end, where he silently seized the Tin Woodman's hand.

Meantime, the beast had smelled the Tin Soldier and found he was the last of the line.

"That's funny!" growled the Hip-po-gy-raf; "I can smell straw, but I can't find it. Well, it's here, somewhere, and I must hunt around until I do find it, for I'm hungry."

His voice was now at the left of them, so they started on, hoping to avoid him, and traveled as fast as they could in the direction of Mount Munch.

"I don't like this invisible country," said Woot with a shudder. "We can't tell how many dreadful, invisible beasts are roaming around us, or what danger we'll come to next."

"Quit thinking about danger, please," said the Scarecrow, warningly.

"Why?" asked the boy.

"If you think of some dreadful thing, it's liable to happen, but if you don't think of it, and no one else thinks of it, it just can't happen. Do you see?"

"No," answered Woot. "I won't be able to see much of

anything until we escape from this enchantment."

But they got out of the invisible strip of country as suddenly as they had entered it, and the instant they got out they stopped short, for just before them was a deep ditch, running at right angles as far as their eyes could see and stopping all further progress toward Mount Munch.

"It's not so very wide," said Woot, "but I'm sure none of us can jump across it."

Polychrome began to laugh, and the Scarecrow said: "What's the matter?"

"Look at the tin men!" she said, with another burst of merry laughter.

Woot and the Scarecrow looked, and the tin men looked at themselves.

"It was the collision," said the Tin Woodman regretfully. "I knew something was wrong with me, and now I can see that my side is dented in so that I lean over toward the left. It was the Soldier's fault; he shouldn't have been so careless."

"It is your fault that my right leg is bent, making it shorter than the other, so that I limp badly," retorted the Soldier. "You shouldn't have stood where I was walking."

"You shouldn't have walked where I was standing," replied the Tin Woodman.

It was almost a quarrel, so Polychrome said soothingly:

"Never mind, friends; as soon as we have time I am sure we can straighten the Soldier's leg and get the dent out of the

Woodman's body. The Scarecrow needs patting into shape, too, for he had a bad tumble, but our first task is to get over this ditch."

"Yes, the ditch is the most important thing, just now," added Woot.

They were standing in a row, looking hard at the unexpected barrier, when a fierce growl from behind them made them all turn quickly. Out of the invisible country marched a huge beast with a thick, leathery skin and a surprisingly long neck. The head on the top of this neck was broad and flat and the eyes and mouth were very big and the nose and ears very small. When the head was drawn down toward the beast's shoulders, the neck was all wrinkles, but the head could shoot up very high indeed, if the creature wished it to.

"Dear me!" exclaimed the Scarecrow, "this must be the Hip-po-gy-raf."

"Quite right," said the beast; "and you're the straw which I'm to eat for my dinner. Oh, how I love straw! I hope you don't resent my affectionate appetite?"

With its four great legs it advanced straight toward the Scarecrow, but the Tin Woodman and the Tin Soldier both sprang in front of their friend and flourished their weapons.

"Keep off!" said the Tin Woodman, warningly, "or I'll chop you with my axe."

"Keep off!" said the Tin Soldier, "or I'll cut you with my sword."

"Would you really do that?" asked the Hip-po-gy-raf, in a disappointed voice.

"We would," they both replied, and the Tin Woodman added: "The Scarecrow is our friend, and he would be useless without his straw stuffing. So, as we are comrades, faithful and true, we will defend our friend's stuffing against all enemies."

The Hip-po-gy-raf sat down and looked at them sorrowfully.

"When one has made up his mind to have a meal of delicious straw, and then finds he can't have it, it is certainly hard luck," he said. "And what good is the straw man to you, or to himself, when the ditch keeps you from going any further?"

"Well, we can go back again," suggested Woot.

"True," said the Hip-po; "and if you do, you'll be as disappointed as I am. That's some comfort, anyhow."

The travelers looked at the beast, and then they looked across the ditch at the level plain beyond. On the other side the grass had grown tall, and the sun had dried it, so there was a fine crop of hay that only needed to be cut and stacked.

"Why don't you cross over and eat hay?" the boy asked the beast.

"I'm not fond of hay," replied the Hip-po-gy-raf; "straw is much more delicious, to my notion, and it's more scarce in this neighborhood, too. Also I must confess that I can't get across the ditch, for my body is too heavy and clumsy for me to jump the distance. I can stretch my neck across, though, and you will notice that I've nibbled the hay on the farther edge—not because I liked it, but because one must eat, and if one can't get the sort of food he desires, he must take what is offered or go hungry."

"Ah, I see you are a philosopher," remarked the Scarecrow.

"No, I'm just a Hip-po-gy-raf," was the reply.

Polychrome was not afraid of the big beast. She danced close to him and said:

"If you can stretch your neck across the ditch, why not help us over? We can sit on your big head, one at a time, and then you can lift us across."

"Yes; I can, it is true," answered the Hip-po; "but I refuse to do it. Unless—" he added, and stopped short.

"Unless what?" asked Polychrome.

"Unless you first allow me to eat the straw with which the Scarecrow is stuffed."

"No," said the Rainbow's Daughter, "that is too high a price to pay. Our friend's straw is nice and fresh, for he was restuffed only a little while ago."

"I know," agreed the Hip-po-gy-raf. "That's why I want it. If it was old, musty straw, I wouldn't care for it."

"Please lift us across," pleaded Polychrome.

"No," replied the beast; "since you refuse my generous offer, I can be as stubborn as you are."

After that they were all silent for a time, but then the Scarecrow said bravely:

"Friends, let us agree to the beast's terms. Give him my straw, and carry the rest of me with you across the ditch. Once on the other side, the Tin Soldier can cut some of the hay with his sharp sword, and you can stuff me with that material until we reach a place where there is straw. It is true I have been stuffed with straw all my life and it will be somewhat humiliating to be filled with common hay, but I am willing to sacrifice my pride in a good cause. Moreover, to abandon our errand and so deprive the great Emperor of the Winkies—or this noble Soldier—of his bride, would be equally humiliating, if not more so."

"You're a very honest and clever man!" exclaimed the Hip-po-gy-raf, admiringly. "When I have eaten your head, perhaps I also will become clever."

"You're not to eat my head, you know," returned the Scarecrow hastily. "My head isn't stuffed with straw and I cannot part with it. When one loses his head he loses his brains."

"Very well, then; you may keep your head," said the beast.

The Scarecrow's companions thanked him warmly for his loyal sacrifice to their mutual good, and then he laid down and permitted them to pull the straw from his body. As fast as they did this, the Hip-po-gy-raf ate up the straw, and when all was consumed Polychrome made a neat bundle of the clothes and boots and gloves and hat and said she would carry them, while Woot tucked the Scarecrow's head under his arm and promised to guard its safety.

"Now, then," said the Tin Woodman, "keep your promise, Beast, and lift us over the ditch."

"M-m-m-mum, but that was a fine dinner!" said the Hip-po, smacking his thick lips in satisfaction, "and I'm as good as my word. Sit on my head, one at a time, and I'll land you safely on the other side."

He approached close to the edge of the ditch and squatted down. Polychrome climbed over his big body and sat herself lightly upon the flat head, holding the bundle of the Scarecrow's raiment in her hand. Slowly the elastic neck stretched out until it reached the far side of the ditch, when the beast lowered his head and permitted the beautiful fairy to leap to the ground.

Woot made the queer journey next, and then the Tin Soldier and the Tin Woodman went over, and all were well pleased to have overcome this serious barrier to their progress.

"Now, Soldier, cut the hay," said the Scarecrow's head, which was still held by Woot the Wanderer.

"I'd like to, but I can't stoop over, with my bent leg, without falling," replied Captain Fyter.

"What can we do about that leg, anyhow?" asked Woot, appealing to Polychrome.

She danced around in a circle several times without replying, and the boy feared she had not heard him; but the Rainbow's Daughter was merely thinking upon the problem, and presently she paused beside the Tin Soldier and said:

"I've been taught a little fairy magic, but I've never before been asked to mend tin legs with it, so I'm not sure I can help you. It all depends on the good will of my unseen fairy guardians, so I'll try, and if I fail, you will be no worse off than you are now."

She danced around the circle again, and then laid both hands upon the twisted tin leg and sang in her sweet voice:

> *"Fairy Powers, come to my aid!*
> *This bent leg of tin is made;*
> *Make it straight and strong and true,*
> *And I'll render thanks to you."*

"Ah!" murmured Captain Fyter in a glad voice, as she withdrew her hands and danced away, and they saw he was standing straight as ever, because his leg was as shapely and strong as it had been before his accident.

The Tin Woodman had watched Polychrome with much interest, and he now said:

"Please take the dent out of my side, Poly, for I am more crippled than was the Soldier."

So the Rainbow's Daughter touched his side lightly and sang:

> *"Here's a dent by accident;*
> *Such a thing was never meant.*

Fairy Powers, so wondrous great,
Make our dear Tin Woodman straight!"

"Good!" cried the Emperor, again standing erect and strutting around to show his fine figure. "Your fairy magic may not be able to accomplish all things, sweet Polychrome, but it works splendidly on tin. Thank you very much."

"The hay—the hay!" pleaded the Scarecrow's head.

"Oh, yes; the hay," said Woot. "What are you waiting for, Captain Fyter?"

At once the Tin Soldier set to work cutting hay with his sword and in a few minutes there was quite enough with which to stuff the Scarecrow's body. Woot and Polychrome did this and it was no easy task because the hay packed together more than straw and as they had little experience in such work their job, when completed, left the Scarecrow's arms and legs rather bunchy. Also there was a hump on his back which made Woot laugh and say it reminded him of a camel, but it was the best they could do and when the head was fastened on to the body they asked the Scarecrow how he felt.

"A little heavy, and not quite natural," he cheerfully replied; "but I'll get along somehow until we reach a straw-stack. Don't laugh at me, please, because I'm a little ashamed of myself and I don't want to regret a good action."

They started at once in the direction of Mount Munch, and as the Scarecrow proved very clumsy in his movements,

Woot took one of his arms and the Tin Woodman the other and so helped their friend to walk in a straight line.

And the Rainbow's Daughter, as before, danced ahead of them and behind them and all around them, and they never minded her odd ways, because to them she was like a ray of sunshine.

Chapter 20

OVER NIGHT

The Land of the Munchkins is full of surprises, as our travelers had already learned, and although Mount Munch was constantly growing larger as they advanced toward it, they knew it was still a long way off and were not certain, by any means, that they had escaped all danger or encountered their last adventure.

The plain was broad, and as far as the eye could see, there seemed to be a level stretch of country between them and the mountain, but toward evening they came upon a hollow, in which stood a tiny blue Munchkin dwelling with a garden around it and fields of grain filling in all the rest of the hollow.

They did not discover this place until they came close to the edge of it, and they were astonished at the sight that greeted them because they had imagined that this part of the plain had no inhabitants.

"It's a very small house," Woot declared. "I wonder who lives there?"

"The way to find out is to knock on the door and ask," replied the Tin Woodman. "Perhaps it is the home of Nimmie Amee."

"Is she a dwarf?" asked the boy.

"No, indeed; Nimmie Amee is a full sized woman."

"Then I'm sure she couldn't live in that little house," said Woot.

"Let's go down," suggested the Scarecrow. "I'm almost sure I can see a straw-stack in the back yard."

They descended the hollow, which was rather steep at the sides, and soon came to the house, which was indeed rather small. Woot knocked upon a door that was not much higher than his waist, but got no reply. He knocked again, but not a sound was heard.

"Smoke is coming out of the chimney," announced Polychrome, who was dancing lightly through the garden, where cabbages and beets and turnips and the like were growing finely.

"Then someone surely lives here," said Woot, and knocked again.

Now a window at the side of the house opened and a queer head appeared. It was white and hairy and had a long snout and little round eyes. The ears were hidden by a blue sunbonnet tied under the chin.

"Oh; it's a pig!" exclaimed Woot.

"Pardon me; I am Mrs. Squealina Swyne, wife of Professor Grunter Swyne, and this is our home," said the one in the window. "What do you want?"

"What sort of a Professor is your husband?" inquired the Tin Woodman curiously.

"He is Professor of Cabbage Culture and Corn Perfection. He is very famous in his own family, and would be the wonder of the world if he went abroad," said Mrs. Swyne in a voice that was half proud and half irritable. "I must also inform you intruders that the Professor is a dangerous individual, for he files his teeth every morning until they are sharp as needles. If you are butchers, you'd better run away and avoid trouble."

"We are not butchers," the Tin Woodman assured her.

"Then what are you doing with that axe? And why has the other tin man a sword?"

"They are the only weapons we have to defend our friends from their enemies," explained the Emperor of the Winkies, and Woot added:

"Do not be afraid of us, Mrs. Swyne, for we are harmless travelers. The tin men and the Scarecrow never eat anything and Polychrome feasts only on dewdrops. As for me, I'm rather hungry, but there is plenty of food in your garden to satisfy me."

Professor Swyne now joined his wife at the window, looking rather scared in spite of the boy's assuring speech. He wore a blue Munchkin hat, with pointed crown and broad brim, and big spectacles covered his eyes. He peeked around from behind his wife and after looking hard at the strangers, he said:

"My wisdom assures me that you are merely travelers, as you say, and not butchers. Butchers have reason to be afraid of me, but you are safe. We cannot invite you in, for you are too big for our house, but the boy who eats is welcome to all the carrots and turnips he wants. Make yourselves at home in the garden and stay all night, if you like; but in the morning you must go away, for we are quiet people and do not care for company."

"May I have some of your straw?" asked the Scarecrow.

"Help yourself," replied Professor Swyne.

"For pigs, they're quite respectable," remarked Woot, as they all went toward the straw-stack.

"I'm glad they didn't invite us in," said Captain Fyter. "I hope I'm not too particular about my associates, but I draw the line at pigs."

The Scarecrow was glad to be rid of his hay, for during the long walk it had sagged down and made him fat and squatty and more bumpy than at first.

"I'm not specially proud," he said, "but I love a manly figure, such as only straw stuffing can create. I've not felt like myself since that hungry Hip-po ate my last straw."

Polychrome and Woot set to work removing the hay and then they selected the finest straw, crisp and golden, and with it stuffed the Scarecrow anew. He certainly looked better after the operation, and he was so pleased at being reformed that he tried to dance a little jig, and almost succeeded.

"I shall sleep under the straw-stack tonight," Woot decided, after he had eaten some of the vegetables from the garden, and in fact he slept very well, with the two tin men and the Scarecrow sitting silently beside him and Polychrome away somewhere in the moonlight dancing her fairy dances.

At daybreak the Tin Woodman and the Tin Soldier took occasion to polish their bodies and oil their joints, for both were exceedingly careful of their personal appearance. They had forgotten the quarrel due to their accidental bumping of one another in the invisible country, and being now good friends the Tin Woodman polished the Tin Soldier's back for him and then the Tin Soldier polished the Tin Woodman's back.

For breakfast the Wanderer ate crisp lettuce and radishes,

and the Rainbow's Daughter, who had now returned to her friends, sipped the dewdrops that had formed on the petals of the wild-flowers.

As they passed the little house to renew their journey, Woot called out:

"Good-bye, Mr. and Mrs. Swyne!"

The window opened and the two pigs looked out.

"A pleasant journey," said the Professor.

"Have you any children?" asked the Scarecrow, who was a great friend of children.

"We have nine," answered the Professor; "but they do not live with us, for when they were tiny piglets the Wizard of Oz came here and offered to care for them and to educate them. So we let him have our nine tiny piglets, for he's a good Wizard and can be relied upon to keep his promises."

"I know the Nine Tiny Piglets," said the Tin Woodman.

"So do I," said the Scarecrow. "They still live in the Emerald City, and the Wizard takes good care of them and teaches them to do all sorts of tricks."

"Did they ever grow up?" inquired Mrs. Squealina Swyne, in an anxious voice.

"No," answered the Scarecrow; "like all other children in the Land of Oz, they will always remain children, and in the case of the tiny piglets that is a good thing, because they would not be nearly so cute and cunning if they were bigger."

"But are they happy?" asked Mrs. Swyne.

"Everyone in the Emerald City is happy," said the Tin Woodman. "They can't help it."

Then the travelers said good-bye, and climbed the side of the basin that was toward Mount Munch.

···——·◄ Chapter 21 ►··——··

POLYCHROME'S MAGIC

On this morning, which ought to be the last of this important journey, our friends started away as bright and cheery as could be, and Woot whistled a merry tune so that Polychrome could dance to the music.

On reaching the top of the hill, the plain spread out before them in all its beauty of blue grasses and wild-flowers, and Mount Munch seemed much nearer than it had the previous evening. They trudged on at a brisk pace, and by noon the mountain was so close that they could admire its appearance. Its slopes were partly clothed with pretty evergreens, and its foot-hills were tufted with a slender waving bluegrass that had a tassel on the end of every blade. And, for the first time, they perceived, near the foot of the mountain, a charming house, not of great size but neatly painted and with many flowers surrounding it and vines climbing over the doors and windows.

It was toward this solitary house that our travelers now directed their steps, thinking to inquire of the people who lived there where Nimmie Amee might be found.

There were no paths, but the way was quite open and clear, and they were drawing near to the dwelling when Woot the Wanderer, who was then in the lead of the little party, halted with such an abrupt jerk that he stumbled over backward and lay flat on his back in the meadow. The Scarecrow stopped to look at the boy.

"Why did you do that?" he asked in surprise.

Woot sat up and gazed around him in amazement.

"I—I don't know!" he replied.

The two tin men, arm in arm, started to pass them when both halted and tumbled, with a great clatter, into a heap beside Woot. Polychrome, laughing at the absurd sight, came dancing up and she, also, came to a sudden stop, but managed to save herself from falling.

Everyone of them was much astonished, and the Scarecrow said with a puzzled look:

"I don't see anything."

"Nor I," said Woot; "but something hit me, just the same."

"Some invisible person struck me a heavy blow," declared

the Tin Woodman, struggling to separate himself from the Tin Soldier, whose legs and arms were mixed with his own.

"I'm not sure it was a person," said Polychrome, looking more grave than usual. "It seems to me that I merely ran into some hard substance which barred my way. In order to make sure of this, let me try another place."

She ran back a way and then with much caution advanced in a different place, but when she reached a position on a line with the others she halted, her arms outstretched before her.

"I can feel something hard—something smooth as glass," she said, "but I'm sure it is not glass."

"Let me try," suggested Woot, getting up; but when he tried to go forward, he discovered the same barrier that Polychrome had encountered.

"No," he said, "it isn't glass. But what is it?"

"Air," replied a small voice beside him. "Solid air; that's all."

They all looked downward and found a sky-blue rabbit had stuck his head out of a burrow in the ground. The rabbit's eyes were a deeper blue than his fur, and the pretty creature seemed friendly and unafraid.

"Air!" exclaimed Woot, staring in astonishment into the rabbit's blue eyes; "whoever heard of air so solid that one cannot push it aside?"

"You can't push this air aside," declared the rabbit, "for it was made hard by powerful sorcery, and it forms a wall that is intended to keep people from getting to that house yonder."

"Oh; it's a wall, is it?" said the Tin Woodman.

"Yes, it is really a wall," answered the rabbit, "and it is fully six feet thick."

"How high is it?" inquired Captain Fyter, the Tin Soldier.

"Oh, ever so high; perhaps a mile," said the rabbit.

"Couldn't we go around it?" asked Woot.

"Of course, for the wall is a circle," explained the rabbit. "In the center of the circle stands the house, so you may walk around the Wall of Solid Air, but you can't get to the house."

"Who put the air wall around the house?" was the Scarecrow's question.

"Nimmie Amee did that."

"Nimmie Amee!" they all exclaimed in surprise.

"Yes," answered the rabbit. "She used to live with an old Witch, who was suddenly destroyed, and when Nimmie Amee ran away from the Witch's house, she took with her just one magic formula—pure sorcery it was—which enabled her to build this air wall around her house—the house yonder. It was quite a clever idea, I think, for it doesn't mar the beauty of the landscape, solid air being invisible, and yet it keeps all strangers away from the house."

"Does Nimmie Amee live there now?" asked the Tin Woodman anxiously.

"Yes, indeed," said the rabbit.

"And does she weep and wail from morning till night?" continued the Emperor.

"No; she seems quite happy," asserted the rabbit.

The Tin Woodman seemed quite disappointed to hear this report of his old sweetheart, but the Scarecrow reassured his friend, saying:

"Never mind, your Majesty; however happy Nimmie Amee is now, I'm sure she will be much happier as Empress of the Winkies."

"Perhaps," said Captain Fyter, somewhat stiffly, "she will be still more happy to become the bride of a Tin Soldier."

"She shall choose between us, as we have agreed," the Tin Woodman promised; "but how shall we get to the poor girl?"

Polychrome, although dancing lightly back and forth, had listened to every word of the conversation. Now she came forward and sat herself down just in front of the Blue Rabbit, her many-hued draperies giving her the appearance of some beautiful flower. The rabbit didn't back away an inch. Instead, he gazed at the Rainbow's Daughter admiringly.

"Does your burrow go underneath this Wall of Air?" asked Polychrome.

"To be sure," answered the Blue Rabbit; "I dug it that way so I could roam in these broad fields, by going out one way, or eat the cabbages in Nimmie Amee's garden by leaving my burrow at the other end. I don't think Nimmie Amee ought to mind the little I take from her garden, or the hole I've made under her magic wall. A rabbit may go and come as he pleases, but no one who is bigger than I am could get through my burrow."

"Will you allow us to pass through it, if we are able to?" inquired Polychrome.

"Yes, indeed," answered the Blue Rabbit. "I'm no especial friend of Nimmie Amee, for once she threw stones at me, just because I was nibbling some lettuce, and only yesterday she yelled 'Shoo!' at me, which made me nervous. You're welcome to use my burrow in any way you choose."

"But this is all nonsense!" declared Woot the Wanderer. "We are every one too big to crawl through a rabbit's burrow."

"We are too big now," agreed the Scarecrow, "but you must remember that Polychrome is a fairy, and fairies have many magic powers."

Woot's face brightened as he turned to the lovely Daughter of the Rainbow.

"Could you make us all as small as that rabbit?" he asked eagerly.

"I can try," answered Polychrome, with a smile. And presently she did it—so easily that Woot was not the only one astonished. As the now tiny people grouped themselves before the rabbit's burrow the hole appeared to them like the entrance to a tunnel, which indeed it was.

"I'll go first," said wee Polychrome, who had made herself grow as small as the others, and into the tunnel she danced without hesitation. A tiny Scarecrow went next and then the two funny little tin men.

"Walk in; it's your turn," said the Blue Rabbit to Woot the

Wanderer. "I'm coming after, to see how you get along. This will be a regular surprise party to Nimmie Amee."

So Woot entered the hole and felt his way along its smooth sides in the dark until he finally saw the glimmer of daylight ahead and knew the journey was almost over. Had he remained his natural size, the distance could have been covered in a few steps, but to a thumb-high Woot it was quite a promenade. When he emerged from the burrow he found himself but a short distance from the house, in the center of the vegetable garden, where the leaves of rhubarb waving above his head seemed like trees. Outside the hole, and waiting for him, he found all his friends.

"So far, so good!" remarked the Scarecrow cheerfully.

"Yes; so far, but no farther," returned the Tin Woodman in a plaintive and disturbed tone of voice. "I am now close to Nimmie Amee, whom I have come ever so far to seek, but I cannot ask the girl to marry such a little man as I am now."

"I'm no bigger than a toy soldier!" said Captain Fyter, sorrowfully. "Unless Polychrome can make us big again, there is little use in our visiting Nimmie Amee at all, for I'm sure she wouldn't care for a husband she might carelessly step on and ruin."

Polychrome laughed merrily.

"If I make you big, you can't get out of here again," said she, "and if you remain little Nimmie Amee will laugh at you. So make your choice."

"I think we'd better go back," said Woot seriously.

"No," said the Tin Woodman, stoutly, "I have decided that it's my duty to make Nimmie Amee happy, in case she wishes to marry me."

"So have I," announced Captain Fyter. "A good soldier never shrinks from doing his duty."

"As for that," said the Scarecrow, "tin doesn't shrink any to speak of, under any circumstances. But Woot and I intend to stick to our comrades, whatever they decide to do, so we will ask Polychrome to make us as big as we were before."

Polychrome agreed to this request and in half a minute all of them, including herself, had been enlarged again to their natural sizes. They then thanked the Blue Rabbit for his kind assistance, and at once approached the house of Nimmie Amee.

NIMMIE AMEE

We may be sure that at this moment our friends were all anxious to see the end of the adventure that had caused them so many trials and troubles. Perhaps the Tin Woodman's heart did not beat any faster, because it was made of red velvet and stuffed with sawdust, and the Tin Soldier's heart was made of tin and reposed in his tin bosom without a hint of emotion. However, there is little doubt that they both knew that a critical moment in their lives had arrived, and that Nimmie Amee's decision was destined to influence the future of one or the other.

As they assumed their natural sizes and the rhubarb leaves

that had before towered above their heads now barely covered their feet, they looked around the garden and found that no person was visible save themselves. No sound of activity came from the house, either, but they walked to the front door, which had a little porch built before it, and there the two tinmen stood side by side while both knocked upon the door with their tin knuckles.

As no one seemed eager to answer the summons they knocked again; and then again. Finally they heard a stir from within and someone coughed.

"Who's there?" called a girl's voice.

"It's I!" cried the tin twins, together.

"How did you get there?" asked the voice.

They hesitated how to reply, so Woot answered for them: "By means of magic."

"Oh," said the unseen girl. "Are you friends, or foes?"

"Friends!" they all exclaimed.

Then they heard footsteps approach the door, which slowly opened and revealed a very pretty Munchkin girl standing in the doorway.

"Nimmie Amee!" cried the tin twins.

"That's my name," replied the girl, looking at them in cold surprise. "But who can you be?"

"Don't you know me, Nimmie?" said the Tin Woodman. "I'm your old sweetheart, Nick Chopper!"

"Don't you know me, my dear?" said the Tin Soldier. "I'm your old sweetheart, Captain Fyter!"

Nimmie Amee smiled at them both. Then she looked beyond them at the rest of the party and smiled again. However, she seemed more amused than pleased.

"Come in," she said, leading the way inside. "Even sweethearts are forgotten after a time, but you and your friends are welcome."

The room they now entered was cosy and comfortable, being neatly furnished and well swept and dusted. But they found someone there besides Nimmie Amee. A man dressed in the attractive Munchkin costume was lazily reclining in an easy chair, and he sat up and turned his eyes on the visitors with a cold and indifferent stare that was almost insolent. He did not even rise from his seat to greet the strangers, but after glaring at them he looked away with a scowl, as if they were of too little importance to interest him.

The tin men returned this man's stare with interest, but they did not look away from him because neither of them seemed able to take his eyes off this Munchkin, who was remarkable in having one tin arm quite like their own tin arms.

"Seems to me," said Captain Fyter, in a voice that sounded harsh and indignant, "that you, sir, are a vile impostor!"

"Gently—gently!" cautioned the Scarecrow; "don't be rude to strangers, Captain."

"Rude?" shouted the Tin Soldier, now very much provoked; "why, he's a scoundrel—a thief! The villain is wearing my own head!"

"Yes," added the Tin Woodman, "and he's wearing my right arm! I can recognize it by the two warts on the little finger."

"Good gracious!" exclaimed Woot. "Then this must be the man whom old Ku-Klip patched together and named Chopfyt."

The man now turned toward them, still scowling.

"Yes, that is my name," he said in a voice like a growl, "and it is absurd for you tin creatures, or for anyone else, to claim my head, or arm, or any part of me, for they are my personal property."

"You? You're a Nobody!" shouted Captain Fyter.

"You're just a mix-up," declared the Emperor.

"Now, now, gentlemen," interrupted Nimmie Amee, "I must ask you to be more respectful to poor Chopfyt. For, being my guests, it is not polite for you to insult my husband."

"Your husband!" the tin twins exclaimed in dismay.

"Yes," said she. "I married Chopfyt a long time ago, because my other two sweethearts had deserted me."

This reproof embarrassed both Nick Chopper and Captain Fyter. They looked down, shamefaced, for a moment, and then the Tin Woodman explained in an earnest voice:

"I rusted."

"So did I," said the Tin Soldier.

"I could not know that, of course," asserted Nimmie Amee. "All I knew was that neither of you came to marry me, as you had promised to do. But men are not scarce in the Land of Oz.

After I came here to live, I met Mr. Chopfyt, and he was the more interesting because he reminded me strongly of both of you, as you were before you became tin. He even had a tin arm, and that reminded me of you the more.

"No wonder!" remarked the Scarecrow.

"But, listen, Nimmie Amee!" said the astonished Woot; "he really is both of them, for he is made of their cast-off parts."

"Oh, you're quite wrong," declared Polychrome, laughing, for she was greatly enjoying the confusion of the others. "The tin men are still themselves, as they will tell you, and so Chopfyt must be someone else."

They looked at her bewildered, for the facts in the case were too puzzling to be grasped at once.

"It is all the fault of old Ku-Klip," muttered the Tin Woodman. "He had no right to use our cast-off parts to make another man with."

"It seems he did it, however," said Nimmie Amee calmly, "and I married him because he resembled you both. I won't say he is a husband to be proud of, because he has a mixed nature and isn't always an agreeable companion. There are times when I have to chide him gently, both with my tongue and with my broomstick. But he is my husband, and I must make the best of him."

"If you don't like him," suggested the Tin Woodman, "Captain Fyter and I can chop him up with our axe and sword, and each take such parts of the fellow as belong to him. Then we are willing for you to select one of us as your husband."

"That is a good idea," approved Captain Fyter, drawing his sword.

"No," said Nimmie Amee; "I think I'll keep the husband I now have. He is now trained to draw the water and carry in the wood and hoe the cabbages and weed the flower-beds and dust the furniture and perform many tasks of a like character. A new husband would have to be scolded—and gently chided—until he learns my ways. So I think it will be better to keep my Chopfyt, and I see no reason why you should object to him. You two gentlemen threw him away when you became tin, because you had no further use for him, so you cannot justly claim him now. I advise you to go back to your own homes and forget me, as I have forgotten you."

"Good advice!" laughed Polychrome, dancing.

"Are you happy?" asked the Tin Soldier.

"Of course I am," said Nimmie Amee; "I'm the mistress of all I survey—the queen of my little domain."

"Wouldn't you like to be the Empress of the Winkies?" asked the Tin Woodman.

"Mercy, no," she answered. "That would be a lot of bother. I don't care for society, or pomp, or posing. All I ask is to be left alone and not to be annoyed by visitors."

The Scarecrow nudged Woot the Wanderer.

"That sounds to me like a hint," he said.

"Looks as if we'd had our journey for nothing," remarked Woot, who was a little ashamed and disappointed because he had proposed the journey.

"I am glad, however," said the Tin Woodman, "that I have found Nimmie Amee, and discovered that she is already married and happy. It will relieve me of any further anxiety concerning her."

"For my part," said the Tin Soldier, "I am not sorry to be free. The only thing that really annoys me is finding my head upon Chopfyt's body."

"As for that, I'm pretty sure it is my body, or a part of it, anyway," remarked the Emperor of the Winkies. "But never mind, friend Soldier; let us be willing to donate our cast-off members to insure the happiness of Nimmie Amee, and be thankful it is not our fate to hoe cabbages and draw water—and be chided—in the place of this creature Chopfyt."

"Yes," agreed the Soldier, "we have much to be thankful for."

Polychrome, who had wandered outside, now poked her pretty head through an open window and exclaimed in a pleased voice:

"It's getting cloudy. Perhaps it is going to rain!"

Chapter 23

THROUGH the TUNNEL

It didn't rain just then, although the clouds in the sky grew thicker and more threatening. Polychrome hoped for a thunderstorm, followed by her Rainbow, but the two tin men did not relish the idea of getting wet. They even preferred to remain in Nimmie Amee's house, although they felt they were not welcome there, rather than go out and face the coming storm. But the Scarecrow, who was a very thoughtful person, said to his friends:

"If we remain here until after the storm, and Polychrome goes away on her Rainbow, then we will be prisoners inside the Wall of Solid Air; so it seems best to start upon our return journey at once. If I get wet, my straw stuffing will be ruined, and if you two tin gentlemen get wet, you may perhaps rust again, and become useless. But even that is better than to stay here. Once we are free of the barrier, we have Woot the Wanderer to help us, and he can oil your joints and restuff my body, if it becomes necessary, for the boy is made of meat, which neither rusts nor gets soggy or moldy."

"Come along, then!" cried Polychrome from the window, and the others, realizing the wisdom of the Scarecrow's speech, took leave of Nimmie Amee, who was glad to be rid of them, and said good-bye to her husband, who merely scowled and made no answer, and then they hurried from the house.

"Your old parts are not very polite, I must say," remarked the Scarecrow, when they were in the garden.

"No," said Woot, "Chopfyt is a regular grouch. He might have wished us a pleasant journey, at the very least."

"I beg you not to hold us responsible for that creature's actions," pleaded the Tin Woodman. "We are through with Chopfyt and shall have nothing further to do with him."

Polychrome danced ahead of the party and led them straight to the burrow of the Blue Rabbit, which they might have had some difficulty in finding without her. There she lost no time in making them all small again. The Blue Rabbit was busy nibbling cabbage leaves in Nimmie Amee's garden, so they did not ask his permission but at once entered the burrow.

Even now the raindrops were beginning to fall, but it was

quite dry inside the tunnel and by the time they had reached the other end, outside the circular Wall of Solid Air, the storm was at its height and the rain was coming down in torrents.

"Let us wait here," proposed Polychrome, peering out of the hole and then quickly retreating. "The Rainbow won't appear until after the storm and I can make you big again in a jiffy, before I join my sisters on our bow."

"That's a good plan," said the Scarecrow approvingly. "It will save me from getting soaked and soggy."

"It will save me from rusting," said the Tin Soldier.

"It will enable me to remain highly polished," said the Tin Woodman.

"Oh, as for that, I myself prefer not to get my pretty clothes wet," laughed the Rainbow's daughter. "But while we wait I will bid you all adieu. I must also thank you for saving me from that dreadful Giantess, Mrs. Yoop. You have been good and patient comrades and I have enjoyed our adventures together, but I am never so happy as when on my dear Rainbow."

"Will your father scold you for getting left on the earth?" asked Woot.

"I suppose so," said Polychrome gaily; "I'm always getting scolded for my mad pranks, as they are called. My sisters are so sweet and lovely and proper that they never dance off our Rainbow, and so they never have any adventures. Adventures to me are good fun, only I never like to stay too long on earth, because I really don't belong here. I shall tell my Father the Rainbow that I'll try not to be so careless again, and he will forgive me because in our sky mansions there is always joy and happiness."

They were indeed sorry to part with their dainty and beautiful companion and assured her of their devotion if they ever chanced to meet again. She shook hands with the Scarecrow and the Tin Men and kissed Woot the Wanderer lightly upon his forehead.

And then the rain suddenly ceased, and as the tiny people left the burrow of the Blue Rabbit, a glorious big Rainbow appeared in the sky and the end of its arch slowly descended and touched the ground just where they stood.

Woot was so busy watching a score of lovely maidens— sisters of Polychrome—who were leaning over the edge of the bow, and another score who danced gaily amid the radiance of the splendid hues, that he did not notice he was growing big again. But now Polychrome joined her sisters on the Rainbow and the huge arch lifted and slowly melted away as the sun burst from the clouds and sent its own white beams dancing over the meadows.

"Why, she's gone!" exclaimed the boy, and turned to see his companions still waving their hands in token of adieu to the vanished Polychrome.

Chapter 24

The CURTAIN FALLS

Well, the rest of the story is quickly told, for the return journey of our adventurers was without any important incident. The Scarecrow was so afraid of meeting the Hip-po-gy-raf, and having his straw eaten again, that he urged his comrades to select another route to the Emerald City, and they willingly consented, so that the Invisible Country was wholly avoided.

Of course, when they reached the Emerald City their first duty was to visit Ozma's palace, where they were royally entertained. The Tin Soldier and Woot the Wanderer were welcomed as warmly as any strangers might be who had been the traveling companions of Ozma's dear old friends, the Scarecrow and the Tin Woodman.

At the banquet table that evening they related the manner in which they had discovered Nimmie Amee, and told how they had found her happily married to Chopfyt, whose relationship to Nick Chopper and Captain Fyter was so bewildering that they asked Ozma's advice what to do about it.

"You need not consider Chopfyt at all," replied the beautiful girl Ruler of Oz. "If Nimmie Amee is content with that misfit man for a husband, we have not even just cause to blame Ku-Klip for gluing him together."

"I think it was a very good idea," added little Dorothy, "for if Ku-Klip hadn't used up your cast-off parts, they would have been wasted. It's wicked to be wasteful, isn't it?"

"Well, anyhow," said Woot the Wanderer, "Chopfyt, being kept a prisoner by his wife, is too far away from anyone to bother either of you tin men in any way. If you hadn't gone where he is and discovered him, you would never have worried about him."

"What do you care, anyhow," Betsy Bobbin asked the Tin Woodman, "so long as Nimmie Amee is satisfied?"

"And just to think," remarked Tiny Trot, "that any girl would rather live with a mixture like Chopfyt, on far-away Mount Munch, than to be the Empress of the Winkies!"

"It is her own choice," said the Tin Woodman contentedly; "and, after all, I'm not sure the Winkies would care to have an Empress."

It puzzled Ozma, for a time, to decide what to do with the Tin Soldier. If he went with the Tin Woodman to the Emperor's castle, she felt that the two tin men might not be able to live together in harmony, and moreover the Emperor would not be so distinguished if he had a double constantly beside him. So she asked Captain Fyter if he was willing to serve her as a soldier, and he promptly declared that nothing would please him more. After he had been in her service for some time, Ozma sent him into the Gillikin Country, with instructions to keep order among the wild people who inhabit some parts of that unknown country of Oz.

As for Woot, being a Wanderer by profession, he was allowed to wander wherever he desired, and Ozma promised to keep watch over his future journeys and to protect the boy as well as she was able, in case he ever got into more trouble.

All this having been happily arranged, the Tin Woodman returned to his tin castle, and his chosen comrade, the Scarecrow, accompanied him on the way. The two friends were sure to pass many pleasant hours together in talking over their recent adventures, for as they neither ate nor slept they found their greatest amusement in conversation.

EXPLORE the WORLD of OZ.

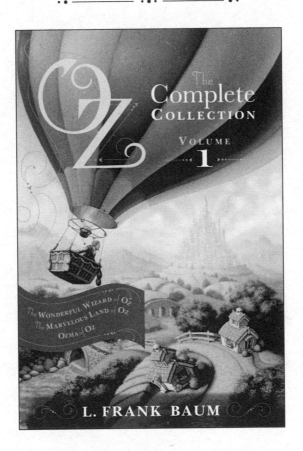

EXPLORE the WORLD of OZ.

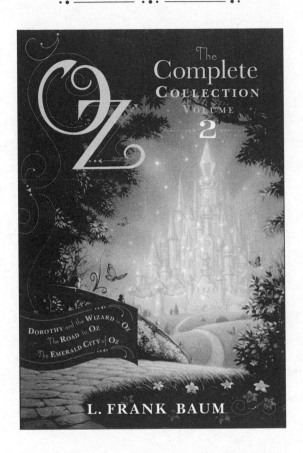

EXPLORE the WORLD of OZ.

EXPLORE the WORLD of OZ.

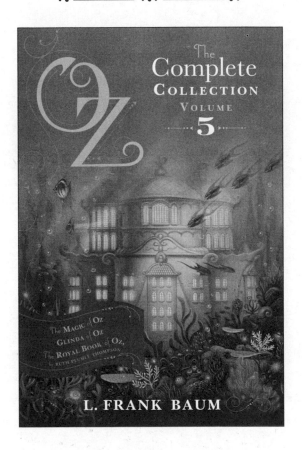